Praise for the novels of Sherryl Woods

"Sherryl Woods writes emotionally satisfying novels about family, friendship and home. Truly feel-great reads!"
—#1 *New York Times* bestselling author Debbie Macomber

"During the course of this gripping, emotionally wrenching but satisfying tale, Woods deftly and realistically handles such issues as survival guilt, drug abuse as adolescent rebellion, and family dynamics when a vital member is suddenly gone."
—*Booklist* on *Flamingo Diner*

"Woods is a master heartstring puller."
—*Publishers Weekly* on *Seaview Inn*

"Once again, Woods, with such authenticity, weaves a tale of true love and the challenges that can knock up against that love."
—*RT Book Reviews* on *Beach Lane*

"Woods…is noted for appealing character-driven stories that are often infused with the flavor and fragrance of the South."
—*Library Journal*

"A reunion story punctuated by family drama, Woods's first novel in her new Ocean Breeze series is touching, tense and tantalizing."
—*RT Book Reviews* on *Sand Castle Bay*

"A whimsical, sweet scenario…the digressions have their own charm, and Woods never fails to come back to the romantic point."
—*Publishers Weekly* on *Sweet Tea at Sunrise*

SHERRYL WOODS
Lilac Lane

mira

mira

ISBN-13: 978-0-7783-0817-1

Lilac Lane

Recycling programs
for this product may
not exist in your area.

For questions and comments about the quality of this book, please contact us at CustomerService@Harlequin.com.

www.Harlequin.com

Printed in U.S.A.

This one is for all the readers who've embraced
my characters and stories through the years.
You've been such a blessing in my life,
and I treasure the friendship you've offered.

Lilac Lane

Prologue

The death of Peter McDonough would have been a blow at any time, but coming as it had on the very day Kiera Malone had finally accepted his proposal of marriage left her reeling. After her first husband, Sean Malone, had abandoned her with three young children, she had vowed never to let another man into her life, much less into her heart. She'd clung to her independence with a fierce protectiveness. She'd made a practice of scaring men away with her tart tongue and bitter demeanor, even knowing as she did so that she was dooming herself to loneliness. Better that than dooming herself and her children to another loss, another mistake.

After the death of his wife, Peter, bless his sweet soul, had waited patiently on the sidelines for Kiera, running his pub in Dublin, supporting her daughter, Moira, in her efforts to make a career of the photography that Kiera herself had thought of as nothing more than a hobby, and making the occasional overture to Kiera.

To Kiera's confusion, not even her best efforts to push him aside and make clear her lack of interest, efforts that had chased off every other man who'd approached her, seemed to dissuade Peter. He took her rebuffs in stride. If anything, his not-so-secret crush had deepened.

More troubling, aside from his thick, curly hair and firm jaw, he had a combination of traits that drew her to him—strength balanced by gentleness, bold determination tempered by patience and a booming laugh that could fill her heart with unexpected lightness. He was, in all respects, a man who knew exactly what he wanted, and he wanted Kiera. She had no idea why.

Moreover, he'd had the support not only of her father, Dillon O'Malley, but of her daughter. Up until then, Moira, like Dillon, had approved of very few of Kiera's choices in life. Yet for once Moira and Kiera's father had conspired to push Kiera and Peter together at every opportunity. Since their approval had been granted so sparingly over the years, she'd been persuaded to be less resistant than usual. What was the harm, after all, when she knew it would come to nothing? Relationships tended to deteriorate over time, even those begun with passion and hope. They ended. At least that was her experience.

But then Moira and Dillon had somehow convinced Kiera to move back to Dublin, where, they'd said, there were more opportunities. They dangled new opportunities like strands of glittering gold, told her any one of them would be an improvement over her dead-end career in a dingy neighborhood pub in a tiny seaside village on the coast north of Dublin where she'd toiled for long hours and low pay for most of her life. Moira had actually had the audacity to scold her for accepting security for her family over any ambitions she might have once had to run a restaurant of her own.

"Where's your confidence and self-respect?" Moira had demanded. "You're a far better waitress and cook than I am. And you've management skills, as well. Look at how well you've kept our family afloat."

Kiera knew the truth of that. Moira was competent, but her heart wasn't in the restaurant business, not even that Irish pub she was hoping to run with her new husband in Chesapeake Shores, Maryland. Luke O'Brien was the attraction there.

Moira's clever argument took another twist. "After all Peter's done for me, it's only fitting that I not leave him in the lurch when I move to Chesapeake Shores. Come to Dublin, where you'll be making at least twice the tips and have the support of a man who's been nothing short of an angel to me. He'd be the same for you. It could be the sort of partnership your life's been lacking."

Kiera noted with some amusement that Moira hadn't suggested *romance*, a word her daughter knew well would have sent Kiera fleeing in the opposite direction.

"He has his own children to step in and help with the running of the pub," Kiera had protested, even though much of what her daughter said made sense.

The prospect of starting over, though, was a scary business. As harsh and difficult as her life had been, it was a niche in which she felt comfortable. With children to support on her own, she'd stopped taking chances. Moira was exactly right about that. She'd put her family first. Wasn't that what a mother was meant to do? The thought of taking a daring risk now was beyond terrifying and yet, perhaps, just a little intriguing.

"His sons have little interest in the pub, much to Peter's dismay," Moira said. "There will be room for you. Peter will welcome the help and the company. If you ask me, he's been a wee bit lonely since his wife's passing."

Persuaded at last—or perhaps simply worn down—Kiera had made the move, but only after telling Peter very, very firmly that he was not to be having expectations of a personal nature where she was concerned. He'd agreed to her terms, but there'd been a smile on his lips and a spark in his blue eyes that she probably shouldn't have ignored.

And there he'd been, day in and day out for the better part of two years, always with a quick-witted comment that made her laugh or a gesture that softened her heart. And his patience truly had been a revelation to her. He'd done not one single thing to make her feel rushed, to make her put up her well-honed guard. Nor was he one to overindulge in Guinness, a habit that would have sent Kiera running even faster after living with Sean's uncontrolled bouts of drinking and subsequent abusive talk.

And so, eventually, one by one, her defenses fell. She found herself looking forward to their late-night talks after the pub closed, to his interest in her opinions. Maybe most of all, she'd basked in his kind and steady company that made her feel secure as she hadn't since the very earliest days of her marriage to Sean Malone. She'd last felt that way before Sean's drinking had started, before he'd walked out the door of their home for the very last time, leaving her with two sons who were not yet ready to start school and a daughter just home from the hospital.

Because she'd made such a show of rebellion in

marrying Sean in the first place, Kiera hadn't allowed herself to go running home to her parents back then. Instead, she'd struggled to make do, surviving on her own, if barely. It was only when her mum lay dying that she'd reconciled with her parents and eventually allowed them back into her life and the lives of her children. Her sons and daughter hadn't even been aware that they had grandparents who might dote on them if given the chance.

Now with all three of her children grown and finding their own paths—albeit in the case of her sons, a path she wouldn't have chosen, the same one their dad had taken—Kiera had been at loose ends when she made the move back to Dublin. She'd perhaps been more vulnerable than she'd allowed herself to be in years.

She couldn't claim that Peter had taken unfair advantage of that. He'd been too fine a man to do so, but the fact was, she'd finally been ready to reach for a little happiness. Peter had offered the promise of that and more. And exactly as Moira had predicted, his sons were happy enough to have her in their father's life and working by his side at the pub. The future looked bright with the sort of promise of love and stability she'd once dreamed of, but never imagined truly finding.

And, then, on the very day she'd said yes, when she'd opened her heart and allowed Peter to put a ring on her finger, a ring he'd claimed he'd been holding on to for years for just such a glorious day, he'd betrayed her as surely as Sean Malone ever had. He'd suffered a fatal heart attack just hours later, and once again, Kiera was alone and adrift. Abandoned.

Wasn't that just the way of the bloody world? she thought, her protective bitterness returning in spades and her fragile heart once more shattered into pieces.

Chapter 1

Moira O'Brien sat in the kitchen of her grandfather's cozy home by the Chesapeake Bay, a home he shared with Nell O'Brien O'Malley, with whom he'd been reunited only a few short years ago after a lifetime of being separated. The air was rich with the scent of cranberry-orange scones baking in the oven and Irish breakfast tea steeping in a treasured antique flowered teapot on the table. Nell had brought it home from Ireland after visiting her grandparents decades ago. She said it had been her Irish grandmother's favorite.

"What should we be doing about our Kiera?" Nell asked them. Though Kiera hadn't even come to Chesapeake Shores for her own father's wedding to Nell or for Moira's wedding to Luke O'Brien on the same day, Nell had always considered her family, embracing her and fretting over her as surely as she did her own children, grandchildren and great-grandchildren. She was the most nurturing person Moira had ever known.

Moira bounced her baby girl on her knee as she considered the problem they'd all been worrying about ever since they'd heard the news about Peter's untimely death right on the heels of the far happier news about his engagement to Kiera.

"Kiera will make her own choices," Dillon said, his tone a mix of resignation and worry. "I know my daughter all too well. Pushing her to bend in the way we'd like will never work. She'll simply dig in her heels out of pure stubbornness, exactly as she did when she married Sean Malone against my wishes all those years ago. Right now she's probably regretting the very fact that she let us convince her to move to Dublin in the first place. She'll be listening to very little of the advice we offer."

"Well, it's sure that my brothers won't be around to support her," Moira said disdainfully. "She hasn't once mentioned them since Peter died. I doubt they come around at all these days except to ask for a handout."

Nell gave her a disapproving look, but Moira knew she was right. Her brothers were following a little too closely in their father's drunken footsteps. "She belongs here with us," she said emphatically, keeping her gaze steady on her grandfather. "You know I'm right. She needs the kind of family we've found here. A steady dose of the O'Briens will restore her spirits. She wasted years on bitterness and regrets after my dad left. I know she'd say she was working too hard to waste time on love, but the truth is she was too terrified to take a chance that she'd be making another poor choice. We can't allow her to do the same again."

To Moira's surprise, it was Nell who promptly backed her.

"I agree that coming here is exactly what she needs," she said, then reached over to stroke the baby's cheek. "And I think our darling little Kate right here and her need for a grandmother's attention is the very reason Kiera won't fight us on this."

Moira saw the light of near-certain victory spark in her grandfather's eyes and knew Nell had hit on the perfect solution. "You're suggesting I throw myself on her mercy, tell her that I'm in desperate need of help with the baby, even though our Kate is perfectly content in Carrie's day care center," Moira concluded.

"Which has been dreadfully overcrowded since the day it opened," Nell claimed with exaggerated innocence.

"Dreadfully," Dillon confirmed, nodding, his expression astonishingly serious for a man who knew they were bending the truth, if not flat-out breaking it. Nell's great-granddaughter's child care business was flourishing, that much was true, but she had more than enough competent staff to manage it.

"If you think it will take more to persuade her, there's your own husband's pub, which is in dire need of an extra pair of hands," Nell added. "You're far too busy with your photography and your travel to exhibitions to help my grandson out as you once did."

Moira nodded. "True enough. Megan would have me traveling once a month if I'd agree to it. I suspect she's exaggerating a bit, but she tells me she's had to turn down requests for shows, because I won't make myself available as often as she'd like. She's got quite a knack for inducing guilt."

"Exactly, but we can use that to our advantage with Kiera," Nell said. "And my health is far too fragile for me to be spending my spare minutes in the kitchen at the pub keeping a watchful eye on the chef to be sure the menu doesn't stray too far from proper Irish recipes."

"Nell, you've given us a scare or two, but in all honesty, you're about as fragile as a steel beam," Moira replied, but she was laughing at the clever strategy. If she handled the performance convincingly, it would play on all of her mum's weaknesses, most especially on her need to be useful while keeping a firm grip on her independence.

"And you're wickedly devious to boot," she told Nell. "Both traits I admire, I might add."

"I'll thank you for that," Nell said, clearly taking it as the praise Moira had intended. "With a contrary family the size of mine, it's always best to have a few tricks up my sleeve. Sadly, most of them are onto me now."

"Isn't this something we should at least be discussing with Luke?" Dillon asked, inserting a word of caution. "If we intend to push Kiera into a job at his pub, he should be brought on board with our plan."

"Leave Luke to me," Moira said confidently. "I think I can convince him of the advantages of having her here. It would allow him more free time at home with me and Kate. Mum is far more experienced at running a pub than I ever thought of being. Not only was she more competent, but she loved it as I never did. She'll be a true asset."

"Are we agreed, then, that once Luke's given us his blessing, Moira should be the one to make the call?" Dillon asked. "It'll receive a better reception than any suggestion that comes from me. Kiera and I have made our peace, but it's tenuous at best." He studied Moira. "How are your skills at bending the truth without getting caught?"

Moira laughed. "An improvement on yours, and that's a fact."

* * *

Luke walked into his house on Beach Lane well after midnight, expecting to find his wife and daughter sound asleep as they usually were. Instead, he opened the door to discover the soft glow of dozens of candles and his wife wearing one of those shimmery gowns that skimmed over her curves and never failed to cause a hitch in his breath in the few seconds before he managed to get it off her.

Suspicion warred with heat, but as usual the heat won. With his gaze locked with hers, he tried to assess the glint in her eyes as he crossed the room and accepted the glass of champagne she held out to him.

"It's been a while since I've had a welcome like this at the end of the day," he murmured, his gaze drifting to the swell of her breasts where the gown had dipped low.

"And it's long overdue, it is," Moira said, her voice soft and filled with promise.

She pushed him back against the cushions of the sofa and settled snugly against him. "I've missed our time like this. Haven't you?"

"It's not as if our love life has been lacking," he commented in a choked voice as her hand tugged his T-shirt free and slipped below to caress bare skin.

"Not lacking for sure," she conceded. "But less spontaneous. You can't deny that. With our schedules so demanding, we practically need an appointment to have a moment like this."

"And you've been missing the spontaneity?"

"Old married couples need an occasional spark to liven things up," she said, and managed to say it with a straight face.

As intrigued as he was by where this was heading,

Luke couldn't seem to stop the laugh that bubbled up. "Old married couple? Is that how you're thinking of us these days? When did we both turn gray and start hobbling around? In my opinion, we've barely left the honeymoon phase."

She frowned at his teasing. "If you're not interested after I've gone to all this trouble," she huffed in typical Moira fashion. She'd always been too quick to take offense.

He brushed a wayward strand of hair from her cheek. "I am always interested in you," he contradicted. "And will be until the day I die. However, Moira, my love, I know you a bit too well to take this seduction at face value. You have something on your mind. Out with that and then we'll get to the rest of the evening as you've planned it."

She looked as if she wanted to argue, but in the end she sighed and sat back, then took a healthy gulp of her champagne. Since Moira rarely indulged in alcohol, Luke figured whatever she was about to tell him was likely to be something she knew he wasn't going to want to hear.

"It's about my mum," she confessed.

Luke's antenna went on full alert. He and Kiera had called a tentative truce since he'd married her daughter, but they weren't exactly close. And though he sympathized with what she must be going through since Peter McDonough's unexpected and sudden death, he couldn't imagine what that had to do with him.

"I was with Nell and my grandfather earlier," Moira continued.

"So they're involved in this, too?" he asked, his antenna now waving as if there were a dozen signals com-

ing at him all at once, none of them boding well. If
his grandmother was involved, there was a very good
chance it involved the sort of sneaky meddling that
terrified everyone in the family. The only person even
better at it was his uncle Mick O'Brien. Thankfully, so
far his name hadn't come up.

"Just tell me," he instructed his wife. "What are the
three of you conspiring about when it comes to your
mother, and what could it possibly have to do with me?"

Moira leaned toward him, her expression earnest.
"You know how devastated she was by Peter's death.
We think she needs a change of scenery if she's not to
go back to her old ways."

"Her old ways?"

"You know, retreating from the world, wallowing in
her misery and bitterness," she explained. "I've already
heard hints of that when we've spoken. She feels betrayed. The walls are going back up. It happened after
my dad left. I can't let her waste the rest of her days
being all alone again. She's still young enough to enjoy
a full and happy life, if only she'll allow it."

Luke recalled how impossible Kiera had been when
they'd first met in Ireland. The only person topping her
in that department had been the woman sitting right
here with him, her skin glowing, the strap on her gown
sliding provocatively low, and her voice filled with passion, albeit of an entirely different sort than when he'd
first walked in the door. What sort of idiot was he to
have redirected that passion to this conversation?

"I'm guessing you three have come up with a solution to save her from herself," he said warily.

"We have," Moira said enthusiastically. "We think
she needs to come here, to be with us, with all of the

O'Briens. She needs to be surrounded by family. It'll show her just how a life is meant to be lived. We'd be setting a good example."

Though Luke desperately wanted to argue, to claim it was a terrible idea to remind Kiera of all the family closeness she'd just lost when Peter died, he couldn't do it. Despite the flare-ups of old family feuds and conflicts, there was healing power in the O'Brien togetherness. He'd experienced it his entire life. And there was healing magic in Chesapeake Shores, as well. He'd have to be hard-hearted to deny that to Moira's mother.

"Fine. She'll come for a visit," he said. "Why would I object to that? When we built our house, we included a guest suite just for such a visit. When you furnished it, I know you did it to your mother's taste, hoping she'd find it comfortable the first time she came. I believe her favorite Irish blessing hangs on a plaque just inside the door."

"She'll find it welcoming, there's no doubt of that," Moira said. "But there's a bit more. We're thinking of something a little longer than a quick visit."

And here it comes, Luke thought, barely containing a sigh. "Tell me."

"I'm going to ask for her help with Kate," Moira began slowly, then added in a rush, "And you're going to give her my old job at the pub." Her smile brightened. "Won't that be grand? With all of her experience, she'll be far more help than I ever was."

He studied the hopeful glint in his wife's eyes and didn't even try to contain the sigh that came. When he didn't immediately speak the emphatic *no* that hovered on his lips, Moira beamed, clearly taking his silence as agreement.

"And you'll talk to Connor about getting her a work visa as your Irish consultant, just as you did for me?" she asked, referring to his cousin, who'd become a first-rate lawyer. "I understand it may be a bit trickier these days with changes in the law, but I have every confidence Connor can manage it."

"I'm a bit surprised you haven't already discussed this with him," Luke said.

"Never before talking to you," she said with a hint of indignation that made him chuckle.

"Then you weren't a hundred percent certain I'd go along with your scheme?"

"Maybe ninety-five percent," she admitted. "You've a stubborn streak that sometimes works against me."

"Pot calling the kettle black," he retorted. "You know you have me twisted around your finger. And what you can't accomplish, Nell can. I'm quite sure she'd have been by first thing tomorrow if you'd put out a distress call."

"But it's not coming to that, is it?" she asked hopefully.

Luke studied his wife closely. "Does it mean so much to you to have her come and stay for longer than a brief visit?"

"I think this change is what she needs. So do Nell and Grandfather. And I owe her, Luke. She gave up everything for my brothers and me. I don't think I realized how hard she worked or how many sacrifices she made until I'd had a taste of working in a pub myself. I used to blame her for not spending more time with us, but now that we have Kate, I can't imagine being away from her as much as my mum was away from us. It must have been hard for her to put work over her children. My brothers may be ungrateful louts, but I'm not."

"No, you're definitely not that," Luke said, though he couldn't help regretting it just a little. Then, again, having Kiera underfoot would be a small price to pay for the joy that Moira had brought into his life. "I'll call Connor in the morning."

Her eyes sparkled. "Seriously? You'll do it?"

"Was there ever any doubt? Now, come here, Moira, my love," he said, beckoning her closer. "Let's not waste this effort you've gone to tonight. I know you think we're somehow going to gain more time to ourselves with this plan of yours, but I have my doubts. I think we need to take full advantage of this bit of spontaneity."

"There will be more chances, I promise," Moira said, launching herself into his arms. "You'll see."

It helped her case that the strap on her gown slid off. After that, Luke could barely think of his own name, much less any arguments he might have wanted to offer.

Moira was thoroughly pleased with her efforts the night before. She might have used a little manipulation to get her way, but she was pretty sure Luke was pleased enough with the reward for his acquiescence.

When there was no response to her tap on the kitchen door at Nell's, she headed for the garden. Sure enough, Nell was on her knees weeding, while her grandfather observed.

She settled into the Adirondack chair next to his. "Shouldn't you be helping?" she asked him.

"Fool woman chased me off," he grumbled. "She claims I don't know a flower from a weed. Now, I ask you, how am I supposed to tell the difference this time of year? They're all just green things poking through the dirt."

Nell glanced up at that. "Wasn't a nursery among your business interests in Ireland?"

"Yes, and others ran it quite successfully," he countered.

Nell turned to Moira. "If he were half as uninvolved in that business as he claims, you'd think by now he'd have let me educate him about the difference," she said tartly. "I think he finds it convenient not to know."

Moira laughed. It was obviously a familiar argument. "Something tells me you're right, Nell. My grandfather has mastered any number of skills over the years. If he's not grasping this one, there's a reason for it."

Nell took off her gardening gloves. When she went to stand up, Moira started to her feet to assist her, only to be waved off.

"The day I can't get up on my own, I'll have to give this up," Nell said. "And since I don't intend to do that until I'm dead and gone, I'll manage."

"At least you got her to take a break for a cup of tea," Dillon said. "I've been trying since I came out here. It's probably stone-cold by now."

Still he poured her a cup and set it on the table beside her chair. "If you'd like a cup, you'll need to run into the house for one," he told Moira.

"Nothing for me. I just dropped Kate off at day care and stopped by here to give you both an update."

"You've talked to Kiera, then?" Nell said.

"No, only to Luke. He's agreed to the plan."

"I've no intention of asking how you persuaded him," her grandfather said. "I'll just accept the outcome as a blessing."

"He's promised to speak to Connor this morning to get him started on the paperwork. Now, if you'll make an airline reservation for Mum, I think we can put our plan in motion," Moira told him.

Dillon nodded at once. "I'll go straight in and do that now, though I'd probably best buy the kind that's refundable just in case she balks," he said. He touched Nell's cheek. "Shall I warm that tea for you?"

"I'm fine with it as it is," she said, covering his fingers with hers and giving them a brief squeeze.

Moira watched the two of them with a catch in her throat. Would she and Luke have that same sort of devotion after so many years? Of course, Nell and Dillon had fallen in love as teenagers, then separated and had families before being reunited. Perhaps that was why they were so grateful for their second chance.

She turned and caught Nell studying her.

"You're pleased by the prospect of having your mother here?" Nell asked. "I know the two of you haven't always had an easy time of it."

"True enough," Moira admitted. "But I think I understand the choices she made a little better now. I want her to finally have some of the happiness she deserves. I think she may find that here. There's a lot to be said for a fresh start."

"Especially in Chesapeake Shores," Nell said.

"Yes, especially in Chesapeake Shores."

Which was why later that very afternoon, as Kate conveniently cried in the background, Moira called her mum and, with a note of desperation in her voice, pleaded for Kiera to come to Chesapeake Shores for an extended visit.

"I don't need to be at loose ends in a strange country," Kiera argued. "Peter's children have offered me a place at the pub for as long as I want to stay on. They'll even boost my pay if I'm willing to take on managing it, so they can go blissfully on with their own lives."

"And you're willing to accept their charity?" Moira asked, putting the worst possible spin on what had no doubt been a genuine and well-meant offer that would benefit all of them, including her mother.

Her comment was greeted with silence, which told Moira her mother had considered the very same thing. They were very much alike in questioning the real motive behind any kindness they might feel was undeserved.

"We're your family, not them. You won't be in the way here," Moira said, pressing her tiny advantage. "I truly need the help, and you should spend a little time with your first grandchild. And with me traveling so much lately, Luke could use your presence at the pub. The customers like chatting with someone with an Irish lilt in their voice. It provides a touch of authenticity."

"So I'm to be the Irish window dressing?" Kiera asked, the once-familiar tart sarcasm back in her voice. "How is that an improvement over accepting charity from the McDonoughs?"

"The job here would be much more than that," Moira promised. "This is a family business, and you're family. It would be almost the same as if it were your own restaurant."

"I doubt Luke would see it that way. Wasn't this pub his dream? Besides, it's not as if I can waltz in and take a job in America," Kiera protested. "I know there are laws about that sort of thing."

"Luke's cousin Connor will handle the legalities of

a work visa, just as he did for me," Moira assured her. "Focus on spending time with little Kate for now. I can't wait for you to see her in person. She's growing so fast, and she's a handful. You'll probably find her to be a lot like me in that respect."

With the baby's pitiful cries to lend credence to her story, Moira gave a silent fist pump when Kiera reluctantly agreed to take the very flight that Dillon had already booked. As she hung up, Moira gave the baby a noisy kiss that changed tears to smiles.

"Now we've only to find a way to make her stay," she said.

And that, most likely, was going to be a far more difficult task. Kiera might be feeling a bit vulnerable at the moment, but it wouldn't last. And when her fine temper was restored, there could be hell to pay for their manipulation.

Chapter 2

Kiera had seen pictures of Chesapeake Shores, some on postcards, but many more taken by her daughter. None, however, had prepared her for the tug of recognition she felt as Moira and Luke drove her through the quaint downtown area with its charming shops, circled the town green with its display of colorful tulips and then turned onto Shore Road en route to their home. To their left, the Chesapeake Bay sparkled in the sunlight. The sky above was a brilliant blue. A few impressive sailboats were taking advantage of the morning breeze.

"It's a bit like a seaside village in Ireland, isn't it?" she said, taking it all in. "The architecture's very different, to be sure, but the feel of it's the same."

Moira beamed at her. "That's exactly how I saw it when I first came to town. I felt at home here almost at once. And you know it was Luke's uncle Mick O'Brien who designed it all from scratch and built on what was once farmland. He's a famous architect, and Luke's brother, Matthew, works for him now."

"It's hard to imagine having the vision to design an entire town," Kiera said, in awe of the thought. "The villages in Ireland go back for centuries and are a hodgepodge of styles jumbled together in cozy harmony. Mick must possess an impressive imagination."

"And I couldn't even build a playhouse for our Kate with the design spelled out quite simply for me," Luke told her. "I had to ask Uncle Mick and Matthew for help. It was a humbling experience."

Kiera knew a thing or two about asking for help, no matter how needed it might be. She sympathized with him. "Did they torment you for asking?"

"My brother will never let me forget it," Luke confirmed, then shrugged off the humiliation. "That's okay, though. He wouldn't know one ale from the next if I didn't draw his attention to it. We each have our own skills."

Kiera laughed, then noted that the comment had been made with a perfect bit of timing. "Ah, and there's O'Brien's," she exclaimed as she spotted the pub. There was no mistaking its Irish heritage with its dark green sign with gold lettering, the same type of sign that could be found on nearly every corner back home. "You've captured the look of it exactly right," she told Luke.

"Thank you. That was the idea."

"Have you thought of adding window boxes overflowing with flowers beneath the windows?" Kiera asked. "That would add another authentic touch. We Irish love our flowers and any chance to display them in a profusion of color. I think they're meant to counterpoint our gray and rainy days."

Luke smiled. "There you are, already earning your keep as a consultant, Kiera."

"I told you she'd be filled with ideas," Moira said. "Just wait until you see inside, Mother. Luke imported an antique bar from a pub in Ireland that we visited.

The son of the longtime owner had persuaded him to modernize. We didn't waste breath telling him what a mistake he was making. Luke just made the deal and we rushed right out the door. You'll swear you're back home again."

"And yet wasn't the goal to give me a fresh start in a new place?" Kiera teased.

Moira regarded her with a serious expression. "But don't you see? It will be easier if it feels at least a little bit like home. I've had hardly a pang of homesickness since I've been here."

Kiera reached for her hand and gave it a squeeze. "I know. I was teasing you."

To Kiera's regret, Moira looked surprisingly startled by that.

"Really?" Moira asked, as if the concept were completely foreign to her.

Kiera sighed. "I suppose I shouldn't be shocked by your reaction. There wasn't much lightness and laughter or teasing when you were growing up. Peter reminded me that I had buried my sense of humor down deep. He helped me recover it. He reminded me that laughter is a gift that gets us through the difficult times. I'd like to hold on to that bit of wisdom at least, now that he's left us."

Moira's eyes immediately turned misty. "Mum, I'm so sorry he's gone."

"So am I. On my good days I'm determined to hang on to the positive memories and treasure the changes he brought to my life. At first I wasn't sure I could do that, but it's almost as if I hear him whispering in my ear that I must, that I can't retreat back into my old ways." She gave her daughter a knowing look. "Believe me, I know that's a concern for you and your grandfather, as well."

"We'll help with it," Moira promised. "And Kate will be the answer to your prayers. It's hard to go more than a minute without smiling at something she's done. She's such a blessing."

"I can't wait to meet my very first grandchild," Kiera told her. "Imagine me, old enough to be a grandmother. There was many a day I wasn't sure I'd survive being a mother, and here you are, a mother yourself *and* a successful photographer."

Luke stopped again in front of a storefront down the block from the pub. There were several stunning, very modern paintings in the windows. Though Kiera knew nothing of art at all, the wildness of these spoke to her on some level she couldn't entirely explain. It was as if she'd experienced the emotions they evoked so vibrantly.

"This is where Moira's works were first exhibited," Luke said proudly. "I know Peter encouraged her, but my aunt Megan is the expert over here who discovered her photography."

"And has nagged at me until I almost believe I have real talent," Moira said. "I wake up some days pinching myself when I see an advertisement for my work in some famous gallery in New York or on the West Coast."

"Peter was so proud of you," Kiera told her. "He bragged about you to every customer who came into the pub and pointed out all of your pictures on the walls. Original works by Moira O'Brien, he'd tell them, then show them the programs from your exhibits in America. He was so pleased that you sent those to him. He loved you like a daughter, you know."

"Stop or you'll have me bawling," Moira protested. "Let's go home, Luke. I want Mum to see our house and meet our Kate. After flying all night, she's no doubt anxious for a bit of a rest."

"I would like nothing more than to hug my granddaughter, then have a hot shower," Kiera admitted. "And perhaps a cup of tea. Then I'll be ready to see your grandfather and Nell and see whatever else the day has in store."

"Nell has invited the whole family for an afternoon barbecue in your honor," Moira told her. "I tried to tell her it might be too overwhelming after your long flight, but she insisted. She wants you to feel welcome. And Grandfather is anxious to see for himself that you're doing okay after everything that's happened."

"When am I to begin working for you, Luke, beyond suggesting window boxes as I just did? If I'm going to be here for a while, I want to pay my own way."

If she hadn't been watching her son-in-law so closely she might not have noticed just the slightest hesitation, the quick glance between him and Moira. "Is there some problem you haven't mentioned?"

"Just a bit of a delay on the paperwork," Luke said hurriedly. "My cousin says there's nothing to worry about. Things like this are just taking longer these days. You might have to wait before officially starting on the job."

Kiera's spirits sank. Her fresh start was clearly more precarious than they'd led her to believe. "There's no job?"

"Of course there's a job," Moira said, casting a defiant look at Luke. "It will just be unofficial for the time being. You'll still be consulting."

"But this consulting work will be an unpaid position?" Kiera asked, determined to clarify her status. "I'll be living here on your charity?" It was exactly what she hadn't wanted, to be a burden on her daughter and Luke. She'd agreed to come for a lengthy stay only because of the promise that she'd be earning her keep.

"You're family, Kiera. There's no charity in this," Luke quickly assured her. "You'll be paid for the work you do, just not as an official employee until we can work out the legalities."

"How long might that take?"

"Connor is certain it will go smoothly," Moira insisted.

"A few weeks at the most," Luke said.

Kiera sighed heavily. "I see." She'd cut her ties with home, only to find herself with an uncertain future.

"I know what you're thinking," Moira said. "And you're wrong. This is going to work out. You'll see."

"Perhaps we should have been more certain of that before I came," she replied wearily.

"Kiera, you can talk to Connor yourself later today," Luke said. "He'll be able to reassure you."

She was suddenly far too exhausted to argue. "Then I'll wait and see," she said, then amended silently, *and try not to feel discouraged.*

But if there was no hope for a reasonably quick resolution to her work status here, then she would have to make a call to the McDonoughs and see if there was any chance she could go back to work for them in Dublin. Even if Luke and her daughter did their best to convince her that she had a place here with them, she'd spent too many years counting on no one but herself to settle for that. The fact that she could make her own way in the world was the one thing in which she'd always taken pride. Now more than ever, she needed to cling to that faith in her own abilities.

All thoughts of that discouraging news flew out the window, though, when Kiera walked into Moira's home and met her granddaughter. With her rosy, round cheeks, halo of strawberry blond curls and blue eyes welling with tears, she was the spitting image of Moira as a baby, as was the temper tantrum she was throwing.

"I'm so sorry," the young girl who'd been babysitting said when they came in. "I wanted her to look perfect for your arrival, but she objected to me changing her, then kicked off her shoes and screamed bloody murder when I tried to put her in her playpen."

Kiera reached for Kate anyway, feeling a tug she hadn't felt since the first time she'd held Moira in the hospital so long ago. The baby gave her a startled look, then settled in her arms with a sleepy sigh, worn out by her tantrum.

"You've a golden touch," Moira said happily. "I knew you would."

Kiera smiled. "Experience," she told her daughter.

Luke laughed. "So Moira's moods started that early?"

"In the cradle," Kiera confirmed. "And just like our Kate, it was hard to hold them against her, when she was so perfect in other ways."

When she glanced at Moira, she saw that tears were tracking down her cheeks. "What?" she asked, worried that she'd upset her within minutes of walking in the door.

"You thought I was perfect," Moira whispered.

"Of course I did. Now I imagine Luke sees you that way, too."

"Love must come with blinders, then," Moira said, smiling. "A good thing, too."

"Kiera, love, you seem awfully quiet," Dillon said, drawing Kiera away from the crowd of O'Briens scattered across Nell's yard. "Are you needing a bit of a rest? I'm sure everyone would understand if you wanted to go back to Moira's or even just inside to lie down in our guest room here for a quick nap."

Kiera saw the genuine concern in her father's eyes and, not for the first time today, wanted to give in and let the tears flow. She'd shed plenty when Peter first died a few months ago, but none since. And as much as she'd wanted to cry when Luke and Moira had filled her in on the delay to her work visa, she'd held back, stayed strong and hidden her panic as she'd learned to do so well over the years. She'd never wanted her children to experience every uncertainty that terrified her.

Now, though, she wanted to feel her father's strong arms around her, comforting her as he had when she was a girl and had skinned her knee or had her heart broken. She wondered what Dillon would think if she just buried her face in his chest and sobbed, as she held on tight.

Instead, she forced a smile. "I'm okay, Dad."

"I'm not convinced of that," he said. "Even after all these years, I can tell when you're in pain. And why wouldn't you be? Peter's death was a shock. And coming here is a huge change." He studied her knowingly.

"It's been a while since you've taken so many risks at once."

Surprised by his insight, she murmured, "You have no idea."

"Do you think I didn't have a few moments of uncertainty when I agreed to pick up everything and leave Ireland to be with Nell?"

She smiled at that. "You, uncertain? I can't imagine such a thing."

"Only a fool doesn't have second thoughts when they risk a big change," he told her. "The brave move forward and do it anyway, because they believe the rewards will be worth it. Having Nell with me for the rest of our lives was worth everything I gave up. And despite how it turned out, I know you're at least a little happy that you had Peter in your life, even if it was for far too brief a time."

A knot formed in Kiera's throat, preventing speech, but she nodded. When she could finally find the words, she whispered, "He was the best man I've ever known."

"And coming here to Chesapeake Shores will be another of those risks that will turn out well in the end," he promised. "You'll look back someday and be unable to imagine being anywhere else." He glanced around until his gaze settled on Nell. His entire expression softened. "I know this is where I belong."

Though she was touched by the sentiment in his voice and on his face, she frowned at his words. "I'm only staying temporarily," she reminded him. "Even if that work visa finally comes through, it won't last forever. Don't be thinking of this move as permanent."

"I'm hoping you'll change your mind about that. We all are." He beckoned a young man over. "Connor, please tell Kiera that everything will work out in the end."

"I'm doing everything I can to speed things along," Connor assured her.

"And I've made a few calls myself," Mick O'Brien said, joining them.

Connor scowled at his father. "Dad, haven't I warned you that your meddling with immigration could actually make things more difficult?"

Mick looked undaunted by the criticism. "Haven't you learned by now that contacts are to be used cleverly when you have them?"

"And now I'm the cause of a family squabble," Kiera said with regret.

All three men laughed. "Not to worry, Kiera," Mick assured her. "Connor and I could squabble over the color of the sky. It doesn't mean anything. One of these days he'll come to respect my judgment, rather than taking issue with my attempts to help. I think standing his ground with me has made him far more effective in the courtroom, though I doubt he'll admit that, either."

"I can't deny that I've had more experience at winning lively debates than most of the lawyers I encounter," Connor said. He grinned at Mick. "I will thank you for that, at least." He gave Kiera a reassuring look. "Stop worrying. Leave that to me."

Mick nodded. "You are in good hands, Kiera."

His words seemed as much of a shock to Connor as they were a reassurance to her.

"Now, why don't we grab some of Ma's apple pie before it's all gone?" Mick said. "I know where there's an extra quart of vanilla ice cream to go with it." He feigned a dark scowl for Dillon's benefit. "Don't tell Ma

I know about her secret stash in the spare refrigerator on the back porch."

"Not a chance," Dillon said. "I'm happy to learn of it myself. Now when she tells me we're all out of my favorite ice cream, I can see for myself if she's fibbing to keep me from overindulging."

Kiera was swept off on the sound of the men conspiring and on the reassurance of Mick O'Brien's confidence. She wanted desperately to believe that Connor had her situation under control, and Mick's faith in his son made her more hopeful than she'd been just minutes ago.

For a few blissful days Kiera allowed herself to recuperate from the unfamiliar effects of jet lag. She indulged in playing with little Kate, who, as predicted, was a constant source of joy, even when her temper kicked in to remind Kiera of how impossible Moira had been at the same age and, truth be told, well beyond it.

But by the end of her first week in Chesapeake Shores, she was anxious to get to the pub and see for herself just how well Luke had re-created a bit of Ireland here on the Chesapeake Bay in Maryland.

To ensure that he couldn't put her off yet again, she was dressed and ready by nine in the morning, the time he usually kissed Kate goodbye and headed to O'Brien's to handle paperwork and such before the pub opened for lunch. She had Kate in her carrier, ready to go along, as well. Moira had gone off to a meeting with Megan to look through some of her latest pictures, which fit in quite nicely with Kiera's plan.

"What's this?" Luke asked, regarding the two of

them suspiciously as they sat on the front porch when he emerged from the house.

"We thought we'd accompany you to work this morning," Kiera said brightly. "We won't stay too long. Moira's just down the street meeting with Megan, so we can catch a ride home with her or walk back on our own, since it's such a lovely spring day with not a cloud in the sky."

Luke raised an eyebrow. "Clearly you've thought of everything."

Kiera nodded. "I tried to be thorough."

"So you've tired of just hanging around the house babysitting?"

"I will never tire of being with my precious granddaughter, but I want to see the inside of this pub of yours so I can start making a contribution. You can tell me what your needs and expectations are, as well."

Luke nodded, an unexpected grin spreading across his face.

"What is it about this that has you smiling?" Kiera asked.

"Your daughter owes me a fancy dinner at Brady's," he said. "I told her your patience was unlikely to last another day. She was sure you'd make it through another week."

"The two of you have been making bets about this?"

Luke immediately looked guilty. "I'm sorry. I probably shouldn't have told you that. It's just something that we do when we see things differently, a way to take advantage of whichever one of us is proven right in the end."

"My Moira isn't enough of a challenge as it is?" Kiera asked.

Luke laughed. "Oh, she will never stop being a challenge, that's for sure, but she's mellowed since she's been here. I think she's mostly content with her life."

"I'm glad for that," Kiera told him. "She didn't have an easy time of it growing up, between never really knowing her dad and me working nonstop just to keep our heads above water. I know she saw how bitter and resentful I was, but I doubt she realized how much of it rubbed off on her and changed her own view of the world. I've seen that mellowing you're talking about since I've been here. I've heard it in her voice when we've talked on the phone. You, your family, this place, it's all been good for her."

"I think maybe it's Megan who's done the most for her. Learning that she has a genuine, sought-after talent has given Moira a self-confidence she was lacking when we met. She was spirited enough, but it was based on sheer grit and stubbornness. Now it's grounded in a sense of self-worth."

Kiera gave him an appraising look. "You know her well."

"I love her," he said simply. "I think I did from the day we met. Knowing her well took a little more time and a lot more understanding."

Kiera was surprised by his openness about his feelings and his maturity. "I think I'm going to enjoy getting to know you better, Luke O'Brien. You're a fine man."

"We'll see how you feel after you've worked with me for a time," he said.

Kiera laughed. "I've worked for a tyrant or two in my day," she said. "You'll hold no surprises if you turn out to be another one."

"Hopefully not a tyrant," he said.

"We'll see what your staff says about that," she said. "Now tell me about them."

On the quick drive to the pub, he ran through the short list of waitstaff, many of whom were college students working part-time. "You'll be working most closely with the chef, Bryan Laramie," he concluded. "Bryan's pretty easygoing, but he considers the kitchen his domain."

"The name doesn't sound Irish."

Luke chuckled at that. "No, Bryan's a New Yorker by birth, a graduate of the Culinary Institute, who landed somehow in Baltimore working at a deli. I've never heard the whole story about that. He doesn't talk much about himself or his past."

"Isn't a deli one of those places known for matzo ball soup and pastrami on rye sandwiches?"

"Among other things, yes."

"Why would you hire someone like that to run the kitchen in an Irish pub?" Kiera asked.

"Of all the applicants, Moira and I liked him the best. And Nell put him to a test with some of her best recipes and he won the position hands down over two others we considered. You'll see. He knows his way around the kitchen and we're building something of a reputation for the quality of our food, as well as for our selection of ale and the fine Irish music we bring in on the weekends."

"Then I'll keep an open mind," Kiera promised.

Luke gave her a worried look. "Kiera, O'Brien's runs smoothly because we operate as a team. We all know our roles and respect each other's contributions, from the waitstaff and kitchen staff all the way through to Moira and me."

"And where exactly am I to fit in?"

"Once you've spent a little time learning the way we operate, getting to know our regular customers and so on, you'll make recommendations just as any of the rest of us might. We're always open to fresh ideas. And anything that ensures our customers of a true Irish experience will be especially welcomed. We'll trust you about that."

It all sounded perfectly reasonable to her, even if offering a little less control than she'd been anticipating. Still, she would have Luke's ear if there were changes she felt needed to be made in the name of Irish authenticity.

"How will you be introducing me to the staff?" she asked. "Am I to be one of them, or a consultant only, as Moira suggested, or a nosy troublesome mother-in-law who happens to be visiting from Ireland and can't keep her opinions to herself?"

Luke gave her a curious glance. "Are you in need of a formal title?"

"Not for my ego," she replied tartly. "But it will be a help to all of us, if I know my place."

"Since I can't give you an official position just yet until Connor settles that paperwork, why don't we just say you're helping out and lending us your expertise from years of working in pubs in Ireland?"

Kiera nodded slowly. "So a voice, but no authority."

"Something like that," Luke said, his tone cautious. "Are you okay with that for now?"

"I'll do my best to make it work," she said. She'd spent years under similar restraint in her old job. She'd had far more freedom and say at Peter's pub, but she could put that aside for now. At least she hoped she could, if only in the name of family harmony.

Bryan looked up from the Irish soda bread he was about to put into the oven to see Kiera Malone regarding him intently, her expression radiating disapproval.

"Something on your mind?" he asked.

"Just observing," she said, backing off a step.

"But you have something to say. I can see that you're practically biting your tongue. Just say it."

Ever since Kiera had been introduced to the staff at O'Brien's, she'd been lurking about, *observing* as she put it. It was driving him a little bit crazy. He didn't like extra people milling about in his kitchen, especially with an unmistakable hint of judgment in their eyes. He'd grown used to being respected, thanks to regular praise from not only the customers, but from Nell O'Brien, who was his go-to person for inspiration with the menu and its execution.

To be fair, from what he'd seen, Kiera was a hard worker in general and she got on well enough with the customers and even the waitstaff. She wasn't still for a minute and was always eager to take on any task that was given to her, even pitching in to help out washing dishes or scrubbing the floor after hours. All of that was admirable.

It was the way she watched him as he worked, though, that made him want to banish her from his kitchen. It was only out of respect for Luke and Moira that he'd kept his mouth shut till now and tried to accept her presence underfoot.

He studied her expression and could tell she was

torn between speaking out and staying silent. "Just say whatever's on your mind before your head explodes," he told her impatiently.

"The soda bread is going to be hard as a rock," she blurted finally.

He frowned at her. "And just why is that?"

"You were pounding it as if you had a grudge against it," she told him.

Bryan drew in a deep breath to try to calm himself before he said something he'd regret. It was true, he'd been taking out his frustration over Kiera's presence on the dough. And, quite likely, she was right. Over-kneading would be the kiss of death for the soda bread. It would likely be inedible.

Rather than admitting as much, however, he simply gestured to the array of ingredients. "Would you like to show me how it's done?"

Her expression brightened at once. "You won't be offended?"

Given that it was his way of saving face when his own loaves of bread were tossed in the trash, no, he wouldn't be offended at all.

"Have at it," he said, instead. "I have other work to do if we're to be ready when the doors open for lunch."

When he turned back a few minutes later, Kiera was lovingly kneading the bread with a touch that stirred an annoying hint of longing. Out of the blue a shocking image of those hands on him, massaging his shoulders at the end of the day, made him more irritable than ever. Images like that were not only inappropriate, they were totally unwelcome. At this rate, the woman was going to drive him to the brink of insanity and she hadn't even been underfoot a full week.

Chapter 3

When Kiera emerged from her room on her day off, she found Moira on the porch with a cup of tea, looking far more relaxed than she usually did during the family's hectic mornings.

"What are you doing all alone out here?" Kiera asked, drawing her robe more tightly around her to ward off the early-morning chill. "And where's your sweater? The air's cool and damp today. You'll catch a cold."

Moira chuckled. "It's been a few years since you've scolded me like that. You call this weather cool and damp after living by the sea in Ireland? Have you been away so long already that you've forgotten what cool and damp are truly like? I remember it clearly. The fog rolling in off the water, the dampness seeping into your bones. This weather today is nothing that a nice cup of tea can't improve. May I get you one?"

"I'll do it for myself in a minute," Kiera said. "So what are your plans for the day? Usually by now you're already out the door with your camera in hand."

"I have the whole day entirely to myself," Moira said. "Luke took Kate over to Carrie's today. The babysitter will pick her up later. Since you're off as well, I thought you and I could do something together, perhaps starting with breakfast at Sally's."

"Why there, when I could fix something for us here?" Kiera asked.

"It's become a tradition for the O'Brien women who have businesses downtown to gather there every morning before they start their workday," Moira explained. "You've been here a couple of weeks now. You should really get to know them. I find listening to them talk about balancing work and family to be inspirational. On my bad days, they help me to believe I can successfully juggle it all."

"I've already met them all," Kiera reminded her.

"At Christmas in Ireland years ago and at Nell's when you first arrived here. That's hardly time to get to know them. I'll bet you can't even put names with faces yet."

Kiera lifted a brow. "Is that a dare I hear in your voice? Your husband seems to think your marriage depends on these little bets you have between you. Are you taking that tack with me, too?"

Moira blinked and color rose in her cheeks. "Luke told you about our bets?"

"He did," she said, chuckling at her daughter's dismay. She had a feeling they weren't talking about precisely the same bets. Some must take an interesting and intimate twist from time to time. It was probably best that she didn't know the details of those.

"Are you daring me to name the O'Brien women when we see them at the restaurant?" Kiera persisted. "Have you forgotten that a good waitress must have a knack for keeping her regular customers' names straight in her head, along with their food preferences and any other details they might reveal over time?"

"Then you're accepting the challenge?" Moira asked, sounding surprised.

"Of course, but what's the reward if I prove myself?"

"I will treat you to a full day of pampering—a manicure, pedicure, all the spa treatments you can imagine, including a new hairstyle."

Rather than succumbing to the temptation of such an indulgence, Kiera bristled. "And what is wrong with my hairstyle?"

"Nothing at all," Moira said hurriedly. "But twisting your hair into a tight knot on top of your head isn't exactly a style, now, is it, at least not of the sort they show in fashion magazines? In your case it's merely a convenience."

"It's the way I've worn it for years. It suits me and it meets regulations at any restaurant."

"Now, there's an explanation to make any woman proud of her appearance," Moira argued. "Besides, the truth is that you do it mostly because it's easy and familiar."

"Haven't you shaken up my routine enough in recent weeks?" Kiera grumbled. "Are you now concerned with my frumpy appearance?"

"You're not frumpy," Moira declared hurriedly. "Just a wee bit dated, perhaps. Most women like a change now and again. I thought you'd be pleased by the prospect. I wasn't trying to insult you."

Kiera sighed. "I know you weren't. And it's a lovely offer. If I win, I'll let you make me over however you like."

Moira's eyes narrowed. "You aren't going to lose on purpose just to thwart my efforts, are you?"

"Girl, don't you know me well enough to know that

I never lose anything on purpose? We're a lot alike in that way."

Moira laughed then. "We are, indeed."

"And what if you win and I can't name everyone? What am I to give you?"

"The chance to spend the day with you at a spa," Moira said.

"Clever," Kiera said approvingly. "You've a knack for getting your own way, no matter what."

"Something my husband has learned very well," Moira replied with a saucy grin.

A half hour later, they walked in the door at Sally's. The brightly lit, cozy café, which was just across from the town green, was crowded with people sipping coffee and having a chat before work. Some had plates piled high with eggs and sausages and bacon. Others had croissants, some raspberry, some chocolate. Both looked delicious. Kiera's mouth watered.

When she could tear her gaze away from the flaky croissants, Kiera immediately spotted several of the O'Brien women seated at a large round table in the back.

"We used to sit in a booth with everyone coming and going as their workdays began," Moira told her as she started to weave her way between tables. "But it got to the point where there were so many of us and none of us wanted to miss anything that we took over the bigger table in back." She leaned closer. "We stole it right out from under some of the men in town, who thought they'd earned a permanent right to it," she confided. "I think that was the real reason we made the move."

Kiera chuckled, pleased by the thought of getting to know some women who weren't intimidated by anyone. She stopped en route to joining them and put a hand on Moira's arm to halt her progress. "Shall we put my memory to the test now before we join them or would you prefer that I demonstrate by greeting them one by one?"

Amusement sparkled in her daughter's eyes. "Your choice."

"Then I'll go and say hello," Kiera said, walking the last few steps to the table and approaching Mick's wife first. "Good morning, Megan. I'd love to know more about those paintings in the window at your gallery. I've been admiring them ever since I arrived. And Bree, how are you today? As soon as Flowers on Main opens this morning, I'll be in to buy some fresh flowers to take home. Shanna, I'll be stopping by your bookstore later, as well. I'm told you carry a fine selection of cozy mysteries. They're my favorite. Heather, the quilt you have in the window of your store is lovely. Did you make it yourself?"

She turned to Moira. "Have I done this to your satisfaction?"

Moira blushed as the others regarded them curiously. "I'm afraid I made the mistake of betting my mum that she'd never remember each of your names. She's gone me one better by noting which shops you own, too."

"Don't you know you should never underrate a mother's hidden talents?" Megan teased, laughing. "Kiera, I think it's a common curse. Children never think we have any skills worth noting."

"I won't make that mistake again," Moira vowed. "This one is costing me a trip to a day spa."

"Oh, what I wouldn't do for a day of pampering," Bree said with a sigh, holding up her hands for inspection. "I have far too many nicks from thorns and floral wire, and my nails are totally ragged."

"Then come along," Kiera said readily.

"Oh, do," Moira chimed in. "It will be fun to have a totally indulgent girls' day."

"Sadly, I don't have anyone to take over for me at the shop today," Bree said. "But if you go again, count me in."

The talk turned to family gossip and bits of town news. Even though Kiera didn't know all of the people whose names were tossed about, there was something surprisingly soothing about being treated as a member of this boisterous group that laughed almost as frequently as they spoke. She felt more a part of them than she had on the day they'd first welcomed her at Nell's. That was a more formal occasion, and while it had been meant to make her feel included, she'd really felt like an outsider who had something to prove. Today she felt accepted. After years of living as if it was her against the world, it was startling how good that simple act of acceptance felt.

Bryan had felt oddly edgy all day. He'd glanced over his shoulder half a dozen times, expecting to see Kiera Malone lurking about, watching him as she had ever since her first unofficial day on the job at O'Brien's. Instead, there'd been no sign of her. And, ironically, that bothered him almost as much as her presence. He was obviously losing it.

"You seem a bit off-kilter today," Luke said as Bryan took a rare break to sit at the bar and have a cup of coffee while the pub was in a lull between lunch and dinner. "Everything okay?"

"Fine," Bryan said. "It's been quieter than usual, don't you think?"

Luke gave him an incredulous look. "Did you not keep count of how many meals you were putting together at lunch? We had an entire busload of tourists come in, along with our regulars."

Bryan felt his cheeks heat. "Well, of course, there were a lot of customers. I was talking about…" His voice trailed off. There was no way to explain without giving himself away.

"Are you, by any chance, referring to Kiera's absence?" Luke inquired, a knowing glint in his eyes.

"Is she not around?" Bryan asked, trying to seem disinterested.

Luke just laughed. "Nice try, my friend, but I know she's been getting under your skin."

"Not at all. It's just that…" Again, he couldn't think of any words that wouldn't either imply too much or be insulting somehow to his boss's mother-in-law. Neither would be good.

"It's just that she's always underfoot in *your* kitchen," Luke guessed.

Bryan sighed. "Something like that."

"Is it too much?" Luke asked, real concern in his voice. "I can tell her to back off, to go through me if she has suggestions."

"That would be making too much of it," Bryan said, though it was exactly what he wanted. "I'm just not used to having someone question every move I make."

Worry continued to darken Luke's eyes. "Is that what she's doing? You know I trust you. More important, my grandmother trusts that you know what you're doing, and it's her opinion we live by when it comes to the food here. Everybody in town enjoys an invitation to Nell O'Brien's table. Since we've been open, they now feel they can have that sort of meal right here anytime they want. I don't want anyone to suggest we don't have faith in the way you're running the kitchen."

"To be honest, Kiera doesn't say all that much unless I urge her to speak up. It's just the look on her face. I know she's biting her tongue to keep from offending me. It makes me nervous."

"Are you sure it has nothing to do with her being an attractive woman?" Luke taunted. "I know she might be a couple of years older than you and I see her only as Moira's mother, but I've seen the way the gazes of some of our regulars follow her when she's in the room. It's little wonder that you're not immune."

Bryan scowled. "This is most definitely not about that," he said flatly. "I'm not saying she's not attractive, just that I'm not interested in her in that way. It would be inappropriate. She's my boss's mother-in-law. That makes her off-limits. Period."

"Said a little too emphatically, if you ask me," Luke noted, laughing. "But I'll take you at your word. If you want me to speak to her, keep her out of the kitchen, just let me know. I've told her that's your domain. I can remind her again."

"That would be making too much of it," Bryan said again, feeling foolish about the entire conversation. It had probably been far too telling. Kiera Malone rattled him, and he wasn't entirely prepared to say why. He wasn't even sure if he could explain it to himself. And he certainly wasn't about to endure Luke's teasing by making some faltering attempt to explain it to him.

* * *

It was well past six when Kiera and Moira left the spa and headed straight for O'Brien's for something to eat. Kiera had a hunch Moira was more excited about showing off her mother's makeover than she was about her own.

Kiera still wasn't used to the image she saw when she looked into the mirror. She looked ten years younger. That's what the hairstylist had told her about the shorter cut, and Moira had agreed. Kiera wasn't sure about ten years, but she did feel lighter and more feminine somehow. And not all of the color in her cheeks was due to the blush they'd applied at the salon. She felt surprisingly good about her new look, though oddly uneasy about showing it off at the pub.

When her daughter held open the door for her at O'Brien's, Kiera hesitated ever so slightly.

"Mum, what are you afraid of? You look amazing."

"I don't feel like myself at all. At my age, there's no need for this sort of nonsense."

"At *your* age?" Moira mocked. "You're far from over the hill. Pretty polish on your nails, skin that glows and a haircut that frames your face is not unnecessary nonsense. Every woman deserves to feel beautiful, whatever her age. As soon as we're inside, I'm going to get my camera out of Luke's office and take some pictures, so you can see yourself as I do."

"The last thing I want is a fuss. I don't want to be the center of attention," Kiera said nervously.

Moira sighed. "Will you please just come inside and graciously accept all of the compliments that I know are going to come your way?"

"Is that supposed to make me less nervous?" Kiera

grumbled, but she did walk into the pub, relieved to see that it was busy enough that she might not even be noticed. Of course, that didn't take into account that Mick and Megan were seated at the bar, as they often were, along with Luke's parents, Jeff and Jo O'Brien.

It was Megan who caught sight of her first.

"Oh my, look at you," she said, coming over to clasp Kiera's icy hands. "You look fabulous, Kiera." She turned to the rest of the family. "Doesn't she?"

"I would hardly have recognized you," Mick said. "I like the new hairstyle. It becomes you."

Jo beamed. "I need someone to take me in hand, as Moira did for you. I haven't had a makeover in years and I am in sad need of one. Being on the athletic field at the high school all day long wreaks havoc with my skin and my hair. Kiera, you're putting all of the O'Brien women to shame with this new look of yours." She grinned at Megan. "Well, perhaps not her. Megan has always been stylish from head to toe."

"It's those trips to Paris I insist Mick take me on," Megan replied. "I sit in cafés and observe what the French women are wearing, then adapt it for Chesapeake Shores. I think I've learned to knot scarves in at least twenty different ways."

"And I always thought there was only one way," Jo said ruefully.

Kiera was happy to have their attention diverted from her for the moment and fascinated by the teasing between the sisters-in-law. It continued to astonish her how well the O'Briens meshed as a family, despite differences in styles, opinions and personalities.

Luke beckoned Kiera over to the bar. "I need a closer

look at this transformation," he said. "Is this the same woman I saw polishing my bar just last night?"

"Okay, okay," Kiera said, laughing at last. "I'm flattered by all the attention, but I wouldn't mind a pint of ale right about now. Is the service in here falling apart without me on the job?"

"Happy to oblige," Luke said at once. "And what about some dinner? You and Moira must be starved after your long day. The special tonight is shepherd's pie."

One of my favorites, Kiera thought to herself. She couldn't help wondering if Bryan had the knack for it, since it hadn't been on the menu since her arrival.

"You stay right here," she told Luke. "I'll get plates for myself and Moira."

Before he could stop her, she walked around the bar and entered the kitchen. "Two shepherd pie dinners," she called out.

Bryan's head swiveled so quickly in her direction, she was surprised it didn't make him dizzy. Then his mouth gaped in a most startling and complimentary way.

"Kiera?" he said, his voice oddly choked.

"Yes. Who else would be barging into the kitchen like this?"

His gaze narrowed. "You look different."

"After the money Moira spent today, I would hope so," she said tartly, then gave him a hesitant look. "Is it a good difference?"

His lips curved slightly at the apparent hint of insecurity in her voice. "You look softer, more approachable," he said, though he sounded as if that was more troublesome than it should have been.

"Ten years younger, that's what the stylist claimed," she said. "Of course, she wanted to be sure of a tip."

"I don't know about that," Bryan said. "You looked fine before." He seemed to be fumbling for words. "But don't all women want to look younger?"

Kiera studied him curiously. There was something oddly charming about his obvious nervousness. Usually he was brusque to the point of rudeness. If there was something about her look tonight, there was also something very different in Bryan's reaction to her. She wished she could put her finger on it, but perhaps it was better that she couldn't put a name to it. That might shift the nervousness straight to her.

"What took you so long?" Moira asked when Kiera finally returned to take her seat at the bar.

"Bryan wasn't giving you a rough time, was he?" Luke asked worriedly. "Or you him?"

"Not at all," Kiera said, placing two plates of shepherd's pie on the bar. It looked just fine, and the aroma was as tempting as any she'd eaten before. "I'm anxious to give this a try. Moira, have a taste and see if it's like what we get back home."

"I've had it before," Moira said. "It's as delicious as any I've ever had, except perhaps that you've made yourself. The only dish you make that's any better is your Irish stew. I have to warn you, though, Bryan's Irish stew has become a favorite here. He takes great pride in it, as does Nell, who taught him how to make it."

Leaving the Irish stew debate for another time, Kiera took a bite of the shepherd's pie and nodded, pleasantly surprised that it seemed authentic. Not bad for a man who'd once been making sandwiches in a deli.

"Does it pass muster?" Luke asked.

"It does," Kiera said. "It's quite good, in fact."

"And will you tell Bryan that yourself? I know it would please him."

"Bryan's ego needs no boost from me," Kiera said, not sure why the thought of praising his cooking felt too much like eating crow.

Luke kept his gaze on her steady. "For the sake of harmony," he suggested.

"Fine, then," she said grudgingly. "I'll tell him." She rose to do just that before she lost the will, but Luke waved her back to her seat.

"After you've finished. A clean plate will speak volumes, too," he told her. "Bryan might not show it, but he could use a bit of reassurance from you from time to time. Nell sings his praises, but that's become commonplace. You're a new test for him and one he's not entirely sure he's passing. He feels as if you're judging him each time you walk into the kitchen."

Kiera was confused. "Isn't that what I'm here for? To find areas that need improvement?"

"Absolutely," Luke said quickly. "And I'm sure Bryan would welcome a suggestion here and there. Have you shared your thoughts with him?"

Kiera thought of how she'd been handling things and realized she'd felt constrained by her lack of real standing. She'd observed and judged, but mostly kept her opinions to herself, storing them up for the time when she'd feel free to speak her mind. She could see now how that silence might make Bryan feel uneasy. He'd probably prefer a tart comment or two to the silence.

"I'll try to do better at making him feel at ease," she said, thinking of the hint of nervousness she'd noticed for the first time earlier. Perhaps she had inadvertently thrown him off his game. That had never been her intention, but they did seem to have gotten off on the wrong foot. There was no denying that.

"I'd appreciate that," Luke said, clearly satisfied by her response.

"I've been cautious about speaking up till now, but if I'm to be honest and more candid with him, then I can't hold back my opinion when I think he's gotten it wrong," Kiera warned.

A smile tugged at her son-in-law's lips. "I wouldn't dream of asking you to," he said. "That would be as wasted an effort as asking the wind not to blow."

Kiera laughed. It would, indeed.

Chapter 4

Rather than being stuck in his closet of an office, Luke had brought the stacks of dreaded pub paperwork that occupied way too much of his time these days to a table by the window that looked out onto the bay. That view, at least, made the prospect of spending the next couple of hours dealing with numbers and invoices slightly less daunting.

He'd barely made a dent in the work when the door at O'Brien's opened and Moira came in with Kate in her stroller.

"Da!" Kate exclaimed ecstatically when she spotted him. She immediately held out her arms.

All thoughts of invoices and supply orders vanished as Luke reached for his daughter. His gaze, though, kept straying to his wife.

"What brings you by? Did you have a meeting with Megan? And why is this little angel with you, rather than your mother?"

"After we all had breakfast at Sally's, I dropped my mother off at Connor's office. There were some forms they needed to go over," she said.

Her anxious tone provided a clue for Luke, but her

pacing was a dead giveaway that something about that meeting was upsetting his wife.

"And that has you worried?" Luke asked, frowning. "Why? Did Connor suggest there might be a problem? Is something holding up the visa application?"

"No, to the contrary, he thinks this will be the last bit of paperwork needed to satisfy immigration."

"That's great news," Luke said, lifting Kate high into the air until she giggled.

"You might want to watch that," Moira warned. "She just ate an entire pancake at Sally's, then went after Mum's eggs. Our little one has the appetite of a horse now that she's trying regular food, but she hasn't learned when to stop."

"Yes, my worrywart," Luke said, shifting Kate till her feet touched the ground and she could cling to his knee to stay upright. "You know, I think she's very close to walking."

Moira regarded him incredulously. "She's not going to be a year old for another month. She's still falling on her bum whenever she tries."

"But that's the point, isn't it?" Luke said. "She's trying. She's not satisfied with crawling."

"I suppose," Moira responded distractedly, still pacing.

"Okay, that's it," Luke said. "Something is on your mind. Tell me. You've learned by now that I'm no mind reader. Is your work not going well?"

Moira shrugged. "Megan's pleased with it, or says she is. She'd like me to do more and faster, but I'm working at a pace that gives me time at home. I've told her I don't intend to sacrifice that."

"And is she pressuring you to do otherwise?"

"She doesn't say it, at least not anymore, but I know she's disappointed. She thought I'd have more free time with my mother here."

"Don't you?" Luke asked, puzzled by her mood and the entire conversation. Communication skills varied widely between the average man and woman, he'd discovered. For him and Moira, it was as if they spoke entirely different languages and, quite possibly in her case, from some universe not yet discovered.

"Of course I have more time than I did. I'm out with my camera almost every day now, while Mum watches Kate," she said impatiently, as if he should already know the obvious answer. "And when my mum is here, Kate's at day care. I've more than enough time. This isn't about work, Luke."

"But it is something," he said, seizing on the admission, albeit an incredibly skimpy one. "If it's not your work or the meeting with Connor..."

"Where I was very pointedly told I wasn't needed," she grumbled.

Uh-oh, Luke thought. "And that offended you?"

"Well, of course it did. It's never pleasant being dismissed, but if you're thinking that's the issue, you'd be wrong."

Luke bit back a sigh he knew would only escalate the frustrating conversation. "Moira, love, just tell me in simple English that my dense male mind can comprehend."

She scowled at his attempt at humor, then sighed herself. "To be honest, I miss being here, working by your side."

He grinned, hoping to lighten her dark mood. "Is it me you miss or the paperwork?" He shoved a stack in her direction. "I'd be more than happy to turn these over to you and go for a long walk with our Kate."

She shook her head, though she did crack a smile. "Nice try, but paperwork was always your domain. I miss the people," she said candidly. "I didn't expect to, since there were days I thought they'd drive me mad changing their orders or complaining that something wasn't just right."

"If this is about the company, then, I don't understand. You're in here at some point every day. You still see everyone."

"It's not the same." She sighed again, then lifted her troubled gaze to his. "You're going to think I've lost it, but I think I'm a little jealous of my mum taking my place."

He was beginning to get what she was saying, but he was far from understanding any of it. "But this was your idea, Moira. Having your mom here, not just for a visit, but working here."

"I know. That's what makes my feelings so ridiculous. Having her here was what I wanted. She and I are getting along better than we ever did back home. I think she's feeling more at home here every day. You should see her now at Sally's in the morning. In just a few short days, she's become one of the O'Brien women. They all turn to her for an opinion and laugh at her stories from Ireland. She's got them all wanting another family vacation over there, I think, so be prepared for that."

Literal minefields had nothing on the dangers of trying to pick his way carefully through a conversation with his wife. "And you're feeling left out? Replaced? What?"

"It's the same as in here, as if I don't know how I fit

in anymore." She covered her face, clearly embarrassed. "Next thing you know, I'll be complaining she's taken my place in our home, too."

Luke bit back a desire to laugh. "I don't think she'll ever replace you with me, Moira," he said, fighting to keep his tone serious.

Another hint of a smile touched her lips then vanished. "I'm not thinking *that*, you idiot. But she is making herself indispensable there, too. I'm surprised at how quickly that's come about."

Luke didn't credit himself with a lot of insightfulness, particularly where his wife was concerned, but he thought maybe he knew what was going on. "Moira, did you by any chance see yourself as your mum's savior when you suggested bringing her here?" He could tell by the flush in her cheeks that he was on the right track. "And has it turned out that, perhaps, she's quite capable of saving herself? That she saw she was heading down an old path and was ready to step in a new direction?"

She regarded him with a narrowed gaze. "When did you get to be so smart and insightful?"

He couldn't quite tell if she was impressed by that or if it was another of the day's annoyances for her. "You've given me plenty of practice at sorting through the hints you toss about," he told her. "I'm learning to put the puzzle pieces together."

"Congratulations," she said wryly. "So how do I fix my feelings, when even I can see that I should be happy that she's adjusting and that things are going so well?"

"Maybe you should try congratulating yourself for assessing what she needed and simply getting her here. It wasn't up to you to fix her sadness, but you insisted she come to a place where she could find her own path to healing."

"I didn't expect it to happen quite so fast," she admitted. "It's as if she's forgotten all about Peter."

There was a despondent, accusatory note in her voice that spoke volumes. "Do you feel as if she's betraying him just because she's choosing to live her life?" he asked.

She frowned at the suggestion. "No, of course not. It's what I hoped for, isn't it?"

"So you said at the time you invited her here, but perhaps you're finding the reality a little more jarring."

She fell silent. Luke waited her out. Moira was never quiet for long.

"Okay, yes," she said eventually. "I saw the blush on her cheeks when she came out of the kitchen the other night after talking to Bryan. There's something between those two. I think it's disrespectful to Peter's memory."

"Ah, so that's what this is really about," Luke said, realizing they'd finally hit on the real source of her misery. She'd adored Peter and hoped her mother would have a future with him. Now she feared that Kiera wasn't mourning him as he deserved. Even if her emotions were contradictory and all over the place, he had to accept they existed and try to console her.

"Moira, for starters, I don't think you need to worry that your mother has forgotten Peter or her feelings for him," Luke said quietly. "I've found her in tears more than once when I've come home late at night, and each time she's said how much she misses him."

Moira looked startled. "You've found my mother in tears and never told me?"

"I caught her in private moments. They weren't mine

to reveal," he said. "As for Bryan, that's another thing about which you're worrying for no reason."

"I know what I saw," she said stubbornly.

Luke laughed. "And I've seen it, too, on Bryan's side, but neither of them is prepared to do a single thing about it. Bryan, at least, is in denial that he has any feelings for your mother at all. He views her as a necessary nuisance, or so he claims. And your mother sees only that they're battling wits over control of the kitchen, since he's rejected every suggestion she's dared to make since I encouraged her to speak up. I'm seriously tempted to make her his sous chef, just to watch the fireworks."

"Don't you dare!" Moira said, then paused and chuckled at last. "Though it might be fun to watch. Bryan's always seemed a bit closed off and quiet. I like him a lot, but the truth is we know very little about him or his personal life outside of the pub. Seeing the two of them rile each other could be entertaining."

"Well, it's something to consider, once your mother's status is clarified and we can officially put her on the payroll," Luke said. "I think she's struggling with how to handle things with her status unresolved. I hope Connor's right that the paperwork will go through soon. She needs that to feel secure about speaking out."

Suddenly Kate released her grip on his knee and hit the floor with a solid thud. Her cries filled the pub. Moira picked her up and cuddled her close.

"I suppose she tired of not getting any attention from either of us," she said.

"Following in your footsteps, perhaps," Luke teased. "Weren't you staging your own cry for attention when you came in the door just now?"

"I suppose you'll hold that over my head," she grumbled.

Instead, Luke pulled his wife and daughter onto his lap. He tucked a finger under Moira's chin and turned her face toward him, then kissed her soundly. "If you ever need reassurance about how important you are in my life, all you need to do is say so," he told her solemnly. "You and Kate are my world."

"More important than O'Brien's?" she asked, a smile on her lips.

"More important than anything." And that was something he needed no coaching to know was exactly the right thing to say.

Kiera had stood outside the door of the pub watching Moira, Luke and Kate for a moment and concluded this time together, just the three of them, was something they needed. She was in the middle of their lives a little more than she ought to be these days.

Since she wasn't due at work for another hour and wasn't needed to help with Kate, she headed for her father's. It was a pleasant morning for a walk along the bay with the sunlight filtered through sprawling oak trees and the sweet scent of lilacs strong in the air.

She found Dillon and Nell in the kitchen, a pot of freshly brewed Irish breakfast tea on the table and the familiar scent of currant scones coming from the oven.

"Are you sure I'm not interrupting?" she asked, sensing she'd stumbled across another cozy, intimate scene that emphasized the emptiness in her life. Funny how she'd gone for years without feeling so adrift and after just a few months of being close to Peter, she felt it with sudden and depressing clarity.

"You're family. How could you possibly be interrupting?" Nell said, pouring her a cup of tea without asking and bringing a warm scone to the table.

The aromas brought back a wave of memories from Ireland that put tears in her eyes.

"Are you missing home?" Dillon asked.

"Yes and no," she said. She gestured at the tea and scone. "These do stir so many memories, but in general I've been quite happy here. In fact, I've been surprised by how well I'm adapting." She gave her father a wry look. "Just as you said I would."

He laughed. "I'm surprised you didn't choke on those words."

"I'm capable of admitting when I've been wrong about something," she said. "In this case, it's not so much that I was wrong, as that you had better foresight than I did."

"And a lovely spin that is," Dillon said, but he was laughing as he said it.

Kiera allowed herself a smile, then debated revealing something that had been on her mind for a few days now.

"There are a few changes I've been contemplating," Kiera told them eventually. "I think I should start looking for my own place. I met with Connor earlier this morning, and he says we should have the last of the details settled for my work visa in another week. If I'm to stay for a few months, if not a little longer, I can't continue to impose on Luke and Moira. They're practically newlyweds. They don't need me underfoot." She gave them both a stern look. "And don't think I haven't realized that I was never needed to care for Kate."

"A child always needs a grandmother, if only to spoil them, and to pass along a little wisdom," Nell corrected.

"And I can do as much if I have my own place," Kiera said. "I'll begin looking as soon as my work status is finalized."

"You mentioned other changes," Nell said. "What are those?"

"Not a change so much, as a desire to feel more a part of Chesapeake Shores. I've spent a little time with your family recently, and they all lead incredibly active, busy lives. I think I've spent my life so focused on work that I've never had the opportunity to take on other commitments. I'd like to give that a try. If I'm to have that full, well-rounded life everyone seems so intent on my having, I think that's the next step."

Dillon regarded her with delight. "I think it's wonderful that you're interested in taking on something new. You'll find that giving back in some way can be incredibly fulfilling."

"I agree," Nell said, her expression turning thoughtful. "And I might have some ideas along that line."

"Of course she does," Dillon said. "Watch out, Kiera. Nell has her fingers in a lot of community pies, so to speak. Next thing you know, you'll find you don't have a minute to yourself anymore."

"That would be just fine by me," Kiera said. "I need more to do and less time to think."

"Then I will see to it," Nell said, looking delighted by the prospect.

"Thank you both for listening," Kiera said. "And for the tea and scone. It felt like a moment out of time. It was..." She searched for the right word. "Comforting, that's it. It felt like home. I think I needed that this morning. Now, though, I need to get to the pub, or Luke and Moira will wonder what on earth has happened to me. Moira will be driving around, thinking I've gotten lost. She watches over me and frets as if I haven't an ounce of sense."

"She just wants to make sure you're happy here," Dillon said. "It's what we all want. Now, would you like a ride back to the pub?"

"Thanks, but I'm fine with the walk. It's a lovely spring morning. Everyone tells me it will soon be too hot here to enjoy a stroll by the water, though I can't imagine such a thing."

She pressed a kiss to her father's cheek and then, impulsively, to Nell's. "I'll see you soon."

"You can count on that," Nell said.

"And there's your only warning to run while you still can or leave yourself to my wife's mercy," Dillon said.

"Stop with your nonsense, Dillon O'Malley," Nell scolded. "I've only Kiera's best interests at heart. She'll tell me the minute she feels overwhelmed—won't you, Kiera?"

"I've always been known to speak my mind. Isn't that so, Dad?" she said wryly.

"True enough."

Kiera left their cottage feeling warmed by more than the familiar tea and scone. How long had it been since she'd truly felt part of a family? Longer than she could recall. It felt surprisingly good.

"You took a long time to get here," Moira told Kiera when she walked through the door at the pub.

"I decided to pay a visit to your grandfather and Nell, so you and Luke could have a bit of time together."

Moira gave her an odd look that Kiera couldn't quite interpret, so she didn't bother trying. "I need to touch base with Luke and see what he wants me to do today."

"Not before you tell me how it went with Connor after the two of you pointedly told me I wasn't needed."

Kiera heard the hurt in her voice. "It was hardly that you weren't needed. Kate was too restless to keep still while we went over so many boring details."

Moira looked surprisingly startled. "That's all it was?"

"What else would it be? Did you think we were keeping secrets from you?" Kiera asked. "You heard the most important part, that he's convinced my status will be resolved within a week or two at the most. As a temporary consultant, I can hardly be taking a job from an American, since being from Ireland is in the job description."

"And you'll be able to stay for how long? Did you discuss permanent residency?"

Kiera frowned. "That was never under consideration, Moira. We're looking at a six-month work visa, perhaps a year at the outside. I don't think we can stretch it further than that."

"You have family here," Moira argued. "You'll have work. You could apply to become a legal resident. *That's* what should have been discussed."

"A discussion for another time," Kiera countered. "I'm not prepared to make such a decision yet."

Her daughter looked thoroughly dismayed by her response.

"Aren't you happy here?" Moira asked. "I thought you were. I thought you'd been adapting really well, in fact."

"Darling, I am happy. This change has definitely been good for me, exactly as you'd hoped. Do we have to take another leap already?"

Now Moira looked oddly guilty. "I just want you to know that we like having you here with us. I know Granddad wants you to stay on."

"Your grandfather knows where I stand on this. We all need to focus on the here and now and not be looking too far down the road just yet." She studied her daughter's expression. "Are you thinking for some reason that I've been feeling unwanted?"

"Maybe I was afraid that I'd made you feel uncomfortable somehow," Moira admitted. "Sometimes I send out mixed signals. Ask Luke. He's been victimized by my mood swings."

Kiera chuckled. "And haven't I known you since the day you were born? Your mood swings come as no surprise to me." She put her hand to Moira's flushed cheek. "You and Luke have been wonderful to me. I'm grateful for everything you've done. It's made things so much easier. I still miss Peter dreadfully, but I realize that life will go on, if I remain open to it. And it's easier here, where I'm not constantly reminded of the loss."

"It will get even easier, you know," Moira said earnestly. "And your life can be better than ever. Luke came into my life just when I was thinking I had nothing of value to offer anyone. And then my photography was discovered by Peter, and then Megan. And now I have baby Kate, too. A few years ago, I could never have imagined such things. I want that for you, too."

"A baby at my age? That might be a bit over the top when it comes to wishful thinking," Kiera teased. "But I appreciate the sentiment."

Moira looked startled for an instant, then chuckled. "Do you have any idea how it makes me feel to see you laughing and making jokes?"

"Which only shows how seldom I allowed myself to enjoy life for far too long. That's changing, Moira, and you're to be thanked for some of that."

"And now you're making me cry," Moira said, brushing at the tears tracking down her cheeks. "I'm going into Luke's office to steal my daughter back and take her home before I scare off the customers with my tears."

Kiera followed Moira to the back, then waited outside the door of the cramped office until she'd gathered up Kate and kissed her husband goodbye.

"See you later, my little ones," she said as they passed by.

Moira paused, her expression startled. "You always used to say that on your way out the door when my brothers and I were young."

"I did," Kiera said. "I'm surprised you remembered."

"Your leaving was the saddest, most memorable part of my day," Moira admitted. "I was never awake to hear you come in at night. I never had that moment of joy, though the boys did. Sometimes I remember lying in my bed, hearing you through the door and feeling so left out."

Tears welled in Kiera's eyes. "And you never once crawled out of bed to join us."

Moira shrugged. "I suppose I thought it would make you mad to discover I was still awake." She gave Kiera a wry look. "Or perhaps I was just being stubborn. I was quite good at that."

"Indeed you were. I hope you've grown up to learn

how important it is to make clear what you need. It was a lesson I learned far too late myself."

"I'm still working on it," Moira said. "Luke reminds me time and again that he's not a mind reader. It forces me to speak up, even when I think he should figure things out on his own."

"It's a much healthier way to live," Kiera said. "Rather than letting resentments build."

Moira hesitated, then said, "One of these days we should talk about my brothers. You rarely mention them. There must be some reason for that."

Kiera stiffened. "They've gone their own way," she said tightly. "But we can discuss that another time. It's past time for me to be earning my keep around here today."

Moira's gaze narrowed. "That cryptic answer is not enough to satisfy me, you know. But I will wait since our Kate needs to get home for some lunch."

Kiera stared after them as they left, then sighed. Her sons were a topic always guaranteed to fill her with anxiety. She'd resigned herself to the reality that they were past her influence. Those memories Moira had of the three of them laughing late at night were from a very distant past, one she doubted they would ever recapture.

Chapter 5

"Would you mind handling the bar for me during lunch?" Luke asked Kiera when she came into his office right after Moira left with Kate. "I've barely made a dent in the paperwork that was to be done this morning."

Kiera gave him a knowing look. "Seems to me you had a bit of a distraction."

"The best kind," Luke agreed. "But it has put me behind, so would you mind helping me out?"

"It's what I'm here for," she told him. "I'm capable of drawing a few pints of ale and making friendly conversation."

"Just be careful you don't do it so well that everyone asks for you and I'm rendered irrelevant."

"As if I could do that," she scoffed. "You've a knack for listening when it's called for or saying something to earn a laugh, when that's needed. Owning a pub like this is the perfect fit for you, Luke. You couldn't do better if you'd been born and bred in Ireland."

He gave her a startled look. "You couldn't have found a compliment that could please me more, Kiera. I wasn't at all sure I had a niche in life when we first met in Ireland," he admitted.

His candor revealed a rare insecurity, especially for an O'Brien. Kiera was touched that he felt comfortable sharing his feelings with her. "How can that be? I thought everyone in your family was born with confidence to spare."

Luke laughed. "It certainly seems that way, but I was the youngest and had none of the passion for a career that everyone else seemed to have. I discovered what I was meant to do while I was in Dublin. The more pubs that Moira and I visited around the countryside, the surer I felt that this could be my calling. Even then, I had no idea how my family would react. They tend to be overachievers. I feared having my own pub here in Chesapeake Shores wouldn't measure up as much of an accomplishment."

"Did they find fault with your choice?" she asked curiously. She knew Mick and Luke's own brother had international reputations as architects and urban planners. His uncle Thomas O'Brien ran a foundation dedicated to saving the Chesapeake Bay from environmental toxins. His aunt Megan, of course, had major connections in the art world, which she'd used to Moira's benefit. His cousin Bree was known for her plays that had been produced locally, by a regional theater in Chicago and even on Broadway. There wasn't a one of them who couldn't claim success in their field. Had they judged Luke's ambition to be less than theirs?

"My father questioned it at first. He thought it was too big a risk, but Uncle Mick got it right away, as did my grandmother. To my father's dismay, they were quite vocal with their support."

"I should think so," Kiera said. "Neighborhood pubs are a fine Irish tradition. Aren't there bars in the States that are similar?"

"I wanted this place to be more than just another bar. I wanted it to be a community gathering spot," Luke said.

He gestured at the arrangement of tables, subtly done to make conversation easier between tables. The antique bar he'd imported from Ireland had space for a dozen people, and a mirror behind it that allowed customers to speak to others seated several stools away and still see their reactions mirrored on the wall. And while the colors he'd chosen reflected the waterfront setting more than an Irish pub might, they were warm, inviting shades of the sea. There was even a bit of a dance floor carved out in front of the area where Irish bands played on weekends.

"Well, if your regulars are to be believed, you've achieved that," Kiera told him. "I myself can see that you've created a place that's comfortable, friendly and the first place to go for the local gossip." She hesitated deliberately, then taunted, "That is if you haven't already picked it up at Sally's in the morning."

Luke laughed. "I like to think we come by a few tidbits of news first right here, if only because Uncle Mick seems to know everything and finds my bar the perfect place to be sharing it. O'Brien's may be my pub, but Uncle Mick reigns over it."

"Now, that has the ring of truth, to be sure." With the time for the pub's midday opening almost upon them, Kiera reminded them both that they needed to get back to work. "You'd best get busy on that paperwork now. Leave the bar to me."

"I'm right here if you need me," Luke told her. "Or ask Bryan. He's filled in a time or two when we've been short-staffed."

"I'll do my best to handle it without bothering either one of you," Kiera said, and headed off to check on supplies. She stopped short when she found Bryan seated at the end of the bar with a cup of coffee.

"And shouldn't you be in the kitchen?" she inquired lightly, trying to calm the unexpected flutter of nerves she got at the sight of him. What was it about him that affected her so? He was annoying, to be sure, but it was more than that. Maybe that impossible nature of his reminded her just the tiniest bit of Sean Malone, which was far from a recommendation.

As if to prove her point about his difficult nature, he immediately bristled at the hint of accusation in her voice. "Kiera, I've been running the kitchen quite efficiently for some time now. I don't need you to tell me how to do it. I believe I've mentioned that before."

She winced. "More than once," she said stiffly. And here they went again, off on the wrong foot, just when she'd been trying to convince both Luke and herself that they could manage to get along. "I wasn't suggesting you don't know what you're doing."

"Really? Haven't you made it your role to be Luke's eyes and ears, when he's not around?" His gaze narrowed as he watched her busy herself behind the bar. "And now what? Are you taking over bartending, too? Were you not satisfied with meddling in how I run the kitchen? For the past week, you've been tossing out suggestions every time you pass through the kitchen door."

She stopped in her count of glasses and stared at him in shock. "Are you suggesting that I'm pushing my way into things that are none of my concern? I don't know what you expect, Bryan. Luke told me it bothered you if I kept silent. Now I'm speaking up too often. You'll have to excuse me if I'm confused by how to make this work with you."

Something that might have been guilt flitted across his face, but she didn't know him well enough to be sure.

"I'm only doing what my son-in-law has asked of me," she reminded him. "If that bothers you, take it up with him."

"Oh, believe me, I have."

Kiera was taken aback by the flat answer. "You've tried to undermine my position here? Why would you do such a thing? Is it your goal to get me fired from my job before I've even begun?"

This time the flush of guilt that spread across his face was undeniable. "No, of course not. Your position is not in question. Luke and Moira want you here. That's all I need to know."

"Then what?"

"I've just tried to clarify what authority you have over what I do."

"So it's a matter of authority, is it? Is it me personally you object to listening to or would it be any woman?" She paused to let her words sink in, then answered her own question. "Wait now. It can't possibly be that since you've no objection to taking Nell's words to heart or Moira's. That leaves only one answer. It must be me. Do I grate on your nerves because I hit a little too closely to the truth from time to time and underline some insecurity of yours about your cooking?"

Bryan looked genuinely distraught by her conclusion, but she was in no mood to be consoled by that. If his patience had worn thin, hers was at an end.

"Kiera, no. Look, I'm sorry," he said. "It's been a bad morning, and it has nothing at all to do with you. I'd been hoping for something, and it didn't work out. There's no reason for me to be taking my foul mood out on you. You just happened to appear as I finished taking the call."

Something in his voice alerted her that whatever that call had been about, it truly had thrown him off his game. His words were as close to a sincere apology as she'd ever heard from him. And there was no mistaking the hint of despair in his eyes, if she paused long enough to see that and not focus on the temper in his tone.

She stopped what she was doing, took his coffee cup and refilled it, then looked him in the eye. "Do you want to talk about whatever's really bothering you? I'm not Luke, but I'm a good listener and I don't spread tales."

A smile flitted across his face at that. "Spoken like a true Irish bartender," he said.

"Spoken sincerely," she countered. "We certainly can't claim to have reached the status of friends. In fact, we're coworkers and barely that, but I'd like to help if I can."

He seemed taken aback by the offer. "I appreciate that, but there's nothing you can do. It's something I'm unlikely to resolve. One of these days I have to accept that."

The resignation in his voice reminded her of times in her own past when she'd wanted to give up. Sometimes it had been her own inner strength or a bit of support offered when needed that had gotten her through. She wanted to offer that to him.

"If it's important enough, you can't stop trying, no matter how many dead ends you encounter," she told him. She thought of how her father had reached out again and again, despite her determined efforts to push him away. No matter how far apart she told herself they were, she'd known if she truly needed him, he would be there. He'd proved it by all he'd done with Moira to get her to Chesapeake Shores when she'd desperately needed to make a change.

She held Bryan's gaze and added earnestly, "It's the trying that will come to matter someday."

He sighed. "I want to believe that. I truly do." He picked up his coffee and headed toward the kitchen. "Thanks for this," he said, gesturing with the cup. "And for the advice."

Kiera watched his retreat and felt something inside her shift. Bryan Laramie was a far more complicated man than she'd ever imagined. And despite every warning bell going off in her head, she couldn't help being just a tiny bit intrigued.

There was always a natural lull between lunch and dinner at the pub. The waitstaff often changed during that time, with some of their part-time college students heading off to class and others showing up for the evening shift.

Normally Kiera wanted nothing more during those hours than to put her feet up for a bit, have a strong cup of tea and say not a single word to another soul. Today, though, with her conversation with Bryan still on her mind, she decided to take a chance and see if she could get to the bottom of his mood. Even as she told herself that pressing him was a bad idea, she stepped into the kitchen, only to find it as spotless as if there had never been a lunch rush, and deserted. Since the back door was sitting open, she peered outside and down the alley behind the building. No sign of him there, either. Going off and leaving the kitchen unsecured wasn't like him, which only worried her more.

Wherever he'd gone and whatever his reason for it, he shouldn't have been so careless, she thought with annoyance. She closed the door and turned the lock, then went back into the dining room and settled at a table just inside the door with her tea and a book that wasn't holding her interest. Her gaze kept straying to the street, but wherever Bryan had gone, he didn't appear to be in any hurry to get back.

Not that she intended to question him or even to lecture him on his carelessness. One testy encounter was enough for today. She was just hoping to see what he had to say for himself when he returned to find he couldn't slip in the same way he'd walked out.

She'd been staring down the street for a half hour or more when Luke joined her.

"Everything okay?" he asked.

"Fine. The lunch hour went smoothly. Will you be wanting me behind the bar again tonight?"

"No, I can take over. Paul called in, so I'll need you to help with serving."

Her gaze narrowed. "It's the third time this week he's called in."

"Finals are coming up soon. I think he's under a lot of pressure to get his grades up. His parents have high expectations for him. He's the first in the family to go to college. He doesn't want to let them down."

The excuse sounded like one her own sons might use

to explain away irresponsibility. "But he has a responsibility to you," Kiera objected. "That matters, too."

"I've told him his grades are the most important thing for the moment. And I have you here to take up any slack."

She nodded, accepting his decision for the generosity it showed. It wasn't up to her to tell him that his employee might be getting off too easily. If Paul was taking advantage of Luke's good nature, he'd learn it soon enough. "Of course," she said.

Luke studied her intently. "Is something else on your mind?"

"Not a thing," she said, though she couldn't seem to stop her gaze from straying once more to the empty street outside.

Luke's expression turned knowing. "If you're wondering where Bryan is, I've sent him on an errand, as I do every day or two around this time."

"Bryan's whereabouts are no concern of mine," she said a little too quickly.

"Perhaps not, but that wouldn't stop you from wondering, I suspect. There are fishermen coming in now. He's gone to check on the catch and buy fresh fish for tonight's menu if he likes what he finds."

"Ah," she said, a weight that wasn't hers to be bearing lifting.

Just then there was a pounding on the back door that startled them both, followed by a very vocal stream of what sounded like colorful obscenities. Luke chuckled. "You locked the kitchen door, didn't you?"

"I thought it needed to be secured with no one back there," she said defensively. "I'll let him in."

"Stay right there. I think it's best if I do it." He

grinned at her. "You might want to stay out of his path for a bit."

"With pleasure," she said. There had already been far too many unsettling encounters. Who knew where another one might lead? Certainly not to the peace and harmony Luke wanted among his staff.

Bryan's day had gone from bad to worse, starting with a call from his private investigator informing him of yet another dead end. He should be used to those by now. If they'd been commonplace nineteen years ago, now there were even fewer leads to investigate, so fewer disappointments to be gotten through. Still, each one cut another slice out of his soul.

Then there had been the odd encounter with Kiera right before the lunch hour. Her offer of a sympathetic ear had thrown him, especially after he'd jumped all over her with his foul temper. He hadn't leaned on anyone in so long, he had no idea how to deal with it.

And, then, just when his equilibrium was balancing out after the rough morning, Kiera—and there was no question that she was responsible, since everyone else knew the routine—had locked him out of the pub's kitchen. He'd been left standing in the alley with heavy buckets of freshly filleted fish on ice. His sour mood had returned and, once more, she was smack at the center of it.

All of that had thrown him completely off his game. Distracted, he'd added far too much salt to the Irish stew and left an entire batch of fish and chips in the hot oil until smoke filled the kitchen. Fortunately, before it could set off the alarms he'd opened the back door and allowed the cool spring breeze to replace the scent of food that was fried beyond hope.

"Were you trying to burn the whole place to the ground?" Kiera inquired as she stood in the doorway of the kitchen, hands on her lush, well-rounded hips, regarding him with that superior attitude that had been getting on Bryan's nerves since the day Luke had informed him that she was there as their latest "consultant," direct from Ireland. Pain in the posterior was more like it, he thought, trying to intimidate her with a glare that always failed to have the desired effect. All of his carefully laid out plans to make peace with her were forgotten in the moment.

"Get out of my kitchen," he ordered brusquely, hoping to stake his claim on the territory once and for all. Of course, she didn't budge. If anything, his ire kicked up the heat in her temper.

"So it's your kitchen, is it?" she asked. Gone in a flash was the more accommodating tone of this morning. "I was under the impression that it, like the rest of the pub, belonged to my son-in-law."

"Technically, perhaps, but it's my domain in here. As I believe I've mentioned before, I don't need you hovering over me every minute. I know what I'm doing."

"Yes," she said, her tone sarcastic. "I can see that from the smoke in the air."

"Have you never made a mistake, Kiera?"

"A lifetime of them," she replied tartly. "But never one that might chase off the patrons of the very place that provides my livelihood."

"Not what I've heard," Bryan muttered, turning away from the woman who was rapidly becoming the bane of his existence. For a while now Kiera had made him seriously question why he'd ever left that deli in Baltimore where he'd been a master of matzo ball soup and pastrami on rye. Even with waitresses yelling their demands and the lunchtime flurry of impatient customers in a rush, it had been a lot less nerve-racking than O'Brien's since Kiera had arrived.

"Should I be telling my customers that fish and chips are off the menu tonight?" she inquired sweetly.

"No, you should not," Bryan retorted tightly. "You should tell them they're being cooked to perfection by the chef. Now go away and let me do just that."

"If you can," she said tartly, then added far more sweetly, "Would you perhaps like me to take over with your Irish stew, since I've been told it tastes a bit saltier than usual tonight? It's been one of my family specialties for years now."

"Go away, Kiera."

Bryan gritted his teeth as she left, changed the oil in the deep fryer and started over. He winced when he realized that Luke had replaced Kiera in the doorway.

"Bad night?" Luke inquired, a barely contained smile on his lips.

"A bad few weeks," Bryan replied, not feeling any need to censor himself. Luke knew as well as he did that Kiera had created chaos since her arrival. She'd taken her role as consultant a little too seriously, questioning everything that went on in O'Brien's. He'd heard her cross-examining the waitstaff and seen for himself the changes she'd made with the location of table setups. In his opinion, the old arrangements of supplies had worked just fine. When he'd caught her in his pantry about to rearrange things, he'd tossed her out. Luke might be willing to overlook her criticism for the sake of family harmony, but Bryan didn't have to do the same.

"Bryan, we've talked about this. She's trying to find her place here," Luke reminded him. "She's a proud woman who wants to earn what little she's being paid. It's not easy being in a new country with few people she knows. And she didn't leave Ireland under the best circumstances. She'd just lost the man she loved."

Bryan heaved a sigh. "Moira has repeated that more times than I can count, and while I appreciate the position both of you are in, I'm just not sure how much more I can take." He leveled a look at his boss. "And before you ask, I have no idea why the woman bugs me. I should let her comments roll off my back. I always intend to do just that. Just this morning I would have sworn we'd reached a truce of some kind, but then she says or does something and before I know it, the battle lines are drawn once more."

"I know it can't be that you simply don't like being told what to do," Luke said. "You took my grandmother's cooking lessons well enough when she was teaching you all of her old Irish recipes. How many times did she ask you to make the same thing over and over before she was satisfied? When she did the same to me, I came close to saying words that no grandmother should ever hear a grandson utter, but I never once heard you complain or say a sharp word. Give that same patience a try for Kiera's sake."

"Nell may have been a tough taskmaster, but she's practically a saint by comparison to Kiera Malone," Bryan said. "And before you say it, the same could be said of Moira."

Luke's eyes widened in surprise. "You think Kiera is more maddening than Moira?"

"At least a thousand percent," Bryan confirmed.

"Really?" Luke asked skeptically. "Then, again, you didn't know Moira back when we first met. Let's just say I found her to be a challenge." He regarded Bryan intently. "Much the same way you look upon Kiera." He grinned suddenly, looking oddly satisfied, as if something he'd been theorizing about had just been confirmed. "This should be interesting to watch."

Bryan regarded him suspiciously. "You're not going to tell her to back off?"

Luke laughed. "I've told her the kitchen is your domain. What more can I do?" he inquired a little too innocently.

"Remind her that this is *your* pub and that she is most definitely not in charge, at least when it comes to me."

"I'll mention it," Luke agreed. "But she's a strong-willed woman."

Bryan regarded him with confusion, but then understanding dawned. "You're actually enjoying this test of wills that's developing between us, aren't you?"

"A tiny bit," Luke conceded. "As long as it doesn't interfere with the pub running smoothly, I intend to enjoy this in much the way my family enjoyed watching Moira tie me up in knots."

"Not the same," Bryan said fiercely. "They thought you needed someone to shake up your life. I'm not looking for a challenge in mine."

"Neither was I," Luke replied. "Lo and behold, though, there was Moira. As my grandmother took great pleasure in reminding me, we don't necessarily get to choose when love comes along."

Bryan gave him a horrified look. "Love? If you think that has anything at all to do with what's going on between Kiera Malone and me, then you need a bit of counseling about relationships."

Luke laughed. "My wife would probably say the same, but I think I'm right about this. All that chemistry will explode one of these days."

"Just pray it doesn't take your pub down with it," Bryan retorted.

As his boss walked away, Bryan got the distinct impression he might be doomed. That deli in Baltimore was looking better and better.

Chapter 6

For the better part of a week following their last confrontation, Kiera managed to steer clear of Bryan. Obviously she had to speak to him when placing orders or relaying special requests from their customers, but there was a deliberate civility between them these days. She should have been grateful, but it was starting to get on her nerves almost as badly as their previous exchanges of quick-tempered words. She knew exactly how to deal with a mercurial temper. Stiff politeness was something else entirely.

"You and Bryan seem to have made peace," Moira said one evening as the crowd was thinning. "I'm not hearing the tart comments and testy tones this week. How did that come about?"

Kiera shrugged. "We're both trying a bit harder, I suppose. Luke has repeatedly told me he wants peace and harmony among the staff. I'm trying to do my part to achieve that. Bryan must be as well, though it doesn't seem to suit him. He cuts himself off midsentence, when we both know perfectly well he wants to lash out and put me in my place."

Moira regarded her curiously. "You don't sound pleased about him making the effort."

Kiera hesitated then admitted, "It doesn't seem quite natural, if you know what I mean. Has Luke gone a step beyond and ordered him to be on his best behavior around me just because I'm your mother?"

"I seriously doubt it," Moira said. "Has he given you instructions to go easy on Bryan?"

"He's stressed again and again that Bryan's invaluable as his chef and that we need to find a way to get along. I've taken that to heart, but I thought Bryan was too stubborn to listen."

Moira smiled. "Well, however it came about, you're doing as Luke wanted."

"Not really. What we're doing is being exceedingly polite whenever we can't possibly avoid each other. That's not the same as real teamwork."

Her daughter carefully banked a smile. "And that's now driving you crazy? Do you have any idea why?"

"I told you before. It's not natural."

"And the bickering felt right?"

"Well, of course not," Kiera said impatiently, knowing that she was making little sense. "Who wants to argue with someone day and night over the slightest thing?"

Moira laughed. "Do you know what my brothers told me about the early days when Dad was still around?"

Kiera stared at her, startled by the change of topic, especially the shift to Sean Malone. Moira knew perfectly well that she didn't like talking about the past in general or Sean in particular. "The three of you talked about that?"

"Of course we did. I was curious about the man I

never got to meet. You never wanted to answer my questions. It always made you either sad or angry, so I stopped asking you and coaxed things out of the two of them. Not that they could be credited with much insight, but their memories were clear enough."

Kiera should have realized that her daughter would naturally be curious about the father who'd abandoned her. And, given Moira's stubborn streak, Kiera also should have known her daughter wouldn't have given up without answers from someone. Just because she'd stopped asking Kiera, Kiera shouldn't have assumed she'd stopped asking at all.

"And what did your brothers tell you?" Kiera inquired. "Not that they could be trusted. They were practically babies themselves."

"They were old enough to remember that before the drinking got so bad, the two of you would argue night and day. *Bickering* is what they called it."

"And they recalled that as being a happy time?" Kiera asked incredulously.

"They said it was always with an undertone of affection and that you always kissed and made up."

Kiera sighed. That much was true. There had been so much heat between them that any conversation could turn from peaceful to all-out warfare in a heartbeat, then end with another sort of passion entirely. She hadn't known her sons were so aware of the pattern. She'd assumed they were far too young to have any real awareness of the stormy dynamics between their parents.

"Did you?" Moira prodded. "Always kiss and make up?"

Unable to speak past the lump in her throat, Kiera nodded. "Until we didn't."

"They noted the change," Moira said, surprising Kiera again. "They said it was as if you both simply stopped caring about making things right and the arguing was all that mattered."

That summed it up nicely, Kiera thought, but concluded they'd delved into the past quite enough for one sitting. And she wasn't sure she liked where her daughter was heading with this.

"Are you drawing some sort of comparison between those days and what goes on between me and Bryan? If so, you couldn't be more wrong." She hoped her firm words would put an end to that, though she was forced to admit she'd wondered about it herself lately. While she hadn't reached any conclusions, she had lectured herself with reminders that it was not a pattern to be embraced yet again.

"I've seen the passion in your exchanges with Bryan," Moira insisted.

"It's not of a personal nature. It's because I care about doing my job, about doing the best I can for Luke and the pub," Kiera countered, satisfied with the spin.

"That's some of it, I'm sure, but I think it runs deeper. I think there's chemistry at work. I'll admit I didn't like it at first. I said as much to Luke. I thought it was disrespectful to Peter, but I'm forced to admit that it's made you come alive. There's been a spark in your eyes and color in your cheeks." She regarded Kiera intently. "That's really all I want for you. I want you to go on living."

"And you think battling wits with Bryan Laramie over his Irish stew or his fish and chips holds the key to that?"

"Maybe. It's not as if you have to rush into something with him or anyone else. Just keep an open mind, the same way I'm trying to do."

"Moira, darling, I love that you want to see me happy, but some sort of romance with a man who gets on my last nerve is not the answer. The only thing I feel when I see Bryan is the desire to shake some sense into him."

Moira laughed. "Exactly."

"You have a very odd understanding of the way relationships should work," Kiera concluded. "I suppose I'm to blame for that, since I set no example at all for you. Your dad was long gone and I never let another man into our lives until you pushed me toward Peter. He was another sort entirely. He was kind, respectful and steady, exactly the sort of man capable of giving me the life I'd never had."

To her surprise, Moira looked deeply troubled by her words. "You would have settled for that?"

"It wasn't settling," Kiera said indignantly. "I was reaching for happiness. Why would you say such a thing? You and your grandfather believed that Peter was perfect for me. Now you're questioning it?"

"I know. I'm surprised myself. It was just hearing the way you described him, as if he were a comfortable fit."

"And what's wrong with that? At my age and with my background with your father, comfortable holds a great appeal."

"A few months ago, I would have agreed and seen nothing at all wrong with it," Moira told her. "But it implies that you're past passion, like a woman who chooses shoes that don't hurt her feet over those that make her feel feminine and sexy."

Kiera didn't like the analogy, but she was forced to

admit she could see the truth of it. "Perhaps that's where I am in my life."

"I don't believe it. I've seen a difference when you're around Bryan," Moira said, then grinned. "I don't like saying it, because you're my mother, after all, but it reminds me of the way things are between Luke and me. There's a lot of heat and electricity when the two of you are in the same room."

It was a bit frightening to have her daughter romanticizing the situation. Kiera had to put an end to the speculation or any attempt at matchmaking it might inspire. "If there are any sparks at all, and I'm not saying there are, it's only because he's infuriating," she responded emphatically.

Moira clearly wasn't persuaded. "And just saying so brings you alive in a way I've never seen before," she replied, then slipped off the bar stool and gave Kiera a kiss. "Something to think about."

Kiera would think about it, alright. But only long enough to question whether her daughter had taken complete leave of her senses.

Kiera's six-month work visa came through the day after her disconcerting conversation with her daughter. She almost wished there'd been some glitch that she could have used as an excuse to pack up and run back to Ireland, back to comfortable and steady in an environment that soothed her. That, however, was not to be, and the truth was, she really wanted a while longer to soak in the world of the O'Briens and Chesapeake Shores itself.

One certainty, though, was that she needed to have a good sit-down with Luke and define her position at the pub more precisely. Even more essential, she needed to make good on her plan to find her own place now that her future here was settled for a few months at least.

Luke and Moira continued to assure her they were content having her living in their guest room, but even their spacious house was too crowded to have a mother-in-law in residence for more than the brief time she'd already spent there. And after last night's chat with Moira, she didn't want her daughter watching her every move and analyzing it, especially when it came to her personal life.

The very next day at Sally's, she decided to address the problem without giving Moira a chance to try to talk her out of it.

"I need a place of my own," Kiera announced, appealing to Luke's sister, Susie O'Brien Franklin, when the O'Brien women were gathered for coffee at Sally's. She'd been told Susie's history with ovarian cancer and heard the story about her recent adoption of a baby girl. Though Susie and her husband, Mack Franklin, had faced tragedy, it was her triumphs that had been the focus of the telling. Kiera had also been told that Susie knew every piece of property available for sale or for rent in Chesapeake Shores.

As she'd expected, Moira regarded her with dismay. "Mum, I've told you again and again that Luke and I are happy to have you," she protested. "Your visa's only for six months. Why move out for such a short time? You'll barely have time to get settled. You don't need to find your own place until you decide if you'll be staying indefinitely."

"And your grandfather has said the same," Kiera told her patiently. "He and Nell have invited me to stay with them. This is for the best. I don't like being underfoot. After you and your brothers went off on your own, I grew used to being in my own space, answering to no one."

"And I know the perfect place," Susie chimed in eagerly before Moira could present another argument against moving. "I haven't even had time to post the listing. It just came in last night, when Uncle Mick finished the renovations. It's just a little cottage, no more than a guesthouse, really, on a piece of property that even has its own tiny glimpse of the bay. It's completely furnished. The owner was forced to move into a retirement home because she could no longer maintain the property on her own, so she's renting the main house and the guesthouse separately to cover her costs."

"The house on Lilac Lane," Bree O'Brien Collins guessed, her eyes lighting up. "Jake always took care of the landscaping there. He still does most of it, but now—"

She was clearly about to say more when a sharp look from Susie silenced her. Whatever the message between the two women, Bree stumbled over her words only slightly before adding, "There's no place in town that has more beautiful lilacs this time of year."

"It sounds lovely," Kiera said, letting the awkward moment pass. "There's nothing more wonderful than the scent of lilacs filling the air on a spring breeze."

"If it appeals to you, Kiera, let's go see it," Susie said at once. "Rental properties in Chesapeake Shores never last long. Once the listing is out there, it won't take long to rent. You'll want to grab it right away. I'll get the key from the office and drive you over."

"Kate and I are coming, too," Moira insisted. "I don't

want you rushing into something just to avoid being underfoot."

Kiera rolled her eyes, but agreed to have an entourage as she inspected the cottage.

A half hour later as she roamed through the cozy, freshly painted, furnished rooms, all of them filled with natural light, new hardwood floors and with the scent of lilacs drifting through the front door they'd left open, Kiera was charmed. Her daughter questioned the size of it, but Kiera found it perfect for her needs. It even had a tiny guest room, should her granddaughter ever spend the night. It reminded her of quaint cottages by the sea in Ireland. And there was, indeed, that glimpse of the bay that Susie had promised. The view was no doubt better from the main house, but this would definitely do.

"This is perfect," she said happily.

The rent was a delightful surprise, too, low enough to be easily covered by what Luke had insisted on paying her at the pub now that all of the legalities were settled. He'd handed her the first check just last night. There were absolutely no drawbacks that she could see, at least not until she walked outside and saw Bryan Laramie stalking across the lawn, a scowl on his face.

"What's this?" he demanded.

Oblivious to his brusque demeanor or choosing to ignore it, Susie beamed at him. "I've found a renter for the cottage," she announced cheerfully. "You and Kiera will be neighbors. Isn't that perfect? You'll be able to ride to work together."

Bryan looked not one bit happier about that idea than Kiera was. She whirled on her daughter. "Did you know about this?" she asked Moira. "Were you just playing devil's advocate to trick me into agreeing to this house before I realized who I'd have as a neighbor? After our talk last night, I'd think you would know better."

"Mum, that would be far too devious, even for me," Moira replied, though the feigned innocence in her tone was defied by the laughter she was trying to keep contained.

"And you?" Kiera said to Susie. "Is this the reason you silenced Bree so quickly back at Sally's? Was she about to mention my new neighbor?"

"I rent properties, nothing more," Susie said, though her grin gave her away, as well.

There had been a plot afoot, no question about it, one of those O'Brien conspiracies she'd heard so much about. Apparently Moira had seen this day coming and conspired with Susie to make this happen. She wouldn't be surprised to learn that Moira'd had a hand in choosing paint colors, since they suited her so perfectly.

If she hadn't fallen in love with the cottage at first glance, Kiera might have walked away from the deal, from the whole sneaky lot of them, in fact. One glance into Bryan's challenging gaze had her changing her mind, though. She would not be chased off by his dark scowl or by the exchange of knowing glances between her daughter and Susie. No matter their roles in planning this, the mere thought of making Bryan's life uncomfortable provided the possibility of more entertainment than she'd had in years. If there were other reasons for planting herself quite visibly in his path, well, it was probably best if she didn't think too long or hard about those.

Bryan drove down the winding narrow road that was Lilac Lane, still stewing over the discovery that his new neighbor was to be Kiera Malone. She'd moved in the day before. He'd watched her taking a few suitcases into the house and fought the temptation to offer help. He knew her well enough to realize she would have taken it as an insult. She took her desire for independence to amazing heights, and any offer of help from him would have been regarded with special disdain.

This morning, as he rounded a curve, the very woman plaguing his thoughts appeared from nowhere in the early-morning haze. Muttering a curse, he hit the brakes.

"Do you have a death wish?" he inquired, his heart still racing from the close call. "Only an idiot would walk down the middle of the road on a day when the visibility is next to zero."

"It's not exactly a road, now, is it? It's a private lane. You're the only person living on it with a car."

"So you thought you'd test your luck with me? After all the encounters we've had at the pub, didn't it occur to you that I could be the most dangerous driver of all, at least where you're concerned?"

She shrugged. "My Moira believes you're a gentleman. And Luke sings your praises. While my own opinion is less enthusiastic, I can't imagine you're any more dangerous behind the wheel than you are in the kitchen."

"Where you seem to think my skills are lacking," he reminded her. He sighed. "Would you like a lift?"

"With a dangerous man such as yourself?"

"I promise to try to get us both to the pub in one piece."

"Then it would be rude of me to refuse."

She slid gracefully into the passenger seat, her movements exposing just a bit of the creamy skin above her knee. Bryan had a hard time tearing his gaze away until he reminded himself that this was Kiera Malone, his boss's mother-in-law, and a woman who seemed destined to turn his previously contented existence into chaos. These uncomfortable, wayward thoughts needed to be tamped down.

"Kiera, do you suppose it's possible for us to call a truce?" he asked, his tone far more plaintive than he would have liked. He'd heard that her work visa had been approved, so he had to find some way to make a lasting peace with her. She clearly wasn't going anywhere, at least not for months.

"Were we at war?" she inquired tartly as if she'd been unaware of it.

"Not exactly war, but we seem to have differences of opinion about everything. You tried rearranging the spices in the pantry at the pub, for heaven's sake. And I've caught you trying to move my pots and pans around, as well."

"I thought there were more efficient arrangements," she told him. "If you'd given them half a chance, you would have seen that."

"The arrangements I had were perfectly fine," he retorted, then waved off the argument. In the overall scheme of things, it was inconsequential, even if he'd said otherwise when he'd caught her.

"Kiera, surely we can find common ground. We both like your daughter, for one thing. And I, at least, respect Luke. I doubt he'd have you working at the pub if he didn't think you'd contribute to the ambience he's worked hard to create. You obviously have experience at pubs in Ireland that I lack. Your father and Nell, people I admire, are in your corner, as well. Could that be our starting point, the people we have in common?"

She studied him with a narrowed gaze. "Does it matter to you so much that you and I truly get along? We both know my stay here will only be for a few months. Then you'll be rid of me and able to go back to doing things your own way in the kitchen, even if those ways are mostly wrong."

Bryan's temper, held carefully in check for at least five minutes, went from simmer to boil in a heartbeat. "Wrong? Shall I pass on that opinion to Nell, since I'm doing the Irish dishes exactly as she taught me."

"Is that so?" she asked skeptically. "And the menu as a whole? Did she add the she-crab soup, something I doubt you'd find in an Irish pub?"

"It was a concession to the expectations of those visiting Chesapeake Shores, added with her full approval. As were the steamed crabs and the oysters in season."

"And those odd cheesy things, were they her suggestion, too?"

"Are you referring to the crab quesadillas?"

She nodded.

Bryan hesitated. While it was true that Nell had agreed to the experiment, she'd railed against the fact that no such thing would be on a pub menu in Dublin. She'd been won over after she'd tasted one, then added a word of caution. "But only as an occasional special," she'd insisted. "Unless popular demand suggests otherwise."

Popular demand had pushed them right to the top of the pub's specialties on the lunch menu, Bryan was proud to report a few weeks after he'd introduced them. He glanced over at Kiera.

"There's no reason traditional Irish pub food can't be blended satisfactorily with regional dishes," he told her. "It makes us unique."

"I would think the Irish menu, the selection of ales and music would do that quite nicely all on their own," she retorted. "Is there another such restaurant in the vicinity that I've not yet seen? In Ireland there's a pub around every corner and they see no need to deviate from the traditional. It's the individual atmosphere and the collection of regulars that provide the draw."

"From a much larger pool of customers," Bryan argued. "Believe it or not, Kiera, Luke and I were making a success of this pub with the input from Nell and Moira."

She paled at that. "So I'm not needed at all, is that it?"

He saw the flicker of pain in her eyes and felt a momentary pang. He knew Luke wanted her to feel welcome, and that Moira, Dillon and Nell were hoping she'd find a permanent home in Chesapeake Shores. Her place at the pub was a critical element of that dream.

"I didn't mean that," he said, even though the words didn't come easily. For a man who'd uttered few apologies in a lifetime, he seemed to be making a habit of it since Kiera had come around. "I just meant that not every single thing needs to be changed. I'm sure you have some innovative ideas to make us even more successful and authentic. Maybe you could put some on paper and we could talk about them before we open one day, not when I'm in the middle of trying to feed a crowd of people and my temper's already short."

She seemed genuinely startled. "You're actually willing to listen to my ideas?"

"Sure. Why not? I'm as eager to try new things as the next person." At one time he would have been chomping at the bit to make his own innovations. He'd left culinary school eager to make his mark. He'd wanted to impress the food critics and earn raves from his customers. Somehow he'd lost that enthusiasm along the way. He could pinpoint the precise moment, but he'd stopped dwelling on it.

He glanced over and caught Kiera studying him intently, her expression filled with skepticism. Eventually she nodded.

"I'll take you at your word, then," she conceded. "And perhaps we can give that truce of yours a try, as well."

Bryan pulled into a parking space behind the pub, shut off the engine and turned to her. He was surprised to see a faint spark of excitement in her blue eyes. It gave them the brightness of sapphires, he decided, then shook off the thought as another of those unexpected and inappropriate digressions he should be avoiding.

He did not need to be noticing Kiera Malone's bright eyes or her lush hips or the creaminess of her skin. He didn't need to start thinking of her as a woman at all, he reminded himself fiercely.

Because in his past experience, females did little beyond driving a man crazy and then leaving him with a broken heart. He'd had enough of that to last a lifetime. In fact, years later, he was still recovering from the last time.

Chapter 7

Deanna Lane sat in the doctor's office at the University of Virginia campus health center, her nails biting into the palms of her hands. She'd been feeling lousy for over a week. Her energy level, which usually kept her going from dawn till midnight, had fallen to a new low. She could barely force herself to crawl out of bed in the morning.

With finals coming up in another week and the semester due to end, she normally would have waited to see her family doctor back home in Richmond, but she was afraid whatever she'd caught would play havoc with her ability to study and keep her grades up. Her roommate had noticed her pale complexion and lack of energy and asked point-blank if she was pregnant, but that wasn't even remotely possible. She was dating, but not seriously enough for there to be any chance of that.

In her premed courses, she'd learned just enough to be terrified that she might have some sort of blood disorder or cancer. That was the danger of all those courses, she'd been told. They could make even the healthiest student susceptible to hypochondria. Before they knew it, they'd start imagining they had a dozen fatal illnesses by the time the semester ended. Surely that's all this was, her imagination working overtime. Mononucleosis would be a much more logical explanation. A light case of an energy-sapping flu even more likely.

When Dr. Robbins, who was not only one of the physicians, but a professor and Deanna's adviser and mentor, came into the room her expression gave away nothing.

"Well," Deanna prodded. "What's the verdict? What do the blood tests show?"

"That you're perfectly healthy," the doctor said, giving her a reassuring smile. "Deanna, your blood work is absolutely normal in every respect."

The reply should have reassured her, but Deanna wanted answers. She needed solutions, not a pep talk. "Should we be doing other tests of some kind?"

"I honestly don't feel they're necessary right now."

"Then why am I feeling so crummy?" She mentally flipped the pages of various textbooks. When nothing obvious jumped out at her, she seized on her psychology course. "Am I depressed?"

Dr. Robbins fought a smile. "Do you think you're depressed?"

"No, but there must be some explanation. You looked for mono, right?"

"You're a college student. Of course I did," she replied patiently, "though we haven't seen many cases on campus this year."

"Help me out here. I need to figure out what's going on and fix it," she said in the goal-oriented way that had driven her all her life.

"Okay," Dr. Robbins said. "While I can't find anything specific in your test results to go on, my educated hunch is that you're staying up way too late studying, panicking a bit over finals in your premed classes and already thinking ahead to that summer job you're planning to take back home working for your stepfather."

That all made perfect sense, but Deanna wasn't entirely convinced. "This isn't all in my head, Dr. Robbins. It can't be."

"Oh, the symptoms are real enough," she said. "But trust me, they'll go away once you get some rest and put your exams behind you. One of these days you'll grasp the significance of the mind-body connection. I believe it's possible to make yourself sick and to make yourself well," she said, then added, "though an educated diagnostician and physician certainly can play an important role."

She leveled a somber look into Deanna's eyes. "There's another thing that might be at work here, something we've talked about before. Perhaps you need to admit to your stepfather that you really don't want to work in his construction business, not only for this summer, but definitely not forever. I know that decision you made has been weighing on you."

Deanna winced, almost regretting that she'd confided in this woman she'd come to trust. "It's not that I don't want to work with him," she insisted. "It's just that…" Her voice trailed off.

"It's just that your heart is in medicine. Don't you think he'll understand that, especially given how much time the two of you spent in hospitals when your mother was ill? From everything you've told me, he's a reasonable man. And you are taking premed courses."

"Of course he's reasonable," Deanna responded defensively. She hesitated before admitting, "But I haven't exactly mentioned the courses I'm taking."

Dr. Robbins was clearly startled. "Why on earth not?"

"It's just that he's been a little lost since my mom died last year," Deanna explained, wondering if perhaps she hadn't been making excuses just to keep from disappointing him. "When I came back to school last fall, he asked what I needed for tuition and room and board and then he wrote the check. I didn't want to upset him by telling him I was changing my major from business to premed."

"I'll bet he'd be more upset if he found out you're going along with this job for the summer just to please him and giving up the chance to volunteer at Johns Hopkins Hospital, which is what you really want to do. You told me that money for school isn't the issue, and volunteering will give you all sorts of practical experience. My alma mater is eager to have you there."

"I know you're right," Deanna conceded, sighing heavily. "But I dread having that conversation with him. He's really looking forward to my being home for the summer. It's just the two of us now."

"And there it is," the doctor said, a note of triumph unmistakable in her voice. "There's the guilt that convinces me all the more that we're dealing with anxiety. Believe me, I see this a lot. I'm certain it's the primary reason you're feeling so lousy right now."

"I suppose," Deanna conceded reluctantly. If it was the explanation, it came attached to a whole lot of emotional baggage she wasn't ready to deal with.

The doctor leveled a hard look at her that had her squirming. She could guess what was coming.

"There's one more subject you need to speak to your stepfather about," Dr. Robbins reminded her. "We've discussed this before, too. You need to find out more about your family medical history. You know your mother's, but you know nothing at all about your biological father's. Your stepfather may have those answers or, at the very least, he may be able to tell you how to find them."

It was, indeed, another conversation Deanna had been avoiding, another layer of that emotional baggage that kept piling up. "I feel as if asking him anything about my biological father will seem like a betrayal. Ash has been the only father I really remember."

"You're injecting emotion into it," the doctor chided. "And there is some of that, to be sure, but Deanna, really, this is a medical necessity. You've had enough premed courses already to understand that. Genetics is a critical component of understanding what medical risks you might be facing. Will you promise to sit down with him and discuss it? Surely you must have other questions, too, especially since your mother never told you much about your father or what happened between them."

"She left him," Deanna said flatly. "That's enough for me. She must have had her reasons." Even as she spoke, though, she couldn't help wondering if blind loyalty to her mother—and to Ash—hadn't been misguided. She knew plenty of stepchildren and adoptees who craved information about their biological parents, and no one thought less of them for not being happy with the family they had. Had she been afraid of the answers she'd find? She had no idea.

"Well, I'm not going to force the issue. However, the

medical questions could loom large one of these days. Think about that."

Deanna nodded. She knew the doctor was right. And it wasn't as if she hadn't had questions of her own over the years about the man she barely remembered, but none had seemed urgent enough or important enough to upset her mother by asking. And Ashton Lane had been all the father she'd ever needed. Rocking the boat hadn't been in her nature.

Dr. Robbins looked satisfied. "Okay, then. Let me know soon if you decide you want that chance to work at Johns Hopkins this summer. I'll make the arrangements. As for the way you're feeling these days, I recommend you put everything else on hold for at least twenty-four hours and get some sleep and something besides pizza and caffeine into your system. I think rest and good food will do wonders. I know you think you don't dare take any time off right now, but your studying will be far more effective if you're rested and relaxed. Stop by again in a couple of days if you're not feeling better."

"Thank you." Amazingly, she felt better already as she left the office. Perhaps it was just being reassured that she didn't have anything dire or maybe it was simply talking to someone who understood the dilemmas in her life.

That improvement in her outlook lasted for the rest of the afternoon, right until she looked at her caller ID and saw that her stepfather was calling. Then all of the panic washed over her again.

When Deanna answered the call, she forced a cheerful note into her voice. "How are you?"

"Super," he said at once, his tone almost bright enough to fool her. "I was wondering if you might be able to get home this weekend. I know you must be stressed out over finals and that you'll be home in a couple of weeks, but—"

Thinking of her conversation with Dr. Robbins, Deanna cut him off. "I'll be there tomorrow."

He seemed taken aback by her quick agreement. "Are you sure you can spare the time?"

"Absolutely. I'll make the time." Richmond was practically around the corner from Charlottesville. She could attend classes tomorrow and be home by dinnertime. Maybe she could kill two birds with one stone, get some of the rest she so desperately needed and get a few things off her chest, as well.

Deanna stared at the magazine clipping that her stepfather had handed her as they sat in their favorite restaurant on Friday night. It was a review in a regional publication about an Irish pub in Chesapeake Shores, Maryland, that was earning raves for its atmosphere and authentic cuisine. The chef was Bryan Laramie, a name she knew all too well, even if her other memories were blurry.

Tears gathered in her eyes as she read through the clipping again. Surely it wasn't possible that her father had been this close by, just over a hundred miles away, for all these years.

"It can't be the same person," she said, but when she looked into Ashton Lane's familiar brown eyes, she saw the truth. "How can this be? I thought he was in New York."

"That's where he was when your mother first left. I have no idea how he ended up in a small town on the Chesapeake Bay. I saw the article a couple of days ago, though, and checked it out. This is your biological father, Dee. Since he's this close, I thought you needed to know. I knew I was taking a chance of upsetting you this close to finals, but I was afraid if I waited, I'd come up with a dozen reasons not to tell you at all. We've never really talked about your father, and a part of me wanted to keep it that way." He searched her face. "Should I have waited?"

She shook her head. "No." Confused, though, she lifted her gaze to his. "What should I do now?"

All of her life, Ash had been there to guide her decisions. It felt natural to turn to him now, but she could see the discomfort in his eyes.

"That's not up to me," he said gently. "What you do with this information is up to you."

Deanna could barely make sense of any of it. Talk about timing. She'd gone for months at a time, even years, without a single thought of her biological father coming into her head, and now he seemed to be ever-present in her thoughts and in her conversations.

She studied Ash, wondering how he must be feeling about this. His expression gave away nothing. He'd spent his life running a small, but successful family construction business in Richmond, where he'd grown up. He and her mother had met when Deanna was still a toddler. She wasn't entirely sure of the circumstances, though somehow he'd ended up giving her mother a job and then, a couple of years later, they'd moved in together. He'd adopted Deanna when she started school and wanted to know why they didn't have the same last name. Her mom and Ash had never had children of their own, and Ash had doted on Deanna as if she were his flesh and blood. In so many ways she'd had an ideal, happy childhood.

"You know you're the only father who matters to me, don't you?" she asked him urgently. "Knowing that Bryan Laramie lives close by doesn't change that."

"You've been the best daughter any man could ask for," he assured her. "But you must have questions. If you need to have them answered, now you know where to look. I'll support whatever you want to do. I'll go with you, if you want to see him and need me there. Whatever you want."

That was Ash, Deanna thought. He'd been endlessly devoted during her mom's battle with cancer, by her side in the hospital, providing round-the-clock care toward the end, never once complaining about the sacrifices he made to be with her. "This is where I belong," he'd told Deanna when she'd asked about the impact his absence must be having on the business. "The company will get by."

Now he was ready to put his own feelings aside to support her.

"I need to think about all this," she told him, desperate for some time alone to sort through all the emotions raging through her. How could her father have been so close and never come looking for her? What sort of man did that? Not the kind she could imagine inviting into her life at this late date.

Perhaps, though, she should see Bryan Laramie at least once, get the answers about her medical history that Dr. Robbins had told her she should have, answers that might come into play even years from now in some medical crisis or another or when she was thinking of having children of her own. Perhaps that one contact would be enough. It wasn't as if there'd been this huge void in her life all these years. Ash had filled that. He'd been there, strong and understanding and always ready with a bit of wisdom or a laugh.

No, this was strictly a practical decision, she told herself. And in the morning, she would explain all of that to her stepfather, along with how she was feeling about the job at his company and the allure of the chance to spend the summer at one of the country's premier medical centers. Ironically, that job would put her in even closer proximity to Chesapeake Shores and her father. Maybe that was exactly the sign she'd been needing to guide the decision she'd dreaded making about her future.

"God works in mysterious ways," her mother would often tell her when speaking of the day she'd met Ashton Lane. Now Deanna had her own example as proof of that.

Bryan had tossed restlessly all night long. Some of that could be blamed on Kiera and that new look she'd gotten a couple of weeks ago at the spa, a feminine look that had caught him off guard and made his breath hitch in a way he'd been avoiding for a long time now.

Over the years he'd dated any number of women, many of them attractive, but not a one had gotten to him as Kiera Malone did. That made her dangerous and made these dreams that stirred him in the night even more disturbing.

Better those dreams, though, than the ones that came after, the familiar ones that rarely changed. There were always a baby's cries, the whispered words he couldn't quite make out and, when he awakened, the same emptiness that he'd felt on that morning nearly two decades ago when he'd discovered his wife and baby had vanished without so much as a note of goodbye.

A morning run didn't help. Nor did a cold, bracing shower, nor a pot of very strong coffee. Nothing helped. He felt the pain as sharply as he had on that first day when he'd realized that his wife and child were truly gone. And every single time he'd hit a dead end in his search for them, the pain had been his companion, the dreams the reason he fought sleep.

No matter how often he told himself to let it go, to end the hunt and move on with his life, he couldn't quite put aside the way his daughter had giggled when he held her in the air, the way her smiles had moved him. He'd loved his wife with all his heart, but their baby girl had stolen his breath away.

Not a day went by that he didn't try to imagine what Deanna must look like now, where she might be, what direction her life had taken. When he thought of the woman who'd run away with her, his feelings were mixed. The part of him that had loved Melody and her wild spirit still ached at times, but then he remembered what she'd stolen from him—the future she'd stolen from the three of them—and he hated her for that.

Other people got over failed marriages, he told himself repeatedly. They recognized the mistakes they'd made and either fixed them or repeated them. He'd recognized his; he knew that on too many occasions he'd chosen work over his wife and child. Melody had repeatedly tried to make her point about that, but she hadn't stuck around long enough for him to try to fix the problem. Instead, she'd tired of waiting. One day she'd simply packed up and left. Maybe there'd been someone else waiting for her, though he'd never had any reason to suspect her of cheating. More likely, she'd simply given up and done the one thing she could think of that would punish him for not putting their marriage first.

He might have forgiven that, but the lack of contact, the inability to even see his precious daughter from time to time, had filled him with rage at first. He'd gone to court once seeking help, but he'd found none. Instead, he'd met skepticism that his wife would take his child and flee if she hadn't had good reason to do so. The implication that he might have abused her or their daughter was unmistakable. None of them had understood that a wife and mother might be immature enough to simply want retaliation. So he'd gone back to spending a fortune on private detectives.

Then, once the trail had gone cold in Baltimore, he'd abandoned hope, though he'd taken the job in the deli there on the very unlikely chance that one day they might cross paths. Of course, they never had. And inertia had kept him there for fifteen years.

When Luke had advertised for a chef for his new pub in Chesapeake Shores, Bryan had seized on the chance to make a fresh start. The change of scenery had, indeed, been good for him. He liked the quiet little town along the bay. He liked and respected the O'Briens. He had a garden behind his rented house. Working it in the early morning, his hands in the cool dirt, watching the herbs and vegetables grow and ripen, gave him a certain serenity. He'd found some peace here, at least during the day.

At night, though, that was another story. At night the dreams came back. He wondered if PTSD was a little like this, sneaky and devastating when it turned up to

shatter calm. All he wanted these days was calm, the
chance to be a little creative in the kitchen, to grow the
restaurant's fresh vegetables and herbs in his own garden, to enjoy a morning run or a glass of wine on his
back deck from time to time. That's it. He didn't need
anything else. Or anyone, he amended. Perhaps he was
every bit as selfish and self-absorbed as Melody had
once accused him of being.

Now, though, Kiera Malone had come along and
made him wonder about the narrow life he'd chosen.
If he were going to change his solitary ways, he most
certainly wouldn't choose a woman who annoyed the
daylights out of him or one who was here only temporarily. What would be the point, then, in letting her into
his life only to watch her fly off to Ireland? Better to
keep his distance.

Satisfied with the stern talking-to he'd given himself, he drank one more cup of coffee for good measure, then headed to O'Brien's, convinced that Kiera
could do nothing at all to get under his skin today. He
wouldn't allow it.

Sadly, within the hour, the vow was broken and the
pesky woman had managed to trip his temper and his
lust just by walking into his kitchen with an Irish tune
on her soft pink lips and a couple of "wee little suggestions" for his menu.

Kiera wasn't sure what she'd done wrong, but at
Bryan's fierce scowl and command that she leave his
kitchen, she backed through the door and headed for
Luke's office.

"I suppose now you're going to complain about me
to your son-in-law?" Bryan asked, following her.

Kiera whirled around. "I was going to do no such thing," she said, standing toe-to-toe with the infuriating man. "If you and I have a problem, then we'll work it out between us like the adults we're meant to be, though right at the moment I'm not so sure your maturity rises to that level."

Bryan's cheeks flushed. "Kiera, I'm sorry. You're right. I'm behaving like an idiot. I had a terrible night and I'm taking it out on you. Again. I swear I'll stop doing this. I'll bite my tongue off before I utter another sharp word."

She regarded him with amusement. "I appreciate the commitment, but I've serious doubts about you being able to keep it. You're not cut out for staying silent, any more than I am."

He laughed, and it was a fine sight to see. It warmed her heart.

"You're right about that," he conceded, "but I can vow to try. Bring those suggestions of yours over to a table and let's talk them through."

She studied him and noted the weariness in his eyes, as well as the sincerity behind his apology. "Okay, then. Would you like a cup of coffee while we talk?"

"I think I've probably had more than my share this morning, as it is."

"Tea, then. I keep some chamomile here for occasions when I'm feeling restless and uneasy."

"I'm not a big fan of tea, but perhaps I should give yours a try," Bryan said.

"Ah, you're more amenable already," she said approvingly, busying herself with pouring boiling water over a tea bag she'd retrieved from her supply.

She put the cup on the table in front of him. "Would

you be wanting to talk about whatever ruined your night's rest?"

"Are you suggesting I'm in need of counseling? After the display I just put on, I shouldn't be surprised."

"Not counseling," she corrected. "Perhaps just a friendly ear."

Bryan studied her curiously. "Do you take in stray puppies that have nipped at you, too?"

Kiera chuckled at the comparison. "No, I've subjected a few people to my own quick temper from time to time. I've wanted forgiveness and understanding for that, so it's only reasonable that I return the favor."

"I appreciate the offer, but the story's too long and dull for the time we have before the pub opens." He beckoned to her. "Let's see that list you stuffed in your pocket when I ran you out of the kitchen."

She pulled the crumpled paper from her pocket and smoothed it out, then met his gaze with an earnest expression. "I'm not trying to tell you how to do your job. At least that's not how it's meant. It's just that I'm a fresh pair of eyes and I've had years of working in a restaurant in Ireland, which gives me some level of competence."

He smiled. "And you're Irish," he said. "I get it. I'll try to be more open-minded, rather than taking offense."

She looked skeptical. "Can you do that?"

"I can try."

"Okay, then. I was thinking perhaps that the lunch menu could use a few hearty sandwiches. I've listed them on here. These would be found in countryside pubs all over Ireland. To be honest, I think they're on the menu because they're not only appealing to a farmer who might be going back into the fields, but because it takes a lot of ale to wash them down."

Bryan chuckled at that. "An interesting observation," he said as he scanned her suggestions, which seemed to rely heavily on thick bread, cheese, meats and tomatoes in season. "It would be like working in the deli again," he muttered disparagingly.

Kiera frowned at his comment. "And there goes the open mind you promised."

"Sorry. You're right. Why do you think these might work, aside from selling extra ale, perhaps?"

"Because they're a staple of an Irish pub, especially in the countryside. We want people who come here to have a truly Irish experience. One or two options like these on the menu give them a better picture of what they might find if they were to pull into a pub on the side of the road anywhere in Ireland. For anyone who's traveled there, it will be a pleasant reminder."

She sat quietly as Bryan seemed to weigh her argument. "Fine. We'll try them as specials here and there and see how it goes."

Kiera beamed at him. "You're really going to take my suggestion?"

"As an experiment," he cautioned.

"That's good enough." She leveled a steady look into his eyes. "Was it so difficult, then, giving me this tiny victory?"

Bryan laughed. "No, Kiera, it was almost painless."

"Then perhaps we can try it again sometime," she said. "I want to be on the same team with you, Bryan."

An odd expression flitted across his face at that, and he almost knocked over his cup of tea in his rush to stand. "I need to get back to work."

"You don't want the rest of your tea?" she asked innocently, well aware that he'd stopped drinking it after the first cautious sip.

"You and I will find our way to peace, Kiera, but I doubt I'll ever give that chamomile tea of yours another chance. It's worse than medicine."

"But even better for you," she told him. "Sometimes it takes a bitter pill to cure what ails you."

"I'll take the ailment," he said vehemently.

"You'll let me know if things get bad enough that you change your mind," she told him. "I won't hold the shift in attitude against you."

He shook his head at that, a smile tugging at his lips. "Good to know."

And then he was gone.

A moment later, Luke came out of his office to join her. "Did you and Bryan work things out?"

"Nothing to work out," she said.

"That's not what the shouts from the kitchen earlier suggested."

"I believe his day got off to a wobbly start. It was nothing to do with me." She studied her son-in-law's worried expression. "Don't be fretting about this, Luke. Bryan and I will find a way to work together. Today was a good first step in that direction."

"Thank you."

"No need. I've had a good bit of experience dealing with obstinate men. One more will be no challenge."

Though this one was showing signs of being far more complicated than those she'd dealt with in the past.

Chapter 8

Though it was Saturday morning, Ash was already up and dressed for a construction site when Deanna joined him at the kitchen table. She poured herself a cup of coffee and reached for a doughnut that was a familiar part of their Saturday ritual. Ash was always out of the house at dawn to bring home the fresh doughnuts from their favorite bakery. She and her mom had loved that sugary treat. She wondered if he still followed that routine when she wasn't home or if this was his way of trying to create normalcy on a day that was anything but routine.

"Going to work on a Saturday?" she asked as she selected a still-warm doughnut with maple icing. "That's new."

Ash shrugged. "The house is just too empty without your mom," he admitted. "For a long time after she died, I used Saturdays as a chance to catch up on all the work I'd missed. Now it's become a welcome habit. I was already dressed for it this morning before I remembered that today isn't the same. You're home."

He studied her intently. "How did you sleep last night? I hope my dropping the news about your father like that didn't keep you awake. I'm sure it was upsetting to be hit with it out of the blue."

"Amazingly, I slept better than I had in a while," Deanna confessed. "I don't know if it was being in my own bed and away from all the craziness that comes with studying for finals or if it was finally having some concrete piece of information about my father that I hadn't even realized I wanted."

"Have you made any decisions about seeing him?"

"Will it bother you if I decide to go to Chesapeake Shores?" she asked, watching him closely. She wasn't entirely sure that she wasn't looking for even the slightest excuse not to go.

Though Ash hesitated, in the end he shook his head. "I always thought this day would come eventually. If I were thinking only of myself, maybe I would have kept that information from you, but I knew how wrong that would be. That's why I dragged you home so close to finals, to get it out in the open before I could change my mind. As hard as it is for me to believe sometimes, you're an adult now. You have to make your own choices."

"Even when I'm afraid the choice I make might hurt you?"

"Even then," he told her gently. "Dee, I'll be fine, whatever you decide. You and I have had years as father and daughter. You've been an incredible blessing. How could I possibly begrudge the man who gave you life the chance to get to know you? You exist because of your mother's marriage to Bryan Laramie. That's an inescapable fact."

She took a sip of her coffee to buy time, then dared asking, "Did Mom ever tell you why she left him?"

"Not really. She just said things had been going wrong for a long time and she wanted to start over."

She nodded. "That's pretty much all she ever told me. Do you think things were really bad? Could he have been an awful person? Would it be a terrible mistake for me to even consider letting him into my life or even meeting him? Like you said, I'm an adult and I've had you, an amazing stepfather, for all these years. It's not as if I need a dad. Maybe there's no reason to rock the boat."

Even as she said the words that could let her, let *both* of them, off the hook, she wasn't sure what response she was hoping for.

"You read that article," Ash reminded her. "The people the writer interviewed in Chesapeake Shores seem to regard your father very highly. Their comments were glowing about him, about the excellent menu he's created at that pub and about the pub itself. Don't you think he sounded like someone you might like to know?"

She thought about how everyone interviewed had spoken of Bryan Laramie—or at least his food—in such positive terms. "That's what I thought, too." She hesitated, then admitted, "It made me wonder if Mom really told me the whole story. He seemed to have a lot going for him in New York in the restaurant business. If that's true, though, how did he end up in some little town in Maryland?" The pieces just didn't seem to mesh. "We must be missing something." She looked to her stepfather for guidance. "Don't you think so?"

An odd expression flitted across Ash's face. It almost looked like guilt. Deanna frowned. "Is there something *you're* not telling me?"

He was quiet for so long, she thought he might not

answer, but then he set aside his coffee and leaned toward her. "There is something you need to know, something your mother and I kept from you. I'm just not sure I can find the words to explain."

Her heart thumped unsteadily. "What, Ash? What could you and my mother possibly have kept from me that's so terrible? Is it about my father?"

"No, this is about your mother and me."

Deanna didn't understand and told him just that.

"Just hear me out," he said, but then fell silent, his expression more deeply troubled than Deanna could ever recall.

"To be honest, after a while I almost forgot about all this myself or at least managed to tell myself that it didn't change anything," he said eventually. He gave her a long look, his expression oddly wistful. "We were so happy together, the way a family was supposed to be. The day I met you and your mom was the very best day of my life, and not a day went by after that when I wasn't grateful for everything we had. I stopped thinking about the one thing we didn't have."

The knot in Deanna's stomach tightened. "Just say it, Ash. You're scaring me. We were a great family. All of my friends envied how close we were. They loved coming over here. They said their parents never laughed and teased each other the way you and Mom did, as if you were practically newlyweds."

The color actually seemed to drain from his face then. Deanna regarded him with dismay. "I've really upset you, when I was trying so hard to do the opposite. What did I say?"

"It was a lie," Ash responded bluntly, the ugly word left hanging in the air between them.

"Don't be ridiculous," she said, thoroughly confused. "I know exactly how wonderful our life was. I was here every minute. I remember everything from the day we moved into this house."

"You don't remember a wedding, do you?" At her stunned silence, he gave a curt nod. "Of course not, because there wasn't one, Dee."

"There must have been one," she protested, searching her memory for something, anything to prove him wrong. Not one single image came to mind. Frowning, she asked, "Did you and Mom elope or something?"

"No. There was never a wedding. We couldn't get married because your mother never divorced your father. I suppose at some point after she disappeared, he could have sought to resolve things by divorcing her on grounds of abandonment or something, but she wouldn't file the paperwork to divorce him and he never tracked her down to file, either."

Deanna stared at Ash in dismay. The cozy, sun-splashed kitchen suddenly seemed to darken, as if a cloud had passed overhead. "That can't be. She left him years and years ago. They must have gotten a divorce."

"They didn't," he said flatly. "Believe me, I would know. It's something we argued about again and again, but she was afraid if she filed for divorce, he'd find her, maybe even sue her for custody of you, possibly even accuse her of kidnapping you. I tried to tell her there were no grounds, since she was your parent and there had never been any legal ruling to grant him custody."

Deanna struggled to make sense of what he was telling her, but couldn't. "That's just crazy," she said finally. "When people split up, they get a divorce. I mean even people who don't believe in divorce find a way, an annulment or something. They don't just run off and hide and pretend it's all okay."

"Well, that's exactly what your mom did, and there was no reasoning with her. I told her it was irrational, but it was fear, Dee. I even asked a lawyer about it. He tried to reassure her, too, to talk her into clarifying the whole situation legally once and for all. She said she wouldn't risk it. The lawyer swore he could protect her, that we'd prove that we could provide the best home for you, but she wouldn't take that chance. I have no idea why she was so sure your father would win, but she was obviously terrified. She even threatened to take you and leave me, too, if I forced the issue."

Deanna couldn't seem to wrap her mind around any of it. "Do you have any idea at all why she would be so afraid of what he might do? Had she done something he could use against her in a custody battle or something? Had she run because he was abusive?"

Ash shook his head. "I have a theory, but it's just a theory, Dee, based on the years we spent together. Did you know that your mother's father had sued for custody of her and won, because her mother had some mental health issues? She was apparently quite unstable, possibly manic-depressive, though she was never diagnosed, according to your mother."

Deanna was shocked. "I had no idea. Whenever I asked about my grandparents, she just said her family had been kind of a mess, but that both of her parents were gone now."

"They apparently died around the same time you were born," Ash said. "I don't think your mother had the same problem as her mother, but I think she was terrified that she might develop those same tendencies.

And I think in retrospect she knew that taking you and running away was not the act of someone who was totally rational. In the moment, she wanted to teach your father a lesson, and then it all got out of hand. The longer she stayed away, the harder it would have been to make contact and deal with the consequences."

The explanation—no more than a theory, as Ash himself had said—made a terrible kind of sense. Still, she had more questions.

"But you adopted me. She and I both had your last name. I remember that day as clearly as anything we ever did together. I wore a new pink dress because it was my favorite color. We stood in front of a judge and then we went out to lunch to celebrate. Mom even let me have a sip of her champagne."

Ash smiled at the memory. "It was a wonderful day," he agreed.

"But how was that possible?"

"That same lawyer found a sympathetic judge who was willing to allow both of you to change your names legally, but that's as far as it went. Your mother and I couldn't marry, and there was no adoption."

He held her gaze, his eyes filled with regret. "I'm so sorry, Dee. When all of this happened, the paperwork would have meant nothing to you. You were too young to understand it. Later…" He shrugged. "I always meant to tell you the truth. So did your mom, but then she got sick, and I just couldn't hit you with this while you were worried. You had enough to cope with. It was selfish on my part, but I didn't want it to change the way you treated either one of us."

Shock left Deanna speechless. Nothing about her life was what she had always believed. She'd thought she had this great—perhaps even courageous—mother, who'd dared to take off on her own to get out of a bad marriage. She'd thought they'd both been the luckiest people ever to have found Ash and his warm, loving family. Suddenly her heart seemed to stop.

"Did Grandma and Grandpa know?" she asked.

He shook his head. "It would have broken their hearts to know about all the lies. They loved your mom and you so much."

"And Aunt Karen and Uncle Blake?"

He shook his head. "Just your mom and me. No one else. Like you just now, everyone assumed we must have eloped at some point. We never told anyone otherwise."

"How could you lie to everyone?" she asked, shaken to think that this man in whom she'd placed so much trust her whole life could deceive all of them. "They're your parents, your sister and brother."

"We thought it was for the best. And after a while, it didn't seem to matter. We were so happy. Whatever else you think, Dee, remember that. We *were* happy. That wasn't a lie."

There was such a sad, plaintive note in his voice, Deanna might have felt some sympathy for the position he'd been in, but right now she was still reeling at the realization that her entire life had been based on this huge deception.

"Why tell me now? Is it just because you were backed into a corner?"

"Yes, I suppose so. If you meet your father, it's likely to come up that he and your mother never divorced. I wanted you to learn the truth from me, even if it means you'll never be able to think of me as your family again."

She stood up. "I have to go."

"Now? You're too upset. Stay here and let's talk about this."

"What more could you possibly have to say that would make this any better?"

Ash sighed heavily at the obvious truth of that. "Where will you go? Back to school? Or are you heading to Chesapeake Shores?" he asked worriedly.

"I'm not sure," she said. "School, probably. At least until after finals. I'm not throwing away a whole semester of studies over this." She said the last with a touch of defiance, as if trying to prove to herself and to Ash how brave she was or how little any of it mattered anymore, that the *only* thing that mattered was the future, not the past.

She gazed into Ash's eyes, trying to remember the wonderful, honorable man she'd thought him to be just moments ago.

"I do know one thing for sure," she said. "And I'm not doing this to hurt you, Ash. It's just that I need time to make sense of everything. I'm not coming home this summer. I have a chance to volunteer at Johns Hopkins Hospital, and I'm going to take it."

He looked taken aback by her seemingly out-of-the-blue declaration. "Because it's close to Chesapeake Shores?"

"No, because it fits with what I want to do with my life. I'd planned to tell you even before all of this came up."

Now he looked confused. "I thought you intended to come back here and take over my business someday. This doesn't have to change that. I'd still like you to work with me. The business was meant to be your heritage."

"I used to want that, too, but when Mom was so sick, I realized I wanted to study medicine. I've been taking a few premed courses. I believe it's what I was meant to do. I just didn't want to disappoint you."

He gave her a wry look. "And now you don't think that matters, because I've disappointed you," he concluded.

"It's not about punishing you," she insisted. "It's about doing what's right for me. I hope you'll try to understand."

"All I've ever wanted was for you to be happy. Once you've had time to think, I hope you'll see that's all your mother and I tried to do, to give you a stable family. We might have gone about it the wrong way, but our intentions were good."

"I know you see it that way," she said wearily. "Maybe I will, too, at some point. Right now, though, all I see is the incredible, awful lie our life was built on."

And as much as she'd loved her mother and Ash Lane, she had no idea what it would take for her to feel the same way about them ever again.

Even though it was her day off, Kiera was up with the birds, quite possibly because it seemed as if whole families of them were chirping loudly right outside her bedroom window. It was a lovely sound, if not a restful one.

She brewed her first cup of tea for the day, wrapped herself in a luxuriously soft robe that Moira had given to her, and walked outside to sit and watch the sun creep over the horizon, splashing the bay with the bold colors of a dazzling dawn. A workboat made its way slowly along, the chugging of its motor breaking the silence. She'd been told there weren't as many watermen anymore, but the catch of rockfish and hauls of Maryland blue crabs still kept some in the seafood business as their ancestors had been before them.

She glanced up just as Bryan came around the side of the main house, dressed in running clothes that showed off a body that was still toned and fit. It was a display she'd been better off not seeing, given the nerves he stirred in her as it was. Even so, she couldn't seem to drag her gaze away.

Something must have given her presence away, because he looked in her direction. She held her breath, awaiting a sarcastic comment.

"You're up early," he said, his tone surprisingly pleasant. "Especially for your day off."

"It was the birds. They seem to have a lot to be cheerful about this morning."

"You could close your windows."

"And miss this beautiful morning breeze? An early wake-up call is a small price to pay for this."

He nodded in agreement. "I like to get my run in early, so I can be back in time for this," he said.

"Would you like to join me?"

He regarded her cup with skepticism. "Is that more of your chamomile tea?"

"No, it's Irish breakfast tea," she said with a smile. "But I have one of those fancy, single-serving coffee machines. I could brew a cup for you in no time."

"Let me do it," he said. "That is, if you don't mind my invading your space. I wouldn't want you to miss a minute of the sunrise."

She started to argue on principle, but didn't see the point to it. "If you don't mind, then. The kitchen's not exactly hard to find. There are cups and a ridiculously huge variety of coffee pods right by the coffee maker."

She watched him go inside, puzzling over his amenable mood, then shrugged. It was something to be grateful for, so best not to examine it too closely.

When he returned, he took the seat next to hers on the lawn.

She gave him a quick sideways glance, trying not to linger too long on those impressive muscles. "Do you run every morning?"

He nodded. "Almost daily. It clears my head." He gave her a wry look. "And before you comment, some days it does a better job than others. What about you? What do you enjoy doing for exercise?"

"I've never seen the need to be in such a rush, so running holds no appeal. I walk, something I need to get back to doing more before I lose the habit. Riding to work with you has changed the routine I rely on to keep me fit."

"I haven't noticed that it's changed the way you look," he said, then immediately looked as if he regretted his words.

"Was that a rare compliment I heard in there?" she teased.

"I suppose it was. Was I out of line?"

"There's not a woman on this earth who doesn't want to hear a bit of flattery from a man on occasion. The surprise is that you know how to do it."

"To be honest, I'd almost forgotten how," he conceded.

Kiera studied his face, then dared to ask, "Who was she, Bryan?"

He looked confused. "Who was who?"

"The woman who broke your heart. Or is that too personal a question for me to be asking?"

"I doubt I could stop you asking anything that's on your mind, Kiera," he said ruefully. "But it's not something I care to talk about."

"Perhaps it's time you did," she countered. "If not with me, with someone. Wounds that deep are dangerous if they're allowed to fester. I know that as well as anyone."

"You had your heart broken? Was it by the man who died?"

"I saw Peter's death as an abandonment, to be sure," she said. "But it was Moira's father who broke my heart a very long time ago. I allowed it to change my life in ways I never should have. I lived half of a life for far too long and allowed my pain and bitterness to affect my children. And, so you know, I've only recently discovered the difference between the half of a life I led and a full one. It's easy to mistake contentment for living. I'd hate to see you waste as much time as I did."

Bryan stood then, and the rare companionable moment was lost, quite likely thanks to her pushing her opinions on him again.

"Thanks for the coffee, Kiera."

"And the unwanted advice?" she asked. "I'm sorry for overstepping yet again."

"I've heard that's what friends do," he said, though he didn't look terribly happy about it.

"And are we friends now?" she asked, surprised.

"It looks as if we're heading in that direction. We've shared a sunrise together."

She chuckled. "You sound as if that's only slightly more acceptable than the chamomile tea I forced on you."

He laughed then. "It's several steps above that," he said. "I can see a time when I might come to appreciate the friendship, while that tea will never grow on me."

Surprisingly pleased by his words, she nodded. "Then I'll look forward to that day," she told him.

As he walked away, she couldn't resist one last comment. "Try not to burn the pub to the ground today."

He turned back. "If that's your way of wishing a friend a good day, it could use some work."

The comment surprised a laugh out of her, then one from him, as well. The sounds blended in the morning air.

After the sunrise had concluded its show for the day, Kiera busied herself straightening up her little cottage, which took precious little time. Then, at loose ends and craving one of Sally's croissants, which were almost as decadent as the morning scone and Devon cream she would have had back home, she walked into town.

Though she was later than most of the O'Brien women, she found Megan still seated at the large table in back, frowning over something on her laptop, a half-eaten raspberry croissant still on the plate beside her.

"Would I be interrupting if I sat here?" Kiera asked hesitantly.

Megan blinked and looked up, then smiled. "You'd be a welcome distraction, to be honest. Please, sit. You're late this morning."

"I took time to watch the sun come up, then did a few chores," she said as Sally promptly brought her a cup of coffee.

"Anything else today, Kiera?" Sally asked. "I've a few croissants left."

Kiera thought of the chocolate croissant she'd been craving, then glanced at Megan's svelte figure and considered her own ample hips and shook her head. "This will do for now."

"So is it your day off?" Megan asked when Sally had moved on.

"It is. And what explains you being here so late?"

"I've been dealing with a gallery in Atlanta. It's run by an old friend, who doesn't welcome no as an answer. He's used to getting his own way."

"What does he want from you?"

"A showing by your daughter, as a matter of fact. He's upset that it wasn't offered to him first, and even more annoyed that I can't fit his gallery into her schedule for months."

Kiera regarded Megan with surprise. "Is it because she's already booked? I've had the feeling that beyond taking her camera out every day, she has time on her hands."

Megan hesitated. "Only because that's the way she wants it. I could have shows lined up for her back-to-back, but Moira refuses. She likes being home. She misses Luke and the baby when she's on the road. I thought she might let me fit in a few more shows while you're here, but now you're on her list of excuses, too."

"Me?" Kiera said, shocked. "Why?"

Megan smiled. "Because the other excuses were wearing thin, and she knew it. Now she has a fresh one, her mother visiting from Ireland and her wanting to spend every spare minute with you."

Kiera had the audacity to laugh at that. "Now, that would be a first. She was eager enough to leave me behind in Ireland so she could run off to America chasing after Luke. And when we were together, I got on her very last nerve."

Megan laughed with her. "When it came to Luke, that was love, Kiera. It doesn't count and rules of logic don't apply."

Megan's expression sobered. "Would you be willing to talk to her? Perhaps there's something going on that she won't share with me. If I knew what was holding her back, I could guide her career more effectively."

"Is this Atlanta gallery so important?" Kiera asked, leery of unwelcome meddling in her daughter's professional life.

"Not really. I can handle that just by telling my friend he was too slow trying to jump on the bandwagon, but there are others who are not so easily put off. And Moira needs to capitalize on these opportunities while they're pouring in. Being the eccentric, reclusive photographer can create a certain sort of excitement and demand for a bit. Then experts at the most respected galleries find other artists who are more eager to be showcased and move on."

Kiera stared at Megan. "That's how they see Moira, as eccentric and reclusive?"

Megan chuckled. "It's better than maddening, which is what the family used to call her." She immediately looked guilty. "I'm sorry. You're her mother. I should never have said that."

"Not to worry. It's a word that I might have used my-self a time or two," Kiera admitted.

"Will you speak to her?" Megan prodded.

"If the opportunity arises," Kiera agreed half-heartedly. "But I won't push. This is her career. It's not my place to push. And, truth be told, she'll only balk if I do."

Megan nodded. "It's a parent's dilemma, isn't it? We can see so clearly what's best for our children, but try-ing to tell them what that is will only encourage them to do the opposite."

"I could write a book on that," Kiera said, thinking of her sons.

Megan studied her. "We're not talking about Moira anymore, are we?"

Kiera shook her head. "You met my sons in Ireland."

"And you're worried about them?"

"At my wit's end," Kiera admitted. "To be honest, it was a blessing when Moira encouraged me to come here. I was getting nowhere with either of them, and the worry was almost more than I could bear."

Megan gave her a knowing look. "Are you any less worried with the distance between you?"

"No, but at least I'm not wasting my breath trying to talk sense into them, only to have it thrown back in my face. I've had to bail them both out of trouble a time too many. They need to learn to deal with the conse-quences of their actions."

Even as she made the very firm declaration, she couldn't seem to stop the tears that welled in her eyes at the memory of walking away the last time they'd been jailed for their drunken behavior.

"Kiera, I'm so sorry," Megan said, clasping her hand.

"Is there anything I can do? Would you want them here? I'm sure Mick would find work for them."

"As much as I'd like to see them have a fresh start, they need to learn their lesson first. And I wouldn't want my father worrying every minute that they'd only continue their bad behavior here and bring shame on all of us."

"People do deserve second chances, though," Megan reminded her. "I got one from my family."

"Were you spending your days drunk and your evenings in brawls that got you kicked out of every pub you entered?"

Megan winced. "It's that bad?"

"Worse," Kiera said. "They're their father's sons, no question about it. It's clear I should have kicked Sean Malone to the curb much sooner."

"I thought he left when they were very young," Megan said. "That's the impression Moira gave us. She said she never really knew her father at all."

"Because I kept her away from him, but the boys went looking for him and found him to be a jovial drinking pal. Sean's influence by then was far stronger than my own."

"I'm so sorry."

Kiera saw the genuine sympathy in Megan's eyes and wondered at the friendship being offered by this woman whose life had been so different from her own. "Thank you for listening. It's not something I've wanted to burden my father or Moira with."

"Well, I'm around whenever you need to talk. And anything you tell me will stay just between us." She glanced at her watch. "And now I'd better be getting to work. The gallery should have been open fifteen minutes ago."

When Kiera would have stood, Megan shook her head. "Stay and have another cup of coffee and one of Sally's chocolate croissants. I know those are your favorite. I've seen you looking longingly at my leftovers. Sometimes there's just no reason for restraint. You'll feel better with a little chocolate in your system."

Kiera sat back, taking the suggestion to heart. "I believe I will."

"I'll tell Sally on my way out."

Moments later, with a fresh cup of coffee and a chocolate croissant in front of her, Kiera realized she did feel considerably better than she had. She wasn't sure if that was because of the chocolate, the friendship Megan had offered or simply unburdening herself for the first time about the sons who'd strayed so far from the men she'd hoped they'd become.

Chapter 9

Even though she hadn't set foot in the pub all day long, Bryan hadn't been able to get Kiera out of his head. One minute he was annoyed that she'd once more tried to give him unsolicited advice. The next he felt oddly warmed by the offer of friendship. That she was so willing to make the effort with him, despite his often surly attitude, suggested she was either astonishingly kind or a glutton for punishment. He wanted to believe it was the latter, because genuine kindness was something that had been in short supply in recent years, mostly because he'd done his very best to discourage it.

Kiera, however, clearly wasn't someone he was going to be able to keep at a distance. It wasn't just the physical proximity of her cottage. It seemed it was her nature to ignore barriers or to keep pushing at them till they fell.

He recalled Moira, worrying that her mother was returning to the time when she'd been closed off, lonely and bitter, something to which he could totally relate. Just his luck that she'd apparently changed. Just his luck that she'd apparently developed the same stubborn streak that made Luke's life with Moira so challenging.

Though he hadn't realized he was doing it intentionally, in an attempt to avoid another disturbing encounter, he stayed at the pub well past closing. When Luke paused to question him on his way out, Bryan insisted he had things to organize in the kitchen, supplies that needed to be checked and an order to prepare. Given the skeptical expression on Luke's face, Bryan concluded he might have overdone the list of chores.

"Is that so?" Luke asked, glancing around the spotless kitchen in which not a single thing seemed to be out of place. Then his gaze drifted to the well-stocked shelves with only a scattering of empty spots.

"You gave me an order earlier," he commented, his tone casual, but his eyes dancing with humor.

"And now I'm telling you it might not be complete," Bryan said irritably. "We had a big crowd tonight. I used a lot of our staples. Now we're running low."

"On?"

Bryan scowled at him. "Are you questioning my assessment of what's needed to run this kitchen?"

Luke grinned at that. "Never," he said at once. "I'm questioning your skill at fibbing, either to me or yourself. You don't seem to want to leave here tonight. I'm wondering why. It wouldn't be because Kiera's right next door and you're hoping she'll be safely tucked in bed and therefore no temptation, is it?"

"Kiera has nothing to do with anything," Bryan insisted emphatically, which only seemed to make Luke's grin spread.

"Whatever you say," his boss commented with a knowing look. "Just be sure to lock up when you do leave."

"So you're done badgering me?" Bryan asked, startled.

"For tonight anyway," Luke responded. "Unless you'd really like to sit down and talk this through, man-to-man."

Bryan rolled his eyes at the offer. He'd stopped discussing girl troubles with his buddies in ninth grade. "Nothing to discuss."

"Then I'm going home to my wife, whom I'm happy to admit I'm eager to see."

"Have a good night, then," Bryan said, his relief plain, though he held his breath until Luke was out of sight and he heard the front door of the pub close and the lock turn. Then he released a heartfelt sigh, well aware that his escape from the knowing looks and intrusive questions was only temporary. O'Briens, from everything he'd observed in recent years, seldom kept their noses out of others' business for long. And heaven forbid that Mick O'Brien scent even a whiff of romance. He was the absolute worst of all with his meddling.

Sitting in the shadows outside her cottage, Kiera heard Bryan's car as it drove in, saw the glow of the headlights go out and then heard what sounded like a muffled curse as he came into view.

"You're still up," he said, sounding not the least bit happy about it.

"I am, and since we're stating the obvious, you're later than usual. Any problems at the pub?"

"No, I just had some things to finish up," he claimed.

Kiera didn't entirely believe him, but she let it go. "I'm having a glass of wine," she said. "Would you like one?"

"Are you sure you want company?" he asked. "Especially mine? We parted on a bad note this morning."

"A common enough happening," she retorted. "I can suffer with the company, if you'll tell me why you took off so abruptly. I know I ask too many questions sometimes. Did I hit a nerve again?"

His laugh sounded forced. "You should probably know that I'm a bundle of nerves. It makes me an easy target to hit."

Kiera stood up. "I'll get you a glass of wine and perhaps you'll tell me how that came about."

"Or not," he said, his tone wistful.

She paused, looked into his troubled eyes, then nodded. "Okay, then. I can leave it alone for now. We'll just have a chat about inconsequential things or say nothing at all."

When she came back with his wine, he'd finally settled into the chair beside hers, his long, denim-clad legs crossed at the ankles. He accepted the wine in silence, then glanced her way. "On nights like this, with a full moon and stars scattered about in a pitch-black sky, I can almost believe it's possible to find peace."

Kiera nodded in perfect understanding. "I've just been thinking much the same thing."

He regarded her with surprise. "Are you in need of finding peace, Kiera?"

"Isn't everyone to one degree or another? If life's chaotic enough on a daily basis, the idea of calm holds great appeal."

He smiled at the evasive answer. "Now who's dodging the personal questions?"

"Not dodging them," she insisted. "Just trying not to spoil a rare moment of agreement between us."

She waited several minutes, allowing the night's soothing calm to steal over them before saying, "I noticed your garden earlier. Would you mind if I helped out with some weeding sometime?"

She held her breath, anticipating an immediate rejection. Normally the thought of her invading his space would have annoyed him, but tonight his mood seemed mellower, so she concluded it was a chance worth taking. Perhaps he wasn't quite as territorial about his garden as he was about his kitchen at the pub.

Instead of objecting to her request just on principle, he asked, "Do you enjoy gardening?"

She nodded. "Though it's not as if I'm any sort of expert. I only had a tiny bit of space in Ireland, nothing like what you have here, so I only grew a few herbs, many of them in pots sitting in the wee bit of sun they'd get on my back steps, but I found it soothing."

He smiled at that. "And I find it practical, which just shows even when we have something in common, we're coming at it from different perspectives."

"Does that mean we have to be at odds on this, too?"

"No, the two views can be compatible, I suppose. And I can admit that I like the feel of the sun on my shoulders when I work in the garden and the feel of the soil on my hands. But I also appreciate knowing that the vegetables I've grown are going into the food I prepare at the pub, that my ingredients are organic and grown close by, so they're as fresh as they can possibly be."

"There's a movement toward that, isn't there?" Kiera asked, trying to recall what she'd read.

"Farm to table," Bryan replied. "Restaurants have been built around the concept. Most chefs rely on nearby farmers and markets to meet that goal. Here, for me, it's been even more satisfying to know that much of the produce I use I actually grow myself. And what I don't

have room to grow, I get from a couple of local farmers I've gotten to know. Our eggs and milk are supplied
locally, too. And, of course, you already know that our
fish are freshly caught in local waters and picked up at
the docks on the day we serve them."

Kiera was surprised by the enthusiasm in his voice,
the rare passion. She'd known plenty of cooks over the
years. This was her first experience with an honest-
to-goodness trained chef, a man who cared deeply
about the food he served. Perhaps she hadn't been giving Bryan enough credit. He might not have the experience with Irish dishes that she or Nell had, but she
shouldn't be doubting that the commitment he'd made
to the quality of ingredients he used carried over to getting the recipes just right, as well.

"You're suddenly awfully quiet."

"I've a feeling that I've misjudged you," she admitted. "I've accused you of being careless and inexperi-
enced."

"Walking into a kitchen filled with smoke rather than
the delicious aromas you were expecting could have
given you that impression," he conceded, his tone wry.

"That only happened the one time," she said. "Anyone could have an off night." Because it seemed only
right to admit to her own flaws, she added, "Ask my
children how often their evening meal consisted of a
grilled cheese sandwich, because I grew distracted and
let the meal I'd planned overcook. Interestingly, it happened most often on the nights I was preparing something they didn't particularly like." She chuckled. "I
just realized that. I'll have to ask Moira if it was an intentionally devious game they learned to play with me,

asking questions about homework just when I should have been standing at the stove paying close attention."

Bryan faced her, his expression startled. "Is that an olive branch, Kiera?"

"Perhaps." She smiled. "I suppose we'll have to wait and see what tomorrow brings."

He lifted his glass and waited until she'd lifted hers as well, then clinked the two together. "To peace and harmony."

"To peace and harmony," she said, feeling the oddest sense of something shifting between them.

When he stood to go, regret stole over her, but she forced another smile. "Good night, Bryan."

"Sleep well, Kiera."

Once again as he walked away, he paused and turned back, just as he had that morning. "If you're wanting to weed the garden, you're welcome," he said. "But if I find you can't tell a weed from a tomato plant, we'll be having a discussion about it."

She regarded him very solemnly. "If I have any doubts, I'll ask before I yank something from the ground. Your tomatoes will be safe, I promise."

Quite likely a lot safer than her heart, which suddenly seemed to be opening to possibilities yet again. Her relationship with Peter had begun in just such a way, with baby steps and fragile trust. Did she dare risk such a thing happening again, especially with a man whose secrets had made him so wary?

Deanna had taken her anatomy textbook to her favorite bench beneath a huge oak tree on the university campus with every intention of studying for tomorrow's final, but she couldn't seem to focus. She'd been staring at the same page for an hour now, more aware of the mild spring sun filtering through the leaves than of any of the information she was supposed to be memorizing.

When a shadow fell across the book, she looked up to see her roommate studying her with a worried expression.

"Either you're totally fascinated by how the knee bone connects to the thigh bone or there's something else on your mind. I've been standing here for at least five minutes," Juliette complained. "It was the same when you got back yesterday, as if you were off in another world."

She sat down without waiting for an invitation, then held out a square of Dove dark chocolate, their indulgence when studying. "You look as if you need this. I have more in my purse, if there's a real crisis."

Deanna managed a smile. "Always prepared. Were you a Girl Scout, Jules?"

"I think that's the Boy Scout motto, but when it comes to chocolate, I'm never without it, as you should know after two years of rooming together. So what's going on? I know you saw Dr. Robbins before you took off for the weekend. Did she give you bad news?"

"Quite the contrary. She said I was fine, just tired and overwhelmed with finals. She advised me to take a break."

"And that's why you suddenly decided to go home?"

"Pretty much."

Juliette gave her a disappointed look. "I know you think I'm just some flighty airhead who only came to college to nab a husband, but I'm your friend, Dee. I can't help, though, if you won't open up. What's going on? And I can tell this is about more than finals. If that's all it was, you'd be turning the pages of that book like crazy. I watched you last night and just now. You're still staring at the same page."

Deanna sighed. As much as she could probably use a friend right now, she wasn't quite ready to talk about Ash's revelations. Instead, she said, "I told my step-father I'm not coming home to work for his company this summer."

Juliette's eyes went wide. "Wow! That's huge. How did he take the news?"

"I think he was okay with it." She frowned. "It's not as if I really gave him a choice. I just said it was what I was going to do."

"I thought you were worried about disappointing him."

"I was, but this is something I have to do, and that's what I told him," she said, making it sound far less com-plicated than it had been. She hoped Juliette wasn't per-ceptive enough to see through her nonchalance.

"Okay, so this is what you've been telling me for weeks now that you really wanted to do. You've told your stepfather and he's okay with it. Why don't you look happier? Or at least relieved to have the discus-sion behind you?"

"Maybe reality's setting in and I'm just seeing that changing directions like this is a whole lot scarier than I thought it would be," she said carefully. She thought that sounded perfectly plausible, but she could read the skepticism in her roommate's eyes. Behind that airhead persona was a straight-A student with a kind and gen-erous heart and better intuition than Deanna had cred-ited her with.

"You're one of the bravest, most determined people

I know," Juliette said. "Why the second thoughts? Were you counting on your stepfather to stop you?"

Deanna actually paused to consider that possibility. It would have been less scary to stay on the road they'd always assumed she'd travel. Now, though, after this past weekend, it simply wasn't possible. Too much had changed forever.

"You could be right," she admitted. "Maybe on some level, I was hoping he'd say no and I'd do the safe thing, but it would have been the wrong choice. I wasn't that excited by any of my business courses, and while I loved going to work with Ash when I was little and could wear the little hard hat he'd bought me, construction wasn't in my blood, as it was in his." She was confident of that much at least. And now she had all sorts of reasons to go to Baltimore that were even more compelling.

"So you're going to Baltimore," Juliette said. "Is Dr. Robbins ecstatic?"

"She had the arrangements made within an hour," Deanna said, thinking of the one bright spot in all of this. Her mentor had, indeed, been ecstatic. But, then, she didn't know the rest of the story, either.

Jules held out her hand. "Give me your book."

Deanna regarded her with confusion. "Why?"

"Because if you don't pass that anatomy exam with flying colors, none of this will mean much. I'm going to quiz you until you have it all down pat. I'm counting on your getting your degree in medicine and practicing right here in Charlottesville, so you can take care of my family, which I intend to start within months of graduating."

Deanna chuckled. "Have you narrowed down the candidates you'll consider marrying?"

Jules gave her a wicked grin. "The process is half the fun, but there are a few very good contenders. We'll go over the list one of these days. You can give me your thoughts."

"Given my lack of a social life, do you really think I'm remotely qualified to help you pick a husband?"

"You'll be impartial. Some of them make me a little too giddy, so my judgment goes out the window. I want romance, of course, but I also want this to be a sound, rational decision."

Deanna shook her head at the absurd declaration. "Something tells me you're going to run off to a justice of the peace one night and my opinion won't mean a blasted thing. Neither will anyone else's."

Juliette's expression sobered. "Not a chance. That's what my mother did the first time. And a couple of times after that," she added ruefully. "My careful, methodical way is better, and nothing is going to throw me off course. I plan to marry only once, so I'd better get it right the very first time."

Deanna didn't want to tell her that life had a way of throwing you curveballs, just when you thought you had things all mapped out. Jules would learn that for herself soon enough. Deanna certainly had.

Taking Bryan at his word, early the next morning Kiera went over to the garden he'd planted, eager to spend an hour with her hands in the dirt doing something productive. She knew from her limited experience in Ireland just how close to nature it made her feel, how relaxing it could be.

She was about to tap on Bryan's back door to let him know she planned to work in his yard, but the sound of his voice coming through the open kitchen window halted her hand in midair.

"It's time to give up, isn't it?" he said wearily to someone. "I should have done it years ago."

Kiera was struck by the despondent note in his voice. She had a feeling whoever was on the other end of the line had given him yet more bad news. Perhaps it was the same person he'd been speaking to at the pub a couple weeks ago. That conversation had left him shaken in a way she didn't entirely understand.

Though a part of her wanted to continue listening to try to get a sense of what was taking such an emotional toll on him, she couldn't bring herself to eavesdrop a moment longer. She quickly retreated to the garden and knelt down, trying to focus on the task at hand.

The warmth of the sun on her shoulders would have been soothing at any other time, but she couldn't seem to shake the memory of Bryan's tone. If only he would open up with her, perhaps she could help. Something told her, though, that this was a burden he'd carried alone for a long time—long enough that he was finally conceding defeat. She knew what that was like. Hadn't she given up on her attempts to help her sons straighten out their lives? Hadn't it just about broken her heart to do so, even when she'd known there was no other choice? And hadn't she been second-guessing herself ever since, especially when anyone questioned her about her sons?

She'd been working for a half hour or more when she heard the slap of the screen door closing abruptly and heard Bryan's footsteps on the back deck. He came to a sudden halt, quite likely at the sight of her.

She glanced at him over her shoulder and forced a

bright smile. "I took you at your word and came to do some weeding."

For a moment, he looked flustered, but then he rallied and nodded. "Are my plants safe?"

"Come and see for yourself. I think this pile of wilting greenery beside me is made up entirely of invasive weeds. I've carefully avoided all your neat rows and the plants that have stakes."

He grinned then. "Who knew my approach to gardening would provide guidance to a rank amateur."

"The neat little labels at the beginning of the rows helped, too." She gave him a curious look. "You weren't by any chance unsure you'd recognize what you'd planted, were you?"

"In a couple of cases, I did experiment," he admitted. "I've never grown eggplant before, and I added more than one kind of pepper. Adding jalapeño to a recipe, rather than a sweet red pepper, could be a big mistake."

"And you couldn't plainly see the difference when they're on the plant? They look nothing at all alike."

He shrugged. "Mistakes happen."

"Not to you, I'm thinking. Why would you be growing jalapeños in the first place? There's little need for them in most Irish food."

"But I do love a little salsa when I'm having a cold beer on my deck in the evening. The Irish don't know what they're missing. Weren't you the one who told me it's important to serve foods that make the customers thirsty for more ale? Perhaps I should recommend that addition to the pub's menu."

"And have Nell fainting on the spot?" Kiera asked.

"More likely, I'd be risking your grumbling in my ear," he retorted.

Kiera sat back on her heels and studied him closely. His mood seemed surprisingly light, given the tone she'd overheard not that long ago. He seemed calm, too.

"Is your morning off to a good start?" she inquired tentatively.

"The sight of you working in my garden is certainly a pleasant way to start the day," he said, even though they both knew it wasn't really a response to what she'd asked.

"Well, unfortunately, then, I'm about to ruin things by stopping. It's time for me to get ready for work."

She stood up, brushed the dirt from her knees and was about to put the weeds into a bag she'd brought along for that purpose when he stopped her. "Leave that. I'll finish up."

"Okay, then. I hope you'll let me do this again."

"Anytime."

She was about to leave, when he called her name. She paused and turned.

"I'll give you a lift to work if you want." He hesitated, cleared his throat, his expression oddly uncertain. Finally, he added, "Maybe we'll have time to stop at Panini Bistro for an espresso or something."

Startled, Kiera simply stared for a moment. She almost opened her mouth to say they could get all the coffee they wanted at the pub, but she stopped herself just in time. It was another of those rare olive branches being extended by one or the other of them. They weren't to be ignored.

"That would be lovely," she told him. "Will fifteen minutes do?" she asked, knowing he was usually in a rush to get to his precious kitchen and begin his day.

"A half hour will be fine," he said. "It's early yet. Luke won't be expecting either one of us."

No, Kiera thought, but he would find it fascinating if they not only arrived together, which wasn't that uncommon, but arrived with to-go cups from Panini Bistro. If she knew Luke and her daughter, that was something that wouldn't go unnoticed and she'd likely never hear the end of it.

Chapter 10

Because it was such a pleasant June morning, Bryan asked Kiera if she'd like to sit outside at Panini Bistro where they'd have a view of the bay across the street as well as the warmth of the sun before it got too high in the sky. June weather in Chesapeake Shores could be unpredictable, pleasant one day and unbearably hot and humid the next. Today's sunny blue skies and seventy-degree start was one of the better ones.

"I never miss an opportunity to see the water," Kiera responded at once. "It's one of the reasons I found my little cottage so appealing. There's a glimpse of the bay from the yard."

"There's an even better view from upstairs in my house," Bryan said. "When I leave my bedroom windows open, I can hear the lapping of the waves on the shore."

As soon as the words were out of his mouth, Bryan regretted them. He'd spoken the truth, but it had sounded far too close to an invitation. He couldn't be certain from her expression if Kiera had heard it that way, but he knew absolutely that the provocative image of her in his room, in his bed, wouldn't be going away anytime soon. It shocked him just how powerful that image was.

"Bryan?"

At the questioning note in Kiera's voice, he snapped back to the moment and realized a waitress had arrived and was waiting for their orders. "An espresso for me," he said quickly. "Kiera?"

"I've already ordered a cappuccino," she said, her lips twitching as she tried to hold back a smile.

"Well, that's all, then," he said, then met her gaze. "Unless you'd like something to eat."

"The coffee will do."

"Sure thing," the waitress said, leaving them alone.

"Was your mind wandering?" Kiera teased. "I have to wonder where it went. It must have been a pleasant place."

"Nowhere worth following," he assured her, then focused his attention on the boats chugging along on the bay in the morning sunlight. It was a tranquil picture, far more tranquil than his oddly chaotic thoughts.

It had suddenly occurred to him that he was actually on something that some people would consider a date. When he'd issued the impulsive invitation, he'd given it no thought beyond the momentary desire to have Kiera's company for a little longer before their day started at the pub. They seemed to do better with each other away from that atmosphere. Now he was realizing it was a step, albeit a tiny one, toward a more complicated relationship, something he'd successfully avoided for years.

Because he and Melody had never divorced, he'd considered himself unavailable for anything more than the most casual encounters. He was always honest with the women he'd dated, making sure they understood he wasn't looking for anything lasting. But trying to explain why he wasn't interested in more was too personal to share, so he avoided anything that might be leading toward that uncomfortable conversation. Was he actually willing to have that conversation with Kiera? He couldn't quite envision it, which meant he needed to be very careful about any signals he sent to her.

"For a man who said his morning had gotten off to a good start not that long ago, you're looking increasingly troubled," Kiera said. "Have I said something to make you uneasy?"

"Not at all," he said at once. "I'm just not used to doing things like this."

She stared at him blankly. "Like what? Having coffee?"

He nodded, then chuckled. "Sounds ridiculous, doesn't it?"

"We've had coffee before," she reminded him. "Well, you've had coffee and I've had tea, but it's the same sort of thing."

"That was at the pub. This is entirely different. Can't you see that?" Even as he spoke he knew that he was making way too much of an innocent hour at a sidewalk café.

Kiera simply looked puzzled, but before he could attempt an explanation, Mick O'Brien came striding down the street from the direction of his wife's art gallery and spotted them. He paused at their table, then looked pointedly from Bryan to Kiera and back again. "Well, this is a surprise," he said, grabbing a chair from a neighboring table and pulling it over without waiting for an invitation. "Imagine seeing the two of you here," he said, then pointedly added, "together."

Understanding of Mick's assumption suddenly dawned on Kiera's face, and she cast a frantic look in Bryan's direction.

"We're just taking a few minutes to bounce around some ideas for the pub," Bryan told Mick quickly, hoping to take control of the situation. "Kiera has some thoughts for additions to the menu, isn't that right, Kiera?"

She nodded. "Things that were popular in the pubs where I worked in Ireland," she said at once. "You must have been in your share of pubs over there on your visits over the years, Mick. I imagine you have some thoughts as well about what could be added to the menu at O'Brien's."

"Oh, I shared a few with Luke when he first came up with his plan to open the pub," Mick responded. "I'm surprised you didn't ask Ma to join you," he said, referring to Nell. "She takes a special interest in the pub's menu. She has since Luke opened the place. Authenticity is very important to her, as you surely know, Bryan."

Bryan laughed. "I do, indeed. It's a word I was hearing on a daily basis for quite some time. Now Kiera has taken up the chant. She takes her title of Irish consultant quite seriously."

"Well, certainly no offense to Nell is meant by our talking through a few things," Kiera said hurriedly. "This is just a preliminary conversation. Of course, Nell would have the last word."

"Of course," Bryan said, finding himself vaguely amused by Kiera's discomfort. It was rather nice no longer being alone with his stomach tied in knots. He doubted, though, that Kiera had any idea of where Mick's matchmaking mind was now wandering. It had little to do with the pub's menu or Nell's proprietary interest in it. It was finding the two of them together at this early hour that clearly fascinated Mick. The conversation was nothing more than a diversion for him while he assessed their relationship so he could spread the word to the rest of the family. And he would spread it. Bryan had no doubt of that.

When the waitress brought their drinks, Mick ordered an American coffee for himself, obviously not planning to leave the two of them alone until he'd figured out what they were really doing. Heaven forbid he observed any of the sparks that Bryan himself had been feeling when he least expected it.

"It wasn't long ago that Luke was worried about the two of you coexisting at the pub," Mick said innocently. "Obviously things have improved."

"We're making an effort to get along," Kiera told him. "We've found a few things we can agree on."

"And you're neighbors, too," Mick noted. "How's that working out? Kiera, are you finding the little guest cottage comfortable? We did the renovations there quickly at Moira's request, but if we missed anything, be sure to let me know. I'll have someone take care of it."

Bryan caught an odd expression flitting across Kiera's face and had a hunch it had something to do with Mick's casual mention of Moira's role in the renovations. He was a little taken aback by that, as well. Had there been some plan afoot to push the two of them closer together? If there had been, though, it was a worry for another time. Right this minute, they had Mick and his easily stirred romantic fantasies to deal with.

Bryan looked around, hoping to spot another O'Brien or just about anyone else who might provide a distraction for Mick. For a town crawling with O'Briens, though, for once there wasn't another one in sight.

"Kiera, are you enjoying Chesapeake Shores?" Mick asked as if he hadn't had a chance to ask her before, when in truth they talked almost daily at the pub.

"It's lovely," she said, her expression brightening at the innocuous topic. "You must be so proud when you look around and realize that you created such a warm and welcoming place."

Though Mick looked pleased by her comment, he said, "I designed and built the buildings, but it's those who live here who've made it a community."

"But I've a feeling you and your family set the example," she said.

"And not just here," Bryan added, seizing on the topic himself. Work was still Mick's real passion. It should prove a good distraction. "How many other communities has your company built around the country, each with its own distinct way of blending into the landscape around it? I had a chance to chat with Jaime Alvarez when he was here recovering from his broken leg. He showed me pictures of the project he was working on for you in the Pacific Northwest." He turned to Kiera. "It's nothing like Chesapeake Shores, which suits this part of the world. That community fits perfectly with the environment out there."

"That's always our goal," Mick said. "We want each community to be unique. And if you tell my brother Thomas I said this, I'll deny it, but it's because of him that we take such care with the natural beauty of each location and do as little damage as possible."

"But don't you have to be on the road a lot to oversee such work?" Kiera asked, clearly fascinated. "It must take time to get the feel of a place just right so you know how to design for it."

Mick's expression turned rueful. "In the beginning, when I was building the business, it took too much time, if you ask Megan about it. The only way I won her back after our divorce was to promise to let my chief executive, Jaime, and Luke's brother, Matthew, take over most of the projects. I only travel now when there's a problem to be resolved or a need to deal with the local authorities."

Kiera frowned at that. "I wonder, given that experience, why Megan is less understanding of Moira's desire to stay here with her family, rather than traveling so much."

Mick chuckled. "My wife is a complicated woman," he said wryly. "And she's ambitious, not so much for herself, as for your daughter. She hates to see talent go unrecognized. Moira is wise for standing up to her. Perhaps you should remind Megan how she felt about my being on the road all the time."

"I don't suppose you could draw the parallel?" Kiera asked. "I'm finding that I enjoy her friendship a little too much to be expressing an opinion that goes against what she wants."

"Probably a wise approach," Mick agreed. "But it's not a past I like to remind her of, either. I'll be keeping my opinions to myself, as well." He pushed aside his empty cup and stood up. "I need to run, but before I go, I'll catch up with the waitress and pay our check. Good to see you both. Enjoy your morning. I imagine we'll cross paths again at the pub later."

When he'd gone, Kiera glanced Bryan's way. "That was interesting."

"That's one word for it," Bryan said. He met her gaze. "How well do you know Mick?"

"Hardly at all."

"And his reputation for meddling?"

Kiera looked taken aback. "Is that what turned you into a bundle of nerves at his arrival?"

"By the end of the day, half the O'Briens will be speculating about us," Bryan confirmed. "The other half will be actively trying to find excuses to stop by the pub to see for themselves if sparks are flying. I predict we're going to have quite the assortment of O'Briens dropping in tonight."

Now she looked alarmed. "Surely a man as important as Mick O'Brien has better things to do than spread tales about us, especially when we were doing no more than having coffee together."

"You heard him, Kiera. He's semiretired, which means he's bored. Meddling is what he does to fill his days. With his family mostly settled, we present a golden opportunity. I've witnessed his interference in quite a few relationships since I've been in town. They've turned out well, but little thanks to Mick inserting himself into the middle of them. He thinks he has Nell's knack for it, but believe me, he lacks her subtlety."

Though she didn't look as if she entirely believed him, Kiera lifted her chin with a touch of defiance. "Then we'll just have to set him straight. We'll set all of them straight, if it comes to that. I'm grieving Peter and you..." She hesitated. "Well, I don't quite know what's going on with you, but one thing's for certain, we're more than content just to be civil." Her gaze narrowed. "Isn't that right?"

Though he nodded in agreement, Bryan laughed at her naïveté when it came to O'Brien determination. Even though he wasn't looking forward to what might happen next, it might be fun to watch Kiera trying to squirm out of that particular spotlight. Who knew? Maybe she was clever enough to do what few others in that family had been able to accomplish.

On her drive to Baltimore a few days after the school year ended in Charlottesville, Deanna had deliberately detoured through the little seaside town of Chesapeake Shores. She'd even dared to park across the street from O'Brien's hoping for a glimpse of Bryan Laramie. But while plenty of people had come and gone from the Irish pub during the half hour she remained parked there, none had looked like the man whose picture had been featured in that magazine article.

More than once she'd considered getting out of the car and marching inside to confront her father, but in the end, she simply hadn't had the nerve. She had to make peace with the whole messy situation before she saw him. She had this awful feeling if she did it without careful planning, she'd take one look at him and burst into a flood of tears.

When she'd realized that people were glancing her way, as if curious about why she was simply sitting in her car for so long, she'd finally pulled out of the space and headed on to Baltimore.

In the two weeks since, she'd been so busy getting acclimated to her volunteer summer internship and meeting new people that she'd managed to push aside any thought of what her next step with her father should be. Nor had she made any progress in mending her suddenly awkward relationship with Ash.

She couldn't blame the latter on him. Once he'd gotten over her plan to move to Baltimore, he'd done all he could to be supportive. Perhaps that stemmed from guilt over keeping silent all these years, but more likely it was simply because that was the kind of man he was. Despite their rocky relationship at the moment, she knew in her heart he wanted what was best for her. If medicine was her dream now, he'd back her 1,000 percent. He'd proved that by insisting on paying the rent on her apartment for the summer and offering whatever she needed in the way of furnishings to be comfortable.

He'd called to touch base every few days, not lingering on the phone or pressing her about anything, just letting her know he loved her no matter what. Though she understood his goal was to mend fences and reassure her, the calls always left her feeling vaguely guilty for not being quite ready to forgive and forget.

After a fascinating but exhausting week observing and being a glorified gofer in a cancer research lab, she was more than ready to order a pizza and call it a night. The weekend stretched out ahead of her, tempting her with all sorts of possibilities. She could explore Baltimore's Inner Harbor or drive over to Ocean City, as many of her new coworkers planned to do.

Or she could drive down to Chesapeake Shores.

The tantalizing possibility was always there, taunting her for being a coward, for not being ready to take such a huge step.

When her phone rang, she assumed it was the pizza delivery and answered without even glancing at caller ID. Instead, it was Ash.

"Everything okay there?" he asked cheerfully.

"Everything's going great," she said automatically.

"You sure? You sound tired. They're not overworking you, are they?"

"You are such a dad," she said without thinking. "As if nobody but you should put in a long day."

As soon as the words were out of her mouth, sounding just like something she would have said before everything had changed, she fell silent. So did Ash.

He recovered first. "I'm just saying that it is summer. You should have some fun, too. Any big plans for the weekend?"

"Not really. First I want to sleep for about twelve hours straight. Then I'll decide what I'm up for."

"Is Chesapeake Shores on the list of possibilities?"

"I don't know," she admitted candidly.

"Sweetie, what's holding you back? Do you not want to meet your father, after all?"

"Of course I want to meet him," she said with a touch of impatience, then sighed. "It's just so complicated."

"Because of what I told you about your mom and me?"

"That certainly didn't help. I don't know which situation I need to figure out first. I'm trying to make sense of what you told me, but I can't quite get past the two of you creating this whole big fake-family lie."

"We *were* a family," Ash said emphatically. "Not in the conventional way and not in the way you thought, but we were a family, Dee. Your mom was always your mom, and I was the best stepfather I knew how to be. My parents loved you as if you were my own child. Isn't that what makes a family?"

Deanna's eyes stung with tears. "I wish it were that simple. I know it should be. I know I should focus on the love and the stability that you brought into my mom's life and mine. That really is what counts. I just can't get past the fact that our family was built on a lie."

"I am so, so sorry for that. And I'm even sorrier that it's complicating all the emotions that come along with finding your biological father. Is there anything at all I can do to make it easier? I told you before that I'll go with you to Chesapeake Shores if that will help. You don't have to meet him the first time on your own. I can even stay in the background. He doesn't even have to know I'm there or who I am. I'll just be there if you need me."

A part of her wanted to lean on him, but she knew this was a decision she had to make herself and something she needed to do by herself and in her own time. "I appreciate your willingness to go with me, but I need to do it on my own, when I'm ready. I'll be able to handle it when the time is right."

"Well, just remember that I'm here and that I love you and you will always be my daughter in every way that matters."

She wiped away more tears at his words. That was Ash, strong and solid, even when she knew his heart must be aching. His world had changed, too. She needed to remember that.

"I love you," she whispered.

After a startled beat, he replied, "Love you more," just as he always had.

Their relationship might have had a huge setback, but some things would never change. She took comfort in knowing that.

The rhythm of Kiera's days was becoming familiar and comfortable. Several mornings a week, she worked in Bryan's garden before the sun got too hot. He usually joined her at some point, either bringing her a cup of tea or a bottle of cold water. They'd even gone back to Panini Bistro a couple of times, thankfully with no chance encounters with Mick or any other O'Brien.

While O'Briens had been in and out of the pub more frequently than usual, their gazes speculative, Kiera had done her best to ignore them and taken even greater care to stay clear of Bryan during their visits. She would give them no fodder for their wild imaginings.

Her daughter, however, had been oddly absent for a week now. Kiera couldn't help thinking that Moira had somehow figured out that Kiera knew of her role in the cottage renovations and was giving her mother a wide berth until her temper cooled.

Since it was a matter that needed to be settled between them, Kiera decided it was time to pay a visit to Moira's home on Beach Lane. For one thing, she missed her granddaughter.

When she knocked on the door, she noted that Moira's car was still in the driveway, and she could hear the sound of Kate's giggles drifting through the open windows. It was, she thought, the sweetest sound she'd ever heard.

"Come in. It's open," Moira called out when Kiera knocked again.

She found her daughter in the kitchen on her knees,

cleaning up a splattering of oatmeal that had reached the four corners of the room.

"Did our Kate not like her breakfast?" Kiera inquired, as the little girl in question held out her arms to her. Kiera took a damp cloth to her face and hands before picking her up.

"Your granddaughter picked this morning to throw a fine tantrum," Moira said. She gave Kate a sour look. "And now, for you of course, she's all smiles."

Kiera laughed. "That's the way it sometimes works. Any idea what set her off?"

"Her beloved father left for work, abandoning her, or so she seemed to assume. Apparently I make a poor substitute."

"Ah, I lived through that a time or two. Of course, it wasn't that your father had left for the day, since he'd never been around, but simply that I was not enough for you."

"Was there a logic to it?" Moira inquired plaintively. "Something that I can do to avoid such a scene?"

"Not that I was ever able to determine. It did always seem to happen when I was in a rush to be somewhere. You were particularly fond of mashing the oatmeal into your hair, then screaming like a banshee when I had to wash it out."

Moira sighed as she wiped up the last of the oatmeal from the floor. "Then it seems this little apple didn't fall far from the tree." Her gaze lifted to Kiera's. "Mum, how did you do it with three of us and no help at all?"

"There were plenty of days when I didn't cope all that well," Kiera confessed. "I just prayed you wouldn't notice. With three of you, if you'd figured out my weaknesses, I wouldn't have stood a chance."

"But you survived," Moira said, a note of what sounded like awe, or perhaps hope, in her voice.

"I survived. You will, too. And you do have help, more than you could possibly need, if you'd simply ask for it."

"Pure stubbornness," Moira admitted. "She's a wee little girl. I should be able to manage this."

"There's a wide path between should and can. You need to learn when to cross to the other side and hold out a hand to your husband or me or anyone else in this town who'd be happy to have your back. Now, sit down, hold your daughter and I'll make us both a cup of tea."

Moira took Kate from her, then chuckled. "You're more like Nell than you probably realize. You think a cup of tea is the solution to every problem."

"It's usually a good start," Kiera told her.

"So what brings you by this morning? Did you have some instinct that I was at my wit's end?"

"Not at all, but it's been a few days since we've crossed paths. I was wondering if there was a reason for that."

A guilty flush spread across her daughter's pale-as-cream complexion. Kiera nodded without a word being spoken. "I thought so. You heard that Mick revealed your part in getting that cottage ready for me. And after you'd played the part of indignant daughter so well, insistent that I stay here under your roof."

"I had to be convincing, didn't I? Are you furious with me?"

"I'm wondering why you felt the need to pretend you didn't want me to move there in the first place, since moving me into close proximity to Bryan Laramie was clearly part of the plan."

Moira laughed. "Because, just like me, you always do the opposite of what's expected, just to be contrary. If I'd told you I thought it was the right place and that I thought it might bring you and Bryan a little closer, you'd have moved to the outskirts of town just to spite me."

"I thought you believed any friendship between Bryan and me would be disloyal to Peter's memory."

"Friendship wasn't the problem," Moira said. "It was the sparks between you that I found worrisome. So friendship is absolutely all I'm encouraging."

"Carefully noted," Kiera said, not even trying to hide a smile.

"And that's all that's going on between you, right?"

"Absolutely," Kiera said.

"Despite what Mick thinks he saw at Panini Bistro and what Luke and I have seen with our own eyes?" Moira pressed.

Kiera laughed outright at the indignation and worry in her daughter's voice. "You do realize that I'm your mother, and as an adult of reasonably mature years, I have a right to a personal life of my own choosing. Weren't you the very one who reminded me of that several times since I arrived in Chesapeake Shores?"

Moira frowned at the scolding. "I suppose," she said reluctantly.

Kiera nodded. "As long as we've an understanding about that, then I will tell you that Bryan and I have made peace in the name of cooperation and teamwork at the pub. Nothing more."

"And those sparks? I know none of us have just imagined them."

"An interesting outcome," Kiera said.

And one she was not at all ready to examine too closely and certainly not with her daughter. It was enough that they'd kept her up late at night, her thoughts whirling in unexpected ways, ways she'd thought she was well beyond experiencing.

Chapter 11

"Moira, I know it's last minute, and more of a commitment than you prefer in terms of time, but an opportunity like this might never come along again," Megan O'Brien told her as they sat in Megan's cramped office at her gallery on Shore Road.

Ever since she'd first seen Moira's photographs, Megan had been an ardent champion of her work. And thanks to her contacts and credibility in the art world, Moira's career had not only been established, but had taken off in ways she'd never anticipated.

Balancing the opportunities that came her way with her life with Luke and the baby had become a constant tug-of-war. Moira would have been content with life as a stay-at-home mother, but Megan had Luke's sincere backing when it came to pushing Moira to take advantage of the opportunities to show her work to an increasingly expanding audience across the country.

Sometimes, though, like now, she simply had to put her foot down. After a couple of rough mornings at home with Kate, perhaps she should have been eager to escape. Instead, though, it had made her all the more determined not to fail as a mother. Megan needed to grasp that her family came first.

"Not this time," she told Megan very firmly, then seized on what had become her latest excuse. "Megan, you know the timing is off. My mother is here—"

Megan cut her off. "Which should make the decision even easier. She'll be available to help with Kate while you're away."

"It's one thing to have her sit with Kate for an afternoon or evening. It's entirely different to expect her to manage the baby day in and day out, while working at the pub, as well," she said, despite evidence that her mother seemed more than capable of juggling both tasks rather well. Hadn't she had years of experience at just that? Moira was coming to appreciate the toll of that more and more. Her mum was due a break, not more of the same.

"She raised you and your brothers while working," Megan reminded her as if she'd been reading Moira's mind.

Moira recalled those days, her mum exhausted and short-tempered. No, she simply didn't want Kate exposed to that, even if it appeared things weren't remotely the same these days. Kiera had mellowed, just as Moira herself had.

"Talk it over with her, at least," Megan suggested. "This show in San Francisco would open all sorts of doors for you. The gallery there has regulars from not only the West Coast, but from Hawaii, Japan, even China. It'll be your first international exposure."

"I started in Ireland," Moira reminded her, "and there were European collectors when I did my show in New York."

Megan shrugged those reminders off as if they were of no consequence. "You know what I'm saying, Moira. This is another opportunity to expand your audience that simply shouldn't be ignored. My role is to give you the best professional advice I can, and I'm telling you this is an invaluable invitation. Sit down with your mother and Luke. I'll come back to the pub with you right now. We can explain the significance of this to them together. You know Luke will do whatever it takes to support you, and I'm sure your mother will jump on board."

"No way am I subjecting the two of them to you," Moira said. "You're as much of a bulldozer as your husband, Megan O'Brien."

Megan looked pleased by the comment. "Living with Mick all these years was bound to rub off. We both do enjoy getting our own way."

"It wasn't meant as a compliment."

Megan laughed. "I know, but I'll take it as one just the same. So you'll talk to your mother and Luke and let me know tomorrow?"

"As if there was ever any doubt," Moira muttered, then tempered her sarcasm with a more appropriate note of gratitude. "I do appreciate all you've done for me."

"Even when I'm being pushy and demanding?"

"Even then." Moira studied her closely. "You're awfully confident of what the two of them will say, aren't you?"

"I know they both want the best for you and your career," Megan responded a little too carefully.

"You've already talked to them," Moira accused.

"Not to Luke, but I might have mentioned to your

mother that there were opportunities I didn't think you should ignore. Hasn't she said anything?"

"Not a word, which is surprising since she usually doesn't hesitate to speak her mind. We had quite a long chat just the other day and none of this was mentioned. I know she's come to admire you, so it's odd that she didn't rush to do your bidding, unless she's in agreement with me that my place is here."

"Or maybe she was afraid it would be counterproductive," Megan suggested. "Sometimes suggestions coming from a parent don't get the best reception. I've learned that from experience. I imagine your mother has, too."

"We both are known for our stubborn, independent streaks," Moira conceded.

"Don't turn me down just because I tried to involve your mother," Megan said. "Maybe that was overstepping on my part."

"Maybe?" Moira gave her mentor a long look that actually caused her to squirm just a little.

"Okay, it was," Megan conceded. "But if you look at this from every angle, you'll see that it's the next logical step for you to reach your goal."

"I didn't have any goals before I met you. I'm not sure mine are as lofty even now as yours are."

"And that's why you have me, to encourage you to reach higher. You're talented, Moira. You need to dream bigger."

"And to go against my instincts to be satisfied with what we've accomplished already?"

Megan leaned toward her, her expression earnest. "I hope you'll decide against settling for that, when you can achieve so much more, Moira. Let us—Luke, your

mother and me—help you get there. We only want you
and your tremendous talent to get all the recognition
you deserve."

Moira thought of what her mother had said just the
other day about holding out a hand and asking for help,
about accepting it when it was offered. Perhaps she was
being too stubborn for her own good. It surely wouldn't
be the first time, nor would it likely be the last. Perhaps it was time to break the pattern of saying no just
to be contrary.

"We'll talk it over," she promised Megan. "I'll get
back to you."

"Tomorrow?"

Moira smiled at her persistence. "Yes, tomorrow."

Kiera sat in a corner of the pub, bouncing Kate on
her knee. The baby gurgled with delight and reached
for a handful of Kiera's auburn hair. Kiera gently un-
tangled her tiny fingers and placed them around the
grip of a pacifier that so far Kate had been noisily reluctant to give up.

"How about this instead?" she coaxed. "Otherwise,
I'll soon not have a hair left on my head."

In another of her contrary moves, Kate tossed the
pacifier onto the floor.

"Not interested? Okay, what then? There must be
something here that will be more entertaining than tugging on my hair."

"I have something that might do," Bryan said, coming out of the kitchen with one of the miniature fro-
zen all-fruit ices he made just for the baby. He waved a
strawberry-flavored one in front of Kate, who reached

for it eagerly and bestowed one of her best smiles on him.

"She does love those," Kiera said grudgingly. "What made you think of making them?"

Though she hadn't really expected it, Bryan pulled up a chair. Since their truce, he'd taken a few minutes here and there to sit and talk to her. Without him bristling at every word she said, she'd increasingly come to enjoy his company. She especially looked forward to early mornings in the garden, both of them weeding companionably with few words spoken.

"I used to make them for my daughter when she was a baby and teething," he said, not meeting her gaze as he spoke.

The unexpected and very personal revelation took Kiera by surprise. "You have a daughter?"

"I did," he said, his face expressionless. His eyes, however, spoke volumes, the sorrow so deep it almost broke her heart.

"I didn't know. I'm sorry," she said, her voice barely above a whisper.

Bryan shook his head, waving off the sympathy. "It's not that she died. As far as I know she's very much alive."

Once more, he'd caught her off guard. "As far as you know? I don't understand."

"Her mother took her and left when she was barely a year old. I haven't seen or heard from them since."

Surprise turned to shock. "And you haven't tried to find them?"

"Of course I have," he declared impatiently. "I filed missing persons reports. I hired private detectives." He sighed. "But when an adult really wants to disappear, it's apparently easier than you can imagine."

Kiera tried to envision a circumstance in which a woman would take her child and run from someone, vanishing so thoroughly they couldn't be found.

Bryan regarded her with a steady gaze. "Go ahead, ask. I know you're imagining the worst, that I must have done something terrible to drive them into hiding."

"Did you?" she asked evenly, not wanting to believe such a thing was possible. She and Bryan might have had a rocky start, but she'd come to believe he was a good man, albeit one who kept to himself. That distance had served her well, so she'd never tried to bridge the gap. Instead, she'd aimed for civility, a few cautious overtures of friendship and little more. She was no readier for more than he was, despite the undeniable, simmering attraction between them.

"I was neglectful, no question about it," he confessed, the chattiness something new. He seemed intent, though, on making her understand. "I was just out of culinary school in New York, trying to make a name for myself. A chef's hours are never easy, not at a top restaurant that's crowded from opening till closing. The demands to get it right are extraordinary, the stress high. I thought I was doing it all for us, but the truth is, it probably only mattered to me. I was ambitious and believed what I'd been told, that I'd have my own top restaurant one day if I worked hard enough and paid my dues."

Kiera had never worked in anyplace with fiery-tempered ambitious chefs, but she knew the demands of restaurants well enough. "You got caught up in the dream," she concluded.

Bryan nodded. "And look where it got me. I wound up in a deli and then here."

"What exactly is wrong with here?" she demanded, instantly indignant on Luke's behalf. "It's a fine pub and, despite the way I taunt you, you do a fine job."

He looked startled by the faint praise. "A fine job?"

"Don't be letting it go to your head. There's room for improvement."

A rare smile tugged at his lips. "Perhaps Luke was right," he murmured, standing up.

"About?"

"A challenge being just what I need."

He ran his fingers gently over Kate's cheek, now smeared with the stain of strawberries.

As he walked back into the kitchen, Kiera stared after him, even as she wiped the baby's face. She still couldn't quite get over what he'd revealed to her, not just the facts of his past, but his pain. That was something she understood. It gave them something in common. She knew all too well that a bond such as that could be dangerous to a woman who didn't want to risk her heart.

Kiera sat quietly for a time after Bryan had gone, distractedly playing with Kate to keep her occupied. She was so preoccupied that she didn't notice Moira at first, staring at them from just inside the front door of the pub.

When her daughter realized she'd been spotted, she crossed the room and took Kate from Kiera's arms. "What was that all about?" she asked. "You and Bryan? It looked intense."

"Just having a word with each other," Kiera said, reluctant to share what had been said in private.

"Not hurling words *at* each other?" Moira pressed. "That's a pleasant change. It adds to the bond of friendship the two of you are developing."

Kiera thought of the trust Bryan had just placed in her by talking about his daughter and allowing her to see what not having her in his life had cost him. The glimpse inside his heart had shifted things between them yet again.

"It was a good conversation, as a matter of fact." Kiera focused her gaze on Moira. "What is that pink in your cheeks all about? Did you get overheated walking here or did things not go well in your meeting with Megan?"

"A little too well, if you want to know the truth. She's found an opportunity for me to show my photographs in San Francisco."

"That's remarkable," Kiera said enthusiastically. Seeing no such excitement in her daughter's eyes, her own expression faltered. "It is, isn't it?"

"As if you didn't already know the answer to that. I know Megan's been filling your head with information about the opportunities I've been avoiding and trying to enlist you to be on her side."

Kiera saw no reason to deny the truth of that. "And have I added to the pressure on you?"

"No," Moira conceded. "Thank you for that."

"May I say, though, that I don't entirely understand your reluctance to do what Megan is asking of you. You know her judgment is sound in this area. And I was there when she put off one gallery owner, an old friend, to protect you from being overextended, so I saw for myself that she's only pressing you to do the shows that truly matter."

"I didn't realize there were offers she's never even mentioned," Moira said, clearly surprised. "That does make this one seem doubly important."

"It's San Francisco, too," Kiera said wistfully. "Wouldn't you love to see it? Remember when we used to look through those picture books from America and dreamed of traveling there someday even before your grandfather came over here? I never thought such a day would be possible, but here we both are."

"Seeing San Francisco would be nice," Moira admitted. "But this is a big show, bigger than any I've had before. Megan says I'd have to be gone at least three weeks." She shook her head. "No, I can't possibly be away so long."

"And why not, if it's what's needed? It seems like a small sacrifice for such potentially impressive rewards."

"Our agreement was that I'd never be away longer than a week—ten days at the absolute outside. Megan's kept to that promise until now, but she says there's no bending on this. The gallery owner is adamant about the commitment. He wants me there for extensive media coverage, a big opening night party and private meetings with some of his biggest collectors."

"Then you'll go for three weeks," Kiera said decisively. "Luke and I will manage things with Kate quite well. We have Carrie as backup if we need to use the day care." She gave Moira a hard look. "I've seen for myself that Kate loves it there. And the staff seems more than competent to look after her needs. I know perfectly well that I'm here as little more than window dressing, the Irish grandmama come to visit. We settled that weeks ago."

Moira winced. "It wasn't like that."

"Of course it was. You and your grandfather were worried about me and dreamed up as many excuses as you could find to lure me here. You wanted me to feel needed. Don't fret over the deception. I'm grateful. I find I like it here. It's given me time with your grandfather and with you."

"And with Kate," Moira added.

"The best part of all," Kiera agreed. "When you were a wee one, I was never able to experience the joy of the moments as I am with Kate."

Moira looked surprised. "You really mean that, don't you?"

Sorrow stole over Kiera at the memory of how little time she'd had for her own children. "Ah, Moira, you've no idea how many regrets I have about the things I missed with you and your brothers. All I could do back then was keep my head down and put one foot in front of the next to be sure we had food on the table and clothes that wouldn't shame you."

Moira sighed. "I suppose I never stopped to think about how difficult it must have been for you, how much you were missing. I just wanted a mum who was home, who baked cookies and such."

"You've had a taste of my cookies," Kiera reminded her wryly. "Were you really missing so much?"

The comment drew an unexpected burst of laughter. "Perhaps not so much." Moira studied her intently. "You really wouldn't mind helping out while I'm away?"

"It's what I came for," Kiera assured her. "And it would be my pleasure. Perhaps Luke, Kate and I could come to the opening of your exhibit and spend a day or two, if we wouldn't be in the way. I wouldn't mind getting a glimpse of San Francisco myself."

Moira studied her, as if looking for any hint of reluctance, then seemed to come to a conclusion. "Then
that's exactly what we'll do," Moira said. "I'll talk it
over with Luke and we'll work out the details. You
should see more of the country. Truth be told, you were
right about the daydreaming I did when we looked at
those books. I wouldn't mind riding on a San Francisco
cable car and seeing the Golden Gate Bridge. I just don't
like being parted from Luke and the baby."

"Which is why we'll turn part of the trip into a family vacation, something that was all too rare when you
and your brothers were young. That's another of my
regrets."

"You took us to the beach," Moira said. "I remember those Sundays when you'd pack a picnic and we'd
take the train to the shore."

"If you treasure those memories, I'm glad," Kiera
told her. "But there should have been so many more. I
made it harder than it needed to be by not reaching out
to my father. There's a lesson in that for you."

Moira laughed. "Yes, I can see that."

Kiera reached over and took her daughter's hand.
"I'm proud of you, Moira."

Moira seemed stunned by her praise. Kiera couldn't
miss the sheen of tears in her eyes and realized how
rarely those words had probably been spoken. She'd
never meant to be so stingy with them, but time had
rushed by and then it was almost too late. Seeing how
touched her daughter was, she realized that no matter
how old or independent a woman was, no matter the
depth of her pride or the loudness of her claims not to
need anyone, she was never beyond wanting the approval of someone she loved.

* * *

Kiera was eager for a chance to speak to Bryan about everything he'd told her earlier in the day, but he seemed to be deliberately avoiding her. He even made it a point to come to the bar when it was at its busiest to inquire if she'd mind getting a ride home with Luke.

"I have a few things that will keep me here later than usual. There's no need for you to wait around."

Though she'd been about to argue, something in his expression told her it would be a waste of her breath. Her silent acquiescence, though, didn't mean that she was ready to let the subject drop. Nor did she intend to wait long for answers.

At home after Luke dropped her off, she poured two glasses of wine, turned off the lights in her kitchen and walked over to Bryan's deck to wait. She knew he'd breathe a sigh of relief at finding her house dark and that he'd assume she was inside, asleep.

It was one in the morning when he finally pulled into the driveway and cut the engine. She imagined he was feeling relieved and fairly pleased with himself as he came around back and was about to step onto his own deck.

"Nice try," she said calmly, then held out the wine. "You might want to take a sip of this before you start commenting on me invading your privacy. It might put you in a mellower mood."

"Or you could go home without interrogating me," he suggested, even as he took the glass. "That would work, too."

Kiera laughed. "And let you get away with opening up a particularly complicated subject, then trying to sweep it right back under the rug?"

"That would be the kind way to handle what was probably a misguided moment of candor on my part. I should never have said anything, Kiera. It's old news."

"Not that old. It obviously continues to trouble you years later. All those calls that have left you depressed and moody are tied in to what you told me earlier, aren't they?"

He sighed and took a seat beside her. "I've never stopped searching," he confirmed. "But now it's time. There has been nothing but dead ends for years now. A sensible man would have given up."

"Do you remember what I told you after that first call that left you so distraught?"

"That someday just making the effort would be what mattered?"

She smiled. "So you do listen to me on occasion?"

"I listen to every word you utter," he said. "I just pick and choose what to ignore."

"What a ringing endorsement of my wisdom," she teased. "May I give you an example to explain what I mean?"

"The wine seems to be taking effect, so why not?"

"When I married Sean Malone all those years ago, as you may have guessed, it was against my parents' wishes. It caused a huge rift, and I vowed never to speak to them again. As you also might have noticed, I have a stubborn streak. I would have kept to that vow, no matter how much I might have wanted to change things."

She glanced over and saw that he was listening intently. "But through all those years," she continued, "even when I remained stubbornly silent, my father kept reaching out. I knew he and my mother would be there, if I bent even a little and turned to them. Of course, I waited far too long and bent only when my mother was ill and dying, but my father had made it easier to take that step even then simply because he had never given up on me."

She held Bryan's gaze. "It will be the same someday for you and your daughter. If you can show her that you never gave up the search, that your love remained steady and constant, it will mean more to her than you can possibly imagine right now when you're feeling as if all is lost."

Bryan was quiet for so long, Kiera thought perhaps she hadn't reached him, after all, but then she caught the sheen of tears on his cheeks in the moonlight and felt her own eyes sting with unshed tears of her own. When he reached for her hand, she took his in a firm grip and held tight. She wondered how long it must have been since he'd had someone beside him, someone willing to share this aching pain so that he didn't have to face it alone.

Though she couldn't know the answer to that, she realized that it had been years since she'd given herself so unselfishly to someone else to help ease the person's burden. Perhaps she was doing for him what Peter had done for her, providing shelter from an emotional storm that seemed to be unending.

Chapter 12

"What was she like, your daughter?"

Kiera's softly spoken question cut through the silence of the night. If it had been up to Bryan, he would have sat quietly on his deck, letting the mesmerizing sound of the waves and the occasional chirp of some nocturnal bird be the only interruptions to the peace that had stolen over him since Kiera had forced him to think about all the years he'd lost with his child. He'd taken some comfort from her words and from her tight, reassuring grip on his hand.

Now it seemed, though, that she wanted to stir this particular pot some more. No surprise there, he thought, resigned to ripping a little more of the scab from the old wound and exposing it to light.

"I don't remember much. She was practically a baby when they left and too many years have passed," he said with the futile hope that it would be enough to stave off her curiosity. The truth, of course, was that he recalled every detail vividly, and Kiera clearly saw that.

"But there's an image that's stayed in your head—a picture or a memory—that's kept you from giving up the search," she insisted. "Tell me about that."

So he did, slowly at first, reluctantly. He recalled the way Deanna had smelled of strawberries after splashing in the bubble baths she loved, the enchanting giggles that had made him laugh, even when there was no rhyme or reason for it, the weight of her in his arms, the feel of her breath on his cheek as she slept against his chest, trusting in him to keep her safe. That was the thing, there was so much trust between a young child and their parent, and he'd failed her.

Bryan sighed heavily at the end of his recitation. As sweet as those memories were, they made his heart ache all over again.

Kiera must have sensed this, because she never once released her grip on his hand, only squeezed it from time to time.

"She was my little angel, the most amazing gift I'd ever been given," he said, surprised to find that his voice cracked on the words. "And then she was taken away, through no one's fault but my own."

"If we were all punished for our careless failure to realize how important some things are in our life until too late, we'd all be alone and miserable," Kiera said in an attempt to console him. "It's why we're given second chances. And, remember this, Bryan. It was your wife's decision to go, not yours."

Others had said the same, but he'd argued with them as he did now with her. "She wouldn't have left if I'd truly listened to her complaints. I thought I did. I thought I saw how unhappy she was and I was trying to make changes, but I ran out of time. She was clearly far unhappier than I'd ever imagined, her patience worn too thin."

"Sometimes we can only know what another person is thinking if they say the words in plain English."

Bryan gave her a rueful smile. "I believe she did. More than once, in fact. I was just arrogant enough not to recognize the depth of the pain and desperation behind the pleas or the finality when she truly had reached her limit. Each time we fought and she stayed, I thought I had a little longer. And then, one day, without my recognizing the difference, she'd reached her limit. I never saw it until she was gone."

"Still, to take a child from her father, especially a loving father, is unforgivable," Kiera said, apparently choosing to take his side, even though he didn't deserve it.

He leveled a considering look at her. "And yet you kept Moira from Sean Malone, didn't you? Were you as much at fault for that as my wife was for leaving me?"

To his surprise, she didn't bristle. Instead, she held his gaze solemnly, making her words more powerful.

"Not in the same way," she declared evenly. "Sean always knew exactly where we were and that the door was open, if he chose to walk through it. He never did. His sons eventually went in search of him and embraced the man they found, despite his neglect. Moira never showed any interest in that. If she had, I would have done my best to broker some sort of relationship between them, though not of the sort my sons have found."

The last was said with a level of bitterness and dismay that took Bryan aback.

"What does that mean?" he asked.

"They've joined their father carousing in bars at the end of their workdays. They've lost jobs and the women in their lives because of it. They've spent more than a night or two jailed because of their brawls. I finally stopped answering the calls that came in the middle of the night. I thought I was being a terrible mother, but Peter called it tough love."

Bryan read the questions in her eyes, and this time he was the one to offer her hand a reassuring squeeze. "Peter was right, I suspect. Men eventually have to learn to live with the consequences of their actions. That's what I'm trying to do, what I've been working on for so many years now."

"Perhaps all parents have regrets of one sort or another. In the case of my sons, I can't help wondering if things would have been different if only I'd raised them better," Kiera lamented. "Taught them right from wrong."

"They were raised in the same household as Moira," Bryan contradicted. "She learned those lessons well enough. You can't deny that. Her moral compass is steady and sure."

"But boys and their fathers," she countered. "It's a special bond, and if the father's not around, they can hate him for abandoning them or in their imaginations they turn him into some sort of hero. And, as my boys did, they set out to emulate him, even when it's the last thing he deserves." She shook her head. "Enough about that. We were talking about your daughter. She'd be how old now?"

"Not quite twenty."

Kiera smiled. "A young woman, then. And beautiful, if she got your coloring and your eyes."

Startled, Bryan glanced over and laughed. "You've taken note of my looks, Kiera Malone?"

The teasing, slightly flirtatious question clearly flustered her and charged the atmosphere around them.

"I've always been partial to blue eyes," she said as if it were of no consequence when it came to him. "They remind me of the sea." She gave him a steady, challenging look. "And the Irish rogues I've known have all had black hair. It's not necessarily a recommendation, but it is lovely coloring on a woman."

"I see."

"Don't be thinking that I'm flattering you, Bryan."

"Of course not. Nothing personal meant at all."

"Exactly."

But with her cheeks flushed pink and the spark of temper in her eyes, it felt suddenly very personal and they both knew it.

"It's late. You should go, Kiera. You need your rest." He stood up. "I'll walk you home."

"Nonsense. It's right next door and the path is lit."

He walked down the steps from the deck, simply ignoring her argument. She was still muttering under her breath when they reached her back door.

"What was that?" Bryan asked, trying not to laugh.

She tilted her head up and met his gaze, her expression still defiant. "I said you're stubborn."

Unable to resist, he bent down and touched his lips to hers. "Right back at you. Good night, Kiera."

Despite a day filled with unexpected revelations and uncomfortable questions, he felt surprisingly lighthearted. He tried assuring himself that it had nothing to do with that impulsive kiss that could barely be described as such, but he had a feeling he'd only be lying to himself. A quickly stolen kiss between a man and woman their age didn't amount to much, but he couldn't help thinking that between them, it was a beginning.

The audacity of the man, Kiera thought indignantly, even as her fingers touched her lips, which still seemed to burn from that faint, but unmistakable kiss. What had he been thinking? She'd done nothing to invite such a liberty. She hadn't even wanted him to walk her home, much less kiss her outside her door like a schoolgirl on a first date. Had she sent some signal without meaning to that the kiss would be welcomed?

Maybe American men were different. Maybe a quick peck was no more than a courtesy at the end of an evening. Hadn't she seen many a casual acquaintance exchange a kiss on the cheek at the pub since she'd arrived? And this was no more than that. Maybe he'd even landed on her lips by accident.

"You're being a silly old fool," she chided herself aloud. "It meant nothing, no more than a handshake."

Then why had her blood seemed to heat and her pulse started to race? "Because you're a silly old fool," she said again, hoping the message would sink in.

Tomorrow it would all be forgotten.

Unfortunately, that meant she still had to get through what turned out to be an unexpectedly restless night. After tossing and turning and remembering and precious little actual sleep, she got out of bed early and decided to leave the house quickly before she was likely to cross paths with Bryan. She needed to clear her head, shake off this odd, unfamiliar restlessness.

Even as she slipped away, feeling like some sort of thief stealing through the dawn, she was making up excuses for her behavior. She reasoned that she needed to see her father and Nell, anyway, and one of Nell's scones and a cup of bracing tea would be welcome. That those were likely to be accompanied by a few probing questions still seemed more alluring than another disconcerting encounter with her neighbor.

"My goodness, we haven't seen this much company this early in the morning in quite some time," Nell said when she opened the door to Kiera. "Come in. The sky looks as if it might open up with an early-morning shower any minute now."

Kiera hesitated. "You already have company? I had no idea. I didn't see a car. I can come back later."

"Nonsense. Dillon and I love starting our day with some good company and lively conversation. And I've just taken a fresh batch of my orange-cranberry scones from the oven. You'll have one while it's still warm."

Since Nell was already heading toward the kitchen, Kiera was left with no choice but to follow. Before she'd even reached the doorway, though, she heard two male voices, one with the distinct Irish lilt of her father, the other with what she'd come to recognize as the lingering hint of New York. Bryan! The very man she'd been trying to avoid. Her step faltered.

"Kiera?" her father called out. "Come in and join us. What brings you by?"

Her glance landed on Bryan long enough to note the running clothes that suited him so well and to see the spark of amusement twinkling in his eyes. He knew she'd been avoiding him. Of course he did, because he was arrogant enough to think she spent more time thinking about him than she did.

She scrambled for an excuse that had nothing whatsoever to do with Bryan. "Nell's been searching for a project for me. I'm here to see what she's found."

Nell nodded as if it made perfect sense. "And your timing couldn't be better. I have a committee meeting coming up tomorrow that I'd very much like you to attend. It's for the Chesapeake Shores fall festival."

Kiera was unfamiliar with all of America's special holidays. "Is this an American holiday, then, like your upcoming Fourth of July celebration?"

"Actually it began years ago as a way to extend the summer tourist season into the fall months," Nell explained. "It's sponsored by my church, but the whole community gets involved. It had gotten a little stuffy with the same old activities year after year, but I added some fresh voices to the committee last year, and the new additions they came up with were a rousing success. I think you'd bring in even more exciting ideas."

Before Kiera could answer, Nell turned to Bryan. "What about you? It's time you got more involved in the community, as well. This will be the perfect way to meet some new people and share your ideas."

Bryan looked about as enthused as if Nell had invited him to join the circus. "I work in the pub. I know plenty of people."

"You hide out in the kitchen the majority of the time," Nell responded.

"Would you have me cooking on a hot plate behind the bar?"

Dillon choked back a laugh and even Kiera had to fight a smile, but Nell merely leveled a stern look at Bryan. "I'll expect to see you tomorrow."

Now Bryan looked a little desperate. "I really don't have the time."

"My grandson is a big supporter of this event," Nell informed him. "Luke will see that you have the time. The first meeting is tomorrow morning at nine, right here." She turned her gaze to Kiera. "I'll expect you both."

"I'll be looking forward to it," Kiera said with enthusiasm, casting a defiant look at Bryan. She pointedly looked from him to the increasingly gloomy skies, then stood. "I'm afraid I'm going to have to take a rain check on the tea and scone, though. I want to get home and ready for work before it storms."

Her father seemed to take his cue from her. "I'll drive you, just in case it doesn't hold off."

For once Kiera didn't argue.

"Bryan, would you like a lift, as well?" Dillon offered.

"Thanks, but no. I need to finish my run. I'll just be jumping in the shower after that, so a little rain won't matter. I'm going to spend another minute or two wasting my breath trying to convince Nell I'll be no help on this committee of hers."

Dillon chuckled. "Good luck with that. Once my wife's mind is made up, it's unlikely to change."

"Like some others I know," Bryan said.

Kiera walked past him and followed her father outside. When they were on their way, she felt her father's curious gaze studying her from time to time.

"Did I sense some tension between you and Bryan just now?" Dillon asked.

"We've never had an easy time of it. I've been getting under his skin since I arrived," Kiera responded.

"But today, it seemed to be the other way around."

Leave it to her father to develop a deeper level of

perceptiveness at exactly the wrong moment, Kiera thought wryly.

"The truth is that I came over this morning in an effort to avoid him. The last thing I expected was to find him in your kitchen." Even she could hear the grumbling note in her voice suggesting that he was somehow lending aid and comfort to the enemy.

"Is that a problem?"

She drew in a deep breath. "No, of course not," she said, trying to infuse her voice with a different tone entirely. "Is this a regular thing, then? These visits of his?"

Dillon still seemed puzzled by her reaction. "He stops by from time to time when he goes for his run," he explained. "He and Nell talk about menu ideas for the pub. She's become quite fond of him."

"I'll have to keep that in mind and time my own visits accordingly."

Dillon gave her a quick, worried glance. "Has he done something to offend you, Kiera? Moira seemed to think you all were getting along swimmingly these days."

"Moira's an optimist," Kiera said.

At her father's chuckle, she swallowed her annoyance and laughed with him. "Okay, it's not a word I'd normally associate with Moira, but in this case it fits. She and Luke want Bryan and me to get along. We're doing the best we can. Too much contact may test our fragile peace."

Her father gave a nod of understanding. "And now Nell has put him right in your path yet again with this committee of hers. I can ask her to change her mind. It's clear he wants no part of it anyway."

"I wouldn't give him the satisfaction," Kiera said.

"Okay, then, whatever you want."

Kiera evaded his knowing gaze and sighed. As if she had any bloody idea what that was!

"Well done," Dillon enthused when he got back to the cottage and joined Nell in the kitchen.

"I thought so," Nell responded. "It's clear there's something going on between those two. Every time their eyes met, sparks flew. They just need a nudge here and there."

"They're both going to fight the attraction, no question about that," Dillon said. "And we need to be subtle or Kiera, at least, will move heaven and earth just to defy us."

"The committee was just the first step and, frankly, one I hadn't even envisioned until they both turned up here this morning and gave me the perfect opening to throw them together. Just wait until they hear what I have in mind," Nell said, her expression filled with anticipation.

"Tell me."

As she described her plan, Dillon sat back in awe. He'd watched Mick O'Brien meddle in various family romances, but the man had obviously learned from a matchmaking genius.

"Well, what do you think?" Nell asked. "Will it work, or am I going too far?"

"Pure genius, given their competitive natures," he said. "But a word of caution. If it seems that you or I are involved in some sort of scheme, Kiera will balk. She and I are just starting to bond. I worry that this could cause another rift between us."

His concern seemed to put a damper on his wife's

enthusiasm, but within moments her expression brightened again. She stood up and dropped a kiss on his
cheek. "I'll enlist a little help with the plan. The suggestion won't come from me at tomorrow's meeting,
so you will be able to deny you knew a thing about it.
What is it those lawyers we watch on TV call it, plausible deniability?"

Dillon chuckled. "Who knew those shows would
serve a useful purpose? So where are you going now?"

"To Sally's. I'll plant a few seeds here and there,
and if I know my granddaughters, by tomorrow they'll
have turned this into their own idea and added a few
embellishments."

"Nell O'Brien O'Malley, should I be worried that one
day this devious streak of yours will be used against
me?"

She laughed. "What makes you think it hasn't been
already?"

Since in her eagerness to get away from Bryan and
those knowing glances of his she hadn't lingered at
Nell's long enough for a scone, Kiera decided she deserved one of Sally's croissants to replace it. Perhaps
the gathering of O'Brien women she was likely to find
there would prove more settling to her nerves than the
way her day had started.

Today Connor's wife, Heather, Kevin's wife, Shanna,
and Bree were lingering over coffee when she arrived.
The three had distinctive personalities that were echoed
by the clothes they chose, Bree's flamboyant and colorful, Heather's soothing, and Shanna's classic.

"May I join you or are you about to leave?" Kiera
asked.

"Please join us," Bree invited, pulling out the chair next to hers. "We've been commiserating over getting drawn into Gram's fall festival planning again."

Kiera brightened at once. "You're on the committee, as well? That's great news!"

"She's asked you to come to tomorrow's meeting, too?" Bree asked.

"Of course she has," Heather said. "Have you ever known Nell to let an able-bodied person escape her clutches when she's planning her favorite community event?"

"Forget able-bodied being part of the criteria," Shanna said. "Poor Jaime Alvarez was still on crutches when she corralled him into helping last year."

"Well, this year she's added both Bryan and me into the mix," Kiera said. "I'm excited about it."

The other three women exchanged glances.

"Maybe that will let us off the hook," Heather suggested hopefully.

"Not a chance," Bree said ruefully. "I don't think there's an O'Brien alive who's ever successfully squirmed off Gram's hook once she's set it."

Kiera heard the grumbling complaints and couldn't imagine why they weren't more enthused. "It honestly sounds like so much fun to me. Is it really such a burden? I've never had a chance to work on a community event like this."

"We need to stop trying to scare her off or Nell will never forgive us," Heather said. "It really is fun."

"Maybe the first ten years," Bree groused. "I've been doing it since I was old enough to take flyers around town and climb on chairs to post them in shop windows. You'd think, given how many O'Briens have come along since then, that she'd cut the rest of us a break for time served."

Shanna laughed. "Oh, stop acting like a martyr. You know perfectly well that there's not a one of us who wouldn't do anything Nell asked. She has her hand in half a dozen or more community projects. We're all in awe of her energy and we're trying to figure out where it comes from. Personally, I think she takes some magic elixir."

"There's no elixir. It's pure O'Brien stubbornness," Bree said.

"Maybe that explains why you and I don't have it," Heather told Shanna with exaggerated resignation. "We weren't born with O'Brien blood."

Kiera suddenly realized that the complaining was something that simply came with the territory. She suspected Shanna had been right, that the level of love and respect they all felt for Nell would make them all willing to walk over hot coals for her. Being on this committee might be a chore for them, but it was a more welcome responsibility than they'd ever let on.

Just then Bree turned to her. "You've really never been involved in planning any sort of community event?" she asked as if such a thing were unthinkable.

"Never," Kiera told her. "Back home, I never had the time. I tried to take Moira and her brothers to festivals and the like, but there were so many temptations and there were times when money was too tight for me to give them even those small trinkets or treats."

"Then we're going to make sure this is a wonderful experience for you," Bree vowed. "If there's one thing that Chesapeake Shores knows how to do right, it's our special events. You'll see on the Fourth of July.

And the fall festival is even more amazing, especially since Gram decided to shake it up a little. I think even she was stunned at how well the kissing booth and the dancing went over last year. We're really going to have to use our imaginations to top that."

The mention of the kissing booth sent Kiera's imagination soaring off once again to the feel of Bryan's lips on hers, albeit fleetingly, the previous night. She stood hurriedly before anyone thought to question the sudden flush in her cheeks.

"I'll see you all in the morning, then," she said.

She heard a few murmurs about her abrupt departure, but in her haste to go, it barely registered that the woman who'd just come in Sally's door was Nell.

Chapter 13

After waiting for Kiera to leave, Nell crossed Sally's and stared into the upturned faces of her granddaughter and the wives of two of her grandsons and saw suspicion written all over them.

"What?" she asked innocently, pulling out a chair and joining them,

"Your timing is impeccable as usual, Gram," Bree noted. "Kiera's just left so I have a feeling your arrival was no coincidence."

"You know I like visiting with all of you here from time to time," Nell responded.

"Agreed," Bree said, then waited patiently.

Nell frowned at her, but felt compelled to add, "I like catching up on all the family gossip."

It was obviously not the best answer she could have given. The three young women exchanged amused glances.

"And Sunday dinners at Mick's don't keep you up-to-date?" Heather asked. "There's very little that escapes your notice there. The rumor is that you have eyes in the back of your head and the kind of hearing that people half your age would envy. And the visits to the pub during the week usually fill in any blanks."

Nell studied her with a narrowed gaze. "Are you suggesting that I have an ulterior motive for wanting to spend time with you this morning?"

"That is exactly what she's suggesting," Bree confirmed. "I'm inclined to agree. So what's up? We've already heard that you corralled Kiera and Bryan to be on your festival committee this year. Given that those two reportedly get along like oil and water, despite what my father thinks he saw when he ran into them at Panini Bistro a few weeks ago, what's going on in that devious mind of yours?"

Nell regarded them with as much indignation as she could muster since Bree and Heather, at least, had pretty much caught her. "Devious, is it? Is that any way to speak to your grandmother? I thought I taught you to be more respectful of your elders."

Bree merely laughed. "Nice try playing the grandmother card, but we all know you too well. What are you up to? And how are we involved?"

As much as she'd hoped to get their involvement without them being aware that they were being manipulated, she saw that simply wasn't going to happen. They'd known her too long and, in some troubling ways, were too much like her. She might have passed the meddling gene on to Mick, but until now she'd thought it had skipped right over the next generation. Apparently not.

"Okay, if I come clean, do you all swear that you won't reveal my plan, not even to your husbands, cousins or siblings? I suppose I should mention parents, aunts and uncles, too, just to cover all the bases."

Bree laughed. "We'll keep our lips tightly sealed," she promised.

"Unless we think someone could get hurt," Heather corrected mildly.

"Nobody is going to get hurt," Nell said impatiently. "The goal is to have people living happily ever after."

"Isn't it always?" Shanna murmured.

Nell turned to her. "I heard that."

"I meant for you to," her granddaughter-in-law said, undeterred by Nell's scowl.

The girl had spunk, Nell thought. They all did. It was hard to hold your own among the O'Briens without it. She couldn't help thinking that was a good thing. Shanna had needed every ounce of it when she'd first met Kevin, who'd been grieving the loss of his first wife and struggling to raise his little boy alone. She'd had her own difficult crosses to bear from the past, as well.

Nell leaned forward then, noting that all three of them did the same. "Okay, then, here's what we're going to do."

As she described her plan, she saw them nodding, their eyes lighting with anticipation. At the end, she sat back. "What do you think?"

"Ingenious," Bree admitted.

"Will you all take the lead on this tomorrow, as if the idea's just come to you? Dillon's afraid if it comes from me, Kiera will assume it started with him and balk on principle."

"I wouldn't worry about that," Heather said. "She seems to be under your spell, too."

"But if it backfires and hurts her relationship with her father, I'd never forgive myself. Their bond has been healing and growing stronger since she's been here. I can't put that at risk," Nell said.

"Not to worry," Bree said. "We'll take the heat. This could actually be kind of fun. If there are any of those sparks that Mick saw when he caught them together, everyone in town will enjoy getting a chance to fan the flames." She hesitated, then asked, "Why are you willing to risk Dillon's relationship with Kiera, though? Are you so certain that Kiera and Bryan are a good match? He seems a gentle, lost soul in some ways, and she, well, she does have a bit of a temper."

"Which is exactly why they're so well suited," Nell said. "Dillon swears he sees some of Peter's steadiness in Bryan and that it's what Kiera needs in her life. As I've gotten to know them both, I tend to agree. And every relationship needs a little heat and conflict from time to time."

"This could cause some tension at the pub, though," Shanna cautioned. "How will Luke feel about that?"

"He'll have to deal with it for the greater good," Nell said blithely. "I expect him to do his part, too. That's why I've invited him to tomorrow's meeting, too."

"Invited or commanded?" Bree asked with a grin.

"It was an invitation," Nell said defensively, then shrugged. "With a little grandmotherly guilt tossed in."

"What about Moira? This is her mother we're talking about," Shanna reminded them. "Shouldn't she be consulted?"

Nell shook her head. "I think it's best if she's not drawn into this. Her relationship with her mother is at stake, too. She needs to be able to claim quite honestly that she's no more than an innocent bystander."

"Nine o'clock tomorrow, then," Bree said. "Suddenly—and I never thought I'd say this—I can't wait."

The other two women nodded in agreement. Nell barely resisted the urge to give them a high five. She didn't want to risk celebrating too soon. There were any number of ways this plan of hers might go awry. She was counting on Bryan's competitive spirit and desire to be taken seriously as a chef, but Kiera was a bit of a wild card. She was feisty enough to take the bait just on principle, but she could just as easily see right through the scheme and want no part of it.

Kiera was so eager to join the O'Brien women at Nell's the next morning and get her first taste of being a part of a community event that she was the first to arrive at the cottage. Nell had already added extra chairs around the kitchen table and had set the water for tea on the stove to boil. The aroma of scones wafted from the oven, a new flavor Kiera couldn't quite identify beyond being especially mouthwatering.

"What can I do to help you get ready?" she asked her stepmother, suddenly realizing that she was actually becoming comfortable thinking of Nell in that role. She'd expected it to be a more difficult transition, certain that she'd resent the woman who had taken her own mother's place. Somehow, though, knowing that Nell and her father had shared a teenage passion so long ago and were being given this second chance by the grace of God made it easier. It certainly helped that Nell had never pushed, but only opened her arms to welcome Kiera into her life and into the O'Brien family.

"Your father helped me before he left for a walk,"

Nell said. "Just come and have a cup of tea until the others arrive."

"I'm surprised you haven't put my father to work on your committee. The way I hear it, no one in the family escapes from playing a role."

Nell laughed. "And Dillon won't, either, be assured of that. On the day of the event, I have him running in a dozen different directions to do my bidding."

"I'll bet he loves it," Kiera concluded, thinking back to his workaholic ways with his various businesses in Dublin. "I've never seen him so happy and relaxed. Thank you for that."

"I'm not sure it's credit I deserve," Nell told her sincerely. "He claims I'm trying to be the death of him, but being involved has brought him a great deal of satisfaction, I think. And it's made him feel at home in Chesapeake Shores." She gave Kiera a lingering look. "He wants the same for you, you know."

"I'm more at ease here with every day that passes," Kiera acknowledged, then felt compelled to add, "It will be difficult, I suspect, when my time here is over."

The light in Nell's eyes dimmed a bit. "You're so certain you'll be going back to Ireland?"

Kiera nodded, though perhaps not quite as convincingly as she might have just a few short weeks ago. "It's my home, after all."

"As it was your father's, but I like to think he considers this to be his home now."

"Because of you and all of the O'Briens," Kiera said. "And it helps that my daughter has made her home here, too."

"You could do the same, Kiera. Are there things

drawing you back to Ireland, things you miss? Your sons, perhaps?"

"It's where I belong," she said simply, unwilling to get into the subject of her sons just as others were about to arrive. It was too complex a subject for a one- or two-word response.

Nell looked as if she might press her about the two grown sons she rarely spoke of, but instead she said only, "Perhaps you'll come to think of Chesapeake Shores that way one day soon, as the place you belong. Getting involved with this fall festival could be a first step if you open your heart to the possibilities. You already have family here and soon you'll have friends, as well."

Kiera might have considered it another example of Nell's eternal optimism, but she caught the gleam in the older woman's eyes and wondered if there was something behind Nell's words that ought to worry her. Before she could ask a single probing question, the others came in, the women in a chattering cluster with Bryan and Luke dragging behind. Neither of the men looked overjoyed at being included.

As soon as everyone had something to drink and a place to sit, Nell took charge.

"Okay, then, you all know why we're here today," she announced. "It's that time of year again. We need to finalize our plans for this year's fall festival. We added some innovations last year that did very well, but we can't rest on our laurels."

"Gram, it's not even the Fourth of July yet," Bree protested, though it was a half-hearted protest at best. She obviously knew that particular battle was already lost.

"Which means we're already late getting started,"

Nell countered. "I've been distracted. It's time we get focused."

"Thanks to you the fall festival has been running like a well-oiled machine for years now," Heather re-assured her. "I know perfectly well that all of the committees have been working since last fall to put things in place. I'd wager the vendors are already signed up and the advertising and press release ready to go out. We could start after Labor Day and it would still run like clockwork."

"Well, of course we could," Nell retorted impatiently, "but some things can't be left to chance. I've no doubt we could 'phone it in'—is that the expression they use for putting absolutely no effort into something?—and pull off a lovely event that would be a crowd-pleaser, but a few fresh tweaks will keep things lively. I think we can all agree that last year was the best event we've had in years."

Kiera listened to the exchange with amusement. It was clear, even to her, that Nell had an agenda. She also knew Nell would reveal it when she was good and ready.

"Exactly what tweaks do you have in mind?" Luke asked his grandmother suspiciously. "And why are Bryan and I here? You never ask the men in the family to be on the planning committee. You count on us to be the muscle."

"Muscle, is it?" Bree mocked, holding up her arm to point to her biceps. "I have muscles, but it's never gotten me out of these meetings."

"Stop with your bickering," Nell scolded. "I swear, sometimes I marvel at the idea that you've all reached adulthood, when you still sound like children."

Kiera laughed aloud at that, even as Heather and Shanna looked away to cover their own grins.

"Now, as I was saying, we need fresh ideas. Anyone?"

"Let's eliminate the obvious," Bree suggested. "You and the church ladies agreed years ago that there would never be any sort of baby contest or beauty pageant as part of the town's fall festival."

"And that's still the case," Nell agreed. She paused, her expression thoughtful. "That said, it doesn't mean we shouldn't have a lively competition of some kind that will draw interest from around the region. Any thoughts along that line?"

Shanna's eyes lit up. "A bachelor auction," she suggested excitedly. "That could raise a ton of money for the church."

"You're a happily married woman," Nell chided. "What interest could you have in a bachelor auction?"

"None of us is dead," Bree pointed out. "There's no shame in looking, even if we can't bid."

"Well, I'm not even going to consider a bachelor auction, so you can just settle down," Nell said. "It's not suitable for a church event."

"You disapproved of the kissing booth, too, at first," Heather pointed out, "but you have to admit it was a huge success."

"It was," Nell agreed. "And despite my reservations, it will be back this year."

"Your change of heart isn't because it was successful, Gram. It's mostly because it irritated Father Clarence," Luke suggested.

Nell's flushed face proved his point. "Well, he needs

to move into the current century," Nell murmured. "But I'll deny it if you tell him I said that."

"And haven't you told him that to his face more than once?" Luke teased.

Nell frowned at him. "We're getting off topic."

Bree's expression turned thoughtful. "There is one idea that came to me last night, so I did a little bit of research. I think it would fit quite nicely into the fall festival if the setup wouldn't be too complicated."

"Tell us," Nell said eagerly.

"It seems there are quite a few of those cooking shows on TV that draw huge audiences," she began, only to be interrupted by Heather.

"I watch *Top Chef* myself," Heather chimed in. "And *The Chew* and a couple of others. Giada De Laurentiis is my absolute favorite. I've even tried some of the recipes. Of course, those are usually the nights Connor and I end up eating at the pub."

"See," Bree said triumphantly. "That's exactly what I'm talking about. What if we were to have a cooking competition?" Her expectant gaze went around the room, then landed on Kiera as she added, "Amateurs and professional chefs alike can compete."

"Interesting," Nell said, as if mulling it over. She looked at Heather and Shanna. "What do you think?"

"I think it sounds fantastic," Heather said at once.

An innocent smile spread across Shanna's face as she turned her gaze on Kiera. "Perhaps we can put to rest once and for all whether Bryan's or Kiera's Irish stew is the best. I've heard that's come up at the pub a time or two."

The room erupted into laughter. The others seemed to be blissfully oblivious to Bryan's suddenly stony expression and Kiera's panic. Whatever peace they'd managed to achieve was about to be tested in some very public forum. Perhaps that was a good thing. Their truce had led to a couple of emotionally risky encounters.

"Gram, I don't think this is such a good idea," Luke protested. "The kitchen wars behind the scenes at O'Brien's are bad enough. We've no need to take them public."

"Not even if we can raise a lot of money at a dollar a taste with the winner being the one who gets the most tokens at the end of the day?" Nell inquired as if she were still exploring all the angles. "We can charge a small entry fee to go toward prize money and open the competition to anyone else with an Irish stew recipe they'd like to enter. Or maybe we should have multiple categories with amateurs competing against a chef in each one. Luke, you could assemble a team of judges, too."

"Why do we need judges if everyone in town is going to cast a vote?" Luke asked reasonably, apparently abandoning any hope of trying to win an argument with his grandmother.

"Then assemble the team of participating chefs," Nell said readily. "Then we can determine what specialty each of them will prepare, and invite challengers."

"I like that," Bree said. "The more entries we have, the more excitement we can generate."

"I like it," Shanna said.

Nell nodded in satisfaction. "Okay, then. All in favor?"

Kiera had listened silently up till now, but after one glance in Bryan's direction and catching his increasingly horrified expression, the competitor in her roared to life.

"I'm game," she said, obviously startling them all. If this had been Nell's trap, Kiera couldn't seem to find fault with it. "It's for a good cause, after all. And I imagine Bryan won't want me showing him up. He'll agree." She turned a challenging gaze on him. "Won't you, Bryan?"

"I'm pretty sure I was doomed from the minute I walked in the door," he muttered, then shrugged. "Sure. Why not?"

Luke groaned. "And just when the two of you were starting to get along so well."

But, of course, that was precisely the reason Kiera was willing to give it a try. She and Bryan were getting along a little too well these days. It scared her to death. And this was a surefire way to guarantee there would be some nice, safe distance between them once more.

Deanna was sitting in the break room in the research center trying to make a decision about what she might do for the upcoming Fourth of July holiday. It was only a few days away, and it seemed everyone she knew had already made plans.

The Baltimore newspaper that someone had left lying open to an upcoming events page seemed to offer a surprising number of alternatives. Any one of them might be fun and might delay the oft-postponed trip she'd been meaning to take to Chesapeake Shores.

Then, as if fate were stepping in to taunt her, she spotted the headline on a sidebar article touting the charm of the holiday in the beachside town of Chesapeake Shores. A picture of the very shops she'd noticed on her drive through town decorated with red, white and blue bunting made it look like the quintessential small-town celebration. There was a band playing in the gazebo on the town green and a sea of children waving American flags and eating ice-cream cones.

One of her coworkers, another intern here for the summer, leaned over her shoulder. "That looks like fun," Milos Yanich commented. Though he'd been born in Ukraine and grown up in Europe, his English was flawless with only an occasional hint of an accent to give away his roots. He pushed his dark-rimmed glasses back into place, then gave her a hopeful look.

"I've never been to an all-American Fourth of July celebration," he said wistfully. "Are you thinking of going?"

"Maybe," she said.

"Is this town close by?"

"Not too far," she said.

"Have you been there before?"

"I passed through once, but I've never spent any time there," she told him.

Now there was no mistaking the hopeful look that spread across his face. "Then why don't we go? We need a day away from the lab to clear our heads. Sitting inside on a holiday would be a terrible waste, I think."

Deanna hesitated. There were a dozen reasons she should stay away from Chesapeake Shores and two compelling reasons for going. One of them was standing right before her. The other was the man she'd spent weeks now avoiding.

Milos clearly misread her silence. "Not as a date," he said quickly. "I have a girlfriend back home. She keeps asking what I'm doing besides work and I have nothing to tell her. You would be doing me a favor. I don't want her to start thinking that I'm boring. We could go as friends, unless there is someone in your life who might object."

"No one," she admitted. She could hardly explain that she would be tempting fate by going to the very town in which her father lived. What if they accidentally crossed paths? Would he recognize her? That would be highly unlikely since she'd been less than a year old the last time he'd seen her. She would recognize him only because of that photo in the well-worn article she kept in her purse.

Maybe this was what she needed to do, spend a little time in Chesapeake Shores, in his world. If she started to feel more comfortable there it would prepare her for the next time, for the day when she'd go to confront him, to ask why he'd let her go so easily.

"Let's do it," she said, meeting Milos's gaze with a smile. "I definitely don't want your girlfriend to think that your life in America is boring. You should experience an American Fourth of July celebration, and the newspaper says this is the best sort of place to do that."

"Will they have a parade?"

"I imagine so." She glanced at the article again and confirmed it. "Yes, there's a parade at noon."

"And fireworks at night?"

She laughed at his eagerness. He was usually such a somber young man, dedicated to the science that had drawn them both here for the summer. "I think fireworks are probably a requirement for any self-respecting Fourth of July celebration."

"I will buy you hot dogs and ice cream," he promised. "Those are traditional, too, are they not?"

"Very traditional," she agreed, catching just a bit of his enthusiasm. She suddenly realized it had been years since she'd been to any kind of Fourth of July celebration herself. As a child there had been backyard barbecues and neighborhood fireworks in the park, but the Chesapeake Shores celebration promised to be in a class by itself.

Somehow, too, Milos's exuberance steadied her nerves. If she concentrated on showing this young man a good time, making sure he experienced this most American of holidays as it should be experienced, she'd forget that at any moment she might come face-to-face with her biological father.

Chapter 14

"So now, thanks to Gram, the whole town will be taking sides," Luke grumbled to his uncle Mick O'Brien later that evening at the pub. Though the room was crowded and noisy, only Mick was seated at the bar and he was the only O'Brien who'd arrived, giving Luke the perfect opportunity to vent.

Clearly unsympathetic, Mick chuckled. "Which means you finally understand that your sainted grandmother's got a devious streak. Something tells me this is about far more than Irish stew. The topic alone is not exactly newsworthy, even among the regulars who've overheard a few of the squabbles between Bryan and Kiera."

Though Luke thought he already knew the answer, he asked for Mick's perspective, hoping he'd gotten it wrong. "Such as?"

"She's stirring the pot," Mick said as he sipped his pint of Guinness. "And I'm not referring to the stew that's always simmering on the stove in your kitchen here."

"You're suggesting she sees some sort of future for

Bryan and Kiera," Luke concluded. "And that she's decided to meddle."

The prospect was disconcerting. It was one thing for
him or Moira to do a bit of scheming here and there, but
Gram's involvement would take it to a whole other level.

"You've said it yourself," Mick confirmed. "There's
a spark between those two. I've seen it for myself, as
you know. You've assumed it was mostly a test of wills
over control of the kitchen. Ma sees something else entirely. She's just doing her part to fan those particular
flames. I imagine Dillon's put her up to it, not that she'd
need much encouragement to meddle in a possible romance. The goal was never to simply get Kiera here
for a visit. They both believe family belongs together.
They're looking for a way to make sure Kiera stays. Her
work visa will come to an end eventually."

"This fall," Luke confirmed, then sighed as the
pieces fell into place. "Not long after the fall festival,
in fact."

"And there you have it," Mick said, lifting his pint of
ale. "Quite the coincidence, wouldn't you say?"

"Was Gram this devious when you, Thomas and my
dad were growing up?"

"I'd like to think we were always one step ahead
of her," Mick said, then gave him a rueful grin. "But
the truth is, we never stood a chance. When it comes
to getting her way, there's no one on this earth more
talented than Nell O'Brien. And I say that as someone
who knows quite a bit about controlling things so they'll
turn out the way I want them to."

Moira picked precisely that moment to join them, a
scowl on her face. "Are you by any chance referring to
this crazy idea of Nell's to have Bryan and my mother

competing on a stage at the fall festival?" she asked, her tone making clear what she thought of the plan.

Luke sighed. "That's exactly what we were discussing. I don't think Gram had any idea of what sort of strain it could put on their relationship or the tension it could create here in the pub."

"Oh, she knew," Moira said. "Nell doesn't miss a thing. And we've talked about the need for some harmony between them. I thought we were close to achieving that, but have you been in the kitchen tonight? The tension's so thick we could carve it with one of those knives Bryan's always sharpening."

Luke studied his wife. "I thought you were growing used to the idea of some sort of romance developing between your mother and Bryan. Are you opposed now?"

"Not opposed. I just think this is the wrong way to go about it," Moira said. "Things were moving along at a nice, slow, steady pace, giving them both time to get used to the idea."

"And you?" Luke suggested.

She scowled at him. "Okay, yes, I need time to adapt, as well. It wasn't that long ago that she was engaged to a man I'd loved and admired for years. I don't like to think of her heart as being quite so fickle."

"So it's not Bryan you object to?" Mick asked. "Just that Ma's trying to move things along too fast?"

"Something like that," Moira agreed.

"Or is it that you wanted to be in charge of the match-making?" Luke asked carefully. "And now my grandmother's taken charge?"

Moira scowled, then sighed. "Okay, maybe that, too."

"And it goes back to your wanting to be the one to

save Kiera and give her a new life," Luke added, risking his own marital harmony by pointing out the obvious.

"Okay, yes. I'm selfish," Moira admitted with a huff. "I wanted to be the one responsible for giving her a happier life, for introducing her to Bryan and nudging that along at a nice even pace, so she'd be in too deep before she even realized what was happening."

"But, Moira, you brought your mother to Chesapeake Shores. It's because of you that these possibilities for her future exist at all," Mick said. "If your thought is for your mother's future, what does it matter who else helps her to reach that end?"

Luke glanced at his uncle. "You say it as if it's a rational thing," he said.

"Which it's not," Moira admitted. "Her happiness is what matters. Of course it is. If Nell's scheme works, God bless her for it. I just hope it doesn't backfire in the short run and make things around here unbearable. We don't dare fire either one of them."

Just then the door to the kitchen slammed open and Kiera stepped into view.

"Out of my kitchen!" Bryan's shout echoed throughout the pub, drawing suddenly fascinated glances and a flurry of whispers. "I won't have you in here trying to steal my recipes."

"Stealing, is it? There's not a one worth having. The ones locked in my head are far superior."

"Get out!" he repeated.

"My pleasure," Kiera retorted. "I've no need to be around your temper."

The door snapped closed.

Luke sighed. "Too late," he commented. "Moira? Which one will you be trying to calm?"

"I'll talk to my mother," she said, sounding resigned. "You tackle Bryan and see what it might take to improve his mood. I'm thinking it might require more than a pint of ale and a sounding board to calm him tonight."

Mick laughed at the evidence of the turmoil his mother had stirred up. "I'll leave you to it. I don't have any wish to be caught in the cross fire."

"If you happen to cross paths with Gram tonight, give her my thanks for this," Luke said.

"I think she'd probably tell you that it indicates that her mission is on its way toward success," Mick said, walking away to leave Moira and Luke to deal with the latest fallout from one of his mother's clever plans.

"First of all, the competition wasn't Nell's idea. It was Bree's," Kiera told Moira, when her daughter practically pushed her onto a stool at the end of the bar and demanded to know how she'd allowed herself to be drawn into the whole festival cooking battle.

"If you think Nell wasn't right in the thick of it, you're delusional," Moira said impatiently. "Things in the O'Brien family tend to go exactly the way she wants them to because she knows how to set them into motion. Nell's a clever one, and most people underestimate her. They think she's far too honorable to be so sneaky."

"That's a terrible thing to say about a woman who's been nothing but kind to you and your grandfather," Kiera scolded.

"You're taking her side, when I'm trying to point out that she's set you up?" Moira asked indignantly.

"Assuming you're right, I'm not sure I see that it matters. This whole thing came about to benefit the fall festival."

"Again, you're missing the big picture," Moira insisted. "What happened just now with you and Bryan, that's the real goal. She wants the fireworks between you to be so loud and so noisy that the entire town and most of the surrounding counties will show up for the cooking competition at the fall festival to watch you compete with your Irish stew. All the other participants are pure window dressing. You two are the main event. It's not a position I thought you'd care for."

"It's all to benefit the festival," Kiera repeated, stubbornly refusing to concede her daughter's point.

"Fireworks," Moira repeated, then explained patiently, "Between you and Bryan. Fireworks leading to romance. That's the end result Nell is going for."

As her daughter's words sank in, Kiera felt her heart lurch. Wasn't that exactly the opposite of what she'd thought to achieve when she'd agreed to this competition? She'd wanted the distance back, the safety of having the man barely speaking to her.

She thought back to what had happened in the kitchen just moments ago. It hadn't felt all that safe, if she were being totally honest about it. It had felt exhilarating. The sparks hadn't pushed them apart. Instead, they had drawn her toward the flame...exactly as Moira seemed to believe Nell had intended.

"Oh dear," she murmured, recognizing the trap at last.

Her daughter gave a nod of satisfaction. "You're getting it now?"

"I'm afraid so."

"And you'll be on your guard?"

Kiera nodded. She'd be on her guard, alright. Unfortunately at the moment she was having a little difficulty deciding exactly whom the enemy might be.

Preparations for the town's Fourth of July celebration were in full swing all over Chesapeake Shores. Storefronts had been draped with red, white and blue bunting. Small flags had been added to all the planters along Main Street and Shore Drive, and the flowers had been changed out to a selection of red, white and blue blooms, all contributed by Bree from her Flowers on Main shop and her husband Jake's nursery.

In keeping with the color scheme, Sally's was offering raspberry and blueberry croissants. Ethel's Emporium had been stocked with flags of every size and holiday-themed T-shirts. Even her selection of penny candy had an abundance of red cherry, blueberry and coconut coloring. Snow cones were similarly swirled with the appropriate colors and flavors.

Every store was offering holiday discounts in anticipation of the crowds that would be coming for the parade, the arts and crafts festival on the green and the fireworks.

"It's like something out of a picture book," Kiera said as she walked across the green with her father on the day before the holiday. She glanced at him. "What's your favorite part?"

"The parade," Dillon said at once. "Everyone's included. The town's veterans lead it off, wearing their uniforms. Businesses create floats, each one trying to outdo the next, and none of them the least bit professional. I think that's the charm of it—that they're made out of love of the tradition. The high school band plays.

Half the kids in town join in and walk the parade route just to be a part of it."

Kiera studied her father's expression. "You've really come to love it here, haven't you?"

He nodded. "And that's no disrespect to the life I had in Ireland or to my roots there. It's a matter of adapting to where I am now and the people I've come to love as my own family."

"I wonder if I'll ever know that sort of peace and acceptance," Kiera said wistfully. "I keep saying that my home is in Ireland, but when I think back to my life there, it was never easy, not as an adult. I wonder what it is that's drawing me back there."

"It's not always the place," Dillon told her. "It's the idea of the place, the memories it holds, even the bad ones, because there's a sense of security in that. This new place holds a lot of uncertainty for you now. It's not familiar." He held her gaze. "Just remember one thing while you're considering what's right for your future. Home isn't just a place. It's family, and you have that here, Kiera."

Impulsively, she hugged him. "I'm so glad you and I have found our way back to each other," she told him quietly. "I know it's my fault that it took so long. You can't imagine how deeply I regret that, especially that I had so little time with my mother before we lost her."

"It's in the past. The shame would be not to hold tight to what we've found again."

She met his gaze. "You're saying I should stay," she said, wishing he would make it so much easier by making it a demand, not a suggestion. But as they both knew, the decision was hers to make, not his. If he tried imposing his will, no matter how welcome it might be

on the one hand, on the other it would only stir her rebellious temper.

"I'm saying that you'll do what's right for you when
the time comes that the decision has to be made. Just
don't be swayed by expectations, mine or yours."

"Mine?"

"You've a knack for thinking that you don't deserve
more from life, Kiera. You expect the worst to come
your way. Remember that, and that you have a choice.
You can still reach for your dreams. It's never too late
for that."

It was a lovely sentiment, but she'd stopped dreaming years ago. All the ones she'd ever had had proved
elusive.

Dillon smiled. "I can see you building up to an argument," he told her. "Here's the thing to remember about
dreams. They don't come true just by wishing for them.
Life gives back what you put into it. Work hard and you
can achieve even the most impossible of dreams." He
held her gaze, his steady and reassuring. "You know
quite a lot about working hard, my darling girl. Put that
to good use and the rest will follow."

Kiera wished it were as easy as he made it sound.
Even through her usual skepticism and doubts, though,
she felt just the tiniest glimmer of hope.

With the sun already burning down soon after dawn,
Bryan was glad he'd gotten out even earlier than usual
for his morning run. As he turned onto Lilac Lane, he
found himself hoping to spot a bit of color in his garden, specifically sunlight glinting off auburn hair setting off fiery sparks.

As much as he hated to admit it, he missed the early

mornings he'd spent with Kiera in the peacefulness of his garden. They'd exchanged few words, just worked companionably side by side to defeat a common enemy: the weeds that seemed to grow even more robustly than the vegetables.

He sighed. It was this crazy cooking competition they'd been drawn into; Kiera eagerly from what he'd been able to tell. She seemed oddly happy about the battle lines drawn between them and the end to their truce. It shouldn't bother him the way it did. In fact, he should be thrilled not to be bumping into her in his own backyard. He liked his solitude. He'd been content with his own company for years. Why did it bother him so much now to have no one around to listen, to offer a supportive comment or even a feisty retort?

When he'd reached his back deck, he glanced over at the small cottage next door.

"Blast it," he muttered to himself and went back down the steps and across the small patch of grass separating the houses. He banged on the back door impatiently.

"What on earth?" Kiera demanded when she opened the door. "Is the world coming to an end?"

Bryan winced. If he'd come over to make peace, he'd gotten off to a shaky start.

"It's hot out," he said.

She stared at him unblinkingly, as if he'd announced the sky was blue. "So it is," she said. "I'm told that's not uncommon for July."

"What I meant to say was that it's too hot for you to be walking to work today," he said. "I'll be leaving in a half hour, if you'd like a lift."

She hesitated for a split second, then nodded. "I'd be grateful. Thank you."

Suddenly he didn't know which was worse, the shouting that had become routine once again, or this infernal politeness. Did he want to set off an explosion by mentioning it, though? He opted instead, for a nod. "Okay, then. I'll see you in a half hour."

And in the meantime he was going to have a very long talk with himself about acting like an idiot. This morning had been a good reminder that women turned men into bumbling fools. It was probably far wiser to avoid going down that path again.

For a man who'd issued an invitation for her to ride to work with him, Bryan seemed to have used up all his words for the day. He hadn't spoken since Kiera had climbed into his environmentally sensible Prius, grateful to have the air-conditioning blasting.

"I haven't seen much of you recently," she said to break the silence. At his disbelieving glance in her direction, she added, "I meant away from work."

"I thought that was how you wanted it," he said. "I've followed my usual routine, but you seem to have come up with a completely different schedule. You're gone by the time I get back from my run."

"I like to walk into town while it's still cool. I enjoy getting together with some of the O'Brien women at Sally's."

"And the garden? I thought you enjoyed weeding."

"I wasn't sure you wanted me around," she said. "I've done a little when I've gotten home. Luke's let me off earlier in the evening recently, and it's still light out."

Bryan stopped at an intersection and gave her a long

look. "Did he change your schedule to minimize the amount of time we'd have to start a ruckus at the pub?"

She gave him a rueful grin. "He never said such a thing, but I suspect so. I thought perhaps you'd asked him to set it up that way."

"I'm not going to tell Luke how to run his business," Bryan said. "The scheduling is up to him."

"You know," Kiera began, not entirely sure she ought to be opening up this particular can of worms. "When I agreed to do the cooking thing for the festival, I didn't expect things between us to go back to the way they were at the beginning."

"What did you expect?"

"That we'd have a friendly rivalry that would benefit Nell's church and the town."

"And?"

"There is no *and,*" she insisted, but she couldn't quite meet his gaze.

Bryan turned his attention back to the road. Silence fell between them again. She sensed that somehow she'd disappointed him. Had he known she wasn't being entirely honest?

"Okay, there was more to it," she said eventually.

"Something that couldn't have been resolved just by talking to me?"

"How, when you were the problem?"

She could tell her candor had startled him by the clenching of his jaw. He didn't reply, his concentration focused on parallel parking in a tight space in the alley behind the pub.

When he'd turned off the engine, he faced her. "How was I the problem? I thought we'd made peace, that we were getting along, getting to know and respect each other."

"We were."

"And that was a bad thing?"

She nodded. "I realize it can't possibly make much sense to you, but that scared me. I was growing comfortable talking to you, especially on those quiet nights on your deck. It reminded me of another time, another man."

"Your ex-husband?"

She laughed bitterly at that. "Hardly. Sean wasn't much for quiet conversation. No, it was Peter."

"The man who died."

"After Sean, I'd allowed no one to get close to me. I made it my mission to protect my heart from any more pain. It was easy enough to ignore the occasional drunken pass some man might make or to say no to the few who might have put my heart at risk."

She allowed herself a smile. "Then there was Peter. He made no demands. He listened. He gave me reasons to laugh. It was insidious, if you know what I mean. The little exchanges that meant nothing in themselves, but added together to become trust and caring and, over time, love."

There was sympathy in Bryan's eyes. "And then he died."

"And then he died," she agreed simply. "He broke the trust, and my heart."

"And you panicked because you felt it happening again," Bryan said. "You were starting to trust me?"

"I know the signs now, you see. And I couldn't allow it."

"So you and I are going into this crazy cooking competition just to put some sort of an artificial barrier between us?"

She shrugged at how ridiculous it sounded. "So it seems."

To her surprise, Bryan laughed. After a startled moment, she found herself laughing with him.

"It might have been easier just to slap me when I kissed you," he told her. "That would have gotten your message across loud and clear."

"If I'd been thinking at the time, that would have been a good solution," she agreed. "But you caught me off guard."

His gaze searched hers. "And you didn't find it all that unpleasant, did you?"

"Do we really need to talk about that kiss?" she asked, flustered by his candor.

"I think we should," he persisted.

"Why?"

"Because right this minute I am seriously considering doing it again."

Chapter 15

Kiera stared at Bryan in alarm, his crazy pronouncement hanging in the suddenly charged air between them.

"Have you listened to nothing I've said?" she demanded.

"I heard every word. In my experience, the best way to face fear is head-on."

"And in some twisted way that calls for another kiss, when I've already admitted that the first one rattled me and declared it a huge mistake?"

"I don't recall the word *mistake* being used," he said, clearly enjoying the fact that he'd flustered her so thoroughly.

"I'm using it now," she said quite firmly. "It was a mistake, one that there's no reason to repeat."

"Not even as a way to determine if the first time was merely a fluke?" he asked, eyes twinkling. "Perhaps it was just that I caught you off guard, as you said. Now that you've fair warning, you can rally all your carefully crafted defenses and another kiss might have no effect at all. You could put all your worries to rest."

"You're crazy," she declared, though on some level

she found his argument persuasive. Downright tempting, in fact. Perhaps she was a little crazy, too, when it came to this.

"Not crazy at all," he insisted. "I am proposing a rational way to test the situation and determine if the outcome was unique or a likely pattern. It's scientific research, if you think about it."

Feeling a desperate need to escape before he put his theory to the test, Kiera reached for the handle of the door, but before she could wrench it open, Bryan gently touched her shoulder.

"Don't run, Kiera. Let's settle this here and now."

She turned back and saw that there was compassion and understanding in his eyes, no hint of laughter. If he'd been even the tiniest bit amused, she might have fled. Instead she sat back, the internal debate overwhelming her.

While she wrestled with warring emotions—longing and common sense—he reached over and skimmed the pad of his thumb across her lips, his touch as gentle and fleeting as the whisper of a butterfly's wings. Her lips parted at the sensation he stirred. Longing was winning.

To her surprise, he took her hand and placed it on his chest. "Can you feel my heart beating, Kiera? It's pounding. I'm as terrified by what we might discover as you are."

She regarded him with wonder. "You are?"

"Believe me," he said seriously. He framed her face with his hands, then closed his eyes and kissed her oh-so-gently, just as he had the first time, but there was nothing sneaky or quick about this kiss. He lingered, explored and left her head spinning when he finally released her.

He was the first to sigh. "Not a fluke, then."

She nodded, breathless. "Not a fluke."

She wanted to find that every bit as terrifying as she'd predicted, but somehow she couldn't. She found it reassuring. She didn't want to. She wanted to be able to regard him with a cool, distant look and act as if it hadn't mattered, as if it hadn't shattered another layer of the protective wall she'd been trying to build once more around her heart.

"What now?" she asked, her voice shaky.

To her surprise, Bryan looked every bit as confused as she felt. "I wish I knew," he said softly, then smiled as he glanced behind her. "What I do know is that we have an audience. Luke and Moira are standing at the kitchen door of the pub, both of them a bit slack-jawed. I suspect we're going to have a few questions to answer when we go inside."

"We could start the car and drive away," she suggested hopefully, feeling like an embarrassed teenager who was about to be cross-examined by a critical parent.

Bryan chuckled. "You have met Moira, haven't you? Does your daughter seem the kind to be put off? Running away now would only delay the inevitable."

"Or you could go in and take the heat and I could go off and enjoy my first Fourth of July in America with my granddaughter, rather than leaving her with a sitter for the holiday. It's a day families should spend together."

"Isn't the sitter taking her to Mick's for just that reason?" Bryan asked.

Kiera sighed. "Yes, but I could take her." She warmed

to the idea. "I think that's the most reasonable plan. It would be the gentlemanly thing to do."

"How long do you think it would be before Moira catches up with you?"

"If the pub's as busy as it's likely to be today, she won't be able to get away. It could be hours."

"And will your explanation be any easier then? Or will it be harder, since you'll also be explaining why you abandoned your duties at the pub on one of its busiest days of the summer?"

He was probably right, but she didn't have to like it. "I'm the mother. I don't need to have an explanation," she said stoutly, knowing that it was an argument that would hold no water with her persistent daughter.

"Now you're catching on. Just tell them to butt out. That's what I intend to do." He gave her a long look. "Ready?"

She sighed heavily. "As I'll ever be," she said.

One of these days she'd have to focus on how, at this stage of her life, she'd managed to find herself in such a fix.

"You and Kiera seem to be getting along much better today," Luke said, cheerfully greeting Bryan as he walked into the kitchen.

"You should be grateful," Bryan retorted, reaching for his apron and going straight into the pantry to collect the ingredients for the day's special—bangers and mash with onion gravy—for those who wanted an Irish twist to the traditional hot dogs and French fries that would be available at booths on the town green.

Sadly, Luke didn't take the hint and disappear while he was in the pantry.

"You've been asking for a return to peace and harmony. I'm working on it," he told his boss.

"So that kiss I witnessed was for the benefit of the pub?" Luke asked, clearly amused.

"That's what I said," Bryan confirmed.

"And you took no personal pleasure in it?"

Bryan stopped what he was doing and scowled at Luke. "Are you asking as my boss?"

"I was, but now I'm asking as the concerned son-in-law," Luke said.

"Then I'm telling you to butt out. Kiera and I are adults. We're figuring this out day by day. Once we have any notion where this might lead, we'll be sure to let you know."

Luke looked surprised. "Then you think it might lead somewhere? There are feelings involved?"

"I'm not thinking about it at all at the moment. I'm trying to get ready to cook for the legions of customers likely to wander into your pub today."

"Fair enough, but if Kiera's heart gets broken and I have to deal with the fallout, I may not be able to protect you from Moira's wrath."

Bryan nodded. "I'll keep that in mind. I notice, by the way, that you don't seem to be too concerned that my heart might get broken. Haven't you told me repeatedly that Kiera's not an easy woman?"

Luke laughed. "From my vantage point, it seems to me you're handling her just fine."

Luke left the kitchen then and Bryan sighed. If only that were true.

The quiet, sleepy little town Deanna recalled from her previous visit was nowhere in evidence as she and

Milos drove into town on the Fourth of July. The streets of downtown Chesapeake Shores had been blocked off and were packed with people. They were directed to an already crowded parking lot by the high school on the outskirts of town.

"I thought this was a small town," Milos said, his eyes wide. "It looks as busy as London."

Deanna laughed. "Perhaps it seems that way at first glance today, but I promise that the last time I was through here, it was a typical small village. Look around. There are no skyscrapers, and I think there might only be one traffic light. I don't even think there's a McDonald's or a Taco Bell, and definitely no Starbucks. All the businesses are local, or at least that's how it seemed the day I drove through."

"Why did you come here?"

"I'd read about it somewhere," she said. "And I needed a break on my drive to Baltimore." It was simple enough and mostly true. The reality was far too complex for a day like today, with the sun already beating down and only a slight breeze stirring off the water. She glanced at her watch. "The parade doesn't start for a half hour. What would you like to do first?"

Not that there were many options with the crowds seeming to move as one toward the town green.

"There are booths over there," Milos pointed out. "I will buy you something, a souvenir for bringing me to my first American Fourth of July celebration."

"You don't need to do that," she objected.

"A flag at least," he argued. "We'll need one to wave when the parade starts."

His excitement was contagious, and Deanna found herself being swept along with it. With flags in hand, they found a spot along the parade route and waited until they could hear a band playing in the distance. "It's starting," she said, glancing up the street in the direction of the sound.

An hour later the last charming float had passed by and the crowd was dispersing, most of them heading toward the green and the arts and crafts festival there.

"Are you ready for a hot dog?" she asked Milos.

"Let's walk around first and see the shops," he said.

Deanna had to admit she was curious about this town where her father had settled. She let herself be led down Main Street, where they passed Sally's, which seemed to be jam-packed, despite the competition from the food vendors on the green. They peered in the windows at the flower shop, the bookstore and a souvenir shop before turning onto Shore Road with its cafés and galleries.

Deanna caught sight of the sign for O'Brien's and tugged on Milos's arm. "Let's walk on the other side, by the water," she suggested, unwilling to pass directly in front of the restaurant, as if she might be tempting fate.

With Milos willingly following her, she crossed the street and walked out onto the town pier, where they lingered to watch people fishing. Then they started along the waterfront. Deanna kept her gaze focused on the bay, where an increasing number of boats seemed to be gathering in anticipation of the fireworks coming later.

"Wait!" Milos said, stopping suddenly.

"What?"

"It's a pub, just like in Ireland," he said excitedly. "I went to Trinity College in Dublin for a special program and went to many of the pubs there. Have you been to this one?"

"No," she said carefully, panic starting to rise as she sensed what was coming next.

"Then we must go," he said eagerly. "It looks busy, but the line is not too long."

Deanna balked. "I thought you wanted hot dogs and ice cream."

"We have all day. We'll be hungry again. I want you to try something from my life in Europe."

There was no way around it, not without revealing why she didn't want to walk inside that pub. She told herself she was being ridiculous. Sure, she would be putting herself right in her father's path, but even if he came out of the kitchen and looked directly into her eyes, what would he see? A college girl enjoying a meal with a friend. A stranger. Nothing more.

And if she caught a glimpse of him, one she'd been longing for, what was the harm in that? It would be an icebreaker of sorts, a way to make it easier when she faced him with all of her questions. She would have the advantage of familiarity, albeit no more than a glimpse.

"If it means so much to you," she said, though she didn't quite manage to keep her reluctance from her voice.

Milos studied her. "Do you really not want to go?"

Feeling guilty for stealing some of the fun from the moment for him, she shook her head. "Of course I want to go. Let's do it."

Inside, they left Milos's name with a hostess, then ordered soft drinks at the bar and studied the crowded restaurant.

"Is it like the pubs in Ireland?" she asked him.

He smiled. "Exactly." He grabbed a menu from the stack beside them and glanced through it. "The special

is bangers and mash with onion gravy, one of my favorites," he said happily. "Thank you for agreeing to come
to Chesapeake Shores today. I was looking forward to
an American tradition, but now I have a taste of something familiar to look forward to, as well."

He seemed so pleased by all of it that Deanna
couldn't help being glad she'd relented. Just then a
young woman came to lead them to a table in the corner. "Kiera will be your waitress," she said with an authentic Irish lilt in her voice. "She'll be right with you."

Moments later an older woman rushed over, looking frazzled. "I'm sorry for the delay. It's been a bit
of a madhouse today," she said, her apologetic gaze
going from Deanna to Milos and then, suddenly, back
again. Her expression turned puzzled. "Have you been
in before?"

Deanna felt her breath quicken. "No. This is my first
time here."

"You look so familiar," Kiera said. "But then we're
all supposed to have look-alikes, aren't we?"

Deanna forced a smile. "So I hear."

They placed their orders for the day's special and
Kiera hurried off.

"That was strange," Milos said when she'd gone.
"She sounded so certain that she'd seen you before."

"It's not possible," Deanna said emphatically.

But she couldn't help being shaken by the whole exchange. Was it possible that the waitress had seen some
similarity between her and her father? Was that what
had struck her without her even realizing it?

She realized that her friend was studying her worriedly. "Are you okay?"

"I think I just need some air," she told him. "It's

very crowded in here and I think it's getting to me. I'm sorry."

"Go outside and try to find a place on one of those benches across the street," he suggested. "I will ask for our meals to go and join you as soon as I can."

"I'm sorry," she said again.

Outside, the fresh air, hot though it was, helped, as did just being away from the pub. She found an available bench down the block and sank onto it, closing her eyes against the wave of panic that had sent her fleeing the restaurant.

"Deanna?" Milos said quietly, sitting down beside her. "Are you feeling better?"

She forced a smile. "Much," she told him. "And I'm starving."

They ate their meals, disposed of the trash and then walked back to the green to visit the booths at the art festival. Milos was such an easy companion, commenting on everything and clearly enjoying the entire experience that Deanna finally put the uncomfortable moment at the pub behind her and allowed herself to enjoy the day.

After spending the day shopping, walking along the waterfront and throwing a Frisbee in a nearby park, Milos insisted on treating her to hot dogs and ice cream.

"They're going to shoot off the fireworks from the end of the pier," he said between bites. "If we look now, perhaps we can find a place along the shore to watch."

"Let's do that," Deanna agreed.

They'd just found another bench that had been vacated, when the first of the fireworks lit the night sky in a shower of red, white and blue. All around them, there were murmurs of delight and applause from the children nearby.

"Oh my! Look at that," someone with a hint of Irish in her voice murmured from behind them as the next display exploded over the water.

Deanna glanced over her shoulder and spotted the waitress from the pub. There was a man beside her. Deanna didn't need to look at the article in her purse to recognize Bryan Laramie. She'd memorized that image. Her heart seemed to stop for a full minute, before it thumped unsteadily in her chest.

Her father, so close she could almost reach out and touch him. Tears pooled in her eyes, and she had to look away. The tears tracked down her cheeks.

Milos turned his attention from the fireworks to her, worry immediately clouding his expression. "You're crying."

"I always get emotional at these sorts of things," she told him, hoping it sounded believable. "The music, the fireworks. It's all so patriotic and moving."

"It is," he agreed, though he didn't sound entirely convinced that it was the reason for her tears.

Deanna forced herself to keep her gaze on the sky as the show went on, not allowing herself a single peek over her shoulder. She didn't hear Kiera's voice again or that of the man with her. If only he'd spoken loudly enough for her to hear him, she thought. Would she have remembered the sound of that voice? Would a memory have come to her of him whispering loving words as he placed her in her crib? Did grown-ups ever have such memories, even those who had so many more memories to crowd out those early ones? She had no way of knowing.

But very soon she had to find out for herself. She'd delayed confronting the past for long enough.

At home that night, Deanna turned the air-conditioning down until her apartment was almost freezing, then wrapped herself in a comforter. It gave her a sense of security to be in her own personal cocoon.

When her cell phone rang, she almost didn't answer, then saw that it was Ash. He'd be worried if she didn't pick up. She'd told him she was going on an excursion with a friend for the holiday.

"Hey," she said when she picked up. "How was your Fourth?"

"The same as always, a barbecue at the Franklins'. They all asked about you. They were surprised to hear you were at Johns Hopkins for the summer."

"I imagine that was awkward," she said. "Everyone expected me to be working with you."

"I just told them you'd discovered a passion for medicine and were exploring your options in that field. I actually think Janet was envious. Their son is in grad school and still shows no signs of taking an interest in anything in particular."

Deanna laughed. "Greg is going to drift through life as long as they let him and they pay for it."

"I'm afraid you're exactly right," Ash said. "What about your day? What did you do?"

She hesitated, then admitted, "I spent the day with a friend in Chesapeake Shores."

"Oh," he said softly. "And how was that?"

"It was everything a small-town Fourth should be," she said.

"You know that's not what I'm asking, Dee... Did you see your father?"

"I didn't meet him. It wasn't the right time, but I did get a glimpse of him and we ate at his pub."

"That was quite a first step."

"But just a first step. I have to figure out how to take the next one. What if he's forgotten all about me?"

"No father ever forgets his child," Ash said with certainty. "I'm sure he hasn't forgotten you. I imagine, given the way your mother took off, he's wondered about you for years."

"Maybe not. I mean he could have been glad we were gone. Otherwise wouldn't he have tried harder to find us?"

"You don't know that he didn't try. It wasn't that long after you'd left when your mom and I met and your names were changed. The trail could easily have gone cold."

"I suppose."

"I know it must seem scary to think of meeting him for the first time after all these years and not having any idea what to expect. Did you get any sense of him today? What kind of man he might be?"

"Not really, though he's certainly working in a very successful restaurant. It was jammed, despite all the competition from a zillion different food vendors on the town green. The food was delicious, very authentic, according to my friend who lived in Dublin for a while." She hesitated, then said, "One odd thing happened, though."

"What was that?"

"Our waitress at the pub thought she recognized me. She finally dismissed it as one of those look-alike things, but I couldn't help wondering. Do you think I might look like my dad, at least a little? I couldn't really tell from just the one quick glimpse I had."

"It's certainly possible. I thought you took after your mom, but I'd never seen a picture of your dad until I found that article."

"I wish Mom had kept some pictures," she said wistfully. "I asked once and she told me she'd left them behind."

"Not all of them," Ash admitted slowly. "I found one of you and your dad in a box she'd hidden in the back of her closet. Before you accuse me of keeping it from you, I just discovered it last week. I finally decided to tackle cleaning out some of your mom's things. I hadn't been able to face it before. It seemed too final."

"Oh, Ash," she said softly, knowing how difficult that must have been for him and regretting that she hadn't been there to lend him moral support. "You should have waited until I was there to help."

"You've offered before, Dee. The other day the time finally seemed right. Letting go, even though I know they're just clothes and shoes, was harder than I expected."

"What did you do with her things?"

"I've kept all her jewelry for you. Not that she had much—she was never interested in fancy jewelry. I put aside a few other things I thought you might like. Most I donated to a shelter for women trying to get back into the workforce."

"Mom would have loved that," she said.

"About the picture, Dee. If you want, I'll mail it to you."

"Please, yes," she said. "I really want to see it."

"You were just a baby, remember. You're not going to be able to tell if you resemble him."

"Still, it's something I should have when I meet him, to prove I am who I say I am, I guess. He might want proof."

"I'll mail it first thing tomorrow via overnight mail," Ash promised. "When do you think you'll go back?"

"Next weekend," Deanna said, the impulsive words out before she could stop them. Now that she'd said it, it was a commitment of sorts. There would be no backing down.

"I know you've said you want to do it on your own, but I am willing to be there if you need me."

"I know, and I love you for offering. I know none of this is easy for you, either."

"All I want is your happiness, Dee." He hesitated, then asked, "Do you know what you hope to get out of this meeting?"

"Answers," she said simply.

Wasn't that all anybody really needed from the past?

Chapter 16

"It was the perfect end to a perfect holiday," Kiera said, eyes closed, her head resting against the passenger seat as Bryan made his way through the remnants of the Fourth of July traffic, which had been slowed to a crawl by an unexpected storm that hit with driving rain and a fierce wind just after the fireworks ended.

"I think the fireworks this year were the best yet," Bryan said. "And it helped that God added a few bits of lightning in the night sky to put the man-made stuff to shame."

"But the actual storm held off, thank goodness," Kiera said. "I imagine most people got back to their cars without getting soaked."

"If only we could say the same," he responded. "I'm glad I keep a change of clothes at the pub, but you must be freezing with the air-conditioning blowing on your damp clothes. Want me to turn it off?"

"Absolutely not. I'll be fine as soon as I change and get out of these wet shoes," Kiera said. "They got the worst of it. I think we ran through every puddle downtown." She grinned at him. "I think you chose that route deliberately. Were you the kind of boy who never avoided jumping in a puddle?"

He laughed. "I was, as a matter of fact. It drove my mother crazy."

"Moira and her brothers were no better," Kiera assured him. "I grumbled about it, but I couldn't really blame them, especially on a hot summer evening when the splashing helped them to cool off."

"It sounds to me as if their childhood wasn't so rough."

Kiera sighed. "I didn't want it to be, so I encouraged some of the simple little pleasures that other mothers frowned on. Maybe that's how my sons got the idea that it was okay to break all the rules."

Bryan glanced over at her. "Will you ever tell me more about them?"

"One of these days," she promised. "Not tonight. I just want to have a glass of wine and crash. As much fun as today was, I'm exhausted."

"I should probably let you do just that, but I was thinking you might like to have that wine on my deck. The storm has moved on now and it's cooler." He held her gaze for a beat before adding, "I've missed our late-night chats."

The admission made her smile and caused her pulse to leap. She glanced over at him, but his eyes were back on the road. "I'm not sure it's a good idea. We're still trying to sort things out between us."

"A glass of wine and a little conversation, Kiera. It's a good way to wind down after a long day," he said persuasively. "Doctor-recommended, in fact."

Kiera lifted a brow. "Really? What doctor is that?"

Bryan glanced over, a mischievous spark in his eyes. "I believe I found him on the internet."

"An honest-to-goodness authority, then," she said, laughing. "How convenient that you discovered him."

"I think so."

As torn as she was between what she wanted and what was wise, she said, "Honestly, Bryan, I'm not sure I'm up for changing, then changing again for bed."

"Just put on a robe," he said as if it were no big deal to arrive half-dressed at a man's house. "No one's going to see you or judge you. It'll certainly be no more revealing than that blouse that's plastered to you right now."

Kiera glanced down and gasped. Her prim white top had become a revealing, see-through blouse. "Oh dear, I never thought to check to see if I looked a mess after the rain."

"You don't look a mess at all," he said, a sudden spark in his eyes. "You look like exactly what you are, a very attractive woman." He deliberately turned his attention away from her and took studious care with parking, then got out of the car and walked around to open her door. "Get dry and come over," he said as if the matter had been decided. "I'll have the wine ready."

Kiera knew she should say no. She really should, but somehow when her mouth opened, the proper response simply wouldn't come.

"Give me ten minutes," she said, a breathless note in her voice that didn't belong there. If she was making a reckless mistake, well, so be it. She'd made her fair share and lived to tell the stories.

Oh, he was tempting fate, alright, Bryan thought as he opened a bottle of Pinot Grigio and poured two glasses, then took them out onto the deck along with a plate of cheese and some crackers. Wine and a late-night snack outside under a starry sky spelled seduction, pure and simple. He knew it, and Kiera clearly did, as well.

He thought of Luke's perfectly reasonable word of caution earlier and winced. He needed to remember exactly who Kiera was. Not that she was his boss's mother-in-law, but a woman who'd been deeply hurt by the two significant men in her life, albeit in entirely different ways. He couldn't allow himself to be the third.

He thought he was a better man than Sean Malone and healthier, perhaps, than Peter McDonough, but what did that matter when he had no idea what his intentions were? An honorable man would tread carefully under the circumstances.

He took a long swallow of the crisp wine and reminded himself that there was something none of them knew, something he usually kept pushed so far to the back of his mind that it didn't even register. He could very well still be considered legally married. While it might be an easy thing for him to forget after all these years, he doubted Kiera would consider it a small omission. Of all the women in the world who might overlook such an uncertain history, Kiera was definitely not one likely to do so. Caution would have her running in the opposite direction and, perhaps, rightly so.

Which meant he had to tell her before things went any further between them...if only he could find the words.

Though it was a clear night, the stars provided little light, and the slip of a moon added almost none. Still he saw Kiera's shadow crossing the lawn between their houses. He smiled at the sight of her bare feet and the oversize robe she'd belted tightly around her waist. He immediately found himself wondering what she wore beneath the thick white terry cloth that covered her from neck to midcalf. His fingers suddenly itched to tug the belt free and find out.

"Warmer now?" he asked softly as she joined him on the deck.

"Warmer and dry," she said, accepting the glass of wine he held out. She took a sip and sighed. "This is definitely just what the doctor ordered. You'll have to tell me where to find him on the internet. He seems a reliable sort, after all."

"I thought you might come to appreciate him," Bryan said. "Try some of the cheese."

"Not just yet," she said, sighing and closing her eyes. "I think I could fall asleep right here."

"It was a long day," Bryan agreed. "But a good one, too."

"It was. Luke must be pleased. The pub was busy from the moment we opened until we closed for the fireworks. And I heard compliments for the food throughout the day from those who were visiting Chesapeake Shores for the first time. I suspect they'll be back again soon. I must have handed out a hundred copies of the flyer for our upcoming music schedule." She shook her head ruefully. "And I caught Nell handing out a flyer about the cooking competition."

Bryan chuckled. "She's not one to miss an opportunity to spread the word. Did you get a look at her flyer?"

"Not even a glimpse," Kiera admitted. "She claimed not to have enough to go around and to wait until she'd made another batch."

"That's worrisome," Bryan said. "That tells me she

was fairly certain you and I wouldn't like whatever it said."

Kiera sighed. "That was my reaction, too." Suddenly she sat up straight. "Do you have a pen and paper handy? I should probably jot a note to myself to remind Luke to have more copies of the pub's music schedule made."

"Stay still. I'll help you remember."

She glanced his way. "It must be gratifying to you to hear such universal praise for your food."

He smiled. "And it must stick in your craw," he said.

"Why would you say such a thing?"

"Aren't you always telling me that your ways are better?" he reminded her. "And aren't we destined to put the claim to the test just a few months from now?"

Kiera sighed. "And we were having such a pleasant time," she grumbled. "Why would you bring that up now?"

"To be clear, *you* brought it up when you mentioned Nell handing out notices of the fall event, but I'll let it drop. I wouldn't want to ruin one of these treasured moments of peace between us." He hesitated for a long time, then said, "Luke said something today that we should probably talk about."

"About what?" she asked warily, visibly stiffening.

"He warned me not to hurt you."

Kiera turned a dismayed look on him. "He didn't! Why would he do such a thing?"

"Because he saw that kiss this morning and he's concerned about you. And I imagine Moira added her two cents as well and demanded he deal with me."

"Am I not a grown woman capable of looking out for myself?" Kiera demanded indignantly.

"Of course you are, but the people who love you will always be concerned. They want to know I'm not going to take advantage of you."

At last she seemed to relax, and her lips twitched ever so slightly. "And were you considering taking advantage of me?"

He kept his gaze on her steady. "I've been seriously considering seducing you," he admitted candidly.

Her eyes went wide. "And if I were to allow it," she said with an endearing hitch to her voice, "I would consider that to be a mutual decision, not a man taking advantage of a woman."

"It might not be as simple as that," he told her. "There are things you should know before we ever get to such a point, things it's only fair that I tell you so that you can consider all the facts."

She frowned at him. "I don't like the sound of that. Are you an alcoholic, like my Sean?"

He lifted his glass of wine. "I like to think I would not be drinking this if I were."

"And you run miles every day, so it can't be that your health is in jeopardy like Peter, who had no notion at all of how to take proper care of himself."

"My health is good."

"Then what else could put such a dire note in your voice? Do you have some sort of criminal past?"

He could tell that she was deliberately reaching for explanations, each one a bit wilder than the one before. He doubted she would ever land on the truth, though.

"Kiera, you could ask a hundred questions and probably not stumble on the truth. Just let me say this before I lose my courage. I told you about my daughter, about my wife taking off with her years ago."

"Yes. And you told me that she didn't run because you'd ever done either of them any harm."

"That's true." He took a deep breath, then added, "But she left without divorcing me."

Kiera didn't look dismayed. She looked confused. "But it's been years and years. Surely in all that time, one of you…"

Bryan shook his head before she could finish. "I never filed. I wouldn't have known where to have the papers served. As far as I know she never filed, either. Nor was there any attempt at an annulment that I'm aware of."

He fell silent to allow his news to sink in.

"So you could still be married?" she said eventually.

"In all likelihood, I'm still married," he confirmed. "Obviously it would be in name only after all this time, but it would be legally binding. It's never really mattered to me." He held her gaze. "Until now. I wish the situation had been clarified long ago, but it wasn't, so here we are with me in some sort of marital limbo. What might have been simple between any other people, seeing where an attraction might take them, is complicated for the two of us."

"I see." She stared out toward the bay, though it was invisible in the darkness. Still, the gentle waves could be heard lapping against the shore. "That's definitely something to consider, then."

"No one else knows about this. Luke and Moira never asked when they hired me. They know I rarely date, but not the real reason why. I assume they think I'm pretty much a loner, which I have been for years. I've dated off and on, but it's never reached a point where I felt I had to share this information. I'm content with the life I lead. I never minded being alone until you came along. Now, to my surprise, I find I like the companionship and the sparks that fly between us from time to time."

"Sparks can be dangerous," she said with weary understanding. "They can set off a fire that burns out of control. Reason doesn't enter into it. I've spent years trying to avoid just such a thing."

"Which is why it's only fair that you know I may be the worst possible man to ask you to change that." Even as he spoke so candidly, he feared that his words would end whatever had been beginning between them. Still, it had to be said.

To his regret, but not his surprise, she stood up. "I need time to think about this."

"I understand. Take as long as you need," he told her.

She made it all the way to the top step before turning back. She closed the distance between them, leaned down and brushed a shy, hesitant kiss across his lips.

"Good night, Bryan."

"Good night, Kiera," he whispered, smiling as he watched her walk away. He waited until she was safely inside her own cottage before releasing his breath.

Maybe this wasn't quite the end between them, after all.

With her thoughts in turmoil, Kiera left her cottage early in the morning, escaping while she knew Bryan was on his run. She wasn't quite ready to deal with everything he'd told her the night before. To her way of thinking, a married man was a married man and, therefore, off-limits.

But in God's eyes were there ever extenuating cir-

cumstances? she wondered. If so, this would seem to
be such a time, but she doubted a priest or a lawyer
would see it quite that way. In good conscience, could
she? Or would she simply be making excuses for doing
what she knew was wrong?

To her added frustration, this was hardly a topic she
could discuss with anyone. This was Bryan's secret,
not hers, to share.

At Sally's she found only Megan seated at the back
table.

"You're out early," Megan said when she spotted
Kiera. "As busy as everyone was yesterday, I wasn't
sure anyone would get here this morning before I have
to go to the gallery. I debated spending another hour
in bed myself, but Mick is always up with the birds, so
sleeping in is impossible."

"I had a restless night," Kiera admitted. "I figured I
might as well come here and have some strong coffee
and a raspberry croissant. That usually helps."

"I know what you mean," Megan agreed, gesturing
to the same order already in front of her. "What kept
you up? Or is it something you'd rather not talk about?"

"Something I can't talk about, unfortunately. It's an
unexpected situation, and I could use some advice but
can't seek it."

"That is a quandary," Megan said. "You could speak
to me in confidence. I'd never break it."

"I know you can be trusted, as could Nell or my father, but it's not something I'm at liberty to discuss."

"Which means you're left to wrestle with it entirely
on your own. That hardly seems fair." Megan, usually
quick to offer an opinion, hesitated. After apparently
weighing whatever she wanted to say, she met Kiera's

gaze. "I know this may not be right for you, but my daughter Jess is married to a psychologist, if you think he could help. That's entirely different from spreading gossip. Will's a professional and he's very wise. I think all of us have bent his ear from time to time. Even if we catch him on the street, rather than in his office, he keeps what's said to himself."

Kiera thought of the tall, serious young man she'd met at Nell's. His adoring gaze had never strayed from Jess. That must have been Will. "I believe I met him at Nell's on the day I arrived," Kiera said. "I suppose if I can't figure this out, he would be a good person for me to seek out. Thank you."

"Now, since I can't offer any support or comfort about whatever's bothering you, tell me about yesterday. Was the pub as crazy busy as my gallery was?"

"I don't think I sat down or took a breath from the moment the doors opened," Kiera told her. "Everyone was so patient and understanding and they were all talking about coming back again."

"I had lines at the register all day, too," Megan said with satisfaction. "Moira's going to be very happy with the check I have for her. Her photographs were among the day's top sellers. It's a good thing we'd already shipped the photographs for the show in San Francisco or I'd have been tempted to bring those out yesterday to take advantage of the eager crowds with their open wallets. I am going to contact the gallery in San Francisco and suggest he bump up the prices because her works are in such high demand. I think mentioning that her last show was a sellout could spur buyers out there to act quickly."

"I still find it so remarkable that my daughter had

this talent all along and only discovered it by accident," Kiera said. "You've been such a blessing to her, Megan."

"That works both ways. It makes me proud to see her doing so well. And I hear you're going to San Francisco for the show."

"I am and I can hardly wait," Kiera said. "It's only for a weekend, but it will be my first real sightseeing in America."

And, she thought, it couldn't be coming at a more perfect time, just when her life in Chesapeake Shores had taken such a complicated turn.

Bryan had seen very little of Kiera since he'd told her about his questionable marital status. He couldn't blame her for avoiding him, but he was a little surprised by it. He'd thought her more likely to confront the situation head-on, reach a decision and perhaps tell him they no longer had a chance with each other. Perhaps, he thought wryly, the silence was an improvement over that outcome.

He glanced up and saw the very woman plaguing his thoughts standing in the doorway to the kitchen. She was dressed for travel in a neat skirt and a blouse he remembered all too well from the Fourth of July when it had been plastered to her skin. Even in the prim-and-proper outfit, she managed to exude an appeal he was having trouble resisting. How many times in recent days had he wanted to reach for her, to muss her hair, to steal a kiss that would put a lovely pink in her pale cheeks?

"You're getting ready to leave, I imagine," he said, stating the obvious. "You're going to love San Francisco. It's a beautiful city. And be sure you get across the bridge to Sausalito."

"I can't wait to see it all," she admitted, though her excitement seemed oddly tempered.

"But?" he said. "I sense there's something bothering you about the trip."

"Not about the trip. I just can't help thinking that it's the worst time to be going," she said. "We're at the height of the summer tourist season. Luke or I should be staying. Since he belongs there with Moira, I think it should fall to me to be here."

"Nonsense. The kitchen is in my hands," Bryan said. "It's safe enough." He waited, daring her to say otherwise, but she simply nodded. "Okay, then. We have plenty of trained staff to handle the bar and the tables. Nell and Dillon will be in and out, as will Luke's uncle Mick. In fact, I think Mick is looking forward to donning an apron and serving a few pints of Guinness."

"I imagine he is," she conceded. "He seems to fancy his Irish genes have given him a hidden talent for running a pub."

"He certainly has a gift for talking to the customers," Bryan said. "There's a crowd at the bar every night just to listen to him spin a tale. Just go and have a wonderful time, Kiera. You deserve to see someplace new and to bask in your daughter's great success."

She lifted troubled eyes to meet his. "And when I come back, we'll talk," she promised.

"I told you to take as long as you need. I know I presented you with a complicated situation. There's no rush for you to make a decision."

"It's certainly a situation I never envisioned finding myself in, and that's the truth," she said. "If I'd been asked about something like this, I would have considered the answer to be obvious, but it's you and me, Bryan. There's nothing simple about it."

"We can go on as we have been," he told her. "We can remain friends and forget the rest."

She looked startled. "You could do that?"

"I wouldn't want to, but if that was the only choice you gave me, I could manage it." He held her gaze. "Or I could sit with Connor, tell him the story and have him do whatever it takes to clarify the situation legally. That would probably be the sensible thing to do."

"You'd be willing to do that? To tell him so much of your personal story?"

"Perhaps it's time. Past time, more likely. It's something I should have resolved years ago, but I clung to hope for a long time, then just pushed the whole marriage issue aside and tried to forget about it altogether. The only thing I pursued was finding my daughter, and you already know how that turned out. Dead end after dead end. I couldn't bring myself to give up, even though the very detectives I went to kept telling me it was a waste of my money. I thought each new one I hired would see something that the others had missed."

"It seems you have some thinking to do while I'm gone as well, then," Kiera said. "Perhaps it is a good thing that I'll be away for a few days."

"Don't waste a minute of your trip on any of this, Kiera. Just enjoy yourself. Come back with a hundred photographs on your cell phone and as many stories to tell. I'll be eager to hear them all."

She laughed, the sound far more lighthearted than their conversation up till now. "With my daughter a famous photographer, you think there will only be a hundred photos? I'm counting on her filling albums with pictures from this trip. I'll be wanting to show all my friends back in Dublin."

At the careless mention of Dublin, Bryan felt his heart still. Perhaps all the talk and worry about what the future might hold for the two of them was to be wasted time. It was entirely possible that her mind was set on returning to Ireland and that would end the matter.

Now was not the time for that discussion, though. There would be time to explore all of the difficult questions hanging in the air between them when she returned from San Francisco. And that uncertainty gave him just the excuse he needed to postpone that long-overdue conversation with Connor just a little longer.

Chapter 17

Bryan couldn't seem to shake off his impulsive offer to Kiera to speak to Connor O'Brien about his situation, even though he'd decided the conversation could be postponed. Whether things between him and Kiera moved forward or not, he recognized that something had changed inside him. He was finally ready to put that part of his past behind him. He would never give up looking for his daughter, but the marriage was long dead and he needed to let go of whatever legal ties might still bind him to Melody. He still had a future to live, if only he were free to seize it. If he'd learned nothing else from this time with Kiera, he had learned that. Life didn't end after a tragedy. It was right there, waiting for you to grab it.

A couple nights later when he spotted Connor at the bar in the pub with Mick, Bryan came out of the kitchen and joined them. "Connor, I was wondering if I might have a word with you when you have the time. I'd come by your office, but I'm pretty much chained to this place until Luke gets back to town."

"How about your office, then?" Connor suggested,

gesturing toward the kitchen. "Would that work, or is it too busy in there for you to talk?"

"It's mostly quiet tonight," Bryan said. "I can keep up with the orders while we talk, if you don't mind a few interruptions."

"Heather drops the kids off in my office every now and then just to challenge my ability to concentrate," Connor told him. "It'll be fine."

Back in the kitchen, Bryan made quick work of a couple of orders, then turned to Connor. "This is strictly confidential, right?"

"Of course, though if you want to give me a dollar to retain my services, that will make it official that lawyer-client confidentiality is firmly in place." He shook his head. "I've never entirely understood why that dollar makes people feel more comfortable, but it seems to be reassuring."

Bryan handed over the dollar. "I think I get it. It's symbolic, if nothing else."

"So's a handshake, according to my father," Connor said. "I've seen him make multimillion-dollar development deals on that alone."

"And fifty-cent deals with his grandchildren," Bryan added, laughing. "Okay, here's the situation. I'll give you the short version, and you can ask all the relevant questions about whatever I've skipped over."

"That works for me."

Bryan drew in a deep breath, then summarized the history of his marriage, the birth of his daughter, his wife's abrupt departure and his subsequent futile efforts to find them.

Connor had taken a notebook from his pocket as Bryan talked, searched until he found a pen and then jotted copious notes. "The detectives never found a trace?"

"The trail went cold in Baltimore," Bryan acknowledged. "I moved there from New York, hoping that meant they might still be in the area, but it was a dead end. That was years ago."

"Yet you continued to look?"

"I couldn't give up. I can give you all the canceled checks and the reports from the various detectives," Bryan said. "The last one was dated a month ago. This last one was very thorough. He explored every old lead and even followed up on a couple of new ones he thought he'd found online. He'll tell you himself that it was as if they vanished. I had no idea how easily someone could do that."

"Sounds like your wife must have changed her name," Connor said.

"That's what the detectives concluded, too."

"What exactly do you want me to do?" Connor asked. "Are you looking for another investigator to take on the case?"

Bryan shook his head. "No. What I need to know is the legal status of my marriage. I have no idea how to find that out."

"Given how long ago she left and everything you've told me about the way she vanished, I think we could go to court and make a case that she abandoned you and have the marriage declared invalid."

"Would that be complicated?"

"I don't think so under these circumstances, but I'll find out." Connor's eyes sparkled. "I can't help wondering about something."

"If there's anything you need to know, just ask."

"You've gone for years, apparently content to just let things be. I assume this is suddenly so important to you for a reason."

"It's just time," Bryan said, skirting any deeper reasons.

Connor gave him a knowing look. "In my capacity as your lawyer, I can accept that, if you say that's all it is, but as your friend I have to wonder if Kiera is playing some role in this. Everyone in town is speculating about the two of you."

"Thanks mostly to your grandmother," Bryan said ruefully, avoiding a direct answer. "Nell has everybody fascinated with just about everything we do these days. I swear there are bets being placed at the bar. I think Mick's keeping track of them. Unfortunately, I'm not entirely sure if people are betting on Kiera beating me in the cooking competition or on whether we're going to end up together."

"Truthfully, I think there are odds on both," Connor told him, laughing. "My money's on you winning the bet and Kiera winning you. I'm pretty sure my wife bet exactly the opposite. Just so you know, the odds are pretty even right now."

Bryan sighed. "Good to know." If he found that disconcerting, he could only imagine how Kiera was going to feel about it.

Connor grinned at him. "Surely you've been here long enough to know that my family and people in this town place bets on just about anything. If romance is so much as hinted at, the ante goes up. It's just what we do. No offense is meant."

"None taken, but it does add to the pressure, which is all the more reason to get this marriage situation resolved quickly. Can you help me to figure this out once and for all?"

"Of course," Connor said, his expression sobering. "I'll do a little reading and ask a few colleagues in my old office in Baltimore since I've not handled anything exactly like this before. We'll come up with a solution to clarify your legal status."

"Thanks, Connor."

"Not a problem. It beats trying to get people out of traffic tickets. I love a good legal challenge. They're in short supply in Chesapeake Shores, where most people aren't inclined to sue each other over crazy little disputes." He held Bryan's gaze, his expression even more serious. "I assume the end result you're after is to be free and clear to pursue something with Kiera, right?"

"That, and I'm hoping it will be one more step in helping me to let go of my past, something I should have done years ago."

"Take it from me, a piece of paper doesn't always accomplish that," Connor said. "But I'll do my part to get you to that point."

"All I can ask," Bryan said. The rest would be up to him.

Bryan's text came while Kiera was sitting at the airport waiting for her flight home to Baltimore. After a whirlwind three days in San Francisco, she was surprisingly anxious to get back to Chesapeake Shores despite all the uncertainties awaiting her there.

Relieved that Luke was taking a walk with Kate, she studied the text. Saw Connor tonight. He's looking into things. See you soon. Anxious to hear about the trip.

Kiera stared at the terse message and felt something

shift inside her. If Bryan could, indeed, resolve his marital status once and for all, it would make moot all of those decisions she'd made, then rejected, then made again and again. He would be free and she would have to base her decision on her feelings, not on her perception of right and wrong. Feelings were much trickier than hard truths.

"You look awfully serious," Luke said, sitting down next to her with a sleeping Kate in his arms. "I thought you'd be eager to get home and tell everybody about the trip."

Kiera mustered the smile he obviously expected. "It was a wonderful trip, no question about it. Thank you for making it happen. I'll treasure the memories for years to come, especially the chance to see the Golden Gate Bridge and Fisherman's Wharf, to say nothing of watching my Moira being the center of attention."

"You deserved it. You've been a huge help at the pub and with Kate. I know how much it meant to Moira to have you here for her grand success."

"And you and Kate, too. I know she didn't want to see you leave."

"She understands she has obligations to her career," Luke said. "So do I. And she'll be home in another week. I know how much she hates being away, but I've come to look forward to her homecomings."

Kiera smiled at the unmistakable twinkle in his eyes. "I'm sure you have. Perhaps Kate could have a sleepover at my house when Moira arrives next week."

He laughed. "Now, that would be a true blessing."

"Consider it done."

"In that case, I'll have to see that Megan schedules

another show for Moira soon and we'll take another family trip."

"There won't be time for many more," Kiera said softly. "The fall festival will be taking a lot of time between now and October, and when it's over—"

Luke cut her off. "We'll deal with what's next when the time comes, Kiera. You know you have options. Going back to Ireland isn't the only choice."

She wanted to believe there were real options open to her, but she'd learned not to count on things turning out the way she wanted them to. The simple fact that a tiny part of her was already yearning to stay in Chesapeake Shores was tantamount to tempting fate, which hadn't always been so kind to her.

Worry clouded Luke's expression. "Are you okay?"

"Just overthinking things as I usually do," she said.

He glanced at the phone she was still holding tightly. "Was it bad news that had you looking so troubled when I came back just now? Is that what you're overthinking?"

"To the contrary, I'm not exactly sure what sort of news it was," she confessed.

Luke looked predictably bewildered. "Am I supposed to understand that? It sounds like the sort of thing Moira would expect me to grasp, but also the sort that leaves me clueless."

Kiera chuckled. "I'm not sure how you could possibly understand, when I'm not entirely sure myself what I mean."

"A riddle, then?"

She laughed. "Something like that."

Understanding dawned. "Is Bryan somehow involved?"

"He's at the heart of it, yes," she said, then gave Luke a stern look. "But you are not to be nagging at him about it, is that understood?"

"You're awfully protective of him," Luke observed. "That's a change from a few weeks back."

"I'm protective of our privacy," she corrected.

"But he's done nothing to upset you, nothing I need to address?"

"Nothing," she assured him.

Her son-in-law studied her, then nodded. "Okay, then. Just know I'm on your side."

"There are no sides to be taken," she said firmly. And if there were, she thought, perhaps Bryan could use the support every bit as much as she might need it.

Though it had been clear in Bryan's text that he was anxious to see her, Kiera overslept in the morning, then had to rush to get to a festival committee meeting at Nell's. Bryan was outside waiting for her, pacing in the yard.

"I knocked on your door," he said. "I was worried when you didn't answer."

"Jet lag," she said simply. "I slept like the dead and woke up with barely minutes to spare before coming here."

"We need to talk."

"We need to get inside before Nell comes looking for us," she corrected.

"Then we'll talk on the ride over to the pub after the meeting," Bryan said.

"Is it something that can be discussed in a ten-minute drive?"

He sighed. "I suppose not." He gave her a perplexed

look. "I thought you'd be eager to know about what Connor's found."

Despite her impatience to get inside, Kiera paused long enough to caress his cheek. "I want to hear every word," she assured him. "But when I've had a moment to catch my breath so it can sink in."

Looking relieved, he nodded. "Later, then."

"Definitely later."

But, as it turned out, fate once again had other ideas.

The tall, willowy brunette stood hesitantly in the doorway of O'Brien's. It could have been that her eyes were adjusting to the dim light, but Kiera thought otherwise. It looked more like she hadn't quite made up her mind whether to come inside or to flee. Something in that hesitation made Kiera's pulse skip erratically. Surely this couldn't be... She cut off the ridiculous thought before it could fully form. There was absolutely no reason for her mind to go there, except that Bryan's past had been too much on her mind today.

"May I help you?" she asked, approaching cautiously. "Were you meeting someone here?" Recognition dawned on her. "You were here on the Fourth of July. I told you that you looked familiar, but you said it wasn't possible. It's nice to see you again. We're always happy to see returning customers."

The blue-eyed gaze that met hers was clearly a nervous one. "I'm not here as a customer. Not exactly. I'm looking for someone."

"The friend who was with you that day?"

"No, someone who works here, at least I think he does. It's not an appointment or anything like that. It's someone I've been searching for, and I read an article in a magazine about him. Bryan Laramie. Do you know him? Does he still work here?"

Kiera felt her heart race yet again. Some bit of caution told her to tread carefully, revealing nothing until she was certain about why this young woman was seeking Bryan. Again, that sense of recognition washed over her. It was the eyes, the coloring. The truth was right there in front of her.

"And you are?" she asked, needing confirmation of her suspicion.

"Deanna," the young woman responded. "Deanna Lane."

For just an instant relief flooded through Kiera, but before she could even draw a deep breath, the woman added, "It was Laramie once. Bryan Laramie is my biological father."

She spoke the words as if they were foreign to her, as if she wasn't even a tiny bit comfortable with them and needed the practice of saying them. They hit Kiera with a force that nearly took her breath away. She noted the careful distinction that had been made, too. Not her father, but her *biological* father.

All these years of searching, all the unanswered questions and pain, Kiera could only imagine how Bryan was going to react. At the moment, though, her focus was on this terrified young woman who'd obviously used up the last of her courage to admit the truth.

Instinctively Kiera reached out and gave the girl's shaking hand a quick squeeze. "Come with me. You can sit for a moment and gather your composure. I'll get you something to drink."

"I'm only twenty."

Kiera smiled at the honesty. "And I'm only thinking

a glass of cold water with a bit of lemon. It might settle your nerves while I break the news to your father. It's going to come as quite a shock. This moment is something he's been longing for for a very long time."

The girl looked startled. "You know about me?"

"Just that not a day has gone by in the past nineteen years or so when your father hasn't wondered where you were and how you were doing."

Deanna frowned at that, disbelief in her eyes. "Then why has he never come looking?"

"I believe you'll find that's not true, but it's something for the two of you to discuss. I've already said more than enough." She led the way to a table in a darkened corner where the two could have some privacy, brought the tall glass of water and once more patted the girl's hand. It was cold as ice. "Try to take a deep breath and relax. I'll be right back."

In the doorway to the kitchen, she drew a deep breath of her own and gestured for Bryan to disconnect the call he was on. "In a minute," he said impatiently.

"Now!" she said just as firmly. "There's someone here to see you, Bryan. And it can't wait."

He seemed about to argue that there was no time for visiting, but she held up a hand. "Tell whoever you're speaking to that you'll call back, most likely not until tomorrow. You'll need to take the time for this." She leveled a look into his eyes. "Trust me on this."

He searched her face and must have found something there that told him the seriousness of the situation. He murmured an excuse to the person on the phone, then crossed the kitchen to look deep into her eyes.

"Why the fuss? Is it a problem? Where's Luke?"

"The person is here to see you, not Luke." She

touched his cheek. "It's a moment you've been dreaming of."

His eyes widened at that, and the color drained from his face. "Kiera, what are you telling me?" he asked, his voice shaky.

"She's here, Bryan. Your daughter is here."

"Deanna?" He looked as if he hardly dared to believe it might be true after all these years of fruitless searching. "Truly? You're sure?"

"So she says. And she looks enough like you that I believe her. Now, go. Don't keep the poor girl waiting. She's a bundle of nerves."

Kiera stood aside, wishing she had the right to give his hand a squeeze as she had his daughter's, but he brushed past her, then came to a sudden halt. He glanced back.

"What do I say?"

"Start with hello," she said softly. "You'll go on from there."

But hearing the hurt and pain, the accusatory note, in Deanna's voice earlier suggested it wouldn't go so smoothly after that.

As he approached the table where his daughter sat, Bryan felt as if his whole life came down to this single instant. After years of searching, years of hoping and dreaming about this moment, he wanted desperately to get it exactly right. He stood in the shadows, drinking in the sight of this young woman who bore no resemblance to the baby he'd last held in his arms so many years ago.

Instead, she had her mother's wavy hair, though it was the color of his. She had a slender grace, a chin that had a belligerent tilt to it, also reminiscent of her mother. He had no doubt that if he could see her eyes clearly, they'd have her mother's fiery temper flashing in them, as well.

He drew in a calming breath and took the few remaining steps that brought him into her line of sight. "Dee?"

"Mr. Laramie?"

He winced at the formality, the icy tone. "I'm your father, yes. I'd recognize you anywhere. You look exactly as your mother did at your age."

"You're not my father, not in any way that counts," she said, though her voice faltered a bit as if the words and tone had been rehearsed, but didn't fit comfortably now that she was face-to-face with him. Steadying herself, she added more forcefully, "Ashton Lane is the only father I've ever known."

In an instant, Bryan hated this Ashton Lane, the man who'd taken his place in his daughter's life. Railing against him, though, trying to claim his rightful place in her life, wouldn't get them anywhere right now. He prayed for the wisdom to choose his words carefully.

"If that's so, what brought you here?" Bryan asked, trying to hide the pain her words caused him. None of this was her fault. She'd been little more than a baby when her mother had taken her and left.

She clung to her glass of water with a death grip, her gaze on everything in the room except him. "Ash said I should find you, that I'd never be able to move on with my life until I understood how you could abandon us. My mom and me, I mean."

Bryan's temper stirred, but he managed to keep his voice even. "Is that what your mother told you, that I'd abandoned the two of you?"

"It's what happened," she said flatly. "I don't remember you at all. You never sent a single birthday card or Christmas gift. You never paid support." The heat in her voice climbed. "What kind of man does that? What kind of man simply walks away from his wife and child?"

There were years of pent-up emotion behind the accusations, emotions she probably didn't even want to acknowledge, but it told Bryan quite a lot. Whether she wanted to admit that she'd thought about him or not, he'd been on her mind, if only as an elusive concept. And, with either erroneous information from her mother or from her own imagination, every scenario she'd imagined had left him as the bad guy.

Bryan recognized that the angry denials he wanted to utter would only escalate the situation. He took a moment to let his temper cool. Now that she'd said her piece, Deanna seemed suddenly deflated. Perhaps she'd been expecting outrage, after all.

"That's not how it was," he said quietly, pulling out a chair and sitting down to face her. He waited until she met his gaze. "If that's what you were told, I'm sorry to say, it was a lie."

"My mother didn't lie," she said, but the anger had gone out of her voice, leaving a faint question mark in its place.

"Not typically, no," he agreed, because that much was true. The Melody he knew had always been brutally honest. "But in this case, she did," he said evenly, holding her gaze. "And if you like, if you'll keep an open mind, I can prove it."

"How? With a bunch of lies of your own? Why would I ever believe you?"

"I think you want to," he said, understanding that

most of all she needed reassurance. After years of believing she'd been abandoned, how could she be anything except angry and cautious? "I think that's really why you came, to hear my side of things. Isn't that true?"

"I guess," she said, a little of the belligerence fading.

"The reality is that you don't know me at all. And I totally get that. I don't expect you to believe something just because I say it's true," he assured her. "But I assume you're not the kind of person who would dispute facts that you can see in black and white. You can look at my proof, then ask your mother if I'm the one who's lying."

Tears welled in her eyes then. "My mother is dead."

The cold, hard truth blurted out like that shook Bryan. It felt as if it was the second time in his life he'd lost the same woman. This time, though, it came with an undeniable finality. Right now he couldn't even think about what that might mean for his own future. He had to deal with the undeniable pain that truth was causing his daughter.

"I'm sorry, Dee. I'm so, so sorry."

"Why would you be sorry? You walked out on her a long time ago. You never loved her."

Proving that he'd searched for his wife and their baby girl wasn't the same as trying to prove that his feelings had run deep and true. He had police reports, bills from private detectives that stated clearly just how long he'd looked for his family. Feelings couldn't be so easily confirmed.

"Dee, what is it you really need to hear from me? What did you come here to learn? Or did you only come to hurl accusations, say all the things you've wanted to say to me over the years?"

More tears spilled down her cheeks at that. "I don't know," she admitted, her voice cracking. "Everybody kept telling me I needed to do this. They had a whole long list of reasons, some practical like getting a medical history, some emotional like making peace with my past. I've been told I have abandonment issues, though I don't see how that can be since I don't even remember you. And I have a dad, so it can't be that I needed another one."

"I can only imagine how confusing it must be," he said, hearing the confusion in her voice, the longing to make sense of things. "I've wanted to find you for years because a piece of my heart was missing, but now that you're here I can barely find the right words to say. You said the man you consider to be your father convinced you to come."

"In a way. When Ash told me he knew where you were and that he thought I should come, I felt like it was inevitable, you know?"

"Where have you been living all these years?"

"In Richmond."

He thought the terse response was the end of it, but then she added with a hint of pride, "I'm going to school at the University of Virginia in Charlottesville, though, and this summer I got an internship in a medical research program at Johns Hopkins."

"Brains and beauty," he said lightly. "I'm impressed."

She smiled then, and it lit up her face. "That's what Ash says all the time. Ever since I got to Johns Hopkins I've been trying to work up the courage to meet you. I even came here twice. The first time I just sat across the street, hoping you'd come outside. The last time was on the Fourth of July. I came in with a friend, but we didn't stay. I was too nervous to eat. He got our dinner to go. It was delicious, by the way."

Now it was Bryan's turn to smile. "Thank you."

She regarded him nervously. "Was it a mistake, my coming here? Am I turning your life upside down or anything?"

"Not from my point of view," Bryan assured her. "I've been longing for this moment since the day you and your mom left. Will you see this through? Will you stick around and let me show you proof that I spent years looking for you and your mother? Will you listen to what really happened?"

He hated the pleading note in his voice, but he knew he couldn't let her go without fighting for this one chance to make things right, to correct the record, at least.

"I didn't really plan ahead," she said. "I was going to come on the weekend, but I couldn't make myself do it. Again," she added ruefully. "But when I got up this morning, I made up my mind that it was time. I took the day off at work, but that was as much planning as I did. I don't have a place to stay."

"I have a guest room—"

"No." She shut down that idea immediately.

Kiera appeared just then. It was apparent she'd been hovering nearby. For once he welcomed her uncanny knack for knowing when she might be needed.

"Deanna, would you be needing a place to stay for a night or two?" she asked gently. "My cottage is very close to your dad's, but it would give you some space for your thoughts to settle."

"It's an excellent solution," Bryan said, giving her a grateful look. "Will you consider that, Dee? A day or two's not long. We'll only have a start toward getting all the answers we both need, but it's an excellent beginning."

Deanna's gaze held Kiera's. "Are you sure I won't be an imposition?"

"Not at all," Kiera said. "I can take you there now and you can have a bit of a rest."

"And I'll stop by as soon as I get through the dinner rush here," Bryan said. "If there were some way for me to leave now, I would."

He waited for what seemed an eternity as his daughter weighed her options.

"I'll stay," she said at last. "But just for tonight. I need to go back to work tomorrow morning. This summer job is a volunteer internship, but it's important. I don't want them to think I'm irresponsible. And you should stay and finish here for the same reason. If Kiera doesn't mind my staying with her, I could use a little time to let this sink in." She gave him an odd look. "I thought you'd ask me to prove who I am."

He smiled at that. "Even Kiera saw the resemblance, Dee. There was no need for proof."

She pulled a picture out of her purse and handed it to him just the same. "Ash found this recently and sent it to me. I'd not seen it before. It's the only picture my mother kept of the two of us."

Bryan looked at the faded photograph and remembered precisely when it had been taken, on a rare day they'd spent at the park with a picnic. His eyes welled with tears.

"You remember it?" Dee asked.

Bryan nodded. "I have others I'll show you. They're worn on the edges from my looking at them so often. Thank you for agreeing to stay for the night. There's so much I want to know."

"Come along, child," Kiera said.

As the two of them left, Bryan stared after them with a sense of wonder. It wasn't just seeing his daughter for the first time in all these years. It was seeing this entirely new side of Kiera, a woman with compassion and understanding, who'd given him the gift of time to make things right with Deanna.

Chapter 18

"Bryan has a daughter and you knew about it?" Moira was practically shouting in Kiera's ear, her shock and dismay evident. "Yet you never said a word."

"Because it wasn't my news to share," Kiera told her quietly. "And I really can't discuss this now. I'm trying to get Deanna settled in the guest room. Luke's given me the night off to help out. He would have given Bryan the night off, but we agreed that my offering to take over in the kitchen for him, even under these circumstances, wouldn't help the situation given how touchy Bryan is about my invading his space."

"Hold on!" Moira commanded. "She's staying with you?"

"For tonight, anyway. She and Bryan need some time to figure things out."

"Tell me this much at least, because my conversation with Luke was completely unsatisfactory. Unlike the other O'Briens, he doesn't always get the details of the latest gossip straight."

Kiera laughed despite herself. "Be thankful for that. It's enough that Mick has a corner on spreading the gossip."

"Did Bryan know he had a daughter, or did this come as a complete shock to him?" Moira asked. "And where's the mother? Is he married?"

"He knew. It's a very long story, but he's been searching for her for years. He'd only recently given up hope of finding her. And, yes, he was married to her mother."

"They're divorced, then?"

"No, Moira, there was no divorce." At her daughter's dismayed gasp, she said, "I am not getting into this with you now. There's a lot that's yet to be sorted out."

"I can't believe you would do such a thing. You've been getting serious about a man who's still married? You, who always gave us these long lectures about values and such."

Kiera sighed. It was true that she'd tried to teach her children right from wrong, and dating someone married to someone else certainly fell into the forbidden category. None of her lectures had taken serious hold with her sons, but apparently Moira, at least, had heard them well enough to be throwing them back in her face now.

"Moira, not now. I really have to go. If things work out and Bryan can persuade his daughter to come here more often, then you'll meet Deanna for yourself when you get home. At the least there will be answers to all your questions and explanations if you feel you're owed those, too."

Unfortunately, given the tension earlier in the day between Bryan and his daughter and the complexity of the situation, Kiera thought that was simply wishful thinking on her part.

Taking a page from Nell's book, Kiera set about making tea and baking a batch of scones. They wouldn't measure up to anything Nell might make, but the aroma would make the kitchen especially cozy and perhaps make Deanna feel a little more comfortable. She'd just pulled the scones from the oven, when Deanna came in looking refreshed after a shower and hopefully a bit of a nap.

"How are you feeling?" Kiera asked.

"As if I've been put through a wringer," Deanna admitted. "I knew today wouldn't be easy, but I didn't expect it to be so emotional. I felt as if I was being torn between two people, two very different truths. Three, if I add Ash into the mix. Thank you for offering to let me stay here so I've time to sort them out."

"Let that be a lesson, then," Kiera told her gently, setting a steaming cup of tea before her, and then sitting herself. "Every story has two sides, perhaps more. You'd do well to listen to all of them with an open heart and reach your own conclusion about the truth. It's often somewhere in the middle."

"In the gray area," Deanna suggested with a faint smile. "That's what Ash is always telling me, when I'm looking for black-and-white truths."

"He sounds like a wise man."

"He's great," Deanna said enthusiastically. "He really is, but I've been awfully hard on him lately since some things about this situation have come to light. I've felt betrayed and taken it out on him, partly because it's hard to blame my mom now that she's gone."

"And you adored her," Kiera said, seeing it in Deanna's eyes, hearing it in her voice. "You thought she could do no wrong."

Deanna nodded, looking chagrined. "But, of course, everybody can make mistakes."

"And still be a fine person," Kiera suggested.

Deanna took a sip of her tea, her expression thoughtful. "You believe my dad's version of what happened, don't you?"

"I have no reason not to," Kiera said, then felt compelled to add, "But I wasn't there, Deanna, so I'm basing that on my experience with your father. He's been honest with me. He told me all about your mother leaving, about his search for the two of you. He's not spared himself in the telling, either, admitting to the mistakes he made."

"And about never getting a divorce?" she asked skeptically. "I'll bet he never mentioned that."

"Actually he did."

Deanna looked surprised. "That's more than my mother and Ash ever told me. I was still very young when they got together. I thought they'd married, maybe eloped or something, and that I'd been adopted by Ash. Instead, they just had our names changed legally. Why do you suppose my mom let me believe such a huge lie?"

"Perhaps she didn't know how to tell you the truth or were afraid you'd judge her for the decisions she'd made."

"I suppose. Ash thought she was afraid my dad would find us if she went to court to file for divorce, but I don't think it was because she was scared of him."

"Perhaps she was afraid she wasn't immune to him and he'd try to persuade her to come home, back to a time when she'd been unhappy."

Deanna nodded slowly. "Maybe. I wish I knew for sure what she was thinking."

"Someday you'll need to accept that you'll never

know. Even if she were right here in this room, she might not be able to explain it herself. People make rash decisions all the time based on reasons that aren't totally clear, even to them. Then they try to justify them."

Deanna gave her a weary look. "Life's complicated, isn't it?"

Kiera laughed. "You have no idea. It can take a lifetime to figure it out, and then you might only understand the half of it."

Deanna focused on the scone that Kiera had put in front of her. She broke off a piece, tasted it, then took another bite. Eventually she asked, "How long have you known him? My father, I mean."

"Only a few months really. I came here from Ireland to visit my daughter and my father, who are living here now. My daughter's husband owns the pub where Bryan and I work."

"He's the O'Brien, then?"

"One of many of them. It's his family that the pub is named for."

"How on earth did my father wind up working in Chesapeake Shores? I always thought he was in New York."

"Something for him to explain, if you'll let him."

"Do I have a choice? I've come this far. I can't leave without knowing all of it."

"That's an open-minded way of looking at it," Kiera told her. "Would you like another cup of tea and another of these scones, since you've mostly crumbled the first one to bits? I'm more of a cook than a baker, but the scones aren't so terrible, are they?"

"It's delicious, actually," Deanna said with an apologetic shrug as she looked at the plate of mostly crumbs in front of her. "I just don't have much of an appetite right now. But I will take more tea."

Kiera poured the tea, then sat across from her once again.

"Who's the better cook, you or my father?" Deanna asked. Her eyes suddenly lit up. "Wait! When Milos and I were here on the Fourth, we got a flyer about a cooking competition. The two of you are going head-to-head with your Irish stew, aren't you?"

"That's the plan," Kiera admitted. "It's not a position either of us was eager to be in, but apparently our competitive spirit in the kitchen is well-known. There are some who'd take advantage of that to ensure a big crowd at the fall festival."

"It sounds like fun."

"Perhaps you can come back for it."

"I'll be back in Charlottesville in school by then," she said.

She sounded a little bit disappointed by the thought of missing it. Another good sign, Kiera thought, along with all the questions she had for her father and her apparent willingness to listen to his answers.

"I'm not certain of the geography, but is it so far?" Kiera asked.

"Not really, come to think of it. I'll mark my calendar." She took out her cell phone, then looked at Kiera expectantly. Kiera gave her the October festival dates.

"And will you be on my side or your father's?" Kiera teased. "Will family loyalty win out? Or can you be an impartial judge?"

"If your stew is the best, it will get my vote," Deanna promised, just as Bryan tapped on the door, then walked into the kitchen carrying a cardboard box.

"Did I just hear that Kiera's gotten you to take her side in that foolish contest?" he grumbled.

Deanna chuckled. "Kiera said you two were highly competitive. I think I see that. My mother always said I'd take any bet offered. I must have gotten that from you."

"There are better traits you could have inherited," Bryan said, placing the box on the table in front of her.

"What's in here?" Deanna asked, studying it curiously.

"The photos I mentioned to you and the record of every step I took to track you down. I had to have my attorney bring it by the pub."

She peeked inside the box. "There's so much."

"Every investigator report, every police report, the court documents and all of the checks paying for the search."

She glanced at the file on top. "This was only a month ago."

Bryan nodded. "I never gave up, Dee, not even after several investigators told me repeatedly that it was as if the two of you vanished."

She frowned at that. "Are you saying that my mother took me and just left without a word?"

Bryan nodded, then sat. Kiera gave his shoulder a squeeze.

"Would you like me to leave the two of you alone?"

"No," they said in unison.

"I'd like you to be here," Deanna said. "Please."

Kiera gave Bryan a questioning look, but he nodded readily.

"Okay, then," she said, pulling her chair a bit away from the table in an attempt to be less intrusive.

"Why would she leave like that?" Deanna asked.

Bryan explained what their life had been like back then, the long hours at the restaurant, his wife's growing restlessness. Being home alone most of the time with a newborn baby and no family nearby… "I had every intention of cutting back, spending more time at home, but I kept delaying it. One day she simply tired of our life, of fighting to make me see her point of view. In what may have been an act of spite, she took you and left. I don't know if her intent was to punish me by never getting in touch, but that's how it turned out. Maybe it was a test to see how hard I'd try to find you, but then she made it all but impossible."

"When we changed our name," Deanna concluded. "You should probably know that she and Ash never actually married. I just found out that was a lie, too. She'd never divorced you. Ash knew, but somehow they got our last name legally changed to his. It seems most of my life was based on lies."

"One thing wasn't a lie," Kiera said gently, trying to ease the pain she could hear in the girl's voice. "You had people in your life who loved you unconditionally, even the father you hadn't seen since you were a baby."

Deanna's expression brightened. "I need to focus on that, don't I? And let the lies go. I think that's what Ash wanted me to do, too."

"He sounds like a good man," Bryan said. "I'm glad you had him in your life."

"Even though he was never legally my stepfather, I thought he was, and he was the best possible kind of stepfather. I think he'd like you. You've handled me turning up like this with real kindness, even when I was ranting at you."

Bryan smiled. "You're entitled to a good rant or two."

"So are you," she said. "I'm just starting to see that. You lost so much more than I did, didn't you? A wife and a baby you loved, while I had a whole family."

"But now you're back in my life," Bryan said. "I hope you'll come back to visit so we can get to know each other. I really want that second chance for us." When she was about to speak, he held up his hand. "Just think about it. I'm not going to push, at least not as long as you'll tell me how to find you if you stay away too long."

She smiled at that and reached for his cell phone. "There," she said after a couple of minutes of concentration. "All of my information is in your contacts list."

Kiera watched as relief spread across Bryan's face.

"Now, why don't I fix dinner at my place for all of us?" he suggested. "It's late, so I'll make something light."

Deanna shook her head. "It's been an emotional day and it is late. I need to get an early start back to Baltimore in the morning." She lifted a hesitant gaze to his. "Next time? I tasted your food at the pub, but I'd love to have you cook just for me."

Though there was disappointment in his expression, he nodded. "Next time," he agreed. "You'll come next door to say goodbye in the morning?"

"Absolutely. Now, though, I'm going to bed. It's been a long day."

"Good night, Deanna. Sleep well," Kiera said.

"Good night, Dee," Bryan said, his voice choked.

When his daughter left the room, he reached for Kiera's hand. She saw the sheen of tears in his eyes.

"I honestly never thought this day would come," he said.

"And now it has, and with the promise of more," Kiera told him.

"You think she'll keep her promise, that she'll come back?"

"I think she would never have said it if she didn't mean it," Kiera assured him. "Whatever else happened in the past, I think your wife raised a fine young woman. I think you should both be proud of how well she handled today. It couldn't have been easy for her, coming here all on her own to confront you with the only truth she knew."

Bryan smiled. "She held her ground, didn't she?"

"But she also opened her heart, when facts were presented."

"It's only the beginning," he said. "There's so much more I want to know about her. If she has this summer internship at Johns Hopkins, she must be incredibly smart. I want to know about her other interests, too, if there are young men in her life, what her favorite foods are, all of it. I missed so much, Kiera."

"And now you'll have the time to discover every bit of it," Kiera promised. Something told her that Deanna was not one to go back on her promises.

Bryan was on his deck at dawn, coffee made, a batch of chocolate chip muffins fresh from the oven on a plate beside him. He wasn't taking any chances on Deanna leaving town without a goodbye.

He heard a car door open and close quietly in the driveway and held his breath until she came into view.

"How'd you sleep?" he asked.

"Soundly," she said. "You?"

He laughed. "Not a wink. Too much to think about."

"I know. My mind was whirling, too, but I managed to shut it off. Meditation helps."

"I'll have to try that. Would you like some coffee?"

"Of course," she said. "Is there enough to put some in my travel mug for the drive?"

"There's plenty."

She poured the coffee, then peeked under the foil that covered the plate beside it. She turned her surprised gaze on him. "Chocolate chip muffins are my favorite. How on earth did you know?"

"I took a chance that they might be. I used to make them on Sunday mornings," he said. "They were your mom's favorite, too. She fed you bits of them when you were just starting to eat solid food. Of course, you couldn't resist smushing the warm chocolate all over your face."

She laughed. "I'm not so messy anymore, and I never waste chocolate."

"I'll pack these up so you can take them home with you," he said.

"I really should hit the road."

"Of course," he said, though he wanted to beg her to stay and talk.

"May I come back?"

"Anytime you want to," he said, relieved that she'd asked.

"That's what Kiera said, too. She said the guest room was mine whenever I wanted it. I thought I might come back next weekend, if I can work it out."

"Call me if you decide you can make it. I'll try to take the day off. I can show you around Chesapeake Shores."

"I was thinking it might be fun to hang out at the pub

and watch you cook. Kiera said she thought it would be okay. I should learn how to make something in the kitchen besides soup and grilled cheese sandwiches. And it would be something we could do together."

Bryan was more pleased than he wanted to admit that she wanted to be a part of his world. "That works, too. Grilled cheese was your mother's specialty, too, as I recall."

"She got better with other things over time," Deanna told him. "But she obviously didn't love cooking the way you do."

He stood up, took the muffins into the kitchen and packed them in a container, then handed them to Deanna, who'd followed him inside and was looking around curiously.

"How long have you lived here?"

"A few years. Why?"

"Because it's way too sterile. It looks like you just moved in. Even Kiera's kitchen looks homier, and she's only been there a couple of months."

Bryan realized then that he'd never entirely thought of this or any other place as home. He shrugged. "I'm a man. It doesn't take much for us to be comfortable."

"Maybe so, but this is pitiful. I'll work on it," she told him matter-of-factly.

Bryan hid a smile. If it meant she'd be back, she could decorate the whole house in lace and crocheted doilies for all he cared.

Though she was dying to be a fly on the wall while Bryan was with his daughter this morning, Kiera waited patiently until she heard Deanna's car drive off before walking across the lawn to his house. She found him standing at the end of the driveway, staring after the car that had long since left the lane and turned onto the main road.

"She'll be back," she said, slipping her hand into his.

"I know. I'm just standing here marveling at the fact that she was here at all." He turned anxiously to Kiera. "It went well, didn't it?"

"All things considered, I'd say it was a success."

"She wants to decorate my house. She says it's 'pitiful.'"

Kiera laughed. "Are you complaining?"

"Not in the slightest," he said happily. "I'll hand over a fortune so she can do whatever she wants."

"Leave her to do it her way. I don't think she needs your money to make it cozy."

"There's coffee," he told her. "And I saved you a muffin. It seems memory served me well. I baked her favorite and sent her off with most of them."

"Do you feel like talking, then?"

"I want to go over every minute until I believe it truly happened," he admitted.

"Then that's what we'll do," she said readily.

He turned to her. "First, though, there's this." He pulled her into his arms and kissed her slowly and thoroughly.

Kiera laughed when he released her. "That was lovely. What brought it on?"

"Knowing that I'm free to do it as often as I'd like and as often as you'll let me."

She lifted a hand to his cheek. "I thought perhaps the news that Deanna's mother had died would affect you differently."

Bryan climbed the steps to the deck slowly, his expression thoughtful. "It came as a shock," he admitted. "And I'm truly sad for Deanna and for the man who loved the two of them and kept them safe all these years." He met Kiera's gaze. "But I stopped loving Melody a long time ago. My feelings were all twisted up with anger and resentment. When Deanna blurted out the news, all I felt was relief that there was finally an end to the wondering and waiting and praying." His smile held just a hint of sorrow as he added, "It's probably wrong of me, but it brought the clarity I needed, that *we* needed."

"Bryan, even so, we don't know what the future holds for us," she cautioned him.

"No, but at least we're free to discover where it might lead. I'm anxious to get started with that. Aren't you?"

Kiera had mixed feelings, if she was being honest. It seemed he was ready to rush forward, while she preferred the snail's pace they'd been taking. The roadblock of his marriage had been more of a convenience to her than she'd realized or dared to reveal to him now.

She caught him studying her, his expression confused. "You don't seem nearly as happy about this turn of events as I am."

"It's hard to be happy about someone conveniently dying," she said tartly.

He regarded her with shock. "That's not it at all, Kiera. Surely you know I'm not that hard-hearted."

She sighed. "I do know that. I just meant that the news is still fresh. I think you need to take a few minutes, at least, to grapple with it."

"Something tells me you're the one who wants the time," he said slowly. "What I'm less sure of is why."

"You've known from the beginning that I'm not the

kind to rush into these things. I never expected to be in this position at all."

"I see," he said slowly.

"Bryan, I care for you. You know I do."

"But now that there's the possibility of it turning into something real, you're scared," he concluded.

"Terrified," she admitted.

"So am I," he told her. "I have even less experience with relationships than you do, but at least I'm willing to take a risk."

"And I need time," Kiera said. "Can't you give me that?"

"If it's what you need, then it seems I have little choice," he told her. "But I've studied the calendar, Kiera. Time is the one thing we have very little of."

Her heart sank at his words, because he was right. Time was not on their side. The fall festival would be here before either of them knew it. Her visa would expire and she would head back to Dublin.

And unless she found some way to be as courageous as Bryan, it was very likely she'd be going home with her heart broken. Again.

Chapter 19

Nell studied Kiera's expression as they waited for the others to arrive for the fall festival committee meeting. She looked as if the weight of the world were on her shoulders, not at all the way a woman should be feeling if things were progressing nicely with the man in her life.

"Problems?" she asked carefully.

Kiera blinked at the question, then shook her head. "Not really."

"I heard about Bryan's daughter showing up out of the blue. That must have been a shock."

"A happy one," Kiera said, sounding as if she truly meant it. "He's over the moon to have the chance to get to know her after all these years of searching for her."

"And is that taking all of his time?"

"Not at all. And she's a lovely young woman," Kiera added with unforced enthusiasm. "I spoke to her just last night. She's very excited to be coming back on Saturday for another visit. She'll stay with me."

"With you? Why is that?"

"I think she feels more comfortable having a safe refuge just now, a little distance from this man she doesn't even remember. This is a very emotional time for both of them."

"And you don't mind?" Nell prodded, never sure when she might cross a line and stir Kiera's temper. It was every bit as mercurial as Moira's. How they'd both descended from a man as easygoing as Dillon was a mystery.

"Not a bit," Kiera said with a hint of amusement as if she saw right through Nell's cautious questioning, but was willing to endure it to stay away from even trickier turf.

"She's an easy guest," Kiera continued. "And I want to do whatever I can to ease the way for the two of them. I feel a great deal of compassion for both of them. I know how difficult it is to work through an emotional minefield with family you barely know. It took my father and me quite a while to mend fences and feel comfortable with one another, as you well know."

"Still, this reunion of theirs must leave less time for you and Bryan to figure out things between the two of you," Nell persisted. "It's an awkward time to have a third person underfoot."

"There's nothing to be figured out," Kiera said, her tone going flat and defiant.

And there it was, Nell thought with a sense of triumph at the revealing flash of temper in Kiera's eyes. It practically dared Nell to keep probing, but she knew when to end a game as well as she knew how to begin it. She resolved to turn the questioning over to Dillon. Perhaps he could get to the bottom of whatever was bothering his daughter. Despite Kiera's cheerful words about Bryan and his daughter, Nell sensed there was some resentment there. This was the Kiera of old, a hint of bitterness just below the surface. Of course, if she were right, Dillon might very well blunder in and make a mess of it. She'd need to do some careful coaching before sending him on the mission.

"Where are the others?" Kiera asked with a trace of impatience. "I thought we were to begin at nine."

"Nine thirty," Nell corrected, not mentioning that she'd deliberately given Kiera an earlier time to allow for this conversation that was going absolutely nowhere.

"Ah, there they are now," she said, relieved to hear her granddaughter and the others coming in the door. She took note of Kiera's unmistakable disappointment that Bryan wasn't among them. He'd begged off this morning and, since it had suited Nell's purposes, she'd let him.

"Okay, now that we're all here, Luke—why don't you tell us how the cooking competition is shaping up," Nell said enthusiastically, deliberately turning her attention away from Kiera and onto business.

"I know it's the talk of Sally's," Bree said. "Every time I go in there, someone's pulling me aside to find out how it's going. They each have an opinion about whether Bryan or Kiera will win their ethnic main dish category. The split's about fifty-fifty. Some are loyal to Bryan because they know him and have tasted his stew at the pub. Others think Kiera has the edge because of her heritage and her ties to us."

"It's the same at my bookstore," Shanna said.

"And at the quilt shop," Heather added. "In fact, I had an idea. To be sure that all of these people show up for the actual competition and participate in the tastings, why don't we come up with the tokens or coupons or whatever we're going to use and start selling them in advance in all the shops?"

Luke's expression brightened. "I know I could sell a lot at the pub. All of our customers, even the ones just visiting town, are excited about it. They've gotten into the spirit of the competition because they've met both Kiera and Bryan. And some know the other chefs who are participating, too. They might well be drawn back for the festival."

"Fantastic," Nell enthused. "Shanna, could you look into getting something printed, either tokens or coupons, whatever the printer can come up with. Use your powers of persuasion to see if they'll give us a discount."

"Of course," Shanna said at once. "Mack might even be able to do them at the newspaper. I know he'd donate them."

"Of course he would," Bree said. "He'll do anything for Gram. If need be, we can put cousin Susie on the case. He hasn't been able to deny her anything since the day they got married. And now that they've adopted their little girl, he just wanders around in a happy daze all the time."

Nell nodded, pleased with the enthusiasm she was hearing. "Luke, how many chefs were you able to persuade to participate?"

"Counting Bryan, we have ten from around the region, including Baltimore and Washington—and Bryan even recruited an old culinary school friend who has a restaurant in northern Virginia. The entire region will be well represented and their customers might be lured here to support them. It's a much better response than

I'd hoped for. I thought that would be enough for the first year," Luke reported.

"Excellent," Nell said. "And publicity? How's that coming?"

"I've posted the list on the festival website, the town's site, the pub's website, and Mack has put it in the upcoming events section on his newspaper website, too," Luke told them. "We probably have at least two or three challengers for every one of the professionals."

Nell chuckled at his enthusiasm. For a man who'd been reluctant to get involved, he'd done very nicely. "You've done good work, Luke."

"That's not all," he said. "I talked to an appliance store about hooking up stoves that day in return for a sponsorship listing in all the advertising. They're in and will even donate a couple of the high-end models for a silent auction. We'll have a huge tent on the green with the stoves around the perimeter so people can watch the cooking. The tasting tables will be just outside along with the jars for casting votes. I think it's all coming together."

He sat back, grinning as the others applauded.

"Don't be so smug," Bree taunted. "Next year, we'll just put you in charge of all of it. You're proving to be a worthy successor to Gram."

His grin faltered at that. "No way. This is a one-time thing for me."

"We'll see," Bree said. She turned to Kiera. "Kiera, have you been testing your recipe? We'll all come by the cottage one night if you want to try it out on us."

Kiera looked startled, as if she'd been only half listening. "To be honest I hadn't thought of practicing. I've been making my Irish stew all my life."

"It might not hurt to do a run-through, though," Bree said. "When was the last time you made it for hundreds of people?"

Kiera blinked. There was no mistaking the sudden panic in her eyes. "Hundreds of people? I thought there were only a few judges."

"We did talk about that," Nell acknowledged quickly, "but then we decided it would be more fun if everyone had a chance to vote for their favorite."

"And if Gram has anything to say about it, the crowds will be double or triple past years'," Luke said. "She's promoting this thing all over the region. I heard it on a Baltimore radio station the other day. To be sure, we'll only be giving each person a small sample, but it will add up before the day is done."

"Oh dear," Kiera whispered. "Do the others know this?"

"Bryan does," Luke said. "He was there when the announcement came on, but he's used to cooking for a crowd. He took it in stride."

Kiera drew in a deep breath. "Then I suppose I'd better be prepared," she said stoically. "Bree, everyone, would one night next week work? I'm off on Tuesday."

"Then Tuesday it is," Bree said readily. "Everybody in?"

"I'll be there," Heather said eagerly. "I'm dying to see if I'm getting any better at detecting the spices in things. Yours may differ from what Bryan uses."

"But there will be no discussion of that in front of Kiera," Nell said sternly. "Or in front of Bryan. That would amount to giving away insider information."

"Not a word," Heather promised.

"I'll be there, too," Shanna said.

"What about me?" Luke asked. "Aren't I invited?"

"Something tells me you might be in the enemy camp," Bree told him. "I think we'll make this a girls' night. Gram, are you coming?"

"I'll be there," Nell said. "Luke, you'll tell Moira?"

"I can tell her," Kiera said. "I'm with Bree. I'm not entirely sure where Luke's loyalties lie."

"Hey, you're my mother-in-law. You're family," Luke protested indignantly.

"But your pub's reputation is at stake," Bree taunted. "That makes you suspect."

Luke glanced from one woman to the next, then turned to Nell. "Now see what you've done, Gram? It wasn't enough that you stirred up my staff, but now you've got my family divided."

"All in the name of a good cause," Nell said blithely. "And it seems to me things are going along swimmingly."

Kiera's sigh was loud enough to be heard over the laughter. They all turned in her direction. She shrugged off the attention. "I'm just thinking that Nell's playing a little fast and loose with the definition of *swimmingly.*"

Kiera walked into the pub after the disconcerting meeting at Nell's to find Mick seated on his favorite stool at the bar. Since it was only lunchtime, his presence was suspicious. And when he hastily jammed something into his pocket and the man talking to him darted away, her suspicions deepened.

"Mr. Pennington seemed to be in a bit of a hurry," she said mildly. "And you're here much earlier than usual."

"Just catching up with a few people," Mick said.

"And that paper you were quick to hide from me, what was that about?"

"Just a little business."

"You and Mr. Pennington, a man in his eighties, are involved in a business venture?"

Mick managed to keep his gaze steady. "We are."

"Is he building a new house? Wouldn't that be your specialty? Or perhaps he's putting on an addition to that lovely home of his a few blocks from here, the one that's been in his family for two generations? Is it in need of renovations?"

"It's not that sort of business."

Kiera put her hands on her hips and faced him down. She had to give him credit for his steady nerves. He never once so much as blinked.

"Mick O'Brien, are you in here taking bets on this cooking competition? What would the police think about your being involved in some sort of illegal gambling? You're a pillar of the community."

"Call the chief and ask him," Mick encouraged, a grin spreading across his face. "I have a record of his bet right here in my pocket. And you might not want to be so high and mighty with him. He put his money on you."

Kiera groaned. "You're incorrigible."

"If you'd asked Megan, she would have told you that when you first arrived in town."

She marched past him and went into the kitchen, where Bryan was busy chopping herbs he'd brought from his garden.

"Do you realize that Mick is out there taking bets right under our noses?"

Bryan laughed. "And this is the first time you've noticed it?"

"As a matter of fact, yes. And where were you this morning? You missed the committee meeting."

"You would have known that I was going to see one of our produce suppliers if you hadn't taken off so early," he said mildly. "I stopped by to give you a lift to Nell's on my way into town." He practically pushed her down onto a stool and set a glass of ice water in front of her. "Now, what are you really upset about? I doubt it's Mick's betting or my missing a meeting."

She sighed heavily. "This whole cooking thing has gotten out of hand. I just found out I have to prepare stew for hundreds of people. I've never cooked for more than a half dozen in my life."

Bryan tried to fight a smile and lost. "I'd say that gives me an edge, then."

"I don't have pots big enough to make that amount of stew."

"You can use some from here," he said. "Just multiply your recipe."

"I know how to do the math," she grumbled.

"Okay, then what's really bothering you?"

"I thought it might be fun, but everyone's taking it so seriously. What if I give them all food poisoning or something?"

"Has anyone ever gotten food poisoning from your cooking?" Bryan asked with exaggerated patience.

"No, but there's a first time for everything."

"Think of it this way—if they taste mine and yours to judge fairly and get sick, they won't know which stew made them ill, will they?"

She scowled at him. "And that's supposed to be a blessing?"

"Kiera, are you afraid of losing?"

"Losing? What makes you think I'm going to lose? I've been making Irish stew practically my whole life, while you've been making it for how long? A few years?"

"Which would make it doubly humiliating if you were to lose to me."

"I'm not so easily humiliated," she declared, then stood up, her fine spirit restored. She cast a defiant look at him. "But I am not going to lose."

She flounced out of the kitchen before he could see right through her bravado and realize that he'd stumbled onto the truth. How would she ever show her face in the pub again if she lost? What sort of consultant would that make her? She truly would have to go back to Ireland then. And with every day that passed, she wanted a little more desperately to stay.

After her visit to Chesapeake Shores, Deanna was incredibly grateful for her work at the research lab. She could lose herself in reading the detailed case studies, asking the questions she was constantly jotting down on her tablet that was never far away or looking into a microscope trying to see what the expert scientists saw.

The true blessing was their endless patience and willingness to share their knowledge with the young people who were so eager to learn. She, Milos and others might be assigned no more than grunt work, but they had access to so much more if they took advantage of the groundbreaking work going on all around them.

Though she'd already made plans to go back to see

her father on Saturday, once those plans were made, she tried to push all of the resulting emotional turmoil from her mind. Work helped.

As she left for her tiny apartment at the end of the day, she heard her name called by a familiar voice and looked up to find Ash sitting on a bench. She regarded him with dismay, knowing that she'd been deliberately avoiding his calls since meeting her father, uncertain of what to say to him or how to make amends for how harshly she'd been judging him and her mom for keeping so much from her.

She sighed deeply and sat down beside him. "I wasn't expecting you."

"And didn't want to talk to me, obviously."

She nodded. "I'm sorry. It's been a very confusing time."

"Sweetheart, don't you think I know that? I want to help you, not make anything more difficult."

And there was that generosity of spirit that had made her entire life so much easier.

"I owe you an apology," she said softly.

"For what? Being confused? Never. For being angry? You had every right to feel betrayed."

"Stop it!" she said, tears gathering. "You're being too nice."

He chuckled. "I didn't know that was a crime."

She nudged him with her shoulder. "Not a crime. It just makes me feel even worse. You've given me a whole lifetime of love and support, and the very first time you disappoint me, I had no right to act like such a spoiled brat."

This time Ash actually laughed. "Sweetheart, I have seen some spoiled brats in my day, and you don't even come close. You were hurt. Your mother and I kept some pretty big secrets from you. You felt betrayed. I get it."

She searched his face for signs of hurt, but all she saw was the same love and acceptance that he'd never once withheld from her, not even when she'd crashed his beloved classic Chevy Camaro trying to avoid a very slow turtle crossing a busy highway.

"Did you have dinner?" he asked. "Because I'm starving. Is there a good Italian restaurant nearby?"

"There's a great one," she said. "And I'm starving, too."

When they stood up, she walked into his open arms and took comfort from the fact that he still gave the best hugs ever. "We're good?"

"We will always be good."

She tucked her arm through his and led the way to a neighborhood Italian place that was filled with the smells of oregano, tomatoes and garlic.

"The pizza is to die for, but so is the spaghetti and the vegetarian lasagna," she told him.

"Your mom would have approved of that."

She grinned. "That's what I thought, too, the first time I tasted it."

"But I'm in the mood for pizza with the works," he said. "How about you?"

"You read my mind."

After they'd placed their orders and were sipping on their sodas, Ash put his aside. "Are you ready to tell me how it went when you met your biological father?"

"I know you're not going to believe this, but he reminded me a lot of you," she said. "I went in there, guns blazing, taking out all of my pent-up emotional baggage on him."

"How'd he react?"

"He just let me have my say and then he set out to prove that at least some of the things I'd accused him of were completely untrue."

"Such as?"

"I told him how horrible it was that he'd never even tried to find me."

"And he could prove that he had?"

Deanna nodded, still a little shaken by the effect of seeing the proof in black and white. "A great big box full of proof," she said. "The last check to his private investigator was dated just a month ago, as was the man's report that the trail was still cold."

She let Ash absorb that while their pizza was set on the table, the aromas mouthwatering. They each grabbed a slice, blew on it to cool it and took a bite.

"You didn't lie," Ash said. "This is incredible."

"I know. If there could only be one food left in the entire world, I think I'd want it to be this."

Ash chuckled. "And how would your father the chef feel about that?"

She blanched. "Oh dear. Maybe it's not something I ought to mention just yet. That might cut him worse than any of those accusations I was hurling at him."

"If he takes his work seriously, it very well might."

"I'm going back to Chesapeake Shores on Saturday," she said, her gaze searching Ash's face for any sign of disapproval.

"Then things must have ended on a positive note," he concluded.

"We have a long way to go," Deanna told him. "But I want to try while I'm living this close. It'll be harder once I'm back in Charlottesville."

"You only have another year left there," Ash said carefully. "I wasn't going to mention this if things had gone badly, but since it seems your visit was a good one, would you want to consider doing your premed work at Johns Hopkins? I imagine with your excellent grades and the work you've done here this summer, it would be no problem to make the transfer."

She stared at Ash in shock. "I never even considered transferring."

"And you certainly don't have to, if it's not what you want. But with the school's excellent reputation and convenient location, I just thought it might be worth exploring."

"And you wouldn't mind?"

"Not as long as you'll still let me come over here for more of this pizza," he said readily.

"Ashton Lane, have I ever mentioned that you are the most incredible stepfather ever?"

"A time or two," he said, looking thoroughly pleased by hearing it once more. "So it's still true, even if it was never actually legal?"

She reached for his hand and held it tight. "Legal or not, you were the best father, stepfather, mentor or whatever that any girl could ever ask for. And I think my mom would remind you that you weren't too shabby as a husband, either, even if there was no paper declaring you that. I've gotten the idea recently that families can be cobbled together in all sorts of ways. It's the love that counts."

"You're a very wise young lady," Ash told her.

"Not yet," she corrected. "But I'm working on it." She held his gaze. "And when the time is right, I want you to come to Chesapeake Shores to meet Bryan. I really think you two would like each other."

"We certainly have one great thing in common already," Ash told her. "We both adore you. That's a pretty good bond."

While so many things about her past still troubled her, Deanna felt a sudden surge of optimism that with time, all of those unanswered questions would be put to rest and she'd have her very own cobbled-together family, much like the O'Briens she'd heard a little about from Kiera.

Chapter 20

Bryan glanced across the kitchen island at O'Brien's and allowed himself a faint smile at the sight of his daughter with her head bent over as she concentrated very hard on dicing potatoes to precisely the same size. She was wearing jeans and a T-shirt and had her hair pulled back. The tip of her tongue was caught in the corner of her mouth. She glanced up and caught him staring.

"Stop watching me. I'll lose focus and slice off a finger," Deanna grumbled.

"Not if you do it exactly the way I taught you to not ten minutes ago," Bryan said. "Tuck those fingers into a fist away from the blade of the knife."

"And what's to keep the potato from scooting straight onto the floor, then?"

"Your knuckles pressing down to hold it in place," he said, and demonstrated again at a speed that made her jaw drop.

She gave him a hopeless look. "Maybe I'm not meant to learn to cook."

"Have you ever seriously tried before?"

"No." Her expression brightened. "I can scramble

an egg. I stopped burning them after a while. Ash says they're edible now."

"Well, then, when you've been dicing potatoes for a few months, if you're no better, we can talk about the cost of eating all your meals out for the rest of your life."

She frowned at him. "Sometimes you sound so much like Ash, it's uncanny."

The first few times she'd casually thrown Ashton Lane's name in his face, it had hurt, no question about it. Now he was getting used to the easy references and more comfortable with the comparisons. They were no longer tossed out in a way that demeaned him, but only to suggest that he was proving himself just about equal to a man she considered practically a saint.

Bryan finally dared to ask a question that had been on his mind ever since she'd told him she was coming for another visit. "How does he feel about your spending time with me in Chesapeake Shores?"

"To be honest, I think the idea scared him at first, but he's reconciled to it. In fact, he's eager to meet you." She regarded him with a hopeful expression. "Will you agree to it?"

Amused by the impact of that look, he laughed. "Has anybody ever denied you anything you want?"

"All the time," she said with a shrug. "I just keep pestering, though. I'm very stubborn."

"Your mother's influence," he said readily.

"I think she thought it was yours. She never acknowledged being even a tiny bit stubborn."

"Oh, but she was," Bryan said.

Deanna hesitated, then said softly, "Tell me about her, about the two of you. How did you meet? Was it love at first sight?"

He was vaguely startled by the question. Wasn't it something daughters asked their mothers all the time? "She never told you any of this?"

"Not a word."

He wondered if that was deliberate, a way to keep Deanna separated from him in yet another way. The reason, though, didn't really matter. He had an opportunity at long last to fill in the blanks.

He thought back to the exact night he'd set eyes on Melody for the first time. It seemed like a lifetime ago, and yet it still brought a smile to his lips. "I was training in a restaurant in New York. I was on the lowliest rung of the kitchen hierarchy, which meant I mostly cleaned up and did whatever the chef yelled at me to do. It wasn't a very fancy place, though the chef had aspirations and acted as if it were."

"Pretentious," Deanna guessed.

"Exactly. One night your mother came in with some friends. I think they were all a little tipsy. One of them kept sending his dinner back for one ridiculous reason after another. The chef finally tired of it and sent me out to ask whoever was complaining if they'd like to come in the kitchen and cook it themselves."

"And it was Mom?"

"Oh, no, she looked thoroughly embarrassed. When I walked away from the table, she followed me and apologized. She said her friend fancied himself some sort of gourmet cook, even though he'd never once prepared a meal for any of them. She said they didn't take him seriously, and we shouldn't, either. She said she'd just had the best meal she'd ever eaten." Bryan shrugged. "What could I do? I asked her if I could cook for her sometime. I told her it would be even better."

"And she said yes," Deanna guessed.

"Actually, she said no." He grinned at the memory. "But she was back again the next night and the next, by herself. On her fourth visit, she finally said yes."

"Fascinating," Deanna said, her expression thoughtful. "She was a challenge. Something tells me Kiera is, too."

Startled by her insight, he felt his cheeks heating. "What made you draw that comparison?"

She gave him the sort of impatient look he knew that teenagers everywhere had perfected. "Oh, for heaven's sake, anyone can see the attraction when the two of you are in the same room. I just hope I'm not standing in your way, since I'm staying with her."

"Deanna, this entire town is busy sticking its collective nose into my personal life these days. I do not need you jumping onto that particular bandwagon."

"Interesting," she said, laughter dancing in her eyes. "That's pretty much what Kiera said, too. Since I'm not around all the time, I think I need to go looking for an ally who'll nudge things along."

"No, you do not," he said emphatically. "Kiera and I are moving at our own pace."

"Based on my admittedly limited observation, snails move faster than the two of you."

"You've been around how long? About two minutes? You know nothing about it."

She laughed then. "I'll bet you thought it was going to be fun to have your daughter back in your life, didn't you? Are you having second thoughts?"

"Second and third," he said, but he couldn't help going around to where she was seated and planting a quick kiss on her forehead. "But having you here is still the best thing to happen to me in years."

Afraid he'd overstepped when he'd been trying so hard not to push, he backed away, but then he saw the tears in her eyes and knew that kiss had been exactly the right thing to do. If only all of his instincts were that solid. And perhaps if this dream to have his daughter in his life again could come true, then other dreams he'd put on hold years ago might be in the cards, too. A wife, perhaps? Even a restaurant of his own? Who knew where the future might lead, but it was suddenly filled with hope.

Late that night, Deanna thought she heard a low murmur of voices coming through the guest room window at Kiera's cottage. She'd left it open to the faint breeze that was already hinting at fall. She crept over to the window and peered through the shadows until she caught a glimpse of Kiera and her father on his deck. They were seated in chairs side by side, but far enough apart to make any contact awkward. *A snail's pace*, she thought again with amusement.

Since there clearly wasn't anything romantic to be interrupted, she pulled on a robe, grabbed a glass of water in the kitchen and crossed the lawn to join them. She'd missed these sort of late-night talks with her mom and Ash. It was nice to have a new opportunity for that sort of connection.

"I thought you were sound asleep when I came in from the pub," Kiera said, clearly startled.

"I was, but I heard the sound of voices and decided to join you. Is it okay?"

"Of course," her father said.

"I'm not interrupting?" she asked pointedly.

He gave her a sharp look. "Deanna!"

She laughed at the warning note in his voice and turned to Kiera. "He thinks I'm going to start meddling in your relationship," she told her.

Kiera choked on her sip of wine. "I beg your pardon?"

Bryan frowned at her, but she could tell he wasn't really angry. "It seems my daughter fancies herself a matchmaker, and we're not moving at a pace that suits her."

"Correct," Deanna said.

"Since I told her rather firmly to stay out of it, it seems she has a rebellious streak," Bryan said.

"I'm an independent thinker," Deanna corrected proudly.

Kiera laughed. "Well, now that's a trait we might not want to discourage," she said. "The world could use a few more independent thinkers. We just have to keep her away from Nell."

Her father groaned. "Now you've done it."

"Who's Nell?" Deanna asked eagerly.

Kiera glanced at him. "Tactical blunder?"

"I'll say," he confirmed.

"Who's Nell?" Deanna repeated.

"Nell O'Brien O'Malley," Kiera finally told her. "She's married to my father. They met years ago in Ireland, were separated and then found each other again a few years ago. It's a very romantic story, actually."

"And she's one of *the* O'Briens?"

"The matriarch," Bryan said. "She taught me everything I know about Irish cooking." He glanced at Kiera and added diplomatically, "Almost everything. Kiera's added a few tips since she's come."

"But she's not given you her Irish stew recipe, has she?" Deanna teased.

"No, she's kept that a deep, dark secret."

"And that's why the two of you are competing in the cooking contest," Deanna concluded. "And why everyone's talking about it."

"That's only part of the reason," her father said.

"Then what's the rest?"

"It's because Nell is a devious, clever woman," Kiera said.

Deanna glanced at her father for clarification.

"She's matchmaking," Bryan conceded. "And taking full advantage of the fact that Kiera and I haven't always gotten along. She's decided that's the perfect recipe for sparks to fly and people in this town to take sides. And, of course, to raise money for a good cause."

Deanna released a happy sigh. "She's my ally," she said, mostly to herself.

She saw her father and Kiera exchange a resigned look.

"I warned you," Bryan said to Kiera. "It seems my daughter and Nell were cut from the same mold. Thankfully Dee will be going back to Charlottesville any day now and we'll have one less person trying to run our lives."

Deanna thought of her conversation with Ash and came to a quick decision. "There's something you should probably know about that," she told them. "I had a talk with Ash the other night and I've decided to try to transfer to Johns Hopkins for my premed courses. I'm not sure if the paperwork can be completed in time for this next term, but I'm pretty sure they'll let me continue as an intern in the lab until next term while we're working it out." She beamed at them. "I'll be able to see you both all the time. Isn't that great?"

She laughed at her father's bewildered, torn expression. She could tell he was eager to have her close but was also discovering how big a thorn in his side a newly found daughter could be.

The last thing she'd expected when she'd come to Chesapeake Shores to meet him was to find that she'd not only be getting to know her biological father, but that meddling in his life promised to be so much fun.

Kiera waited until Deanna had left for Baltimore and the midday rush at the pub had ended before telling Luke that she and Bryan needed a break.

"We'll be quick, but there's something that needs to be discussed, and it can't wait until tonight."

"Go," Luke said at once. "I've got things covered here for the next hour. Just take your cell phone along in case I'm wrong and a tour bus appears on our doorstep."

"When has that ever happened?" she asked.

"Exactly my point. It's rare, so go."

Kiera went into the kitchen, grabbed a couple of bottled waters from the refrigerator, then stood in front of Bryan. "We're going for a walk," she announced.

She saw him struggle with a smile, even as he said, "Who made you the boss?"

"Not the boss at all, but a woman who needs to talk to a man who's been slamming pots and pans around for the past hour."

"I haven't been slamming anything around."

"I could show you a couple with the dents to prove it. Shall I?" She turned to the current batch in the sink.

"Okay, a walk it is," he said before seeing the evidence. "I'll tell Luke."

"Already done," she said, pulling him toward the door into the alley.

Outside she handed him the bottled water and turned toward the walkway along the bay. A breeze off the water made the air salty, and once again there was the faintest hint of fall in the temperature. She was looking forward to the change of season, the last she'd experience before going back to Ireland.

When she looked up, she caught Bryan studying her. "What?" she asked.

"Perhaps it's your mood we should be discussing," he said. "You were looking a little sad just then."

"I was thinking about how close we are to the end of my time here. I was looking forward to experiencing my first fall in Chesapeake Shores, but then I realized it would be the last season I get to experience."

Bryan stopped and turned her to face him. He kept his hands resting gently on her shoulders. "Kiera, tell me something. If you had your way, what would you do? Stay or go?"

"I'm not certain anymore," she said candidly.

"I think you are." His gaze held hers and he simply waited.

"I've come to like it here," she admitted at last. "Far more than I expected to. I thought if I had a change of scenery for just a bit, it would help after Peter's death, but being here has turned into so much more. There's little Kate, who's such a joy, Moira and Luke, my father." She sighed, avoiding looking at him as she added, "The whole town."

"And am I a part of that? Am I one of the reasons you'd like to stay?"

She took a deep breath, steadied her nerves and resolved to be honest about her emotions for once in her life, to say what was in her heart and take the risk. "You know you are."

He nodded slowly, apparently letting her words sink in, while her nerves struck again, making her jittery as she waited for him to say something, *anything*.

"You know it's a complicated time for me," he said, making her heart sink.

"Of course I do. It's no time for me adding to the pressure. I wouldn't want to, which is why I'll go home as planned."

"You didn't let me finish."

"I think we've said quite enough about this for now," she said tartly, her pride kicking in. "And we came out here to talk about you, not me and certainly not us."

"Kiera—"

She cut off whatever protest he intended to utter. "What was that display of temper in the kitchen all about? I thought you'd be thrilled by Deanna's news. You'll have your daughter close by, and all the time you need to get to know her."

He looked as if he wanted to drag the conversation back to her, but he must have read the determination in her eyes and simply let it go. He thought about his earlier display of temper in the kitchen and tried to explain what worried him.

"She had a plan for her life and I'm interfering in

that. What if this move is all wrong for her and she comes to resent me for it?"

"Did you beg her to move closer? Did you say a single word about this transfer?"

"Of course not. I had no idea it was even an option."

"Well, then, it seems to me to be a decision she reached all on her own, or perhaps with a little help from the man who's been guiding her for most of her life. If they think this transfer makes sense, why would you argue?"

"I don't want to be responsible for throwing her life off track."

"Perhaps you're only helping her to put it onto a newer, better track. She'd been intending to be a doctor when you first met her. She's still intending to be one, as far as I can tell. And isn't this Johns Hopkins one of the best places for training?"

"That's what I hear," he admitted.

"Then is it some other reason that has you skittish? Have you discovered that being a father holds no appeal, after all?"

He regarded her with a shocked expression. "Never!"

"Well, then, if you want my opinion, this is all good. And just for the record, Deanna seems to be a very grounded young woman who takes her goals seriously. I doubt she came to this decision without careful thought. You should be rejoicing that she wants to get to know you better, instead of keeping you on the periphery of her life like some stranger. When she first walked into O'Brien's, that's exactly what she intended, I think."

"Am I overthinking it?"

She smiled. "Yes."

"Speaking of grounded, you're pretty amazing yourself. I hope you know exactly how much I value your opinion. One of these days I'd like to hear your thoughts about something else I've been considering."

Lovely, Kiera thought. And wasn't it every woman's dream to have a man value her for her opinions, just when she'd started to think he might value her in so many other ways?

Moira hung up the phone after talking to her mother on Monday night and turned to Luke.

"I hope to heaven Nell knows what she's doing with this whole cooking competition. My mother is a wreck. I'm to pick her up first thing in the morning, take her to the grocery, then on to a butcher shop if she doesn't like the meat she finds at the grocery, then to a farmers market for vegetables and herbs. When I suggested she just pick a few things from Bryan's garden, she practically bit my head off."

Luke laughed. "Though he won't let anyone see it, Bryan's a bundle of nerves, too. He stands over his stew pot talking to himself, tasting, then muttering. I believe at least three perfectly edible pots of stew have been taken to the homeless shelter today alone to save them from being dumped into the garbage. He may not think they're perfect, but he can't bring himself to waste food when he knows there are so many who'd be grateful for a good meal."

"I don't see how this is bringing them one bit closer," Moira said.

"While the matchmaking gene pretty much bypassed me, I think it's only one piece of a very complicated puzzle," Luke responded. "In an ironic way, they've bonded over their common misery. To be honest, it seems to me they would have found each other on their own, but this might be nudging things along a little faster."

"I suppose," Moira said skeptically. "And time is of the essence since my mother is supposed to leave in just over a month. She won't even be here for Halloween or Thanksgiving or Christmas." Feeling surprisingly weepy, she added, "She won't even see Kate's excitement on Christmas morning. Doesn't every grandmother want to witness an occasion like that?"

"And I imagine Kiera is no exception," Luke said. "We could talk to Connor about getting an extension on her visa."

"She has to say she wants that," Moira said in frustration. "And I think her pride will keep her from asking, especially if Bryan's not the one pushing for her to stay."

"You know your mother better than I do, but would it hurt to just talk to Connor and find out if an extension is even feasible? Then we'd know whether to encourage her if she even hints at wanting to stay."

Moira's expression brightened. "That makes sense. Can you do that tomorrow, since I'm apparently going to be running hither and yon while she freaks out over the perfect ingredients?"

"Done," Luke assured her. "Now come here. I've been feeling neglected since we've had very little of that free time you promised when you invited your mother to come to Chesapeake Shores."

She laughed at him but immediately settled in his arms. "Are you perhaps thinking we could give her yet another reason to want to stay on?"

"I'm not sure I'm willing to ask her to stay so we can have more sex," Luke teased.

Moira nudged him. "That is not what I was thinking. Well, not precisely, anyway."

"Then what?"

"Another grandbaby might be the perfect lure."

Luke's startled gaze met hers. His lips curved. "Seriously? You're ready for another one?"

"Or two," she said. "Perhaps more."

"But only to keep your mother around?" he asked as if to clarify. His gaze narrowed. "Or is this part of a plot to keep Megan from sending you off around the country for these shows of yours? You seem less and less inclined to go just when you should be feeling ecstatic at being in demand."

"What lovely reasons for adding to our family," she responded tartly. "I had no idea you were quite so cynical."

"Realistic," Luke corrected. "There's usually something behind any decision you reach. I'm just trying to understand this one." He studied her intently. "I'm right, aren't I?"

She chuckled. "Yes, my darling husband. Your intuition is rock solid."

"Moira, be serious for at least half a second here. Don't you want the career Megan's offering you?"

She hesitated. "I do and I don't."

"Which means?"

"After a successful show like the one in San Francisco, my head spins at the joy of knowing my photographs make people happy. Plus, I have to admit, it's pretty heady being the center of all that attention. Then as soon as I'm away from that atmosphere, I panic that it was all a fluke and the next show will be a disaster, that perhaps I should stop while I'm on top."

Luke smiled. "You've barely reached the pinnacle and you're already afraid of tumbling down?"

She nodded. "I've not had much experience with success."

"Then shouldn't you treasure every minute of it and trust that Megan will guide you not only to more success, but will tell you the truth about when it's time to stop? Do you not trust her judgment?"

She let Luke's words sink in, desperately wanting to see things his way, to believe in herself as he and Megan so obviously did. "You think I need to make the commitment and go for it."

"I do. You deserve every second of that joy you experienced in San Francisco and in New York before that."

"And we can balance it with our family? I never want that to take second place."

"We can make it work. I promise."

"Even with another baby. I do want that, Luke."

"With another half-dozen babies, if you're willing," he vowed.

Moira grinned. "Then I suppose we should get busy with that and tomorrow I'll tell Megan I'm ready to seize the opportunities she finds for me."

"You could call and tell her now before you change your mind," he suggested.

"Right now I'm thinking only about the joy of making those babies, but if that doesn't interest you…"

"Oh, it interests me," he said, drawing her closer still. "Let's give it a try." He sealed his words with a kiss that stole her breath away just as he always did.

Chapter 21

Kiera knew she was behaving like something of a lunatic as she tore through the grocery store dismissing half of what she found. Moira trailed along behind her with the cart, Kate sitting in the child's seat pointing out everything she recognized on the shelves and crying when it wasn't added to the cart.

"Not today, baby girl," Moira soothed. "We're helping your grandmother shop today."

"Get her the cereal. It's her favorite," Kiera encouraged. "Perhaps that will make her happy, so I can actually think."

"Would it be easier if we waited in the car?" Moira inquired testily.

Kiera winced. "No. I want you with me. I really do. I'm just nervous. I want to get this exactly right."

"To show up Bryan?"

"No, just to prove I know what I'm talking about and can be taken seriously. Otherwise, what use am I?"

"Mum, Bryan takes you seriously. So does everyone else at the pub. You've been a huge help with everything Luke's asked of you. If you'd stop being so stubborn about going back to Ireland, where there's nothing waiting for you, you could have a permanent job and a good life right here."

"I appreciate that you want me to stay out of family loyalty, but this is the big test, isn't it? My make-or-break moment?"

Moira frowned. "Why on earth do you see it that way? There's nothing make-or-break about it."

"Of course there is. If I fail, what sort of consultant can I possibly be?"

Moira left the cart to give her mother an impulsive hug. Kate joined in by lifting her arms toward her grandmother. "Up!" she commanded. "Gamma, up!"

Smiling at last, Kiera picked her up. "Okay, my little cheerleader. I can do this."

"And you might want to start reminding yourself that your presence here is valued because we love you," Moira said.

Kiera nearly burst into tears at that, but kept her head turned away from her daughter and returned her focus to her shopping until she was back in control.

She calmed a bit as she found chicken stock. "Prepackaged," she said with a derisive sniff. "But there's no time to make it from scratch."

She dismissed the lamb as looking too tough, even though meat cooked in a stew could often be a lesser cut. "Do you suppose the butcher will have any better?" she asked Moira.

"I'm sure he will. He supplies the pub with its meat."

"Well, why didn't you say so? I wouldn't have been wasting my time in here. We'll see the butcher and then go to the farmers market."

"It's the end of the season and the middle of the

week. The selection may not be ideal there, either," Moira warned.

"It will be better than anything here," Kiera insisted. "And surely it will be organic."

"Since when has organic mattered to you?" Moira asked, but there was a twinkle in her eyes that suggested she knew the answer and found it telling.

"It matters to Bryan. He takes pride in his garden being organic." Even as she spoke, she saw Moira trying to hide a smile. "Don't even go there. I'm not cooking this for Bryan. He won't even be there tonight."

"Not a word," her daughter promised, leading the way back to the car.

An hour later they had both beef and lamb from the butcher that satisfied Kiera's critical eye. The carrots, onions and thyme were fresh and organically grown.

"We need some pearl barley," she announced, checking her list. "Where can we find that?"

"There's a gourmet store that might have it. Let's check there," Moira suggested. "They have artisan bread to go with the stew. Perhaps a few bottles of wine, as well. And they have a few prepared salads we can grab for our lunch."

Panic struck. "Lunch? Is it that time already? I need to start cooking. Everyone's coming by at six."

"I'll have you home in plenty of time," Moira soothed. "And we can eat a little something while the stew is simmering. You might consider a glass of wine, as well."

Kiera's nerves once again steadied. "Thank you, but wine at this hour will only make me sleepy. I need all my wits if this stew is to be any good at all."

"Mum, you've no need to thank me."

"Perhaps not, but you've calmed me down and you suggested the bread and wine. It never crossed my mind to plan something to serve with the stew. What about dessert? Should we get something from a bakery?"

"I've already told Bree to ask her sister Jess if the chef at the Inn at Eagle Point will send over something with her. She's known for her decadent desserts. It's going to be fine. This is just a chance for you to practice and for family to sample your stew. It's not a dinner party meant to impress anyone."

In her head, when she was thinking even a tiny bit rationally, Kiera knew that. Still, it felt like a test, and one she was terrified of failing. In some ways cooking for Nell and the rest of the O'Briens mattered even more than the outcome of the contest at the fall festival. Because of Luke, this was her daughter's family now, one that had made her feel welcome, as well. She wanted more than that, though. She wanted to belong, to entertain them as an equal, something she couldn't recall ever wanting quite so badly.

"It smells absolutely heavenly in here," Bree declared when she walked into the cottage just before six. She was the first to arrive, and after giving Kiera a quick hug, she headed directly toward the pot simmering on the stove. Lifting the lid, she breathed in deeply. "If this tastes half as good as it smells, you'll win this contest hands down."

The praise was reassuring, but the real test would come later, when the meal was served. Kiera had tasted the stew at least a dozen times and thought it as good as any she'd ever made, but was it good enough? She had no idea.

Bree turned and studied her. "Panicked?"

Kiera nodded. "Ridiculous, isn't it?"

"You should see me on opening night when my play's being performed before a live audience," Bree said. "No matter how it's gone in rehearsal, no matter how confident I am that the laughs will fall in all the right places, I pace around backstage trying very hard not to run to the restroom and throw up. I'm told nerves are part of the process."

Kiera found Bree's words to be soothing, but it was the glass of wine she placed in Kiera's hand that had the real calming effect.

"Remember, you're among friends and family tonight," Bree said.

"Which means you're all likely to be supportive," Kiera said. "Telling me the stew is good when it's awful won't be doing me any kindness."

Bree laughed. "O'Briens can be blunt when it's called for. Not a one of us is known for censoring our words. We expect each other to be tough enough to handle the truth, even when it hurts."

"And that's exactly what I need," Kiera told her. "The truth."

As the women poured into the cottage's close quarters, the cozy rooms filled with laughter. The wine calmed the last of Kiera's jittery nerves, and she found herself able to enjoy the company. She checked her dining room table to be sure she'd put out enough bowls for the stew, enough spoons, most of them borrowed from the pub for the evening.

Satisfied, she went into the kitchen, put the stew into a couple of big tureens and carried those to the table, then added plates of warm bread and the Irish butter she'd discovered to her delight at the specialty market.

"I think we're ready," she announced. "I'd love to seat everyone around a big table, but we'll have to eat wherever we can find a spot to sit."

"It's the company and food that matters, not the seating," Nell soothed. "I'm taking mine outside, so I can enjoy the delightful breeze off the water."

"I'll join you, Gram," Bree said, following her outside.

As Kiera nervously watched, she noticed that they all migrated outside, happy to be together, happy to have a beloved view of the bay.

"Mum, everyone's having a wonderful time. You can relax now. Get your own bowl of stew and come join us," Moira said.

"Yes," Megan said. "It's time for you to sit and bask in the rave reviews I'm already hearing, Kiera."

"I'm not sure I can," Kiera admitted. "Besides, I've eaten enough stew today while I was cooking it. I don't think I could eat another bite."

"Then just bring your wine," Moira said, pushing her toward the door.

She hesitated in the doorway, but her daughter gave her another gentle shove.

Immediately Heather spotted her. "I want this recipe," she called out to Kiera.

"So do I," Nell said.

Kiera's eyes widened at Nell's comment. "You do?"

"Your father's been telling me mine is missing something, and I've had no idea what it could be until I tasted yours. I can't put my finger on it, but I'll know when I see what spices you've used."

"But Bryan's using your recipe," Kiera said.

Bree chuckled at her reaction. "Which means you've got a lock on winning this contest, Kiera! I'm sure of it."

"And you're not just saying that?" she asked worriedly. "You're not just trying to settle my nerves so I show up for the contest?"

Bree's expression sobered at once. "Remember what I told you earlier. We always tell the truth."

"Always," a few more echoed.

"Well, I can remember one time—" Shanna began, only to be shushed by the others.

"Not helping," Bree told her firmly.

Shanna laughed. "I'm just saying we're all capable of a little white lie from time to time."

"But not tonight," Bree countered emphatically.

"Not tonight," Shanna agreed.

Kiera sat back at last, more relieved than she could ever recall being before. Win or lose, she was confident she wasn't going to make a complete fool of herself in front of Bryan or this family.

After that the attention turned to the huge tray of red velvet cupcakes Jess had brought from the inn. It was the perfect way to cap off a night that had made Kiera feel as if she did, indeed, belong.

"Quite a crowd at your place last night," Bryan noted when Kiera got into the car in the morning for the drive to the pub.

"Just a girls' night," she said, unwilling to tell him that it had been a dress rehearsal for her Irish stew, one that had gone surprisingly well. She was still a little stunned by just how well it had gone, in terms of the food and the camaraderie. "We had dinner and dessert."

"And wine?" Bryan asked, sounding amused.

"We had a few glasses," she admitted. "Why did you make such a point of that?"

"Because of the serenading that went on when I got home. Not a one of you can carry a tune, by the way."

Kiera stared at him. "We sang?"

"Oh, yes."

"But I can't sing."

He laughed. "I can attest to that. But you were all very enthusiastic. It was the best homecoming I've had in a while. You don't remember any of this?"

"I remember somebody suggesting we sing a few Irish songs, but things are a little fuzzy beyond that. I'm sorry if we kept you awake."

"Don't be. I got my own glass of wine, sat on my deck and enjoyed the show. Just know that I won't be recommending that Luke bring you all in to entertain at the pub."

Kiera groaned. "I should hope not. In fact, I'd prefer it if you never mentioned this to another soul. My very first girls' night and it got completely out of control."

Bryan gave her a startled look. "Your first girls' night?"

Kiera nodded. "Unless you count a couple of sleepovers when I was very young."

"But surely you had a lot of women friends back home. Didn't you ever get together and kick up your heels?"

"I had three small children at home and a job that lasted practically from dawn to dusk. There was neither time nor money for going out with the girls."

She would have added that there'd been little time

for friendships of any kind, but that made her sound far too pitiful.

She never wanted Bryan to think of her as deserving pity. That also meant she could never fully explain to him or anyone else just how much last night had meant to her. She had, however, given every woman there a fierce hug when they'd left, hoping that would be enough to let them know how much their kindness meant to her.

When Bryan had parked at the pub, she checked her watch and saw that it was still early enough that some of the women were likely to be at Sally's.

"Thanks for the lift," she told him. "I have somewhere I need to be."

Bryan gave her a long look, then nodded. To her surprise, it was understanding she thought she read in his eyes.

"Have fun with the girls," he called after her, proving that he knew exactly where she was going and why.

Just inside the door at Sally's, Kiera noted that there were still three women at what had come to be known as the O'Brien table. She walked over to Sally and told her she wanted to pick up the check for everyone there and ordered her own coffee and croissant while she was at it. Once she'd paid, she joined them in the back.

"Thank you all so much for coming last night," she said when she was seated.

"We were just talking about how much fun it was," Megan told her. "We've enjoyed these morning get-togethers for years, but then we all rush off to work. Family dinners on Sundays are great, but there are children running all over and the men are there. We never get to let our hair down the way we did last night. It was really special, Kiera, and we've vowed to find other occasions to do the same thing."

"I'm afraid we might have let our hair down a little too far," Kiera said. "Bryan caught the whole performance."

The other women exchanged amused looks. "It was time he saw this side of you," Megan said. "Sometimes things get so serious between a man and a woman, they lose sight of the fun that can be had. It happened to Mick and me. There were so many crises and issues and fights when we were married the first time that we forgot how much we enjoyed each other's company and the way we'd always laughed when we were together. Laughter's as important in a relationship as anything else. It gets you through the tough times."

To Kiera's amusement, that set off a lively debate over the importance of laughter versus hot sex that left Megan blushing.

"Too much information," she finally told the others. "Especially for a mother to hear from her daughters."

"Amen," Kiera said with a pointed look at Moira, who'd just joined them and added quite a bit more than her two cents to the debate.

"This has been fun, as always," Megan said. "But I have a gallery to run. Moira, you'll be by later to discuss the upcoming shows I have in mind?"

"I will," Moira agreed.

Megan gave her a curious look. "And you won't be balking before I even open my mouth?"

Moira laughed. "I think you might find me surprisingly agreeable."

"Then please do hurry, then," Megan said.

The women dispersed and Moira walked with Kiera back to the pub.

"You really like them, don't you?" Moira asked.

Kiera nodded, feeling the surprising sting of tears in her eyes at the thought of leaving them, of leaving this whole town and Bryan behind.

"Don't go, Mum. You don't have to," Moira said.

"It's what we planned from the beginning," Kiera said stoically.

"Plans are meant to be changed. Please stay."

But in all of Kiera's struggles, the only thing that had kept her going was having a plan and sticking to it. Straying from that slim grasp on control invited chaos, and she'd had more than enough of that to last a lifetime.

Bryan had a peaceful morning in the kitchen with no one underfoot, but it had left him oddly disgruntled. Apparently he'd grown used to having Kiera bustling around with her comments and unsolicited advice.

Still, he was not expecting to have the peace shattered by Moira tearing through the door in a full-blown mood with him as her target.

"Bryan Laramie, I have no idea what goes on in that head of yours, but you're impressing me lately as a full-blown idiot."

Though he'd grown accustomed to her temper long ago and knew that it usually burned itself out if he simply remained silent, today he wasn't in the mood for it himself.

"What a friendly greeting," he noted in a voice thick with sarcasm. "What set you off today?"

"I've just had a talk with my mother."

Bryan frowned at that. "And what has she been telling you? The last time I saw her, she was in a perfectly pleasant frame of mind and on her way to join her friends at Sally's."

"Well, she wasn't in a pleasant frame of mind just now. She was crying."

Alarm spread through Bryan at once. What on earth might have happened in the past hour? "Where is she? I'll talk to her."

"No you won't. You'll only blunder and make it all worse."

He fought to keep a tight grip on his patience. "Then what is it you want from me?"

"I want you to make her stay in Chesapeake Shores. You're the only one she'll listen to."

"Moira, you're her daughter, the mother of her only grandchild. If you can't talk her into staying, what can I do?"

"The mere fact that you have to ask that just proves what an idiot you are. She cares about you. She won't stay unless you ask. But you can't just ask as if she were a friend you'd miss and think of from time to time. Her staying has to be what you really want."

He sorted through the confusing declaration and thought he saw what she was really saying. "Are you suggesting I propose?" Even as he said the words, his heartbeat escalated straight toward panic.

"Well, why not?" Moira demanded, as if a man asking a woman to marry him were a simple matter. "It's not as if you're still married as you once thought you might be. You're as crazy in love with her as she is with you. If any two people belong together, it's the two of you. Do not be an idiot by letting her leave."

Love? The word hung in the air. It had been so

long since Bryan had even thought in those terms, it was shocking to hear it in connection with Kiera. He couldn't deny, though, that the prospect of her going back to Dublin left him feeling empty inside. She'd slipped into his life and filled some need he hadn't even recognized.

Marriage, though? He'd tried it and been an abysmal failure. Was he any wiser now? Or did he even need to be? Kiera, unlike Melody, was more than capable of telling him what she needed and demanding that she get it. There would be no crossed signals and hurt feelings. With a fiery temperament much like her daughter's, she'd provide a road map. He'd witnessed firsthand how that worked for Luke and Moira.

But what if he pursued the idea that had been nagging at him lately, the possibility that it might not be too late for him to pursue his dream to have a restaurant of his own? Had he learned the lessons well enough from his marriage, or would he revert to old patterns? There was Deanna to consider, too. All were things he needed to take into account before he asked Kiera to marry him.

"Well?" Moira demanded. "Have I gotten through that thick skull of yours?"

Bryan smiled at her. "You'll have to wait and see. And you might want to consider the fact that your mother and I have never even been on what could be considered a date. Marriage would be a giant leap."

"Stop making excuses because you're scared. Sitting around and talking till all hours or spending hours in here cooking together might not be formal dates, but you've gotten to know each other as few couples have."

"Point taken."

"So you'll talk to her about a future?"

"Whatever I decide will be discussed with your mother, not you."

"Well, that hardly seems fair," Moira grumbled, then gave him a hard look. "Just don't disappoint me."

"Moira, I adore you, but your disappointment is not at the top of my concerns when it comes to this."

She looked momentarily startled, but then smiled. "No, and if I'm being rational, which I seldom am, I suppose it shouldn't be."

Once she'd left the kitchen, Bryan tried to resume cooking, but his concentration was shot. Fortunately, today's specials were things he could almost make with his eyes closed. The customers wouldn't suffer because of his distraction, but it was going to be a very long day, and he honestly had no idea how it might end.

Chapter 22

After her visit to Chesapeake Shores, Deanna waited a couple of days to give herself time to seriously consider her impulsive decision to transfer to Johns Hopkins to complete her undergraduate work in premed. Now she was sitting, cell phone in hand, trying to decide if her first call should be to Dr. Robbins to ask for guidance in making it happen or to Ash to tell him about her decision. Even though he'd been the one to suggest it, she couldn't help wondering if he'd be hurt by her final decision to move farther away from home. No matter how supportive he seemed, she knew he'd been counting on her since her mom died.

"You seem deep in thought," Milos said, sitting down beside her. "Is there a problem? I'm happy to listen."

She smiled at the serious young man whose friendship she'd come to value. He was thoughtful and capable of listening without censure. He might turn out to be exactly the sounding board she needed.

Starting slowly to try to put her rambling thoughts in order, she explained what was going on in her life.

"This would be a significant change," he concluded.

She nodded. "That's why I'm so confused. I'm worried about hurting the man who raised me and rushing a relationship with a father I've only known briefly."

"But isn't what's best for your future also important?" Milos asked, pushing his glasses back into place to study her more intently.

"Of course."

"And would you be getting the best education here? If so, isn't that what matters? If it allows you time to get to know your biological father, that is a bonus, yes?"

"Yes," she said, grateful for the fresh perspective.

"And didn't you tell me that your stepfather came to see you recently just to have pizza and talk?"

She smiled, mostly because Milos, unlike many of the men she'd met over her college years, had actually paid attention to things she'd told him. "Yes."

"Then he could do that more often, perhaps, or you could still get home for a weekend."

"You make it sound so simple," she said, laughing.

"I think perhaps it is, when you take all of the tangled emotions out of it."

Impulsively, she threw her arms around him, startling him. "Thank you," she said as he blushed.

"Then you will try to enroll here?" he concluded.

"Yes."

He nodded, a satisfied smile curving his lips. "I'm glad, because it seems I am going to be staying on, too," he told her, beaming at his news. "The arrangements were made just yesterday. Professor Wheeler asked if I was interested, and when I told him I was, he got on the phone and, just like that, pulled strings to make it happen."

"Milos, that's wonderful! Why didn't you mention it sooner?"

He shrugged. "I'm used to the fact that sometimes dreams don't work out." He smiled shyly. "This one did."

"I'm so happy for you and happy that we might get to spend more time together." She hesitated. "That is, if you don't think your girlfriend back home will object."

He sighed. "I think that is over. She knew coming here for the summer was important to me, but I think she's tired of being left on her own. Unlike me, she is very social, what you might call a party girl. She told me she is already seeing other people."

"I'm so sorry."

"It was not meant to be," he said, sounding surprisingly philosophical about it. "And this opportunity will give me the future I want. I want to be part of a team that discovers a cure for cancer or Alzheimer's. I want to do something that matters."

"And I believe you will," Deanna encouraged him. "I've heard Professor Wheeler himself say that you have great promise as a research scientist. It's been evident all summer how much he values your work. He even gave you a small project of your own."

"A very small one," he said.

"Yes, but none of the rest of us was given any independent research to do. That's a real accomplishment, Milos."

"I hope I can live up to his expectations," he said modestly. "I will certainly try my best."

"Between us we will save a lot of lives one of these days," Deanna said confidently. Suddenly she was excited by all of the possibilities ahead of her. "I'd better call my adviser at the University of Virginia and see what she can do about making this transfer official. And then I'll call my stepfather."

"Then I will leave you to it," Milos said.

"Thanks for helping me to clarify things," she called after him.

"You already knew what you wanted," he said. "I did very little beyond listening."

Deanna stared after him. He obviously had no idea just how important listening and a few thought-provoking questions could be.

She made the call to Dr. Robbins and set things in motion, then called Ash several times until she finally caught him as he was coming in the door from work.

"At this hour? It's nearly nine. You're working too hard," she scolded him.

"Are you calling just to check up on me?" he teased, laughing. "Has our relationship flipped on its head?"

"I wasn't, but perhaps I need to start."

"Tell me why you did call," he suggested. "But first let me set down the bag of takeout I brought home with me."

Deanna didn't like the impression she was getting of his lifestyle these days. "What kind of takeout?"

"Would you feel better if I told you it was a giant salad from Whole Foods?"

"Yes, but I'm betting it's Chinese from Imperial Palace."

He sighed. "You know me too well. Now talk to me, while I eat the Kung Pao chicken before it gets cold."

"I've decided to make the transfer to Johns Hopkins," she blurted, aware that the rustling of paper and plastic utensils in the background suddenly stopped.

"I see," he said slowly.

"You sound as if you have mixed feelings," she said worriedly, then reminded him, "It was your suggestion."

"I mentioned it because I thought it might be a good option."

"But now you're having second thoughts?"

"That depends on why you're doing it. If it's for your education, I'm all for it. If it's only about being closer to your father, then it does concern me."

"What if it's both?" she asked.

"Let me just ask you this. If things don't work out between you and your father or get awkward or he has little time for you, any of those things, will you still be happy to be in Baltimore at Johns Hopkins?"

"Absolutely," she said without hesitation. "I'm loving everything about this program here."

"If that's the case, then I'm all for the transfer," he said, though he didn't sound as enthusiastic as she'd hoped.

"Ash, things are going well between Bryan and me," she said, hoping to reassure him. "I think we both want this chance to make up for the time we lost."

"I just don't want you to be disappointed if things don't work out the way you envisioned. Your mother left him for a reason."

"I know, and it probably made perfect sense to her at the time, but a lot of time has passed. He's not the same person, and I'm an adult now. I think I'll be able to decide for myself if he's selfish or too self-involved or whatever it was that drove her away. He's been pretty open about how he put career over family back then."

"He could do that again," Ash cautioned. "It's one thing for you to show up out of the blue and have this happy reunion that lasts for a day or even a weekend, but what happens if you're coming around all the time wanting his attention? He's had years now when he's been able to devote himself to work without any competing demands. The tendency to be a workaholic could be even stronger now."

"It won't be like that. I'm sure of it. Why are you suddenly against this?"

"I'm probably worrying for nothing," Ash admitted. "I just don't want to see you hurt."

"I won't be. My eyes are wide-open and my expectations aren't high. I promise."

"Okay, then. You know you have my full support. Whatever you need from me to make this happen, just ask."

"I love you, Ash," she said, hoping again to reassure him. "That's never, ever going to change."

"Back at you," he said softly. "Keep me posted on what's going on."

"Absolutely."

As Deanna hung up, she couldn't help feeling vaguely deflated. Because she'd always trusted his judgment without question, Ash's concerns had worked their way into her head. It wasn't enough to make her change her mind about her decision, but her earlier excitement had dulled a little. What if she did turn out to be little more than a nuisance in her father's well-ordered life?

She drew in a deep, bracing breath. She'd deal with that when the time came. Right now she was all about seizing second chances.

Kiera opened her kitchen door on a dreary, rainy morning expecting to find Bryan on her doorstep, only to find her father standing there, dripping wet.

"Come in," she said, drawing him inside. "Let me get you a towel to dry off. What on earth are you doing walking in the rain?"

Dillon laughed. "Have you forgotten that a little rain never stops an Irishman? If it did, we'd seldom get any exercise."

Kiera took his soaked shirt and tossed it into the dryer, then she brought him a towel and an old T-shirt of Bryan's that she wore when gardening. It had been freshly laundered the day before. Dillon looked at the logo for an organic farm on the front and gave her a questioning look. "Yours?"

"No, Bryan loaned it to me so I wouldn't ruin my own clothes working in his garden." She saw the speculative gleam in her father's eyes and quickly tried to steer the conversation away from Bryan. "Would you like hot tea or coffee? I have both."

"Coffee, if it's not too much trouble. Nell would have me floating in tea, if she had her way. She thinks a strong cup of tea can solve the cares of the world. Her coffee, however, lacks a certain punch. I'm afraid I've grown accustomed to the espresso at Panini Bistro."

"I'll do my best, but I'm not sure mine's quite that strong," Kiera told him. As she filled her small espresso pot and set it on the stove to heat, she studied her father. He'd aged well. In fact, it seemed he'd grown stronger since moving to Chesapeake Shores, and his skin had a healthy glow from his daily walks. Still, there was no denying that he was aging. She couldn't help wondering how much longer she'd have him in her life. And, if she did go back to Ireland, how much of that time would she miss?

When she handed him his cup of coffee and a pitcher

of cream, he gave her a worried look. "Are those tears I see in your eyes? What's wrong?"

"I was just thinking about how much I'll miss you when I'm back in Dublin."

He gave her a steady look. "There's an obvious solution, but you already know that."

"I can't just decide to stay. There are regulations."

"Which can be readily handled, if it's what you want. Connor knows the law and Mick has contacts just about everywhere, it seems. Both would step up to help."

"I know, and I appreciate that," she said.

"But?"

"I never mentioned a *but*," she said defensively.

"You didn't have to. It's Bryan, isn't it? You've come to care for him. You want him to be the one to ask you to stay."

She sighed, unable to deny it. "I'm being foolish at my age to think that way."

"Nonsense," he said. "From everything I've seen, Bryan is a fine man. If he matters to you, that tells me a lot. You're a cautious woman, Kiera, and after Sean, why wouldn't you be? It's made you leery, but it's also made you a good judge of people."

"It's not Bryan's worthiness that's in question. It's whether or not he has feelings for me." As soon as the words crossed her lips, she covered her face. "Listen to me. I sound like an insecure teenager."

"When it comes to love, we all feel a bit insecure at the beginning."

"You didn't when you followed Nell to Chesapeake Shores."

"No, but I had our history on my side. I knew the love was still there, even after all the years we'd spent apart. Claiming a second chance was less about taking a risk than about what I might be leaving behind."

"Your businesses?"

"Heavens, no! It was past time to turn those over to others. It was Moira, who still needed me, and you. People around here talk of the O'Briens as a fine example of family. We know they've had their difficulties, but they're united just the same. I wanted us to be united, too. I feared if I left that might never happen for you and me. We were making strides, but trust needs nurturing, and I wouldn't be there to do the work. That's why I was so delighted when you agreed to come here. I'd like us to be a united family for whatever time I have left."

"You're making a very strong case for me to stay, regardless of what happens between Bryan and me," Kiera admitted. "And it's not as if I haven't considered it."

"But knowing there's a future with Bryan would tip the scales," he guessed.

She nodded. "He shouldn't have that power, I know, but I don't know if I could bear to just sit by and have the occasional chat with him when my feelings have grown so strong." She frowned. "I didn't want them to, you know."

Dillon chuckled. "I'm sure of that. But fate sometimes takes things into its own hands. And if something is fated, then it usually happens, even if it's not on our timetable."

"Well, I don't have time to wait around," she said in frustration.

His full-throated laugh filled the kitchen. "You sound just as you did when you were three and your mother's cookies didn't bake fast enough."

"Impatience is one of my well-known flaws," she conceded.

"Then perhaps a change of topic is in order. When will you tell me what is going on with my grandsons?"

Startled not only by the topic, but by the fact that it had taken him all these weeks to broach it, Kiera said simply, "It's not a subject I like talking about."

"Because?"

"I'm ashamed of them and the decisions they've made," she said, busying herself by pouring more coffee for her father even though his cup was half-full. "I was hoping you'd never have to find out."

"They're in trouble?"

"Quite likely in jail, since that's where I left them. And before you judge me, I bailed them out of jams more times than I can count. They considered it their due, not the slightest motivation to change their ways. I might well have gone on doing it out of guilt, but Peter convinced me I was doing them no favors. He said perhaps a longer stay behind bars would get through to them as nothing else had."

She'd kept her head turned as she recited all this, but finally dared a look at Dillon. He seemed troubled, but not at all surprised. "You knew, didn't you?"

"I'd heard a few things. I knew if they were hanging out with Sean Malone, sooner or later there would be a bad ending. Peter told me the rest. Ever since you arrived, I've been waiting for you to mention it."

"I said it before. I was ashamed."

"Their behavior isn't your fault, Kiera. They're grown men."

"They're my sons and I was the one who raised them."

"And then they fell under their father's influence at a time when they were old enough to know right from wrong."

"It breaks my heart," she said softly. "I lost them and I don't know quite how. I tried so hard to do right by them, by all three of my children."

"Moira is a testament to your efforts," Dillon told her. "Boys need a strong male role model, and sadly, they chose their father."

"If I'd invited you back into their lives sooner, it could have been you."

"There's no turning back the clock, Kiera. You did the best you could. Would you like me to go to Ireland and see what I could do to help them? I still have friends who could easily intercede."

She shook her head. "They've been helped too often and given no thanks for it. I won't allow them to do the same to you."

"They could come here. There are only petty crimes on their record, brawls and drunk-and-disorderly sorts of things. I think we could overcome that. They could have a fresh start."

"And likely disrupt the lives of too many people I care about in the process," she insisted. "No, I won't have it."

"Think about it, Kiera. Second chances aren't just for a few lucky souls. They might turn their lives around. Just consider it."

She sighed heavily. "I'll consider it because you asked, but I think it would be a grave mistake."

"And if you still feel that way in a few days or a few weeks, I'll abide by your decision. Just remember that family doesn't just include those who play by all the rules. It embraces the rule-breakers, too."

He stood up and retrieved his shirt from the dryer, then kissed her forehead. "I'm around if you want to talk about this or anything else."

She stood and gave him a fierce hug. "You'll never know how much I appreciate that or how much I truly missed it when we were apart all those years. I still treasure all the walks we took when I was a girl, the talks we had, yet even with all that, I lost my way for a while."

"And found it back again," he reminded her. "That's what matters in the end."

She followed him to the door and watched as he strode down the driveway, seemingly oblivious to the rain that was more of a soft drizzle now. She smiled at that. To him, it must have felt like home.

Bryan had been about to leave his house and get Kiera, when there'd been a knock on his front door, the one only strangers or deliverymen used.

He opened it to find a man in his late forties standing there, dressed in pressed jeans and an oxford cloth shirt with the sleeves rolled up to reveal tanned, muscled forearms. Well-worn construction boots hinted at his profession.

"You're Bryan Laramie," the man said. There was a surprising certainty in his voice.

Bryan nodded. "And you are?"

"Ashton Lane, Deanna's stepfather," he replied without hesitation, then amended, "Well, unofficially, anyway."

Bryan surveyed him again and, despite his reservations, liked what he saw. There were no pretensions here, and the fact that he'd come to the house showed he was both discreet and confident.

"Come in," Bryan said. "I don't have a lot of time before I leave for the restaurant, but can I get you a cup of coffee?"

"To tell you the truth, I had more caffeine than I needed working up the nerve to come here," Ash confided with unexpected candor. "I'm pretty sure my daughter would have a fit if she knew I was here."

"But you're concerned about her," Bryan guessed. "And curious about me."

"In my position, anyone would be," Ashton said.

Bryan nodded. "Then let's talk. Hopefully I can put your concerns to rest. Let's sit in the kitchen. It's cozier in there. At least that's what Dee says. She thinks the rest of the house is too sterile and the kitchen only marginally better since she added some colorful dish towels on her last visit. She's eager to redecorate the whole place."

Ashton laughed at that. "Watch her. She has a mind of her own and a stubborn streak."

"So I'm discovering."

"For your sake, be glad her thoughts of decorating have moved beyond the Disney princess phase."

Bryan laughed. "Amen to that!"

Though his guest had declined coffee, Bryan poured him a glass of ice water and added a wedge of lime, mostly to keep himself busy and his own nerves in check. This promised to be more intense than any job interview he'd ever gone on, the stakes higher. They both used the few moments of silence to size each other up, making little pretense that they were doing anything else.

"Can I ask how you feel about Deanna turning up in your life out of the blue like she did?"

Bryan sat across from him and looked him directly in the eye. "I don't know how much she's told you, but I've been searching for her and her mother since the day they left. I've shown her all the reports, the checks to the investigators, every bit of proof I have that I never gave up on her. Having her show up here was like a miracle."

"She's not disrupting your life?"

"To the contrary, I can't wait to get to know her. How do you feel about that?"

"I've loved that girl unconditionally since the day I met her and her mother. If having you in her life makes her happy, I'm all for it. I just don't want to see her hurt because the novelty wears off for you and you lose interest."

"Not going to happen," Bryan said flatly, trying not to be offended. It was, after all, a fair question. "You've had her with you nearly her entire life. I had her for a little more than a year when she was a baby. She's a grown woman now. That's a lot of catching up to do."

He studied the man seated across from him and saw only concern on his face. "I hope you won't try to stand in the way of that. I know how much Dee respects and loves you. I'm sure she'd never do anything to intentionally hurt you, but we both want this chance, I think. We need it."

Apparently his sincerity got through to Ashton Lane, because he nodded. "She's going to change schools to be closer to you. You know that, right?"

"She mentioned it."

"Please don't make her regret it. That's all I'm asking."

Bryan hesitated before replying. "Will it hurt her academically or hurt her future, if she makes this change?"

"No. When it comes to her education, she'll be fine, but we both know that's not the only thing behind this decision. She wants to figure out how you fit into her life."

Bryan understood the other man's concern and nodded. "We'll figure that out together. I don't want her to regret this decision any more than you do."

Ashton stood then, looking reassured. "I'm glad I came. I think we understand each other." He hesitated, then added, "We might not want to mention this visit to Dee, though. She'll kill me for meddling."

Bryan laughed. "Given that she's already looking into ways to meddle in my life, I won't give her a lot of sympathy on that point."

For an instant Ashton looked startled, but then he chuckled. "Watch yourself. If she's after something, she usually finds a way to get it."

"Already noted," Bryan said. "Thanks for coming. I appreciate that you're looking after her. More, I appreciate the way you've cared for her all these years. She's a lovely young woman, and that's all because of you and Melody."

"Thank you for saying that. You'd have every right to resent me."

"I can't say I don't, just a little, but it's because of all the years I lost, not because you were the father she needed, when I couldn't be."

"I imagine if Dee has her way, we'll be seeing more of each other," Ashton said.

"Definitely. She's already mentioned it. I'll look forward to it." And very much to his astonishment, he found that he actually meant it.

Chapter 23

Bryan was oddly quiet and distracted as he drove Kiera to the pub after their late start.

"You've never said why you were running late this morning," she said, hoping his reply would pave the way for a conversation about his mood.

"Unexpected company," he said tersely.

"The car from Virginia that I saw in your driveway when my own unexpected company left?" she suggested.

He nodded.

"I'm guessing it must have had something to do with your daughter," she said, putting the pieces of the puzzle together herself with very little help from him. "I'm also sensing that you don't really want to talk about it."

He gave her a wry look. "Yet that hasn't stopped you from peppering me with questions."

"Of course not," she said, smiling. "I've learned that it's better in the end to push until you get things off your chest, rather than waiting around until the thought occurs to you to unburden yourself to a friend."

"Sometimes I forget just how well you've come to

know me," he said. "And, for the record, I'm not sure how I feel about it."

"You'll get used to it," she said lightly, hoping for a smile, but none came. "This was about Deanna?" she prompted.

"Yes, it was Deanna's stepfather or surrogate father or whatever the name would be for a man who never legally adopted her or even married her mother."

Before Kiera could leap in with a comment, he added, "Through no fault of his own. It's obvious that the man loved both of them and that he cared for Dee as if she were his own. I respect him for making the best of the awkward situation Melody put him in."

"Then you do recognize that Deanna had a good life because of him," Kiera said mildly.

"Well, of course I do. And I'm glad of it. It used to make me physically ill thinking about all the terrible things that might have befallen them or what circumstances they might be living in. Melody was a good person and loved our daughter, but I was very aware of her flaws. She could be reckless and impulsive. Do you know she took only a few hundred dollars from our bank account when she left? How long were they supposed to live on that? I'd have been more reassured if she'd taken everything we had. I suppose she was determined to send the message that they no longer needed me or the income I'd provided at such a high cost to our family. For years I kept an account set aside just in case she ever hinted that they needed help."

"But she had already turned to another man," Kiera said. "And this mood of yours this morning is because you're just a wee bit jealous that it was him, not you in their lives all those years?"

He sighed. "I know it makes me look petty."

She smiled at that. "No, it makes you human. Most men would have mixed emotions. And some would have written all of it off years ago and simply gone on with their lives without a moment's regret or a thought about the woman and child who'd left. Sean certainly forgot all about us until his sons turned up to become his drinking buddies."

Kiera heard the trace of bitterness in her voice and waved off the comment before Bryan could redirect the conversation to her past. "Why did Ashton Lane want to see you?"

"To make sure I didn't intend to treat Deanna like some shiny new toy, then abandon her when I grew bored with parenthood."

Kiera regarded him with indignation on his behalf. "You would *never* do that!"

"Of course not, but I can't really blame him for needing to be reassured, especially since she's leaving the University of Virginia to be closer to me. Haven't I worried about the same thing?"

Though she hesitated to insert herself into the already complicated situation, she knew that she had a rapport with Deanna that Bryan hadn't yet achieved. She was the objective outsider whom the girl had chosen to trust with her own concerns and fears, perhaps in a very small way a substitute for the mother she'd lost.

"Would you like me to talk to her about all this the next time she comes for a visit?" she asked carefully. "Or do you want to do it yourself?"

"As much as I hate admitting it, I think she does trust you to be honest with her."

"She wants to trust you," Kiera said as another driver

tooted his horn to encourage them to move on. "It's just harder because for years she's perceived what happened years ago as all your fault. Her mother did nothing to change her view of that."

"Why would she? She blamed me for putting my work over our family, and she was right. I did do that."

"You're not the first man to make that choice." When he would have spoken, she held up her hand. "That's not a defense of your actions. It's just that her actions are the ones that stripped you and your daughter of a relationship. Leaving, if that's what she needed for herself, is understandable. Deliberately keeping your daughter from you is less forgivable. As deeply hurt as I was by Sean's betrayal, I left the door open for him to see his children. It was his own choice not to walk through it until it became convenient for him because his sons had a little money to spare to feed his need for his evening pints of ale."

Bryan sighed. "In my case, I know we're way beyond the point of laying blame at anyone's doorstep. We need to deal with where we are now, to find a way to relate as father and daughter, when neither of us has any experience at it."

"She does," Kiera suggested mildly. "Not with you, but with Ashton Lane. Perhaps she can show you the way, show you what she needs, if you're patient and follow her lead."

She caught the smile tugging at the corners of Bryan's mouth. "What?" she demanded.

"You, of all people, suggesting patience."

Kiera laughed. "It hardly matters if I'm incapable of following my own advice," she told him. "This is about you."

"And I'm in unexplored territory," he said.

"You're not there alone," she reminded him.

He pulled into his usual parking spot behind the pub and turned to her then, his gaze on hers steady. "And you have no idea how much that means to me. Kiera—"

Her breath caught at the intensity of his gaze, but before he could complete his thought or reach for her as she thought he might, *hoped* he might, there was a tap on the driver's side window. Startled, they both turned to see Deanna standing beside the car, a beaming smile on her face.

"Surprise!"

To Kiera's regret, whatever Bryan had intended to say or do was lost, but she couldn't be too dismayed when she saw the genuine pleasure that spread across his face at the sight of his daughter. He was out of the car in an instant.

"I wasn't expecting you," he said.

"I know," Deanna said, laughing. "That's what makes it a surprise." Her expression faltered. "Is it okay? I know I should have called ahead. Kiera, do you mind if I stay for a few days? The summer program is over and I thought I'd spend some time here, but only if I'm not in the way."

Kiera climbed out of the car. "You couldn't possibly be in the way. You're always welcome."

"Was there anything in particular you'd like to do on this visit?" Bryan asked.

Though she wasn't sure Bryan saw it, Kiera caught the mischievous gleam in Deanna's eyes when she responded. "I was thinking I'd like to meet this Nell I've been hearing so much about. Do you think that would be possible?"

"Of course," Bryan said, clearly eager, especially this morning, to agree to any request Deanna made. "She'll be in today to see how my Irish stew is coming along for the competition."

"Won't the two of you be far too busy then?" Kiera asked, giving him a pointed look that obviously had no effect.

"Of course not," he said, frowning at her. "Dee, why don't you go on into the kitchen while I finish up a conversation I was having with Kiera just now."

When she'd gone, he turned to Kiera. "I thought you wanted me to follow her lead."

"I do," Kiera said. "But you just played conveniently right into her hand in a way I don't think you intended."

Bryan looked bewildered.

"Your daughter is looking for an ally in her meddling," Kiera reminded him patiently. "She's hoping to find one in Nell."

To her surprise he didn't look nearly as dismayed as she'd expected. "And that's suddenly okay with you?" she asked.

He gave her a surprising grin. "Maybe so."

And with that tantalizing remark hanging in the air, he walked away, leaving her to wonder exactly when the world had turned topsy-turvy.

"Mum, what on earth is wrong with you this morning?" Moira demanded when Kiera had lost count of the pub's liquor inventory for the third time.

Her mother blinked and stared at her. "I don't know what you mean. I'm fine."

Moira shook her head and guided Kiera to a table in a corner, left and returned with a cup of tea.

"You're most definitely not fine," Moira said. "You're distracted. You keep gazing toward the kitchen with this odd expression on your face. Is it Bryan? Or his daughter? Has something gone wrong? Has Bryan upset you?"

"You act as if Bryan's the only thing I might have on my mind," Kiera said indignantly. "My life does not revolve around Bryan Laramie or any other man, for that matter."

Moira wasn't buying that for a second. She'd hoped that her conversation with Bryan the day before would nudge him off dead center and spur some action, but what if he hadn't taken that next step, after all? What if she'd only made things worse? It wouldn't be the first time that her good intentions had gone awry. Luke would happily point out a few other occasions. She simply did not have Nell's finesse when it came to meddling successfully.

"Mum, I can't help if you don't talk to me," she said in frustration.

"Who said I needed help?"

Moira was about to throw up her hands and go back to counting bottles of whiskey when her mother added, "What do you suppose is going on in there?"

Moira followed her mother's gaze. "In the kitchen?"

"Of course in the kitchen. There's no one else about in here this morning. Luke's gone off to see a supplier."

"Deanna was trying to follow Bryan's instructions when I came through there an hour ago," she said. "Are you worried about whether they're getting along?"

"It's not the two of them who concern me," Kiera said. "Nell's joined them."

"Okay," Moira said slowly, trying to grasp the problem, then giving up. The workings of her mother's mind eluded her. "Nell's not likely to cause problems for them."

"Of course not."

"Is it the idea of her teaming up with Nell to meddle with your relationship with Bryan? Luke said Bryan had mentioned something about that a few days ago."

"And then apparently forgot all about it," Kiera said with disgust. "But that's not on my mind at the moment. Do you not recall Nell asking for my Irish stew recipe when she was at the house?"

Moira now caught a bit of her mother's alarm. "You didn't give it to her, did you? Not before this cooking competition?"

"Do I look as if I can be taken in that easily?" Kiera snapped. "I told her it was all in my head, but that I'd write it down and get it to her soon."

"Then that's all okay," Moira said, relieved.

"Or is it? Nell has been making the stew for years. She tasted mine and knew at once there was a difference. They could be in there experimenting right this minute. Bryan's a skilled chef. He knows spices. Between the two of them, they could come up with an even better version."

Moira was honestly stunned that the stupid contest was what was weighing on her mother's mind. "This is about stew? The distraction? The heavy sighs? All of it?"

"The contest might not matter to you, but it does to me, and I've told you why."

"The whole make-or-break thing about your reputation," Moira concluded. "And I told you that you were worrying about nothing."

"I'm entered in this contest because a few clever

people—yes, that includes you and Nell—manipulated me into it. Don't make fun of me because I'm taking it seriously."

"Do you want me to go in there to see what's going on?" Moira asked.

Kiera looked startled. "You'd spy?"

"It's *my* pub, *my* kitchen," Moira said. "Okay, technically, it's Luke's, but I have a right to pass through anytime I choose to."

To her surprise, Kiera drew herself up. "An interesting point. I should have thought of it myself. I work here. I have a right to be in there, too. You stay here. I'll go in there and see what the three of them are up to."

She stalked off, her chin lifted defiantly. Moira called after her. "Let me know if you need backup."

Kiera only waved her off and replied, "I've got this."

Moira chuckled. The sight of her mum standing up for herself was something to behold. Maybe Kiera really didn't need her to run interference on any front these days, and wouldn't that be a wonderful testament to how much she'd changed since coming to Chesapeake Shores!

To Kiera's surprise and faint dismay, she found Nell and Deanna huddled in a corner of the kitchen chatting like old friends, while Bryan worked on lunch prep and the stew simmered away on the stove unattended. She sniffed the air but could detect no discernible difference between it and his past attempts. Perhaps she'd overreacted and there was no conspiracy to steal her recipe, after all.

"Did you need something?" Bryan asked, regarding her with amusement.

"Just some water," she said.

His lips quirked. "And there's none of that at the bar?"

"I meant ice for the water."

"I checked the ice maker myself this morning. Is it not working now?"

She scowled at his ready answers. "Okay, it's the wedges of lime and lemon I need. Have you put those out there as well and I somehow missed them?"

He laughed then. "They're ready to go and in the fridge where they usually are. Deanna cut them herself."

Deanna looked up at that. "It took me three times as long as it would have taken him to get the wedges just right, but I think the entire task was meant to keep me out of his way while he made that batch of stew. He doesn't trust me near that. He's convinced I'll make a mess of it and ruin his chances of beating you."

"It's a reasonable assumption," Bryan said, but he was grinning.

"Indeed," Deanna said. "There is strong evidence that my medical career should not veer toward surgery. My skills with a knife are in serious doubt."

"They wouldn't be if you'd practice," Bryan said.

"How, when you won't let me?"

"I left you on your own to do those lime and lemon wedges, didn't I?"

"And encouraged Nell to coach me," Deanna retorted.

Nell and Kiera exchanged a look and dared to laugh.

"They're sounding like a typical father and daughter, aren't they?" Nell observed.

"Certainly the way Dillon and I always interacted,"

Kiera confirmed, reassured by the whole exchange. "And still do on occasion."

She retrieved the limes and lemons and left the three of them still taunting each other. It was only after she'd returned to the bar that it occurred to her to wonder exactly what Deanna and Nell might have been huddling about in the corner where Bryan was unlikely to overhear them. That was a worry for another time.

As well as things had gone ever since Deanna's unexpected arrival in the morning, Bryan remained alert to every nuance in her voice, every hint that she wasn't yet entirely at peace with the past as he'd described to her.

Tonight she'd asked once more to see the box of proof he'd shared with her, then if he had any more old photo albums from their days as a family. He'd seen the expectant look on her face and known she was after more than pictures. She wanted evidence that those pictures and those times had mattered enough for him to keep them. The ones in the box she'd seen before evidently weren't enough to satisfy her.

He'd produced everything he had, all of it carefully preserved, and delivered it to Kiera's during his break at the pub. When he'd left, Deanna was removing each item—from her hospital bracelet and baby blanket to the silver spoon the chef he'd worked for had given her, from a baby rattle to tiny outfits, from framed photos to stuffed animals—and examining each one intently. He had the sense she was trying to stir memories, no matter how unlikely they were to come.

The look on her face and the tears in her eyes haunted him while he finished up his work at the pub. He couldn't help wondering how long it would be be-

fore she trusted him even half as much as she obviously
trusted Kiera. There was some sort of magical connection between the two of them. He was glad of it on
the one hand, but on another, he couldn't help wishing
that the bond between him and Deanna was as strong.

Patience, he reminded himself sternly, as he was
about to open Kiera's back door when he arrived home.
Hearing voices, though, he paused.

"No one understands the heartbreak of being abandoned more than I do," Kiera was telling his daughter.
"There's a difference, though, between a deliberate act
and one that comes about through no fault of the other
person. Your father never chose to abandon you. And
whatever flaws he had that drove your mother to leave,
it was her choice, not his. And you were not the cause of
any of it. If anything, you were an unintended victim."

Deanna quickly jumped to her mother's defense, only
to have Kiera chuckle. "Did I say I was blaming her? I
imagine your father could drive a saint to desperation
from time to time. I know there are days I'd like to walk
out of that pub and never look back, but I'm older than
your mum was when she left and better able, perhaps,
to stand my ground. I'm willing to stick around and
fight for something I believe has value."

Her words struck a chord deep inside him. Bryan
couldn't help it. He stepped into view. "You're saying
I might have value?"

Both women regarded him with startled gazes.
"You've been eavesdropping?" Kiera demanded.

"I just arrived. I didn't want to interrupt what
sounded like an intense conversation," he said in his
own defense. "Rather than talking about my supposed

crime, let's talk about what you said. You suggested I have some value."

Kiera's cheeks turned bright red, but she didn't back down. "I said that these feelings between us might have value. And if you hadn't been listening in to hear it yourself, I'd be denying I ever said it."

He winked at Deanna, who was regarding the two of them with sudden amusement. Her serious conversation with Kiera about the past seemed to be forgotten for the moment.

"Am I in the way?" Deanna asked, though she showed no signs of leaving.

"Stay," Bryan commanded. "I might need a witness. I do believe that Kiera Malone just said she had feelings for me."

"That's what I heard," Deanna confirmed.

"So now it's two against one?" Kiera asked indignantly. "That's a fine thing after all I've done to mediate between you."

"I think perhaps the three of us united would be a force to be reckoned with," Bryan said, looking from one woman to the other.

"What on earth is that supposed to mean?" Kiera asked. "United against what?"

"I've been thinking recently that it might be time I made a few changes in my life. I wasn't quite ready to talk about it, but this might be the perfect time."

At his words, Deanna looked alarmed. "You're not thinking of leaving Chesapeake Shores, are you?"

"Absolutely not," he assured her. "This has become home to me, and that's especially true since it means you'll be close by."

"Then what?" Kiera asked, looking thoroughly puzzled.

"Is it the two of you?" Deanna asked hopefully. "Are you going to ask Kiera to marry you?"

Bryan laughed at her eagerness, all the while wondering if Kiera was freaking out. "If I were, would I be needing you to announce my intentions?"

Deanna looked chagrined. "Sorry. But is that it?"

"That's a subject for another time," he said, aware of the tiniest hint of disappointment on both of their faces, though Kiera was quick to hide it. "This is about work, about a dream I once had that I put on hold."

A smile broke across Kiera's face as if she'd grasped the significance of his enigmatic remarks, but Deanna still looked confused. They waited expectantly.

"It's not that I'm not loyal to Luke," he said quietly. "But I'm thinking perhaps the time has come to strike out on my own. The pub has established its own unique niche. Brady's has had a monopoly on fine dining in Chesapeake Shores for far too long. Kiera, would you be interested in helping me give them a run for their money? I have some ideas that aren't suitable for a pub that I think would be welcomed by the locals and the tourists."

"What sort of ideas?" Kiera asked suspiciously.

"Perhaps a blend of various ethnic foods with a touch of elegance, all farm-to-table. Does that appeal to you?"

Kiera's gaze narrowed. Some of her delight seemed to have dimmed. "So this is strictly a business proposition?"

Deanna shook her head, laughing. "Dad, get a clue!"

Bryan regarded the pair of them innocently. "Were you hoping for more?" he inquired, his gaze on Kiera steady.

"And if I was?" Kiera asked.

"Well, I'm surely not going to propose marriage with my daughter sitting right here. Go away, Deanna."

"Stay. Go." She grinned. "He seems a little indecisive to me, Kiera. Think twice before you say yes."

When she was gone, Bryan pulled Kiera to her feet. "Will you say yes?"

"I haven't heard a question yet, at least not beyond asking me to leave my son-in-law's pub to join forces with you."

"I was thinking the restaurant's first big event could be our wedding reception. What do you say, Kiera? I think it's time we ended our kitchen wars and became a team in every way."

"Where is this coming from, Bryan? You've never hinted at such a thing before. We've never even gone on a formal date."

"If it's courting you need, I'll do it, though I am seriously out of practice."

To his surprise, she touched a hand to his cheek, unexpected tears in her eyes. "I'll consider it," she said softly. "But only after we finish what we started."

"Meaning?"

"We've that fall festival competition to get through or we'll disappoint Nell."

"You're bringing that into this? One thing should have nothing to do with the other," he protested.

"You beat me fair and square, Bryan Laramie, and you'll not only get the trophy, you'll get me, too."

"You're joking," he said.

"Do you believe your Irish stew is the best?"

"I do."

"Then you'll put it to the test."

"With stakes that high, I won't be above bribing every single person in town to vote for mine," he warned.

"You'd cheat?"

"To win your heart, I think I'd do just about anything," he said solemnly.

And, as surprising as it still was to him after all these years of being on his own, he meant it. Having his daughter back in his life was monumental and he'd be forever grateful, but Kiera was the piece of his heart that had been missing.

Chapter 24

At the first opportunity the next morning, Deanna stole away from Kiera's and made her way to Nell's cottage. Before knocking on the door, she stood outside, drawn by the cottage's charm, its spectacular garden, filled now with the colors of fall, and its view of the bay, which was even better than the one from her father's deck.

Just as she was about to tap on the door, it swung open to reveal an older man with a shock of thick white hair, slightly stooped shoulders and a broad, welcoming smile.

"Something tells me that you're the long-missing daughter of our favorite chef," he said. "And I'm Dillon O'Malley."

"Kiera's father," Deanna concluded. "I've been hearing stories about you."

"At least some of them good, I hope."

"All of them," she assured him. "It's your own wife and daughter sharing them, after all."

"Ah, but Kiera hasn't always spoken so highly of me. I'm sure she's told you that, as well."

"She mentioned it," Deanna admitted. "But only to

help me see that father-daughter relationships could be complicated. In my particular circumstances, I found that to be comforting."

"Indeed. Now, come in. Nell's expecting you. She's in the kitchen taking fresh scones from the oven right now," he said, gesturing toward the back of the house. "I'll leave the two of you to your tea and visit."

"Don't let me chase you off."

"You're not. Don't tell my wife, but this is the time of day I sneak away in search of a decent cup of coffee," he confided.

Laughing at the idea of him needing to keep his caffeine habit from Nell, Deanna let him go and headed in the direction of the kitchen that he'd pointed out, though she honestly didn't need his directions. The aromas would have drawn her exactly this way.

"There you are," Nell said. "Sit down and tell me what's happened since yesterday. I sensed you had a bit of news when you called."

"You have no idea. I think our meddling days are at an end." Barely containing her own excitement, she announced, "My father's proposed to Kiera. I was right there for every word. Well, almost. He threw me out at the end, but to be honest, I lingered just outside the kitchen door."

Nell looked stunned. "You're sure of this? As stubborn as the two of them are, I thought it would take more of an effort."

Deanna nodded. "So did I. I was looking forward to conspiring with you. After all, my father's gone all these years since my mom left without replacing her, though there were complicated reasons behind that. They could have been overcome, if there'd been someone important, though. And, from what you told me yesterday, Kiera's been hesitant about commitment, as well."

"But she said yes this time, of course," Nell said confidently.

Deanna chuckled. "How well do you know Kiera? Weren't you the one who repeated just now how stubborn she can be?"

Looking even more startled, Nell sat down. "She turned him down?" she asked with evident disbelief. "Stubborn is one thing, but this…" She shook her head. "I never expected this."

Deanna explained the deal that had been reached the night before. "Thank goodness I eavesdropped, even though I know it's a very bad habit to get into. I stood there rooting for her to say yes right away, but I have to admit, I thought this was pretty clever on her part. It ups the ante for your competition, too, by the way, whether that was her intention or not."

"Clever to make him wait, perhaps, but awfully risky. What if something goes wrong? What if she wins, your father is humiliated and withdraws his proposal? Men can do some incredibly stupid things when their pride's been hurt, especially in public."

"You probably know a lot more about that sort of thing than I do," Deanna admitted. "I suppose it's up to us to see that my father wins this contest."

Nell nodded. "Yes, of course. And that's exactly what we'll do, even if some people conclude that I especially am being a traitor to a family member to suggest such a thing. I can hardly reveal why it's so vital, now, can I?"

Deanna regarded her worriedly. "I hadn't thought of what people might think of your role in this. I can do all of the campaigning. No one will think a thing about it if I'm trying to rally people to my father's side. The only trouble is, no one in town knows or respects me as they do you."

"I've been called worse than a traitor from time to time," Nell said, waving off the concern. "In the end everyone will see why it was necessary for me to take Bryan's side. Besides, he works for my grandson and has been using my recipe at the pub. Some will think that I'm defending that out of my own sense of pride and loyalty to Luke."

"Will they forgive you for taking sides against Kiera, though?" Deanna asked worriedly. "Especially Dillon?"

Nell shrugged. "I've had to earn forgiveness a time or two in my life. I can do it again."

Deanna nodded slowly. "Then where should we start?"

Nell's expression turned thoughtful. "First we have to determine what we're going to tell people. Perhaps we should use the truth, after all. A subtle whisper here and there should spread the word in no time. Everyone likes knowing they've played a part in the outcome of a good love story. That might be our best tactic."

"I agree," Deanna said with enthusiasm. "What next?"

She wasn't at all surprised when Nell got a sheet of paper and began making a list, divvying up people they could contact and making notes for Deanna on the best approach to take with each of them. Deanna concluded military strategies were probably decided with only slightly more attention to detail.

"If you handle these, I'll get to the rest, either directly or indirectly," Nell said, handing her a sheet of paper. "Once word is out that I'm campaigning for the enemy and how high the stakes are, word will spread through town like wildfire."

"Will you tell Dillon what you're up to? It is his daughter you'll be campaigning against," Deanna said. "I'd hate for there to be a rift between you, even for a cause that he'll consider a good one in the end."

"You've no need to worry about Dillon. I'll explain what's going on and swear him to secrecy. No one wants Kiera to stay in town and find happiness with your father more than he does."

Deanna beamed at her. "I wish I'd had a grandmother like you," she told Nell. "My own grandmother on my mom's side died long before I was born and, needless to say, I never knew my father's mother. Ash's mother is very sweet, but she would never engage in something so devious."

Nell regarded her with concern. "Perhaps you shouldn't, either. Meddling is considered by some to be a very bad habit."

"But it's so much fun," Deanna said. "I can hardly wait."

Nell studied her for an instant, then laughed. "Deanna, you'll make a fine addition to the O'Briens, even if the connection is a couple of degrees removed."

Amazingly, though the complex family ties Deanna had appreciated all her life had been extraordinary, the very loose ties to the O'Briens promised to bring something very special to her life.

Bryan found Luke and Mick O'Brien huddled together in the pub two days before the fall festival. Their whispers were a dead giveaway that something was going on, and their expressions suggested they didn't like it.

"What's wrong?" Bryan asked, pouring himself a cup of coffee and joining them at the bar.

"Nothing," Luke said, backing away quickly, his expression suddenly neutral.

"Not a thing," Mick confirmed, though he wasn't nearly as quick to hide his troubled expression. The paper he'd hurriedly stuffed into his pocket suggested otherwise.

"Is this about the bets you're taking on the cooking contest?" Bryan demanded. "I know all about those, and I know Moira doesn't approve. Nor do Nell or Kiera."

"If they knew what we know, they'd be even more upset," Mick said. "I suggest you pretend you haven't seen or heard a thing."

"Now there's a comment deliberately designed to stir my imagination," Bryan said. "Since I'm at the center of this, I think I deserve to know what's going on."

The two men exchanged a long look.

"I think we ought to tell him," Luke said. "He is one of the competitors, after all."

Mick looked less convinced. "This could mean nothing, though. There's no reason to stir the pot, so to speak."

Bryan met his gaze and waited. Mick had never been known to keep a secret for long. And, contrary to his statement, he liked nothing more than to stir the pot.

"Okay, then," Mick said at last. "Up until a few days ago, the bets coming in were in Kiera's favor. After she had that tasting at her cottage for the women in the family, they started campaigning on her behalf. Everywhere

I went, it seemed women were shoving a handful of bills at me and putting it all on Kiera to win the contest."

Bryan wasn't at all surprised by the support. Those women had come to consider Kiera one of their own. He'd heard the raves about her stew and assumed they were well deserved. That only made him want to try harder. Now, of course, he had an added incentive that even Mick and Luke couldn't possibly know about.

"Judging from your expressions, something's changed," he said.

"In a dramatic way," Mick confirmed. "I've never seen anything quite like it. Practically overnight, the tide turned in your favor. Those very same women were coming to me with new bets and adding more money. Their husbands were, as well. It's as if they know something."

Bryan frowned at that. "You don't suppose someone's planning to sabotage Kiera's stew, sneak in and dump a box of salt in it or something like that to ruin the taste of it."

"Not in Chesapeake Shores," Mick said adamantly. "People here might love to place a bet from time to time on the craziest of things, but none have so much money at stake that they'd stack the odds in their own favor."

"Besides, we've heard rumors that Nell is behind it," Luke admitted. "She might campaign hard, but she would draw the line at cheating. She and your daughter have been going all over town rallying support for you. I can't understand it. It makes sense that Deanna would want you to win, but my grandmother? She's cheerleading against her own husband's daughter. I imagine Dillon's fit to be tied."

"She could be doing it for the sake of the pub," Bryan

suggested, though he was beginning to think it wasn't about that at all. He could easily envision his daughter blabbing about the proposal to her new ally and the two of them forming a misguided team to back him. "I am the chef here, after all. Our reputation is at stake."

"That doesn't sound like Gram, though," Luke said.

"No, this seems more personal," Mick agreed, though it was evident he hadn't a clue about what she was up to or why.

Trying hard not to laugh, Bryan debated enlightening them. He knew exactly what had spurred this sudden campaign on his behalf. That deal he'd made with Kiera that would guarantee that she'd accept his proposal of marriage *if* he won the cooking contest.

Luke studied him with a narrowed gaze. "You don't seem that surprised about any of this," he told Bryan. "Do you know what they're up to?"

"I have an idea," he admitted.

"Then, please, tell us," Mick said. "If there's some conspiracy afoot, I need to know about it. Did you put them up to it?"

"Absolutely not," Bryan said. "If I win, I want to do it fair and square."

"Can you get them to back off, so people will know that whoever wins did it fairly?" Luke asked. "The last thing we need is rumors that there was cheating of some kind going on."

"Much as I hate to admit it, I don't know my own daughter well enough yet to have much influence over her. She seems to be under your mother's spell, Mick. Perhaps you're the one who should be taking a stand. Will Nell listen to you?"

Mick sighed heavily. "There's little chance of that.

If Ma has some mission she's dedicated to, especially one that might put her at odds with her own husband, then she's not going to listen to me."

"Then I guess we'll just have to sit back and see how this plays out," Bryan said. "Luke, you might want to tell the folks in charge of parking, setting up chairs and the like to be prepared for record-breaking crowds this year. And if it was your brother-in-law Mack who made those tickets people will use to vote in the cooking contest, let him know he should probably double or triple the original order. Something tells me that we're going to be selling a whole lot of Irish stew."

Kiera hadn't intended to eavesdrop, but she'd overheard just enough of the intense conversation Bryan was having with Mick and Luke to understand that there was a conspiracy going on to ensure that Bryan won the cooking contest. And since Nell and Deanna were involved, she knew precisely why they were determined to affect the outcome.

Letting the door close quietly, she went right back through the kitchen and out into the alley, then headed to Sally's. When she found none of the O'Brien women there, she moved on to Bree's Flowers on Main shop next door.

She found Bree arranging a mix of orange, gold and bronze mums in a tall vase with branches of fall leaves. The effect was stunning.

"It's for the front table at the inn," Bree told her. "What do you think? Is it impressive enough?"

"It's breathtaking," Kiera said honestly. "I thought your real talent was writing, but you have quite a knack for this, as well."

Bree beamed. "To Gram's despair, I grew up yanking the wrong things out of her garden, but the one thing I did learn to her satisfaction was how to arrange flowers. It's a nice counterpoint to staring at a blank computer screen when I'm having writer's block." She studied Kiera intently. "What brings you by? Something tells me you're not here for a bouquet of flowers."

"I overheard something at the pub just now. I think there's a plan in place to ensure that Bryan wins the Irish stew contest."

Dismay spread across Bree's face. "Who's involved?"

"Well, it was Bryan, Luke and Mick talking, but they were saying that Bryan's daughter and Nell are behind it."

Bree's expression turned thoughtful. "I suppose that makes sense. Deanna was bound to support her father, and Bryan is using Nell's recipe."

"If that were all it was about, so be it," Kiera said. "But there's something you don't know." She explained the deal she'd made with Bryan. "I didn't think he'd get a bunch of allies to try to steal the victory right out from under me. It should be about the best stew." She regarded Bree intently. "Shouldn't it? That's why you all were spreading the word about mine, because you liked it, right?"

To her dismay, Bree laughed. "Ah, Kiera, surely you know that none of this was ever about the stew. It was a way to keep the sparks flying between you and Bryan. Now that the job has been done effectively and a marriage proposal's on the table, do you honestly think there's a single O'Brien who won't do whatever it takes to seal the deal?"

"But how on earth can I marry a man who'd win by cheating?" Kiera asked.

"I doubt Bryan, Deanna, Nell or anyone else sees it that way. They're only trying to ensure your happiness. It's a little mixed up."

"A little?" Kiera asked incredulously.

"Okay, a lot, but it's the O'Briens we're talking about. Love and family trump everything else."

"Well, our deal is off if that's the way he wins," Kiera said stubbornly. "And that's the last I intend to say about that."

She marched out of the flower shop with her chin up and her temper ready to take on anyone who crossed her today, including Bryan and every one of the sneaky O'Briens, starting with Nell. What she'd do about Deanna, who was staying under her very own roof, was something she'd have to consider very carefully. The girl was, after all, just trying to support her father, and even Kiera was wise enough not to want to tamper with that bond.

Attendance at the fall festival had never been higher. Though the crowd milled about the various booths buying crafts and jars of homemade preserves, it was clear that anticipation for the cooking contest was running high. It was all anyone was talking about. And while people were sampling desserts and other specialties from the participating chefs, the lines for the Irish stew were the longest. Kiera watched in amazement. It was clear everyone in Chesapeake Shores now knew about the outrageous bet between Bryan and Kiera. Despite Kiera's declaration to Bree, the O'Briens were now oddly unified in telling every person they met on the town green that a vote for Bryan was a vote for love.

Dillon pulled Kiera aside as she was about to start the preparations for making another gigantic batch of her stew. "Do you want to win this wager?"

"You know my stew is the best," she said.

"Not what I asked. Do you love this man or not?"

She shrugged. "I just don't want to make it easy for him, which it seems everyone in town has conspired to do now. Nell and the others have turned it into some romantic fantasy. It's not about the stew at all, anymore."

"Kiera, my darling girl, you don't make loving you easy on anyone," her father said, his tone wry. "What will you do if your stew wins? Will that make you happy, to win the prize and lose this man you've come to love? And don't be denying to me that you love him, because it's been plain as day for a while now."

"I wasn't going to deny it. As for what I'll do at the end of the day if I happen to win, you'll have to wait and see. Given the way the O'Briens are trying to stack the deck against me, it seems unlikely to come to that."

At six that evening, as the sun was setting and the final votes were being counted, she and Bryan stood nervously on the stage on the town green waiting for Nell to announce the winner of the Irish stew cooking contest.

Eventually Nell stepped to the microphone, her expression shaken. "Ladies and gentlemen, the winner of the first annual fall festival cooking contest by one vote is… Kiera Malone!"

The announcement was greeted by a hesitant mix of cheers and stunned silence.

Kiera wasn't sure what she expected to find when

she looked into Bryan's eyes, but it certainly wasn't the gleam of satisfaction she found there.

"You wanted me to win?" she asked, shocked.

"You deserved to win. Even I voted for you. A whole bunch of times, in fact. I wasn't entirely sure if I'd bought enough tickets, but then Dillon said he'd buy a few more."

Kiera was thoroughly confused and not entirely sure what to make of this turn of events. "But the stakes...? Didn't you want the victory?"

"If you're asking if I didn't want *you* enough, the answer's no. I didn't want you this way. I want you because my love is enough for you, not because my Irish stew is better than yours."

She felt a smile spread across her face then. Her own very large gamble had paid off, after all. "In that case, then perhaps you can steal that microphone from Nell's hand and make an announcement of your own."

"What announcement would that be?"

"One that's sure to please this crowd, even the sneaky O'Briens, who believe that love conquers everything. You can tell them that I might have won the trophy, but you won an even better prize. You got the woman *and* her trophy."

Bryan laughed, exactly as she'd intended, proving that he understood her as few men did.

"You're a very complicated woman, Kiera Malone," he declared.

"But life with me will never be dull."

"That's the bonus I'm counting on," he said, taking the microphone from Nell.

He repeated exactly the words she'd suggested, then went down on one knee in front of her with a ring in hand. Kiera saw the satisfaction on her father's face, on Nell's and on Moira's. Even Deanna was cheering as Kiera let him slip the ring on her finger.

Bryan rose and drew her to him for a long, lingering kiss that stirred the crowd as nothing else had. With her heart filled with joy, she couldn't help thinking that a little of that Chesapeake Shores magic she'd heard so much about had indeed rubbed off on her.

* * * * *

Turn the page for a special sneak peek at
Midnight Promises
by #1 New York Times *bestselling author*
Sherryl Woods
coming soon in paperback from MIRA Books.

Prologue

The bride wore a cocktail-length, off-the-shoulder gown in shimmering off-white satin and an antique lace mantilla—a family heirloom—reluctantly provided by her soon-to-be mother-in-law.

At the front of the small Roman Catholic church in Serenity stood the man who'd changed Karen Ames's mind about love, convincing her that the past was just that, over and done with. He'd promised her enduring love, a true partnership, and he'd shown her those traits time and again during their long courtship.

At a tug on her skirt, Karen leaned down to look into the excited face of her six-year-old daughter, Daisy.

"When are we getting married?" Daisy asked, practically bouncing up and down in anticipation.

Karen smiled at her eagerness. After too many years with no father figure around, Daisy and Mack had fallen as deeply in love with Elliott Cruz as Karen had. And in many ways, it was his kind and generous relationship with her children that had convinced Karen that Elliott was nothing like her first husband, a man who'd abandoned them all, leaving behind a mountain of debt.

"I want to be married to Elliott," Daisy said with another tug in the direction of the altar. "Let's hurry."

Karen checked her four-year-old son to assure that Mack hadn't stripped off the tie she'd put on for him earlier or managed to douse his new suit with soda. She also assured herself that the wedding rings were still firmly attached to the pillow he would carry down the aisle.

Dana Sue Sullivan, her boss, friend and matron-of-honor, touched a hand to her shoulder. "Everything's good, Karen. How are your nerves?"

"Dancing a jig," she responded candidly. "And then I look inside and see Elliott waiting there, and everything settles."

"Then keep your eyes on him," Dana Sue advised. "And let's get this show on the road before these two leave without us."

She glanced down at Daisy and Mack, who were already inching from the foyer into the church.

At some signal Karen didn't even notice, the organist began to play for their entrance. Daisy took off down the aisle almost at a run, scattering rose petals with enthusiasm. Then, at some whispered comment, she grinned, glanced back at her mother and slowed to a more sedate pace. Mack was right on her heels, his expression solemn, a tiny frown puckering his brow until he'd safely reached Elliott's side.

Dana Sue followed, winking at her husband who was sitting at the front of the church, then smiling broadly at Elliott, who was running a nervous finger under the collar of his shirt.

Karen took a last deep breath, reminded herself that

this time her marriage was going to be forever, that she'd finally gotten it right.

She lifted her gaze until she met Elliott's, then took that first confident, trusting step down the aisle into the future that promised to be everything her first marriage hadn't been.

1

Now that fall was just around the corner, Karen Cruz was experimenting with a new navy bean soup recipe for tomorrow's lunch at Sullivan's when sous-chef and friend Erik Whitney peered over her shoulder, gave an approving nod, then asked, "So, are you excited about the gym Elliott's going to open with us?"

Startled by the seemingly out-of-the-blue question, Karen spilled the entire box of sea salt she was holding into the soup. "My husband's opening a gym? Here in Serenity?"

Obviously taken aback by her puzzled reaction, Erik winced. "I take it he hasn't told you?"

"No, he hasn't said a word," she responded. Unfortunately, it was increasingly typical that when it came to the important things in their marriage, the things they should be deciding jointly, she and Elliott didn't have a lot of discussions. He made the decisions, then told her about them later. Or, as in this case, didn't bother informing her at all.

After dumping the now inedible batch of soup out, Karen started over, then spent the next hour stewing over this latest example of Elliott's careless disregard for her feelings. Each time he did something like this, it hurt her, chipping away at her faith that their marriage was as solid as she'd once believed it to be, that he was a man who'd never betray her as her first husband had.

Elliott was the man who'd pursued her with charm and wit and determination. It was his sensitivity to her feelings that had ultimately won her over and convinced her that taking another chance on love wouldn't be the second biggest mistake of her life.

She drew in a deep breath and fought for calm, doing her best to come up with a reasonable explanation for Elliott's silence about a decision that could change their lives. It was true that he did have a habit of trying to protect her, of not wanting her to worry, especially about money. Maybe that was why he'd kept this news from her. He had to know she'd react negatively, especially right now.

They were, after all, planning to add a baby to their family. Now that her two children from that previous disaster of a marriage—Mack and Daisy—were both settled in school and on an even keel after the many upheavals in their young lives, the timing finally seemed right.

But between Elliott's fluctuating income as a personal trainer at The Corner Spa and her barely above-minimum-wage pay here at the restaurant, adding to their family had taken careful consideration. She'd wanted never again to be in the same financial mess she'd been in when she and Elliott had first met. He knew that. So where on earth was the money to come from to invest in this new venture of his? There was no savings for a new business. Unless, she thought, he intended to borrow it from their baby fund. The possibility sent a chill down her spine.

And then there was the whole issue of loyalty. Maddie Maddox who ran the spa, Karen's boss, Dana Sue Sullivan, and Erik's wife, Helen Decatur-Whitney, owned The Corner Spa and had made Elliott an integral part of the team there. They'd also gone way above and beyond for Karen when she'd been a struggling single mom. Helen had even taken in Karen's kids for a while. How could Elliott consider just walking out on them? What kind of man would do that? Not the kind she'd thought she'd married, that was for sure.

Though she'd started out trying to rationalize Elliott's decision to keep her in the dark, apparently the strategy hadn't worked. She was stirring the fresh pot of soup so vigorously, Dana Sue approached with a worried frown.

"If you're not careful, you're going to puree that soup," Dana Sue said quietly. "Not that it won't be delicious that way, but I'm assuming it wasn't part of your plan."

"Plan?" Karen retorted, anger creeping right back into her voice despite her best intention to give Elliott a chance to explain what had been going on behind her back. "Who plans anything anymore? Or sticks to the plan, if they do have one? No one I know, or if they do, they don't bother to discuss these big plans with their partner."

Dana Sue cast a confused look toward Erik. "What am I missing?"

"I mentioned the gym," Erik explained, his expression guilt-ridden. "Apparently Elliott hadn't told her anything about it."

When Dana Sue merely nodded in understanding, Karen stared at her in dismay. "You knew, too? You knew about the gym and you're okay with it?"

"Well, sure," Dana Sue said as if it were no big deal that Elliott, Erik and whoever else wanted to open a business that would compete with The Corner Spa. "Maddie, Helen and I signed off on the idea the minute the guys brought it to us. The town's been needing a men's gym for a long time. You know how disgusting Dexter's is. That's why we opened The Corner Spa exclusively for women in the first place. This will be an expansion of sorts. We're actually going to be partnering with them. They have a sound business plan. More important, they'll have Elliott. He has the expertise and reputation to draw in clients."

Karen ripped off her apron. "Well, isn't that just the last straw?" she muttered. Not only were her husband, her coworker and her boss in on this, but so were her friends. Okay, maybe that meant Elliott wasn't being disloyal, as she'd first feared, except, of course to her. "I'm taking my break early, if you don't mind. I'll be back in time for dinner prep, then Tina's due in to take over the rest of the shift."

A few years back, she and Tina Martinez, then a single mom struggling to make ends meet while she tried to fight her husband's deportation, had split the shifts at Sullivan's, which had allowed them both the flexibility they desperately needed to juggle family responsibilities. Karen was still thankful for that, even though they were both working more hours now that their lives had settled down and Sullivan's had become a busy and unqualified success story.

Though she'd thought mentioning Tina would reassure Dana Sue that she wasn't going to be left in the lurch, Dana Sue's expression suggested otherwise.

"Hold on a second," she commanded.

Then, to Karen's surprise, she said, "I hope you're going someplace to cool off and think about this. It's all good, Karen. Honestly."

An hour ago, Karen might have accepted that. Now, not so much. "I'm in no mood to cool off. Actually I'm thinking I just might divorce my husband," she retorted direly.

As she picked up steam and headed out the back door, she overheard Dana Sue say, "She doesn't mean that, does she?"

Karen didn't wait for Erik's reply, but the truth was, her likely response wouldn't have been reassuring.

Elliott had been totally distracted while putting his seniors' exercise class through its paces. Usually he thoroughly enjoyed working with these feisty women who made up for in enthusiasm what they lacked in physical stamina and strength. Though it embarrassed him, he even got a kick out of the way they openly ogled him, trying to come up with new reasons each week to get him to strip off his shirt so they could gaze appreciatively at his abs. He'd accused them on more than one occasion of being outrageously lecherous. Not a one of them had denied it.

"Honey, I was one of those cougars they talk about before they invented the term," Flo Decatur, who was in her early seventies, had told him once. "And I make no apologies for it, either. You might be a little out of my usual range, but I've discovered recently that even men in their sixties are getting a little stuffy for me. I might need to find me a much younger man."

Elliott had had no idea how to respond to that. He wondered if Flo's daughter, attorney Helen Decatur-Whitney, had any idea what her irrepressible mother was up to.

Now he glanced at the clock on the wall, relieved to see that the hour-long session was up. "Okay, ladies, that's it for today. Don't forget to get in a few walks this week. A one-hour class on Wednesdays isn't enough to keep you healthy."

"Oh, sweetie, when I want to get my blood pumping the rest of the week, I just think about how you look without your shirt," Garnet Rogers commented with a wink. "Beats walking anytime."

Elliott felt his cheeks heat, even as the other women in the group laughed. "Okay, that's enough out of you, Garnet. You're making me blush."

"Looks good on you," she said, undisturbed by his embarrassment.

The women slowly started to drift away, chattering excitedly about an upcoming dance at the senior center and speculating about who Jake Cudlow might ask. Jake was apparently the hot catch in town, Elliott had concluded from listening to these discussions. Since he'd seen the balding, bespectacled, paunchy Jake a few times, he had to wonder what the women's standards really were.

Elliott was about to head to his office when Frances Wingate stopped him. She'd been his wife's neighbor when he and Karen had first started dating. They both considered her practically a member of the family. Now she was regarding him with a worried look.

"Something's on your mind, isn't it?" she said. "You were a million miles away during class. Not that we present much of a challenge. You could probably lead us without breaking a sweat, but usually you manage to show a little enthusiasm, especially during that dancing segment Flo talked you into adding." She gave him a sly look. "You know she did that just to see you move your hips in the salsa, right?"

"I figured as much," he said. "Not much Flo does surprises or embarrasses me anymore."

Frances held his gaze. "You still haven't answered my question."

"Sorry," Elliott said. "What?"

"Don't apologize. Just tell me what's wrong. Are the kids okay?"

Elliott smiled. Frances adored Daisy and Mack, though both were unquestionably a handful. "They're fine," he assured her.

"And Karen?"

"She's great," he said, though he wondered how truthful the answer really was. He had a hunch she'd be less than great if she found out what he'd been up to. And truthfully, he had no idea why he'd kept these plans for opening a gym from her. Had he feared her disapproval, anticipated a fight? Maybe so. She was rightfully very touchy when it came to finances after going through a lousy time with an ex-husband who'd abandoned her and left her with a mountain of debt.

Frances gave him a chiding look. "Elliott Cruz, don't try fibbing to me. I can read you the same way I could read all those kids who passed through my classrooms over the years. What's wrong with Karen?"

He sighed. "You're even sharper than my mother,

and I could never hide anything from her, either," he lamented.

"I should hope not," Frances retorted.

"No offense, Frances, but I think the person I really need to be talking to about this is my wife."

"Then do it," Frances advised. "Secrets, even the most innocent ones, have a way of destroying a marriage."

"There's never any time to talk things through," Elliott complained. "And this isn't the kind of thing I can just drop on her and walk away."

"Is it the kind of thing that will cause problems if she finds out some other way?"

He nodded reluctantly. "More than likely."

"Then talk to her, young man, before a little problem turns into a big one. Make the time." She gave him a stern look. "Sooner, rather than later."

He grinned at her fierce expression. No wonder she'd had quite a reputation as a teacher, one that had lived on long after she'd retired. "Yes, ma'am," he said.

She patted his arm. "You're a good man, Elliott Cruz, and I know you love her. Don't give her even the tiniest reason to doubt that."

"I'll do what I can," he assured her.

"Soon?"

"Soon," he promised.

Even if it stirred up a particularly nasty hornet's nest.

When she reached The Corner Spa at the corner of Main and Palmetto, Karen paused. She was beginning to regret that she hadn't followed Dana Sue's advice and taken a slow walk around the park to calm herself down again before arriving here to confront her husband. Even she knew it was probably a terrible idea to do it, not only when he was at work, but when she was still completely furious about being left in the dark. Nothing was likely to be resolved if she started out yelling, which is what seemed likely.

"Karen? Is everything okay?"

She turned at the softly spoken query from her former neighbor, Frances Wingate, a woman now nearing ninety who still had plenty of spunk, even if her age was slowing her down a bit. Despite her own lousy mood, Karen's expression brightened just seeing the woman who was like a mother to her in so many ways.

"Frances, how are you? And what are you doing here?"

Frances regarded her with a perplexed expression. "I'm taking Elliott's exercise class for seniors. Didn't he tell you?"

Karen heaved a frustrated sigh. "Apparently there's quite a lot my husband hasn't been sharing with me recently."

"Oh, dear, that doesn't sound good," Frances said. "Why don't we go to Wharton's and have a chat? It's been ages since we've had a chance to catch up. Something tells me you'd be much better off talking to me than going inside to see Elliott when you're obviously upset."

Knowing that Frances was absolutely right, Karen gave her a grateful look. "Do you have the time?"

"For you I can always make time," Frances said, linking her arm through Karen's. "Now, did you drive or shall we walk?"

"I didn't bring my car," Karen told her.

"Then walking it is," Frances said without a moment's hesitation. "Good thing I wore my favorite sneakers, isn't it?"

Karen glanced down at her bright turquoise shoes and smiled. "Quite a fashion statement," she teased.

"That's me, alright. The ultimate fashionista of the senior set."

When they reached Wharton's and ordered sweet tea for Frances and a soda for Karen, Frances looked into her eyes. "Okay now, tell me what has you so out of sorts this afternoon and what it has to do with Elliott."

To her dismay, Karen's eyes filled with unexpected tears. "I think my marriage is in real trouble, Frances."

Genuine shock registered on her friend's face. "Nonsense! That man adores you. We chat after class every week, and you and the kids are all he talks about. He's as infatuated now as he was on the day you met. I'm as sure of that as it's possible to be."

"Then why doesn't he tell me anything?" Karen lamented. "I didn't know he was seeing you every week. And earlier I found out that he's planning to open some sort of gym for the men in town. We don't have the money for him to take that kind of risk, even if he has business partners. Why would he take on something like that without even talking it over with me?"

She gave Frances a resigned look. "People warned me about these macho Hispanic men. I know it's a stereotype, but you know what I mean, the ones who just do whatever they want and expect their wives to go along with it. Elliott's father was like that, but I never thought Elliott, of all people, would be. He was such a thoughtful, considerate sweetheart when we were dating."

"Are you so sure he's keeping you in the dark deliberately?" Frances inquired reasonably. "There could be a lot of explanations for why he hasn't mentioned these things. With two children and two jobs, you're both incredibly busy. Your schedules don't always mesh that perfectly, so time together must be at a premium."

"That's true," Karen admitted. She often worked late at night, while he left for the spa early in the morning. They were sometimes like ships passing in the night. Their schedules weren't great for real communication.

"And when you do have time off, what do you do?" Frances persisted.

"We help the kids with their homework or drive them to all these endless activities they're involved in, then fall into bed exhausted."

Frances nodded. "I rest my case. There's not much time in there for the kind of heart-to-heart talks young couples need to have, especially when they're still adjusting to being married."

Karen gave her a wry look. "We've been together awhile, Frances."

"But you've only been married and living together for a couple of years. It took time for your annulment to come through. Dating is very different from being married and establishing a routine. It takes time to get in a rhythm that works, one that gives you the time alone you need to communicate effectively. I imagine Elliott's as anxious for that as you are."

There was something in her voice that gave Karen pause. "Has he said something to you? Please tell me you weren't in on this whole gym project, too. Was I the only person in town he hadn't told?"

"Stop working yourself into a frenzy," Frances said, though her cheeks turned pink as she said it. "Elliott and I did have a chat earlier, but he didn't mention a thing about any gym. Just now was the first I've heard about that. He told me that he's been putting off talking to you about something important because you're both so busy. He never got into the specifics with me."

"I see," Karen said stiffly, not entirely relieved by the explanation or by the idea that more people had been talking behind her back.

"Don't you dare make more of that than is called for," Frances scolded. "I asked him why he was so distracted in class today. He hemmed and hawed and finally admitted he'd been keeping something from you. I told him there was no good excuse for not communicating with a spouse." She gave Karen a pointed look. "Notice I said communicating, not yelling. Real communication involves listening, as well as talking."

Karen smiled weakly, duly chastised. "I hear you. But how on earth do we find the time to really sit down and have those heart-to-heart talks we used to have when we were dating? Right now we need all the hours at work we can get. And even if we could find some time, babysitters are too expensive for our budget."

"Then you'll let me help," Frances said at once, her expression eager. "Since you married and moved to a new home with Elliott, I don't see Daisy and Mack nearly as much as I'd like. They're growing like weeds. Soon I won't even recognize them."

Karen immediately regarded her with guilt. Though she'd taken the kids by often right after she and Elliott had married, the visits to Frances had dwindled as their schedules had grown more complicated. How could she have been so selfish, when she knew how much the older woman enjoyed spending time with Daisy and Mack?

"Oh, Frances, I'm so sorry," she apologized. "I should have brought them by more often."

"Hush now," Frances said, giving her hand a squeeze. "That was not my point. I was about to suggest we work out one evening a week when I'll come over and stay with them, while you and Elliott have a night out. I imagine I can still oversee a little homework and read a bedtime story or two. In fact, I'd love it." She grinned, an impish light in her eyes. "Or you can bring them to my place, if you'd rather have a romantic evening at home. I'm sure I could handle a sleepover now that they're older."

Karen resisted, despite the obvious sincerity of the suggestion. "You are so sweet to offer, but I couldn't possibly impose on you like that. You've already done way more for me than I had any right to expect. When times were tough, you were always there for me."

Frances gave her a chiding look. "I consider you family, and if I can do this for you, it would be my pleasure, so I don't want to hear any of this nonsense that it's too much. If I thought it were, I wouldn't have offered. And if you turn me down, it will only hurt my feelings. You'll be making me feel old and useless."

Karen smiled, thinking that Frances was definitely neither of those things. Chronologically her years had added up, but her spirit was young, she had dozens of friends, and she was still active in the community. She spent a few hours every day making calls to housebound seniors just to chat with them and make sure there was nothing they needed.

She nodded at last. "Okay, if you're sure, then I'll

talk it over with Elliott and we'll check with you about setting an evening. We'll give it a test run and see how it goes. I don't want Mack and Daisy to wear you out."

Frances's expression radiated delight. "That's good, then. Now, I should be running along. I'm playing cards tonight at the senior center with Flo Decatur and Liz Johnson and I'll need a nap if I'm to be alert enough to make sure they're not cheating. For otherwise honorable women, they're sneaky when it comes to cards."

Karen laughed as she slid out of the booth and hugged her friend. "Thank you. I really needed this talk even more than I needed to confront my husband."

"Confrontation is all well and good," Frances told her. "But it's best not done in anger." She gave Karen's hand another squeeze. "I'll expect to hear from you in the next few days."

"I'll call. I promise."

"And when you get home tonight, sit down with your husband and talk to him, no matter the hour."

Karen smiled at her. "Yes, ma'am," she replied dutifully.

Frances frowned. "Don't say that just to pacify me, young lady. I expect to hear that the two of you have worked this out."

Clearly satisfied at having the last word, she left.

Karen watched her go, noting that there wasn't a person in Wharton's she didn't speak to or offer a smile on the way.

"She's remarkable," Karen murmured aloud, then sighed. "And wise."

Tonight would be soon enough for that talk she intended to have with Elliott. She would use the extra time to think through the situation, figure out exactly why she was so upset and find a way to discuss it all calmly and rationally over dinner. Frances had been exactly right. Yelling wasn't the mature way to resolve anything.

And unlike the passive woman she'd once been, Karen also knew that the strong, confident woman she'd become wouldn't allow resentment to simmer too long or let the whole incident slide in the interest of keeping peace. She'd deal with this head-on before it destroyed her marriage. At least she'd learned something from her marriage to Ray: what not to do.

Pleased with her plan, she paid for their drinks and headed back to Sullivan's, where Dana Sue and Erik greeted her warily.

"Oh, don't look at me like that," she said. "There are no divorce papers being filed. In fact, I never even saw Elliott."

Erik breathed a visible sigh of relief.

"Where were you, then?" Dana Sue inquired.

"At Wharton's with Frances, the voice of reason," Karen told them.

Dana Sue grinned. "Did she give you one of those sage lectures that makes you feel about two-inches tall? When she was my teacher, she could just look at me with one of those disappointed expressions and practically reduce me to tears. She was the only teacher I ever had who could pull that off. It even worked on Helen."

"No way," Erik said, looking impressed. "I didn't think anyone intimidated my wife."

"Frances Wingate did," Dana Sue said. "She had the best-behaved students in the entire school. We didn't turn into full-fledged Sweet Magnolia hellions until later." Her expression suddenly sobered as she turned back to Karen. "So, have you stopped being mad at me and Erik?"

"I was never mad at either of you," she told them. "I knew you were just the messengers."

"And Elliott?" Dana Sue prodded.

"I still have plenty to discuss with my husband," Karen said. "But at least now I think I can do it without throwing pots and pans or those nifty little dumbbells at the spa at him."

"Word has it that Dana Sue was pretty good at turning pots and pans into weapons back in the day," Erik commented, giving Dana Sue a taunting look.

"Only because Ronnie deserved it," Dana Sue retorted, her tone unapologetic. "The man cheated on me. Fortunately he learned his lesson and I haven't needed a cast-iron skillet for anything other than cooking since then."

After a very tense afternoon, Karen suddenly chuckled. Impulsively, she crossed the room and hugged her boss. "Thank you for giving me my perspective back."

"Glad to be of service," Dana Sue said. "Now, if no one has any objections, let's get these dinner preparations underway before our special of the night is grilled-cheese sandwiches."

"On it," Erik said at once. "Thoroughly decadent chocolate mud pie coming up."

"And I'll get started frying chicken," Karen said, thankful that her relief would be here soon. "When Tina gets here, she can take over and I'll finish up salads before I head home."

At least here, she thought as she settled happily into

her routine, peace and harmony once again reigned. Something told her, though, that it was just the calm before the storm.

Don't miss
Midnight Promises
by #1 New York Times *bestselling author*
Sherryl Woods,
coming soon wherever
MIRA books and ebooks are sold.

www.Harlequin.com

afterword

Beginning with the first book I ever wrote way back in the early 1980s, readers have always asked if my settings were real or fictional, especially the small-town settings in so many of my series. Though I have written a number of books in real and recognizable big cities—Miami, Los Angeles, San Francisco and New York, among others—the vast majority of my settings have been small towns and were the products of my imagination.

That doesn't mean they weren't inspired by a very real town, and in just a few weeks, I'll be introducing readers to that town in a nonfiction book—*A Small Town Love Story: Colonial Beach, Virginia*. This tiny beach community of some 3,500 or so year-round residents on the Potomac River has been the home of my heart throughout my life. I spent summers there as a child and a teen, and I've been returning ever since to the house my parents bought when I was only four years old.

There are rich memories and romantic daydreams around every corner. Colonial Beach has a quirky, wonderful past and is full of captivating storytellers. Its quintessential small-town flavor makes this real-life town every bit as charming and fascinating as any town I've ever created.

So for all of you who've always wondered about who or what might have inspired this story or that one—from Trinity Harbor to Chesapeake Shores, from Serenity, South Carolina, to Whispering Wind, Wyoming—*A Small Town Love Story: Colonial Beach, Virginia* will give you some insights. I hope you'll be fascinated by the town's history and charmed by some of its residents—and maybe, if you're lucky, you'll get to visit someday. In the meantime, check your local bookstore for this glimpse into some of my favorite memories and the people who make life in Colonial Beach worthy of a story of its own.

All best,
Sherryl

Returning home has never been so bittersweet in this acclaimed novel from #1 *New York Times* bestselling author

SHERRYL WOODS

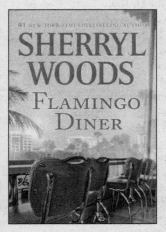

Flamingo Diner has always been a friendly place where everyone knows your name. Unfortunately, in the small town of Winter Cove, Florida, it is also the place where everyone knows everything about you. As a teenager, Emma Killian didn't recognize what a remarkable business her family had created, and so she moved away.

Now her father's tragic death has brought her home to face a mountain of secrets, debts and questions about why and how her beloved father died. As Emma grapples with her out-of-control family, the responsibility of keeping Flamingo Diner afloat and a pair of well-meaning senior-citizen sleuths, she finds support from an unlikely source.

Onetime bad boy Matt Atkins is now the Winter Cove police chief. Matt has always had a penchant for trouble and an eye for Emma. Now it seems he's the only one who can help Emma discover the answers to her questions...and give her a whole new reason to stay home.

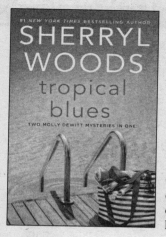

SHERRYL WOODS

36975	FLAMINGO DINER	___	$7.99 U.S.	___ $9.99 CAN.
33034	ROUGH SEAS	___	$7.99 U.S.	___ $9.99 CAN.
33028	TROPICAL BLUES	___	$7.99 U.S.	___ $9.99 CAN.
33008	HARBOR LIGHTS	___	$7.99 U.S.	___ $9.99 CAN.
33006	FLOWERS ON MAIN	___	$7.99 U.S.	___ $9.99 CAN.
33004	THE INN AT EAGLE POINT	___	$7.99 U.S.	___ $9.99 CAN.
32979	MOONLIGHT COVE	___	$7.99 U.S.	___ $9.99 CAN.
32947	DRIFTWOOD COTTAGE	___	$7.99 U.S.	___ $9.99 CAN.
32814	RETURN TO ROSE COTTAGE	___	$7.99 U.S.	___ $9.99 CAN.
31986	ASK ANYONE	___	$7.99 U.S.	___ $9.99 CAN.
31982	ABOUT THAT MAN	___	$7.99 U.S.	___ $9.99 CAN.
31876	PRICELESS	___	$7.99 U.S.	___ $9.99 CAN.
31788	THE CALAMITY JANES: LAUREN	___	$7.99 U.S.	___ $8.99 CAN.
31778	THE CALAMITY JANES: GINA & EMMA	___	$7.99 U.S.	___ $8.99 CAN.
31766	WILLOW BROOK ROAD	___	$8.99 U.S.	___ $9.99 CAN.
31679	THE DEVANEY BROTHERS: DANIEL	___	$7.99 U.S.	___ $9.99 CAN.
31668	A SEASIDE CHRISTMAS	___	$7.99 U.S.	___ $8.99 CAN.
31607	THE DEVANEY BROTHERS: RYAN AND SEAN	___	$7.99 U.S.	___ $8.99 CAN.
31581	SEAVIEW INN	___	$7.99 U.S.	___ $8.99 CAN.
31466	AFTER TEX	___	$7.99 U.S.	___ $9.99 CAN.
31414	TEMPTATION	___	$7.99 U.S.	___ $9.99 CAN.
31326	WAKING UP IN CHARLESTON	___	$7.99 U.S.	___ $9.99 CAN.
31309	THE SUMMER GARDEN	___	$7.99 U.S.	___ $9.99 CAN.

(limited quantities available)

TOTAL AMOUNT $ _____
POSTAGE & HANDLING $ _____
($1.00 for 1 book, 50¢ for each additional)
APPLICABLE TAXES* $ _____
TOTAL PAYABLE $ _____
(check or money order—please do not send cash)

To order, complete this form and send it, along with a check or money order for the total above, payable to MIRA Books, to: **In the U.S.:** 3010 Walden Avenue, P.O. Box 9077, Buffalo, NY 14269-9077; **In Canada:** P.O. Box 636, Fort Erie, Ontario, L2A 5X3.

Name: _____

Address: _____ City: _____

State/Prov.: _____ Zip/Postal Code: _____

Account Number (if applicable): _____

075 CSAS

*New York residents remit applicable sales taxes.
*Canadian residents remit applicable GST and provincial taxes.

mira
Harlequin.com
MSW0219BL